ATLANTIS DYING

ATLANTIS DYING

ANGELA GRAVES

Desert Palm Press

Atlantis Dying

By Angela Graves

©2023 Angela Graves

ISBN (book) 9781954213753
ISBN (epub) 9781954213760

Desert Palm Press
1961 Main Street, Suite 220
Watsonville, California 95076
www.desertpalmpress.com

Editor: Kay Grey
Cover Design: Mich Brodeur eeboxWORX

Printed in the United States of America
First Edition October 2023

Acknowledgements:

I'd like to thank Lee and Desert Palm Press for creating a space for lesbian authors and stories and for believing in this mythological story.

To my editor, Kay Dubrow Grey, thank you for helping me comb through my writing to make it the novel it is now. Thanks to my cover designer, Michelle Brodeur, for the gorgeous interpretation of my written words. Olavi, Lili, and Kristen, thank you all for being such thoughtful beta readers, and for helping me shape this story and deepen the characters. Thank you, Thistle, for decorating the covers of each draft before Momma read them. Nicholas, thank you for giving me time in the summers and evenings to complete this project.

Finally, I'd like to thank my wife, Rachel, for reading every draft and listening to my rambling thoughts until I was able to make them into the novel they are today. Our relationship began with a very different version of this book, and I'm so happy that we get to see it through together.

Angela Graves

Dedication

For Rachel

Chapter One

"SCREW IT. I'M TAKING the ridgeline home," I told Hazel as I walked toward the glorified goat path of a shortcut. My plan was spontaneously brilliant but also likely to get me killed without her help.

Of course, Hazel would probably think I was being stupid, deviating from the Alexa-safe route. I wasn't sure if it was stupid, but I knew I was desperate. Desperate to prove I could finally cross the ridge and even more desperate to get home and rest.

"Are you kidding me?" Hazel asked in one exhale, as she ran to intercept me, eyes wide, voice shrill. It seemed she did think my plan was stupid.

I just shook my head and kept walking, determined.

Hazel had started using the shortcut over a decade ago when we were barely ten. Our parents had probably toddled across as babies if their current capabilities were any indication. It had only ever been me who'd been too clumsy and afraid.

"We're out here to help you," she said. "How's that going to work if you fall down a cliff trying to cut an hour off a hike?"

When I finally stopped moving, half fearful she'd tackle me in her panic, Hazel regained her composure. She stopped in front of me and brushed a few stray hairs toward her braid.

As always, her pale brown skin in combination with earth toned hiking layers helped her blend into the tundra around us. She was made just for this place, or maybe it was made for her. Either way, our mountains were always there to catch her before a fall, and she knew the land like it was family. It was the same for our parents. Our whole village. Just not for me.

"Give me that yarrow, and we'll go home the safe way." She took it from my hand and expertly pulled it apart. The root, stem, and clusters of tiny white flowers each went into different pouches before she packed them in her bag. "We have what we need. Even the long way, you'll be home in time to get a nap before Dad brings Gale and his houseguest over for dinner."

"What?" I already hated whatever she was talking about. "No company! Colored contacts feel like burning ash in tired eyes."

"Don't be so dramatic," she said, barely containing her laughter. "And don't wear your contacts then. It's just Gale and some biology student Dad's been guiding around the area."

"The biology student would probably try to study me if they saw my eyes," I said.

"You have nice eyes, Lex. You don't have to hide them."

She was wrong about my eyes. A luminous emerald would be beautiful, but when it came from the iris of someone's eyes, the effect was far from nice—or so I'd learned from a lifetime of disturbed glances, a lack of eye contact, and even questions about what was wrong with me. Only my immediate family could stand my eyes.

"Let's get home," I said. "I can barely stand. I'm not taking the long way back."

She looked over her shoulder at the precarious trail.

"Actual children use this shortcut," I said.

"You don't need to prove anything."

"And yet, today's the day I prove I'm a true Delmon—I mean, our name basically means mountain. It's pathetic I haven't done this yet." I moved to step past her.

"Fine! Stop." She reached into her backpack again and pulled out a coiled-up length of rope.

"Seriously?"

She was serious. She rigged up some sort of harness on my waist and legs and then did the same to herself with the other end, so we were attached at the hip.

I rolled my eyes as she worked, dreaming about the short walk home on the other side of the ridge. The trail was barely wider than my hiking boots and hugged by a vertical drop on either side, but I shifted impatiently from foot to foot, ready for the nap I'd been promised.

Finally, Hazel stepped out onto the shortcut. "Follow me. And step carefully!"

"I'm always careful," I said. "It's the ground that isn't careful with me."

"Shut up and focus, Alexa."

I was glad to hear the smile in her words. It had taken me a long time to develop any sense of humor about my failure to thrive in our mountain village, and Hazel had been the one to help me finally get there by always accepting me as I was. Mom and Dad had a harder time with accepting, and so I'd endured many years of them always trying to make me more like them.

When I did focus on my steps, I instantly panicked. I was right behind Hazel, three paces along the tight ridgeline. Three paces too far. The ten yards in front of us had never felt more endless. My heart jumped so hard it clogged my throat, and suddenly—I couldn't breathe. When I caught my breath, the air came in panting gasps. I had to fight not to close my eyes as I followed my sister.

A few steps from safety, and my pounding heart seemed to steal the last dregs of blood from my head. The jagged rocks below suddenly spun as the sky above me attempted to take their place. I was passing out.

"Shit, Alexa!" Hazel yelled.

I caught a glimpse of her form jumping toward solid land and twisting to face me before I gave in to the dizziness.

QUEEN KYRA

A regal woman watches a growing grid of dead bodies, row after row, every shoulder touching. It's a stark contrast between such a sight and the scene that should have been depicted. Based on the scattered food tables all over the sprawling flower garden and the fine clothing of the dead, this gravesite had once been a celebration.

Several sword-carrying guards walk among the bodies in the outer edges of the garden. They lift some of the dead and reverently carry them to the rows.

The woman gasps out a single sob and presses her palms to her eyes, but the tears come anyway. When she finally lowers her hands, another woman has joined her.

"Can you heal any of them?" the first woman asks the second, tears now flowing freely.

The second woman has molten gold eyes and olive skin that clings to her bones, but instead of appearing emaciated, a low glow rolls over her, fills her out, rounds and softens her sharp angles, and blends away the harsh to replace it with an incomparable beauty.

"They are all dead, Queen Kyra—drained of their divine lives by Hephaestus's Immortal Death Blades," she says, "but hope is not lost."

She steps away from Queen Kyra and begins walking along the closest row.

Guards drag the remaining bodies away from the neatly gridded dead, toward a large fire between the garden and a thick forest just beyond. They haphazardly toss the corpses into the flames. Other guards feed the blaze and still others form a large pile of swords taken from the dead assailants.

The woman stops in front of a blonde man, covered in several shallow slices.

"My love," Queen Kyra whispers, clearing her tightening throat. "I was too far away to help, but as I ran closer, I watched him block one cut after another while those monsters set after the children."

The other woman takes Queen Kyra's hand. "I never told you this, but my hair was once as black as those human hearts." She points toward the distant pile of burning men. "When I learned how to go beyond healing, to resurrect with my Apollo-given gift, I learned the consequences of using my magic without the approval of the gods. Apollo came to me the first time I saved a life and turned just a few strands of hair white, telling me it would only spread if I continued using my gift in a way for which it was not meant."

"What does it mean now that it has gone all white?" Queen Kyra asks.

"It means that I ignored the gods many times." She pulls out one thick, black lock of hair from under her piles of curls. "When this turns white, my divine life will be no more. My punishment for defying the gods is mortality, and I imagine with this many," She looks across the arrangement of dead, "it will take my mortal life as well."

"What do you mean to do?" Queen Kyra asks.

"I mean to save these people."

Before Queen Kyra can utter a word of response, the other woman's glow brightens across her skin, and keeps getting brighter. In seconds, she's a woman-sized sun. Then the light pours from her body, through her hands. It fills the man under her fingers and spreads like frost on a window, trailing across the bodies. One body after another fills with the same glow. The path of light has engulfed the dead and brightens until it's no longer many glowing entities, but a singular mass.

As quickly as it began, the glow disappears, and in its place hundreds of men, women, and children begin to stir. One after another, they rise from the ground as if waking disoriented from a long sleep.

Queen Kyra looks back and sees the cost of the miracle. The woman's glow fades and leaves behind the cutting angles of bone across her skeletal body. Her once rich skin dulls, and then becomes porous and dry. Her eyes hollow. Fissures begin dancing between the pores, cut deeper, and grow thicker until everything that's left simply crumbles into an ashy cloud.

Queen Kyra chokes on a sob. She looks down at the ash that now covers the man.

He blinks up at her. "Kyra," he says.

* * * * *

When I opened my eyes again, I was lying on the tundra, staring up at my sister, who was winding up the rope and pacing at my feet. The moment her eyes met mine, she knelt next to me.

"Who passes out on a cliff? Did you learn a new level of stubborn down at the university last year?" she jabbed, relief laced into her teasing words.

"Well, we're almost home now." I grinned.

"Seriously, though," she said. "You were out for quite a few minutes. I was starting to freak. I saw you faint in time, but once I dragged both of us to safety—"

She held her palms open to me, showing off the angry red and torn rope burns.

I cringed at the sight. "Ouch—I'm sorry."

She waved my words away. "It's nothing. I helped Mom with a special batch of salve that'll clear it right up. Anyway, you were just lying there." She gestured at me. "Like you were sleeping."

"Well, I can't complain about my nightmares only being faces anymore. It was a whole, weird ass dream this time," I said. "There was a lady with eyes like mine, but golden. Skinny like me too, but it somehow looked good on her."

"Strange. So, you think it's related to your sleep problems?" She was suddenly serious, attentive. Her head tipped slightly sideways as her eyes bored into me. It was the look she had adopted from our mother, when there was a riddle to be solved.

"I think it was my subconscious saying I'm tired of being a freak wherever I go." I said it lightly and laughed as I got up to my feet, but it wasn't exactly a lie.

Chapter Two

I SAT NEXT TO Hazel on her bed while she rubbed a bitter smelling brown salve onto her burned palms. My arms wrapped around my knees as Jane Goodall cuddled in my hoodie pocket doing her little guinea pig purr that let me know she was in her favorite spot. I might not say it aloud, but I wasn't afraid to admit to myself that it was my favorite spot for her as well, especially with how on edge I'd been lately.

"I actually do think that dream today was related to my sleep problems."

"Maybe that's a good sign," Hazel said.

I shrugged. "Maybe." But I didn't think so. The nightmarish flashes had started near the end of my second semester away from home. Every time it happened, I'd woken up sweating and screeching, much to the annoyance of my dorm mate.

Once it had started, every night became a little worse, until I had resorted to avoiding sleep and downing gallons of caffeine. By April, I had been so sleep-deprived that I'd finally flown home in desperation, failing all my courses for the semester.

Now it was mid-July, and my mother had tried every tonic she knew and several she'd invented attempting to help me get some sleep. Nothing had worked, and I was more exhausted than ever. I'd been back home in time to turn twenty with a depressing birthday I hoped to soon forget.

"Maybe I need my head examined by one of those doctors everyone outside our village uses. I've Googled my symptoms, and it could be something beyond Mom's skill."

"I don't believe that's possible," Hazel said.

Our mother was the healer of Oread Basin, and my sister had been her apprentice basically our whole lives, but her official training had started after we'd finished high school. Hazel had gone to her studies with Mom, and our overprotective parents had made me take my first year of college courses online to prove I was ready before they'd let me fly the few hundred miles south to the University of Alaska.

"I can't be stuck back here forever," I whined.

Going away to school had been the first step in my plan to get out and make a life where I wasn't the inferior weirdo. I was going to get a great job in a big city somewhere. I'd finally have a bunch of friends who loved me and never thought I looked strange—maybe I'd get some plastic surgery to make me a little less skeletal. I'd travel wherever I wanted, whenever I wanted. I'd fall in love. And everything would finally be perfect. Too bad I hadn't even figured out what to major in before I ended up back home.

"You aren't going to be stuck, Lex. My apprenticeship with Mom is basically over, so I can go with you now," she said.

"You can't follow me around taking care of me forever. Even if Mom finds the magic formula," I said. "Plus, your boyfriend wouldn't like that."

"Stop!" She slapped me on the shoulder and tried to look annoyed, failing to fully suppress her smile. "Don't you want me tagging along with you?"

"You were the only thing missing from my perfect semester away," I said with a hint of drama, even though it was true.

My parents had adopted me a few months after Hazel was born. We'd been so close from day one, people might have mistaken us for twins, if not for our extreme physical differences.

Hazel, Mom, Dad, and really all hundred or so of the population of Oread Basin were so different from me. My light brown hair did nothing to distract from my creepy luminous green eyes. My skin was much paler than anyone else around town, and I was bony thin. My sister, in contrast, had flowing black hair that splashed over her shoulders, rich and shiny. We were similar in height, but her body was both curvy and muscular.

Everyone in town had Hazel's thick dark hair, her brown eyes, and her solid frame. Most importantly, they all lived effortlessly in our mountain village, nestled in a northern valley of the Brooks Range, far away from other villages and farther from any roads or cities.

The differences were so clear that by the time I was school aged, my parents were forced to admit I was adopted. They refused to give me details, claiming they knew nothing from the closed adoption. I never believed them. Surely there was something they could tell me about my birth parents. About my strangeness.

My parents may have never stopped insisting that I could learn the things they did to make a life here, but I never stopped proving how wrong they were, the near disaster of today being my most recent example. At least it always was a near disaster because my sister was my perpetual savior.

"It's settled then," Hazel said. "You'll face Gale and guest at dinner tonight, and I'll join you at school when you go back."

"I don't think I agreed to that," I groaned, thinking about stupid Gale and the stupid stranger and my stupid contacts.

"Please, Lex," she said. "You can't hide up here forever, and I don't want to have yet another Gale dinner without you!" She was the one whining now.

I'd somehow managed to avoid people other than my family since coming home.

Just once, Dad had tried to make me join him on a guided bear hunt with some people who'd flown in from Fairbanks, but clumsy in my lack of sleep, I rolled an ankle, fell into one of the clients, and sent both of us crashing into a creek.

That was for the best though. Otherwise, I would have just had an intentionally loud fall as soon as I thought someone was going to kill an animal. I'd pulled that move enough times that Dad normally let me skip his hunts.

He'd finally agreed that I could spend a few evenings a week grooming our neighbor's pack horses after hunting trips. It was how I appeased his insistence that I contribute to the community without me having to see other people or help murder animals.

Those horses were the best thing in Oread Basin, anyway. The neighbors had always kept trail and pack horses for people to use when they came to hunt or explore in the area, and I'd grown up helping out with them. When I was old enough, I learned to ride, which was when I'd realized the animals were significantly more sure-footed than me.

"Fine," I said. "I'll have dinner with Gale and the scientist." There was still time to back out.

"Excellent." Hazel got up and headed for her door. "I'm going to help Mom for a bit."

I tucked a hand in with Jane Goodall, keeping her steady as I scooted off Hazel's bed and headed for my own room across the hall.

My room was small and messy, bedding in a wad on the floor from the point in my night where I'd gone to sleep with Hazel because of the freaky face nightmares. My laptop and books from the abandoned semester sat gathering dust on my small desk. Most of my clothes, clean and dirty, were in strategic piles on the floor.

I lifted Jane into her cage on my dresser, went to my floor pile of clean clothes, and replaced my hiking pants with a pair of sweats.

I'd given up asking our parents for money to buy better clothes, since they'd deemed my requested choices a senseless waste of money. The tiny wardrobe of nice clothes that I had was the result of every penny saved from high school and my campus job last year. My blazer and button ups, palazzo pants and slacks all hung neatly in my closet, untouched since April.

They hung next to the one dress I owned, a mint green ballroom dance gown. Mom bought it for me after I'd learned all the dances from the online class I'd begged her to enroll me in. Of course, that purchase then led to her offering me up to teach dance lessons to the community. I was the hero of date night in Oread Basin for my last two years of high school.

My bedside clock told me it was already almost three by the time I was headed downstairs to find food and get an update on my sleep cure from Mom.

In the kitchen, I made some toast before sitting at the table, facing my mom and sister as they worked away on the counter. They used that secret language I'd never understood. The one that turned plants into miraculous remedies for literally everything. Mom had tried to teach me many times, but my efforts reliably ended with useless sludge.

"Have you felt any more rested today?" Mom asked, crushing up some plants in a bowl. Her long black hair was pulled up in a loose and messy bun, as if getting it out of the way had been an inconvenient afterthought. I could see the strength in her arms as she worked away to pulverize the plants. Side by side at work with Hazel, Mom looked like a more grown up, curvier, and softer version of my sister.

I shrugged as I added jam to my toasted bread. "Not really. Did Hazel tell you about my cliffside dream?"

Mom nodded. "Yes. And that you crossed the ridgeline. Maybe wait until you've had a few hours good sleep before you do that again." She didn't look up from her work, but I saw the corner of her lip tug up to reveal her dimple. "I'm impressed, Alexa."

That was rare praise, and surprising given the fact that I'd passed out before getting all the way across. Maybe Hazel had left out some details.

"Thanks, Mom." I kept my response simple so she wouldn't think to amend the compliment.

I gestured at the counter covered in roots, leaves, bowls, and bottles. "This is totally random and experimental, isn't it?" I grinned.

"Experimental...yes." Mom poured the ground plants into a pot on the stove. "Random, absolutely not." She picked up a leather-bound journal and scribbled something inside.

Hazel threw her leather bag over her shoulder and walked around the counter toward the door that led to our backyard. "I'm going for a few more plant cuttings. Want to come, Lexa?"

I worked on my second piece of toast. "Very funny."

She rolled her eyes and smirked at me. "Fine. Just remember you promised to come tonight."

"Yeah, yeah," I mumbled, as she walked out the back door.

Mom walked over to me with a mug in her hand. "You're planning to sleep again."

I nodded even though it hadn't been a question.

She set it next to me. "Drink this first, and sleep on the couch so I can keep an eye on you."

"Thanks, Mom." I downed the warm liquid in three big gulps. It was sweet and earthy.

Before my nap, I ran back up to my room and grabbed my phone. There was no cell service for at least a hundred miles, but the Wi-Fi would allow me to cyber stalk my girlfriend from last school year.

My fingers drifted to the skin right behind my ear as I thought about Claire, touching the tiny pink fireweed that I knew was tattooed there, even if I couldn't see it. I'd met Claire early in the fall semester and by January, after missing each other terribly during my visit home over the holidays, the L word was used, and we'd rushed out for a couple's tattoo. Claire's was on her wrist, but I hadn't wanted to risk the clean, professional look I'd need for my life outside of Oread Basin.

But then our relationship imploded. Because of me. I'd stood her up a couple of times after my sleep issues had started, which had pissed her off. I'd tried to explain what was going on, but she'd had no patience for it. Somehow, we'd kept things going until I flew home, but after a couple of weeks her replies got shorter and fewer. Then one day she stopped answering me.

She sent a final string of texts accusing me of lying about what I was doing and breaking up with me, and I hadn't known how to respond to that. So I didn't.

Instead, I'd taken to stalking her Insta. She was a Fairbanks local but was spending her summer abroad with some friends. I felt a pang of jealousy every time I saw her smiling with the other girls for selfies all over Europe. We'd talked about me going on that trip, not that I could have afforded it, but it still burned to see the kind of life I was missing out on.

According to Claire's latest post, she was in the final days of her trip, and would be finishing her summer in Fairbanks. If I was going to repair our relationship, if I had any hope of her taking me back, if I even made it back, I needed to do something. So I sent a hurried text.

Hey Claire
I'm sorry I had to leave town
We still don't know what's wrong,
but I have a little more energy now

That was a lie, but I'd find the energy if it meant getting back with her.

I'm really sorry u felt abandoned

Some of her final words to me.

I hope ur having a good summer

I slammed my phone face down on the desk before I could see if she'd reply, hoping she wouldn't see it right away. If she responded at all.

Then I went back down and flopped onto our deep cushioned couch, falling asleep to the image of Claire with her arm around some other girl in front of the Mediterranean Sea.

IRENE

A woman sits on a golden slab of rock, skirt fabric bunched up over her knees. Her toes trail across the crystal clear surface of a pond with the rhythmic swing of pale, bony legs, aglow with power. Her hands rest on a warm and pregnant stomach.

A tangle of blonde hair blows along her face and arms in the light breeze, which subdues the heat of the sun pressing against her. Still, she adjusts her canvas sun hat to better shield her eyes.

Suddenly, footsteps rustle through the grass behind her, and she pulls her feet out of the water to turn in their direction. A tall and unnaturally slender woman is striding closer, crimson hair bouncing down her shoulders in time with her movements.

She sits on the rock and stares at the water. "You look worried, Irene," she says. "Do not worry. Everything is planned."

Irene's lips form a weak smile as she clumsily turns her pregnant body and dips her toes back into the pond. "Plans can go wrong, Ivy. And I do not want you punished if I am caught. You have your own child to worry about."

Ivy holds her hand over her own, visibly flat stomach and smiles, blue eyes glowing brighter for a moment.

Irene's eyes fill with tears and her breath shortens into labored pants.

"Irene!" Ivy helps Irene lie down, offering up her lap as a pillow. Then she uses her hand to cover Irene's forehead.

Soon, Irene's breathing returns to normal, though she hasn't stopped crying. "How will I live without her? How can I just give up my daughter?" she asks, voice despondent.

"I wish I had a happy answer, but remember you are saving her from the queen herself," Ivy says.

"I would leave this place forever to be with my baby."

"But Queen Amara would never let the source of our people's peace leave her control," Ivy says. "No. She would send out every one of her hunters to bring you home."

"My gift might be the long awaited source of peace for our people, but it has brought me nothing but torment," Irene sighs.

"My princess!" A dark-haired man steps out of the deep purple trees across the water. A woman follows, stumbling, a few seconds behind him.

The man runs along the edge of the pond with a broad smile as Ivy stands and helps Irene to her feet. He reaches them, and Irene gazes up at his near black, power filled eyes—eyes that almost match the color of his carefully cultivated, shoulder length mullet.

His brown shirt is a durable fabric, visibly damp with sweat, and tucked in. The materials of his belt seem to be miscellaneous fabric scraps, but they're delicately braided to create an accessory that seems out of place on the work clothes.

He folds Irene into his arms and kisses her lips before dropping to his knees, putting both hands on her belly and kissing it.

"No need to wait for me, Damian!" his companion says sarcastically, stumbling up behind him in a pair of bright red cowboy boots and a baggy purple track suit. "I can make my way in these ridiculous boots of yours just fine, thank you."

Irene lets out a short, sharp laugh. "What are you wearing, Penelope?"

"She wanted to fit in with the Earth people and their women are wearing pants now, my love," Damian says. "So, I gave her some of the articles I picked up that time I traveled there on Atlantean business."

"I think her own clothing would have been fine," Irene says, pressing her lips against a smile.

"I told him as much, but he would not let it go," Penelope says. "He is obsessed with his human souvenirs."

Despite her head-to-toe oversized and tacky clothes, Penelope is lovely. Stunning with power, yes, but also lovely. Her curly hair is thick and rich and tussled, ending at her jaw. She wears dangling silver earrings that brush against her long slender neck as she walks. Her eyes match her brown hair in their depth of color, and like the inhuman eyes of the others, they radiate an overwhelming energy.

"How will you get my daughter to safety on Earth?" Irene asks Penelope.

"As soon as you have your daughter," Penelope says, "I will use an invisibility illusion to escape this place and get her hidden on Earth."

"My mother's parents are expecting her," Damien says. "In a Nymph village called Oread Basin."

"And after I deliver the baby to safety, I plan to disappear among the humans. It is time I become a contact on Earth—to help others escape this place."

Ivy adds her part of the plan. "I told Queen Amara that Irene is not due for two weeks and convinced her I needed Irene's assistance on my house calls over the next couple of days." She turns to Irene for a long hug. "And to that end—I must go. I will miss you."

She follows with a hug for Damian and then finally Penelope, holding tightly before kissing her forehead. "Good luck."

"I will have to be more careful without you around to heal me." Penelope grins. "Are you sure you will not run away with me?"

Ivy returns the smile. "Queen Amara has a proclivity for torture, and I am our only healer. I must help here in Atlantis the best I can."

She turns just as her eyes begin to glisten and walks toward the forest. They all watch quietly until the deep purple trunks and branches obscure her.

"We should go," Damian says. "It will be a long climb with Irene so far along."

Irene turns from the forest and looks up the gradual slope of the hillside. It starts gaining elevation just beyond the pond and purple trees. Far away, at the crest of the hill, are the tops of several dark stone arches.

* * * * *

I was out of practice with my contacts, and my eyes were dry, so it was taking longer than usual to put them in. I'd already opted to go casual in jeans and a T-shirt, but there was no way I was skipping the dark brown eye camouflage.

I hadn't been able to get my last dream out of my head since waking from my nap. I knew I was depressed about being back home, feeling so out of place, but now it was influencing my dreams. I had dreamed up all these people—beautiful versions of exactly what I am. I had dreamed that these people were somehow magical and left a baby in my village. And the thing was, it hadn't even felt like a dream. It had felt real. It felt like a memory now, not the fleeting images left over from dreams.

Once my contacts were in place, my eyes were still very green, but the brown of the lenses muted the glow, taking away the alien effect. I spent another few minutes with brushes and powders, trying to soften the look of my bony cheeks and jaw. I didn't have glowing magic, but make-up still worked pretty well.

After I was presentable, I grabbed my phone to see if Claire had replied. Nothing. I hadn't expected much, but it was still a bit deflating.

Claire had been my first girlfriend. She'd been my first kiss, my first everything. Then my stupid brain ruined it all.

Now I was stuck back here where I could count the number of people near my age on one hand, and only two of them were girls. One was my sister, and the other, Ellen Brentwood, had been in love with the only guy our age, other than Gale, since we were five. Small town living was not easy for any kind of dating, and it was brutal for queer dating. I'd talked to some girls online my senior year and when I took my first year of college courses remotely. Unfortunately, when I was never available to meet up in person, it made it hard to have any sort of real relationship. I needed to get out of here.

I micro-analyzed the latest photos on Claire's Insta until I heard Dad call up the stairs for me to come to dinner. Reluctantly, I put my phone down and headed for the kitchen. Dad was waiting at the bottom of the stairs—to hurry me along, no doubt.

"We would like to start eating, Alexa," Dad said, a deep crease forming between his dark eyes as he took in my lackadaisical pace.

"Sorry," I said, moving more quickly.

It seemed that he was going to cling fast to his dinner rituals no matter how old I got. With him, there was always a right way to do things, and that included starving dinner guests until everyone was sitting at the table.

"Hurry up," he said, disappearing back into the kitchen.

I followed. Dad took his seat at the table, across from my mom. Hazel and Gale were on the far side. Gale's black hair had grown out since I'd last seen him. He had it pulled back in a neat ponytail, and he was wearing a flannel shirt almost identical to my dad's.

He beamed at me. "Hey, Alexa! I'm glad you're feeling better."

"Thanks," I muttered, taking hold of the empty seat in front of me, next to the new guy.

"This is Aric Hunt." Gale gestured toward the thin guy sitting at our table.

In fact, he was the only other person I'd seen outside my weird dreams who looked thin like me, practically skin and bones. I got excited as he turned to face me, the sandy blonde back of his head moving to reveal regular brown eyes. For an instant, I'd been sure he'd have the same strange bright eyes as me. Stupid dreams. His thinness wasn't glowing or pretty like my dream pals, either. It just made him look unwell. Just like me.

"Hi." I sat down next to him and busied myself by filling my plate with food from all the dishes on the table except for the salmon.

"Alexa Candace Delmon," Dad said, voice low, staring at me.

I rolled my eyes internally. I hadn't thought he'd pick our regular fight with company present, but here we were again.

"I don't eat animals, Dad," I said carefully. "Don't make it a thing."

"A thing?" His voice raised in pitch. "Your mother spent over an hour on this food. Gale's family provided it. You need to be grateful."

"I am grateful," I said. "For all this other great food."

Dad looked like he was winding up for more, but Mom jumped in to change the subject, as usual.

"You're from UAF, correct?" Mom looked at Aric.

"A biology student, yes. I am here for a field work course," he said.

"So, what's that like?" I asked. "Do you sit in the woods counting birds and caribou all day or something?"

"That is part of it," he said.

"What about you, Gale?" I asked. "What's new?" Maybe if I talked and ate in a hurry, I could keep this whole thing short.

"Aric is staying in my new house for the next month," Gale said. "There's plenty of room for him because I built it to start a family." He looked over at my sister meaningfully.

I almost gagged on my mouthful of food, thankful to see Hazel glare at him.

"This one has two left feet in the backcountry like Alexa," Dad blurted out of nowhere, gesturing at Aric. "I'm not sure field biology is your forte, Son."

That was my dad—not afraid to publicly judge complete strangers for no apparent reason. At least his attention was off my eating habits.

"Reed!" Mom scolded him. "I'm sure that's all part of being a student."

Aric shrugged. "He could be correct. I am...exploring programs."

"Alexa is in her second year," Mom said. "She's also a UAF student."

I groaned internally, having no desire to share my failures with strangers.

"Lex took the ridgeline shortcut today," Hazel changed the subject again.

"I knew you had it in you!" Dad stood up and patted me on the back a little too enthusiastically.

"Ow. Thanks, Dad." I was thankful Hazel hadn't shared the whole story.

"Nice work," Gale told me.

"What is this...ridgeline? Is it something I might try?" Aric asked.

"No, Son," Dad told him. "I get paid to keep you alive." His face suddenly lit up. "Speaking of which, Gale is nearly ready to start guiding on his own."

"Well done," Mom told him.

"Yes," Gale sat up taller. "It's all planned. Reed will join me as we hike south to the Alatna River, but I'll guide the hunt as we float the waters to Allakaket."

"And then you get them loaded on their plane home," Dad added. "Our pilot will be waiting for you."

"Because the girl he fancies grew up in that village," Mom grinned.

Hazel snorted. "No one says fancies, Mom."

The rest of the meal passed with similarly dull conversation about what they all considered news here in Oread Basin. I ended up tuning most of it out while I mentally drafted another text to Claire. That was how I accidentally agreed to go see Gale's new place with him, Aric, and Hazel, and to hang out.

Chapter Three

EVEN THOUGH I'D MANAGED to stall the visit to Gale's house until after ten, at this time of year in northern Alaska, it was still daytime bright, which meant I was fractionally less likely to bite it on a tree root. Hazel called out changes in terrain as we covered the trail through the gnarly branches of the black spruce forest. Even with the daylight and Hazel as a guide, I stumbled several times and even fell as I tried to navigate across a small drainage ditch. Nature really hated me.

Travel got easier for the short time it took us to cross Main Street, the one road in Oread Basin. It was meant for ATVs rather than cars, and it was where the school, the community hall, the village pantry, and a small number of other community buildings could be found. It also led to the airstrip—hopefully Hazel and I would be taking off from there next month.

On the other side of Main, we followed another narrow trail that ended in front of a log cabin with the fresh and unadorned look of new construction.

I followed Hazel up three stairs onto a wide deck where Gale and Aric lounged in a set of folding camp chairs.

Gale jumped up when he saw us. "I have drinks." He hurried over to a cooler next to his front door and pulled out two brown bottles, popping off the caps before handing one to each of us.

I sat down with my beer, recognizing the familiar blue label of the only brand at our general store. It wasn't good, but it gave me something to do as I sat there. Three empty bottles already sat at Aric's feet, though Gale was still working on his first. Hazel and I sat down in the empty camp chairs, the four of us forming a loose circle.

"What do you think of my place?" Gale asked me.

"The view is great," I said, which was true. He had a great landscape view of the distant part of our mountain range.

"I will show you my room," Aric said. "I would like some privacy with you."

"You're wasting your time asking for private time with me," I muffled a chuckle.

"We are both students at the university. I must pull you aside somewhere quiet to ask you about your experience." He tried a different angle.

"She doesn't want to talk about school," Hazel told Aric. "And she's super gay. Lay off."

"She's not lying." I directed my attention to Gale. "Why don't you give us a tour?"

"Great idea!" He hopped to his feet again and headed for the front door with his drink in hand. "Follow me."

We entered his living room, which was filled with natural light from the windows and open to the kitchen. Practically everything—from the kitchen cabinets to the chairs—was hand carved wood, certainly contributed by various community members.

"I had Hazel help me pick the colors in the kitchen...well, everywhere in the house." He fawned over her.

Hazel's shoulders hunched slightly. "I was glad to help." She straightened back up in the very next instant. "I've always loved how everyone in our village pitches in on the new homes."

When we got into Gale's room upstairs, he pointed out the purple bedding. "Do you like the duvet, Hazel?"

I stared at my sister, and when she just nodded at Gale and said nothing else, I turned to him. "Unless you're planning to let Hazel take that duvet to Fairbanks in August, you two should talk."

Gale stared at me, lips pressed flat. "I wasn't aware Hazel was planning to leave."

"Like I said, you should talk," I told him.

I tried to communicate to Hazel without talking, giving her a look that I was hoping said, I'm sorry, but also you need to do this.

"Hey Aric." I gave the sleeve of his T-shirt a brief tug. "Let's get another drink. I guess it won't hurt to compare a few notes about school."

I hurried out of Gale's room, leaving Hazel to figure out her break-up. Aric pulled the bedroom door closed behind him as he followed me.

I heard Gale's voice ask, "When were you going to tell me? You told me we could talk about us after your training was over."

"I told you I didn't want any relationships during my training. And I certainly didn't want you to wait for me, Gale!" she matched his irritated tone.

Aric and I were out of hearing after that.

"So..." I settled back into my camp chair with a new drink. It was already tasting better, a sign of my low tolerance. "What other majors have you tried?"

"A bit of everything." He suddenly seemed more interested in his beer than the topic of our mutual school.

"Well, I'd be glad to just finish my prerequisites," I admitted. "I can't wait to get back there."

"You are not from here." He wasn't asking a question as he tipped his bottle to his lips, gulping it all down in a few large swallows.

"Yeah, I'm adopted." I bristled at his accurate assessment of how out of place I was. "But it's not about that. I left early last semester, and it caused me some relationship problems. I really need to get back there and fix things with my girlfriend."

"Yes," he said. "Your...girlfriend." He walked over to the cooler to open yet another drink for himself and took several large swallows before sitting back down. "You must be aware, that relationship cannot give you offspring."

"Offspring?" This guy was basically a stranger. Why did he think he could talk to me about having babies? "I'm tired. I need to get home."

I got up out of my droopy chair, much more clumsily than I would have liked, and I started walking down the stairs of the porch.

"Wait!" he called after me. "I have things to say—while we are alone."

"I think you've said enough," I called behind me, realizing I was still holding my half empty beer. I tipped it up to finish it off and left the empty bottle on Gale's bottom step. "Tell my sister I went home."

Walking back was a lot harder without Hazel to help me navigate the hazards of Mother Earth. Between that and the tipsy feeling from drinking too quickly, I only made it home after several painful falls.

Before going inside, I cut through the path leading to the neighbor's house. When the trees opened into their lot, I saw the far side of their paddock. All four draft horses munched away side by side at their hay feeder.

"Hey, Yukon." I patted the horse closest to me as I climbed inside the pen. "I've missed you, old man."

I stepped onto the bottom rail of the fence and used it to hoist myself up onto Yukon's smooth chestnut back while he continued eating, unbothered by my added weight. He was the oldest horse here and the only one who'd been around my whole life. He'd been my main source of peace growing up in this place.

I leaned forward and rested my cheek on the crest of his neck while I reached toward his shoulders in a hug. With my eyes closed and my fingers sliding across his smooth coat. The irritation of feeling stuck here and having to spend time with strange creeps seeped out of me until I nearly fell asleep. Deciding I didn't want to also fall off a horse today, I slid back to the ground and made my way toward bed.

The house was already quiet for the night when I got inside, but Mom had left a note on my pillow directing me how to use her latest medicines. The mug on my bedside table was meant to help me sleep and the tin of lotion next to it was supposed to keep my dreams away. I dutifully used both as directed, wondering if the alcohol was going to help or interfere with the experimental concoctions.

KING AMBROSE

A tall blond man stands behind Queen Kyra as she sits at her vanity table crying. "Don't leave me, Ambrose," she says.

"We've been over this, my love." He draws a sword from behind his shoulder and holds it out so he can run his fingers over its floral tooling and the rows of alternating rubies and sapphires just below the blade. The words Immortalis Excessum are engraved down the blade.

"This is the last one," Ambrose says. "Keep it in the vault we built and let no one but our daughters learn it exists."

Kyra's shoulders slump.

Ambrose rests the sword on the vanity, and reaches his arms around Kyra, holding her. His lips kiss softly along her neck and up to her cheek. He finds her fingers with his but jumps at the frosty chills that shoot up his arm.

"Careful, Love," he says, and stands to replace the sword behind his back. "It is not like you to lose control of Demeter's gift to you."

"I do not understand why the prophecy asks me to sacrifice so much." She stands and weaves her fingers into his.

Ambrose leads Kyra to a bookshelf that spans the entire far wall of the room. On a middle shelf, he removes a burgundy leather book labeled Populus ex Progenies Immortalis and presses his index finger into what looks like a chip in the stone wall. All at once, a rectangular seam appears and the stone curves into some recess in the wall.

He reaches for the sword and slides it into the once hidden cavity before returning the stone and book to their places.

He bows his head for a moment before speaking. "I will await the day we are together again. I have said my farewells to Candace and Amara, and they understand. They understand I must do this to bring forth the prophecy, and give them a better life. Please stay here. I do not wish you to see it happen."

* * * * *

Ambrose is standing in a large, mostly empty room. The walls are an uneven dark-stone that curve inward, creating a cave-like feel. In the middle of the room, forming a haphazard pile, are what must be close to a hundred swords covered in the same intricate detailing and jewels as the one he'd just been holding.

A sandy-haired man with glowing sea-green eyes stands next to the pile, looking at Ambrose. "Is it time, King Ambrose?" His voice has a slight tremble.

Ambrose nods. "Thank you for your sacrifice." His words carry enough to create a small echo in the cavernous room. "Your gift will give my fire the strength it needs to finally end the curse of these 77things." Ambrose gestures at the swords.

"I am afraid of not being there for my children," the man says.

"Our sacrifice today is the only way to give your children and mine a future without strife and death. Remember the latest prophecy."

The other man sighs. "If we make this sacrifice, your daughters and my sons will bring the gift of peace with their first child."

"And many more grandchildren after that, the prophecy assures. I want that future for my daughters."

The man nods, fisting and stretching his hands. "Then let us begin—before my nerve evaporates."

Ambrose stands over the heap of metal and breathes deeply for several long seconds until finally, a fire erupts from his fingers, and he pushes it down toward the swords. It touches the edge of the pile, and then it grows, crawling across the blades until all of them are engulfed in flame.

His power goads the fire to burn hotter, and the flame's heat rises until it turns a glowing red, then yellow, then white. Eventually, the metal begins to soften and melt, but as it does, an opposing energy surges up from the swords, through his flames and into Ambrose. It hunts its way inside of him, eating everything up as it backtracks along his fire.

"Now!" Ambrose screams, pain laced into the brief word.

The man grabs Ambrose by the wrist, just above the flow of fire, and the inferno redoubles its efforts against the energy coming back through the connection with the swords. The increase in the blaze sets the weapons to melting again and slows the other, ravenous energy.

When the metal becomes a molten pool, the energy from the swords rears back up and resumes its feast within Ambrose.

An instant later, Ambrose drops to his knees in agony as not only his fire energy, but also the source of his life energy is eaten up from within. Still, he's pushing his remaining heat into the liquid metal until he can't take any more.

He falls forward into the shallow pool of searing liquid, the other man splashing down beside him. Ambrose's destroyed form lets out one continuous and soundless scream. All that's left is anguish and a sense of encompassing nothingness. And then darkness.

* * * * *

I woke screaming, wordlessly frantic in my pain.

Every inch of my body was on fire from within, on the verge of combusting through my skin. My body twisted, limbs shaking violently as I tried to escape the heat.

Someone's voice was crashing into the cracks in my screams. "Hold still..." More screams. "...hear me?" The voice cut through in pieces.

I gasped, quieting my now ragged throat. Hazel was over me, pinning my arms.

"Alexa, you're burning up! What the hell's going on?"

I was searing inside and out, breath coming in tattered pants as the pain continued to flare. For the first time, I noticed a sort of vault at my center, open and pushing heat, but there was nowhere for it to go. It pressed at my fingers, my toes, my face. There was no escape for this heat in my body—this energy that was pushing to find a way out. And I realized I might die for real.

"You're soaked in sweat!" Hazel screeched. "No. You're fucking steaming!" She shook me. "Say something!"

If I could scream, I must be able to talk. "Help me," I whispered. "Something is trapped inside of me!" I sucked in a deep breath as a wave of pain seared across my face where the energy made a new attempt at escape. "I can't stop it. I can't get it out!" I gasped.

"Just hang on, Alexa." Hazel said. "Mom and Dad are bringing ice and medicine. Just hang on."

"I'm trying," I gritted. My breath was coming in shallow huffs, but occasionally, I'd suck in deeply with a sharp wave of agony. As I noticed what my body was doing, I began a slow count in my head, matching my breath to the rhythm.

"Are you still with me, Lex?" Hazel's voice cut into my haze.

I was. Just by managing my breathing, I could better sense my environment. More than that, I was better able to sense what was happening within me. The waves of heat and pain still caused small gasps and temporary loss of focus, but I could think again. "I'm managing."

I tried to imagine the energy going back toward my center. In my dream he'd used the fire energy so easily, but then again, I wasn't him. The energy inside me now was still pulsing out, and it felt like it had an endless source. I was burning up as much as ever.

"Okay, sit up and drink this tea." Mom came in, pushing a mug in front of me. "It'll calm you."

I immediately took a large gulp of the sweet liquid. It was a bit syrupy going down and had a bitter aftertaste that clung to my throat, but the drink had an immediate and powerful effect. I was on my third gulp when I could feel my body separate from my mind. I still noticed the pains and sensations, but I felt outside of myself, and therefore protected from it.

I used the separation to try to understand what was happening inside of me. I sensed the energy coming from my core again, radiating out like a small sun. I couldn't conceive of a way to close it in, but maybe there was a way to make it stop—turn it off and put my body back to normal.

"It's helping," I said. I finished the mug and laid back down. "What's happening to me, Mom?" I sobbed.

Dad rushed in then and threw a sheet over me before pressing bag after bag of ice against my lightly covered skin. It began to cool me, soothing the burn.

"We have to tell her the truth, Reed," Mom cried. "She can't live this way!"

Dad turned toward Mom and gestured at me. "We need to fix this, Fern!" he yelled. "Before we talk about anything!"

"What are you talking about?" Hazel asked, looking between Mom and Dad "What truth?"

"Not now, Hazel," Mom said in that final tone of hers.

I closed my eyes—sensing the energy source inside of me again, that sun that was trying to burn me up. I could feel the heat surging into me—pulsing. My blood. It felt like it was circulating with my blood, but the source wasn't really my heart. It seemed like my heart was just there to move the energy, while the power itself was coming from some infinite place at my core that could never actually be found.

Maybe if I could slow my heart rate, I could keep so much heat from running wild through my body. So I lengthened my breaths, really trying to embrace the calm brought on by the tonic. Soon, the heat was less—not a lot, but I could feel the intensity of the escaping energy slow, get less forceful.

"You feel cooler," Hazel commented.

"I've slowed it down, but I don't know how to turn it off," I said. "How do you turn off a sun?"

"What are you talking about?" She turned to look at our parents and yelled. "What is she talking about?"

"We don't know. Not exactly," Mom said.

"Well, what do you know?" Hazel asked.

"We've been keeping some things secret...trying to protect Alexa."

"Why does she need to be protected with lies, Mom?" Hazel snaps. "That makes no sense."

"There's so much we need to tell you," Mom sighed, sounding defeated. "Alexa has a kind of magic...one we thought we could keep from manifesting." She looked at me. "We thought we'd succeeded when you showed no signs throughout your teens. I see now that we were foolish. There was no stopping—"

"Not now, Fern!" Dad yelled. "We can talk about this when she's not...not..." He picked one of the bags of ice off me and shook it around. "Like this!"

"Magic?" Hazel yelled. "Magic? What the hell are you talking about?"

"Go to your room, Hazel," Dad yelled back.

"Ugh! Whatever! This is insane." She jumped up from her place beside me and stormed out.

"We'll tell you both everything we know," Mom reassured me. "Just try to relax for now. See if you can stop it."

"I don't know how," I cried, tears dripping down the sides of my face.

"Why don't you try to sleep a bit," Mom said.

"That sounds like a horrible idea," I whispered in a panic. "Look what happened last time I slept!"

"No," she said quickly. "My tea will help you sleep, and I'll wake you in a few minutes. Maybe your body will instinctively reset."

"If you say so, but how do I just go to sleep?"

"With this tea, just stop trying to be awake," she shrugged.

I narrowed my eyes at her before closing them. "Okay..." I'd already separated from my body, so I just let that go. Then I let go of my thoughts and slipped into the warm fuzz that I hadn't noticed myself cocooned in until that moment.

Chapter Four

MERCIFULLY, WHEN MOM SHOOK me awake, my body was no longer possessed by fire. I felt no lasting pains, and even the mental fog from the medicine had mostly lifted.

"How long was I asleep?"

"A couple hours—you were calm, so I decided to let you rest."

"Can you tell me what's going on now?"

"Yes, Alexa." She stood up and headed for the door. "We'll talk over breakfast. Dad's making pancakes."

Too distracted to fully dress myself, I grabbed a pair of sweats to go with my oversized T-shirt and hurried downstairs. Even so, I was the last one at the kitchen table.

Mom and Dad were already eating away at their pancakes and eggs, but Hazel was ignoring her empty plate, arms crossed as her foot tapped away under the table.

"Okay." I sat next to my sister, noticing that my parents had abandoned the ends of the table to sit facing us. "Tell us." Then I added, "Please." An afterthought to keep from ruffling my dad's sense of respectability.

"Hazel, Alexa." Mom hesitated for a long moment. "We're not only your parents but also grandparents to Alexa's birth father. Alexa, you're our great-granddaughter."

"You aren't old enough for all that." I could hardly process her words, but I knew my parents weren't great-grandparents.

"Your father and I are both over four hundred years old...and we're Nymphs."

"Seriously?" Hazel snapped. "Stop lying!"

Mom ignored the outburst and continued as she covered Dad's hand with her own. "Just listen. Please. This isn't easy to explain." She waited to make sure we'd stay quiet. "Hazel, you're our biological daughter—"

"And I suppose I'm like three hundred or something." She rolled her eyes.

"Hazel, your mother asked you not to interrupt." Dad narrowed his eyes at her. "And don't be silly. You know how many years you've been alive."

"If you start confusing twenty with three hundred, Sis, I think we need to go file a complaint at the school," I joked to a disappointing lack of response. I guess we were going more for a tense and angry tone this morning. I was too tired for that much feeling.

"Hazel, you're a Nymph," Mom continued. "And Alexa, you're part Nymph as well, but your birth parents, Damian and Irene, asked us to hide you—even from yourself."

"I've seen Damian and Irene," I said. "Well, I saw Damian. It was like I was in Irene's body. Pregnant with myself, by the way. Gross."

"You don't actually believe this shit, Alexa?" Hazel glared.

After my dreams and the fire incident from last night, I was having a hard time being skeptical, so I shrugged and filled my plate with pancakes instead of answering.

"Watch your language, Hazel Dawn Delmon!" Dad was using full names again. Great.

"Sorry." Hazel shrunk back in her chair.

"How did you know about Irene and Damian?" Mom asked.

"I dreamed about them yesterday. The more you talk, the more familiar that dream feels—like one of my own memories. Damian was there with Irene and some other people, and they were like, 'Let's send our daughter to Oread Basin.'"

"That was what caused you to wake in a fever?" Mom asked.

"No. I saw them when I napped on the couch. And I dreamed about a bunch of dead bodies that got brought back to life when I passed out at the ridgeline."

"It sounds like you witnessed the massacre at Queen Kyra's engagement party," Mom said. "We left Atlantis for a safer life right after that and came to live with the Nymphs of this village. That was about three hundred years ago."

"The next queen, Amara, exiled all Nymphs a few decades later," Dad said. "She claimed our kind were tainting the bloodline." He dropped his fork and balled up his fist.

"I wish you'd told me about what you saw in your dreams yesterday." Mom changed the subject. "I may have used different treatments. This is far more serious than simple sleep troubles."

"Well, they just seemed like weird dreams until last night, when I was in the body of a guy who shot fire out of his hands to melt a bunch of swords, killing himself in the process. Before that, I'd thought it was just wishful dreaming because everyone in them had eyes like mine, and they were thin and bony like me too. Is that a thing? If I'm only part Nymph, what else am I? And what does Dad mean about a bloodline?"

Mom took a steadying breath before she spoke. "Your frame and eyes are traits of the Godline people, descendants of the Olympian Gods—"

"You certainly don't get that from your Nymph side," Dad jumped in.

"Yes, Reed, but I was explaining her Godline side now. The appearance of power and fragility in their human-shaped forms became a sort of fashion among the gods and Godline in the early days when they walked with mortals. They enjoyed the fear and obsession it provoked in humans. The traits still show up in their lines."

"Seriously? My body is the victim of an idiotic style from thousands of years ago?" I asked. "Thanks for nothing, stupid gods."

Mom reached over to give my arm a reassuring squeeze and pushed on. "The Olympian gods eventually decided to leave Earth and Atlantis behind. It was sometime after the Trojan War—something about Zeus being tired of all their squabbling over human affairs."

"This is nuts, right?" I asked. "I...I'm not really a descendant of gods."

"Of course, it's nuts," Hazel bumped my arm with her elbow and gave me the smile we saved for each other at the dinner table. The one that said our parents were being ridiculous about something.

"I wish it were not true," Mom said. "But many Godline refused to leave with the Olympians, as commanded. They are who you come from."

"The only issue with the origin of your people," Dad said, "is that when your Godline ancestors refused to leave, it angered the Olympians so much, they left behind a couple of curses that decimated the Godline population over the last two thousand years."

"But that is a detailed history that will take more than one conversation, Reed." Mom gently refocused him.

Then Mom turned to Hazel. "Like we said already, you, me, your father—everyone in the village—we're Nymphs."

"What does that mean, Mom?" She'd lost her hint of humor.

"Nymphs have lived on Earth and Atlantis from the very beginning," Mom said. "While the gods and their early descendants preferred visiting the Mediterranean region or staying in Atlantis, Nymphs formed communities everywhere. Our magic is subtle on Earth, but it's adapted to allow us to live in harmony with the lands we're tied to, even allowing our features to blend with our surroundings. And for those of us who practice, we can use our magic and our land to help and heal people."

Dad had resumed eating but started talking mid-bite. "I don't miss the snobby Godline folk in Atlantis, but I sure do miss the magic. It's woven into the fabric of nature there." He looked at Mom wistfully. "Remember it, Fern?"

"Yes, Dear. Our magic isn't quite so subtle on Atlantis. The form of nature there is only limited by the imagination of the latest Nymph to interact with it." Her eyes went distant for a moment, and then she sighed, blinking back into focus.

"You've been teaching me magic all this time?" Hazel asked Mom, looking hurt.

I understood. They'd lied about everything, but I mostly just felt relieved that the failure defining so much of my life had an explanation. I was the only one here without some special brand of nature magic.

"Yes, Hazel," Mom said. "What we do is magic. Humans do not ask their plants to become medicine. They only work with the natural properties already there."

"I don't know why any of it works, Mom, only how to follow your steps." She was no longer yelling, but her voice had a dangerous edge. "I don't know how to do magic."

"I can teach you," Mom blurted. "Explain how the magic functions in the work you've already mastered. It will allow you to start creating your own recipes." She glanced over at her leatherbound, invented-recipes book. "You can start adding to the journal."

"Were you ever going to tell me?" Hazel asked quietly. "Or were you just going to let me spend my life limited by my ignorance?"

"And no wonder I suck at living here." I joined in, hoping to stay on Hazel's side of the thick tension filling the room. "I've spent my whole life feeling incompetent in this family." I didn't have to reach very deep to get pissed.

"We are sorry for that, Alexa," Mom said. "We really hoped to help you live here using our ways, but your experience—your difficulties are because you do not possess that kind of magic."

No shit.

"What kind of magic do I have?" I asked.

My parents both went silent and looked at each other until the tension filled the room. Finally, Mom sighed and nodded.

Dad started. "You seem to have inherited a Godline gift of some sort. We almost got you through the gifting age. We planned to tell you both the truth after that."

"What's a gifting age?" I asked. The deeper into this conversation we got, the more things about my life made sense.

"The magic in your people is given before birth and shows up sometime between puberty and...well...your age," Mom said. "We almost made it...convinced ourselves you'd been born Giftless. We've been told that happens often now."

"Why wouldn't you want me to have magic?" I asked. "I mean, aside from it almost burning me alive."

"I'm not sure where to even start," Mom said.

"I can start." Dad took over again. "Godline people who live among humans or Nymphs here on Earth—they're in hiding from those in charge on Atlantis. Using their magic, if they have it, will get them found and dragged back there by Queen Amara's hunters."

As Mom took back over, it dawned on me how long they'd been together—the reason they were always so in tune.

"It's why many Nymph villages, like ours, live like humans," she said. "It helps us escape the notice of Atlantis and hide Godline runaways."

"Are you seriously saying Atlantis is real?" Hazel asked. "And I thought you just said we use magic all the time."

"Yes," Dad said. "Atlantis is very real—it's our homeland."

"And Nymph magic is not what they are looking for on Atlantis," Mom added.

"If you say so." Hazel finally began filling her empty plate.

"Okay, but why am I hiding from Atlantis? And what is a Godline gift and what's Giftless?"

"The gift is a specific magical ability in your kind," Mom said. "One power or way of using magic. It's chosen by the Olympian who gifts it, but time passes differently for the gods. They don't always remember, or care, to give a gift in time for the birth of a new Godline child. Those forgotten or refused a gift become the Giftless Godline."

"If the Olympians were so mad about the Godline staying behind, why would they give anyone their magic?" Hazel asked, her curiosity making her forget her temper for the moment.

"The gods are incredibly vain," Dad said. "Now that they can't come down and gather human followers, they seek prestige in the successes of those with their Godline gifts."

"Or at least that's Reed's favorite theory." Mom grinned at Dad. "Who knows why those gods do the things they do. Too much power for too many years is never a good thing."

"Why am I hiding from a world filled with people like me?"

"You were brought to us so Queen Amara couldn't take you," Mom said. "She'd planned to harm you as a way to torment and control Irene."

"Right. Because Irene has a special gift for peace or something, right? There was something in my dreams about it."

Dad set his fork on his plate and shifted to face Mom. "We need to get help for her, Fern. If she started these dreams yesterday, they might already be working on locating her. We need to get her out of the village—for everyone's safety."

Mom nodded.

"I'll contact Lukas right after this," he said.

"Please!" I yelled. "Just tell me what my gift is and how it works. I can't sleep. It's hurting me. It's out of control. And I really hate it!"

"We don't understand how to help with your magic, honey," Mom said. "It's why we need—"

"Who the hell is Lukas and why are we suddenly leaving town?" Hazel asked.

"Lukas is a Godline friend of ours who's also in hiding," Mom narrowed her eyes at Hazel. "He can help Alexa control her gift so she can hide again."

"Hazel was right about all this stuff being hard to believe," I said. "Olympian ancestors? Magic training from a stranger? Someone coming after me here? Really?"

"I'm so sorry, Alexa," Mom said. "Our schooling normally includes comprehensive Godline and Nymph history, but we had a town meeting when we adopted you and decided it would be safest if you only learned what a human would. We thought it would help you blend in with them. Anyway, we tried to honor your mother's wish for us to hide that world from you. So we treated history like mythology in your schooling and left many parts out.

"What about Gale?" Hazel asked.

"His parents gave him the complete education at home," Mom said.

"This is so messed up," I muttered. "Willow? Alder?"

"Yes. All your schoolmates."

"How could you think lying about everything—about who we are, was a good idea?" Hazel asked. "Gale's been lying to me, too!"

"Don't blame that boy for respecting the rules of his parents," Dad raised his voice. "All of these secrets were meant to protect your sister and keep our community safe while doing so. Got it?"

"Got it," she mumbled, staring down at her hands.

"Hazel, you should know something else." Mom hesitated for a few long seconds before sending her next words out in a rush. "Your aunts and uncles who have occasionally come to visit are actually your siblings from when your dad and I lived in Atlantis. I'm sorry we've lied so much."

Hazel closed her eyes and sighed. "Back to Alexa, please."

I took a moment to wonder how I was actually related to my aunts and uncles, but then took Hazel's cue to change subject.

"How would the god people even find me?" I asked. "Why do we have to suddenly leave?"

"The hunters," Dad said. "And the queen's breeding laws."

"Disgusting," Hazel spoke that thought for both of us.

"Indeed." Dad continued. "The vain Godline comes from vain gods. Nymph blood was suddenly diluting the immortal line. Now only Godline pairings are allowed, and the new queen requires results. People are punished for failing her."

"And what does that have to do with hunters and finding me?" I asked.

"Hunters are a profession of elite guards dedicated to dragging Godline people out of hiding and into the queen's breeding cells," he said. "We don't know how they do it, but from everything we've heard, they are very effective."

The picture of my danger was becoming clear—if caught, my choice was torture by an evil queen or being bred like an animal. "So, what now?" I suddenly felt nauseated and lightheaded.

"That's it, Lex? They mention something you find scary enough, and now you're suddenly on board?"

"That's not fair, Hazel." Her words hurt. We'd been in this together, but now her anger struck at me.

"It's just...all the lies! I'm so mad at you two!" She looked over at Mom and Dad. "We could have been prepared for this!"

"I think we all realize that now," Dad nearly shouted. "It is why I've been so patient with your disrespect."

"Ugh." Hazel blew out a long sigh and settled into a resigned slouch.

"Look at the bright side, girls." His lips curled up ever so slightly. "We only kept you in the dark for twenty years. By all means, take a few decades to be angry."

Hazel tilted her head at Dad, eyebrows drawn in thought. "How long will I live?"

"Well, our deaths are one of the things that make us special," he said. "And another reason we hope to return to Atlantis one day. Here on Earth, we simply stop using our magic when we are ready to age. If we do that long enough, our magic will go dormant, we will age, and eventually, die as a human would."

"What's different about Atlantis?" Hazel asked.

"There, we can merge our magic with nature itself, becoming one with the collective magical energies of all our ancestors. That is our true way."

"How long 'til one of those things happens to me?" she asked.

"However long you choose," Mom said.

"I'm guessing that's not how it works for me," I said.

"No. There is something in your magic that perpetually renews your youth and life," Mom said. "I don't understand it beyond that, but I do know it means you can heal almost any wound with enough time, and after you have fully developed, you will never age."

"And that's officially the limit to how many revelations I can have in one day." I stood up from the table.

"That makes two of us." Hazel pushed out her own chair.

"Wait," Mom said. "There's one more thing."

We both waited for her to continue.

"Irene had once been prophesied to rule, but she remains a princess, firmly under the control of Queen Amara. As Irene's daughter, Alexa, you represent potential opposition to Amara's rule."

"Why are you telling us this?" I asked.

"No matter what, Alexa, you can't end up in Atlantis."

"Great. I don't want to go there anyway. As soon as I fix this." I pointed at my own head. "I'm getting back to school."

"When I hear back from Lukas, we'll head to Fairbanks," Dad said. "You two need to start packing."

* * * * *

I tried to pack, but after a few minutes of moving piles of clothes around my bed, I gave up and took Jane out of her cage. It was soothing to stroke her tiny head while holding her against my chest, so that's what I did as I went into Hazel's room.

She was lying on her bed, eyes shut, music so loud in her ears I could hear it across the room. Somehow, she still noticed me come in because she opened her eyes to glare at me.

"What do you want?" She yanked out her earbuds.

"So...we're real freaks, huh?"

"You are, anyway," she grumbled.

"Why are you pissed at me?"

"If they hadn't been hiding you, I would have known the truth," she muttered. "Oh, and you're the reason I've never been allowed to do anything my whole life—always having to look after you and make sure you weren't getting hurt." She turned over sharply on the bed, so her back was to me.

I just stood there, stunned. She wasn't wrong. She'd always made it feel like she wanted to be right there with me, but deep down I'd known she was stuck looking after me.

She flopped back over. "And of course," she stretched out the last word, "you would be some special child my mom and dad have devoted the last twenty years to hiding and protecting. I'm just the lowly biological child who happened to be born."

"Stop it, Hazel!" I snapped. "My whole life was a lie too! And I'm sorry my existence is such an inconvenience!"

She stared at me, lips pressed flat, eyes boring into mine.

"Hazel, please don't leave me alone in this," I said. "Screw them for lying to us."

Our whole lives, we'd never been able to stay angry with each other long. Everything inside of me desperately hoped this time would be no different, even now that everything had changed.

"You're right about that." She sat up. "Screw them." And just like that, her misdirected anger stopped lashing at me.

"All of this is insane." I leaned against her door frame.

"Yeah, like how you're somehow an almost immortal princess."

"How about the fact that you've been performing magic every day since childhood. Maybe you just found the label for it, but you've always been extraordinary. Meanwhile, I'm basically a magic bomb waiting to go off, and I'm being hunted by a royal family that I supposedly belong to."

"Well, when you put it that way, I feel much better about the situation." The tiniest of curves crept into her lips.

"Wallow in my misery all you want." I grinned, testing her mood. "Please just keep being my sister."

"You're still my sister." Her eyes softened. "And I'm sorry I said all that just now. I'm just freaked, and it felt safer yelling at you than Mom and Dad. This is all on them. Not you." She patted the bed beside her.

A knot I only now noticed unraveled within me, and I gave a long sigh of relief as I crossed the room to sit with Hazel.

"Here." I carefully moved Jane into Hazel's lap. "She likes making people feel better."

Hazel started stroking her fingers absently along Jane's back. "I told Gale there was never going to be an us last night."

"I'm sorry I started all that."

"No. You were right. I broke up with him too gently last year and he took that to mean we were on a break. I was too cowardly to deal with it."

"He was way too eager to settle down, but you two were a nice enough couple—I could see why he held out hope."

"We were pretty good together, but I definitely wasn't ready for all that he wanted. Especially not after this morning."

"Yeah."

"Anyway, now that I know about all this magic stuff, I might want to check out some other Nymph villages, meet new people. Maybe become a healer somewhere that doesn't already have one, you know?"

"That sounds cool," I said.

"After you're safe, anyway. I promised I'd help you get back to school, and I will. Fairbanks can be the first stop on my world tour."

"Hopefully Fairbanks is only my first stop as well," I said. "Knowing I lack all nature magic, my original plan is still best—the bigger a city I can move to, the better."

"You know it always bothered me to think about you living far away in some city when I knew I was meant to live here," Hazel said. "But suddenly knowing we aren't getting old any time soon makes it a little easier."

"The idea of living so long is a little hard to believe."

"It's all hard to believe," she said. "We should probably focus on right now, anyway. I'm glad we're headed to town. I wanted to try selling some of my lotions at the farmers' market this year—"

"And you haven't made it to town once this summer because you've been trying to help me with my stupid magical problems. Sorry again, Hazel."

She chuckled. "Yeah, but there's still plenty of season left. And I can get a booth at the State Fair."

"Count me in for the fair. I'll never get over that food or the rides. I'll even take a shift in your booth if you ride that slingshot ride with me."

"I'll never ride that ride. No rational person should like being shot into the sky for the fun of it."

"Suit yourself. Claire rode it with me last year. Maybe she'll forgive me long enough for a fair date." Even though I really wasn't sure what I'd done to make her dump me in the first place, other than maybe becoming too inconvenient.

"Do you think she'll get back with you?" Hazel asked. "What would you even tell her?"

"I sent her a message yesterday, but I don't think she's going to reply. Plus, I'm pretty sure she's found a new girlfriend." One with more money, time, and fewer issues, probably. "You should see them in the photos she's posting. Must be nice to be able to travel the world without a care."

"You can come to some Nymph villages with me on your next summer break."

"I appreciate that, but you and I definitely have different world destinations in mind. Following my sister on her quest for magical development is not the vibe I imagine when I think about traveling the world."

"No worry there. By my calculations, I'm your Great Auntie Hazel."

My laughter erupted as an involuntary bark. "That's so much worse."

Chapter Five

ARIC

A BOY SITS AT the foot of a golden throne mounted on a raised section of flooring. The lower part of a giant room is empty except for one alert and armed man next to the doors on the far wall and, strangely, a heap of dirty rags in the corner nearest him. His child-sized legs, clothed in handsome brown pants, are crossed over each other on the polished white stone.

A woman with silver hair and luminous green eyes looks down at him from the throne. So much power rolls off the surface of her that the frailty of her thin body is impossible to see.

A small series of braids wrap her head like a shining crown, and she's in a flowing, airy fabric that looks like a liquid diamond pantsuit.

"It is good I decided to tutor you on the Queen's Laws myself, Aric. You have learned quickly," she says. "Just a few more questions for today."

"Yes, Mother." Aric's voice trembles between his lips.

"The laws pertaining to forbidden acts?"

"The Godline shall never breed a Nymph because it dilutes the blood of the gods," he says. "The Godline shall never breed a human because the offspring will be a mortal half-breed."

"And?"

"The Godline shall never leave Atlantis for Earth, except on approved business."

"Good, now the breeding rules," she prompts.

"The Gifted Godline shall keep a record of all breeding beginning after the first century of—"

"No!" She stands, eyes flaring with her power. She's out of reach but swings her arm as if she's backhanding him. "Cite the new law!"

An invisible but solid force hits Aric's cheek so hard his body jerks.

He gasps to stop a cry of pain and yells an answer instead. "Two decades!" His body is tense, waiting for another strike. "Gifted Godline shall keep a record of all breeding after two decades of life, changing breeding partners each decade if offspring do not result, and breeding the Giftless only as a last resort."

"And?" She lifts a hand toward him.

"Any Godline who fail to produce offspring must report to the breeding chambers at the queen's discretion."

She begins lowering her arm again. "Tell me why I created these laws." Her voice has softened.

"To save our people from Hera's curse of infertility—to save the Godline," Aric recites.

Satisfied, she slides back into her throne, which is formed by hundreds of thin and twisted golden vines. The seat is rooted into the floor and all over the top and back it's covered in golden buds and roses. "That is enough review for today. We will end on a practical lesson."

The queen looks over at the doors. "Bring him in, Dagan," she tells the guard standing there.

"Yes, Queen Amara," he nods and steps through the door for a moment. When he returns, he pulls a terrified-looking man across the room and stops at the bottom of the steps that lead up to the throne. The two men couldn't look more different. The guard is covered in pristine and shimmering fabrics—fitted dark pants and an ivory top, with fine leather crossing his chest to secure the sword behind him. The other man wears a filthy T-shirt and falls to the knees of his tattered jeans as the guard shoves him to the floor and then returns to his post.

"Tell me why this man is here." Queen Amara says, narrowing her eyes at Aric.

"Because he went to live with the humans, and he married and bred with a human." Aric's voice is shaking heavily now.

"What happens to those who break the Queen's Laws?"

"It is the queen's duty to reeducate them," Aric recites.

"Good. Today you will observe a part of his reeducation." She stands again and walks down to the same level as the man. He has eyes like a terrified animal, and he's frozen in place like one as well.

"We start with a blood bonding. Then he will spend time in the cells for daily reeducation," she says. "Bring my knife."

"Yes, Mother." Aric gets up and walks to a small table beside her throne, picking up an emerald-handled knife with a slender blade and carrying it to her in open palms.

"Stay right here, Son, so you can watch." The man's hand shoves into the air suddenly, and he seems to be fighting with an imaginary force as his palm opens for her. "There are two ways to bond blood," she instructs, stepping up to the man. "Blood bonding can be painless, but traitors must be handled differently."

She slashes the man's hand and then pricks her own, pressing their wounds together. After a moment, the man screams and attempts to twist away, but remains in place, somehow unable to move.

Aric's body becomes tense as he watches, and he starts shaking. Tears form just behind his eyes. Suddenly, he jumps forward, pulling the man's hand away from Queen Amara to interrupt the endless screams.

She waves her free arm in the air, and Aric is slapped hard in the face again with the stinging force of her power. He falls back and cracks his elbow on the marbled floor, blood instantly welling into a small red pool.

"Do not interfere," she yells. "Have the madwoman heal you and get out!" She turns back to the man and the screaming picks up again.

Aric walks toward the pile of rags in the corner, holding his bleeding elbow. Halfway there it becomes clear that the rags are actually a person, hunched over in layers of filthy garments. As Aric gets closer, his steps slow. He hesitates, looking at the figure.

She's familiar.

She's sickly now, but her crimson hair still shows through the layers of dirt. Her bright blue eyes shine out of a filthy face. Ivy. She hums to herself while she rocks a baby doll in her arms.

Aric slows down as he gets closer to her, but she hears his steps and looks up. She laughs and sets the baby doll aside, clapping her hands softly and gesturing for him to come closer. He shakes his head and stays out of reach.

"Go to her," the guard says as he watches them.

"Yes, Dagan, sir." Aric looks back at the woman and walks to her.

She grabs his arm gently and puts her hands over the wound, and the cut in his elbow disappears in a matter of seconds. She smiles up at him, clapping her hands again, and then gestures for a hug, but he turns and runs away.

Aric runs past Dagan, through the heavy wooden doors beside him. It takes all his body weight to pull one open.

He runs through the next room—circular and high ceilinged— toward another set of doors, but another tall guard steps in front of him. This one has glowing amber eyes and long sandy hair.

"Hold, Aric!" he says. "What is the hurry?"

"Apologies, Theron, sir," Aric says. "Let me pass. Please? Just let me go."

"In a moment. What has happened?"

"Mother wanted me to watch her punish someone for breeding a human. I could not watch. I tried to stop her, and she hurt me." His eyes finally well over with tears. "I was scared. I know I am not supposed to be, but I was. The man just kept screaming."

Theron squeezed Aric's shoulder gently. "I am sorry you had to watch that. And that you were hurt."

"The madwoman healed me, but that was most terrifying."

"Aric, her name is Ivy, and she is very kind. She would never hurt anyone. It is not in her nature as a healer. You need never fear her."

"But she is crazy."

"Maybe one day you will understand her better and then she will not scare you so much. May I ask you one last question?"

Aric nods.

"When Queen Amara was punishing the man for loving a human, did you feel it was the right thing to do?"

"It is the law," Aric says. "The queen's duty to reeducate lawbreakers."

"But was it right?"

"Mother says it is."

"That man in there had a family on Earth. He had a wife and two small children he loved. They were ripped from this world, and he is being punished. Does that seem right?"

Aric shakes his head.

"Trust that kind heart."

* * * * *

"Dammit!" Apparently, my dreams were a magical education with a focus on the psychotic people.

I sat up in the dark, blinking, adjusting to the low glow of the midnight sun rimming my bedroom curtains. In the low light, I could see the shadowy outline of my still clean and nearly empty room.

I'd spent the day packing in accordance with Dad's one bag per person rule, prioritizing space for the expensive clothes in my closet before packing in assorted sweats, jeans, T-shirts, and other more practical clothing layers. My make-up, contacts, and school supplies filled out the rest of my bag, which now sat in our detached garage with three others, ready to travel at a moment's notice.

My phone was the only thing I'd left unpacked. It sat on my desk, taunting me, stubbornly refusing to produce a reply from Claire. Maybe she was just busy. Maybe she still hated me. I had no idea. There was still no sign she'd even read my message.

I grabbed my pillow off the floor and jammed it back on my bed. When I closed my eyes again, I begged my brain to give me a pretty dream about a magical party where a clashing outfit was the biggest problem.

QUEEN AMARA

A woman walks through a circular entry room and uses a set of doors that lead into a courtyard, filled with lush greenery and flowers of every color, dispersed in a spiral pattern leading to a sitting area at the center of the walled in space. Blooms change color, petals shifting from pink to red or orange to yellow or blue to purple as she follows a cobbled path through the garden.

When she reaches the center, she drops onto one of several cushioned stone benches, reclining to match the pose of a woman across the open cobbled space from her, but her body remains rigid despite the comfort of the seat.

"Amara, my queen." The other woman's voice is filled with delight. "Why so tense?"

"This is your gift, Helen—your job." Amara's words are clipped. "I have other matters to attend and a staff of servants who could assist you."

Honey colored locks frame Helen's face as she looks at Amara, the rest of her hair pulled up carefully with golden pins. Pins obviously meant to complement her glowing amber eyes. "My queen, I must insist you stay involved in every hunt. You want your people saved from the plague of humanity, do you not?"

"Of course, but I also need to give them back the gifts stolen by the curses from our ancestors and that work is done in the cells."

Behind Helen, a map hangs, suspended between two white columns. Its mahogany frame just longer than the bench she's stretched across. Down the center, like the spine of a book, the map is divided by dozens of minutely labeled arches, each formed by two curved and golden brush strokes. The continents and oceans are familiar under the scripted heading of Earth on one side. Under the heading Atlantis, the other side is covered in unfamiliar landforms and waters. Golden dots mark places across the landmasses of both maps.

"My queen, I have complete faith in your ability to harness the Olympian gifts, but at this moment, I have found one of our people, and we need a strong population, ready for the day you succeed."

"Then tell me," Queen Amara says. "Perhaps this traitor will provide something new to my experiments."

Helen gives a rehearsed sort of laugh. "That is exactly it. Because of your laws, every one of our people, here or in hiding, will serve you as you work to save us."

"The Queen's Laws will save us." The words come from Amara's tongue as if they are well acquainted with being spoken.

"The Queen's Laws will save us," Helen repeats. "I have no doubt you will prove we make our own fate. Not the gods who cursed and left us. Not the prophecies they send through Cassandra."

"Cassandra's prophesies are nothing but tricks and lies meant to cause unrest," Amara says.

"Indeed." Helen pauses, as if hesitating to form her next words. "But the resistance rallies around Cassandra's lies, building hope for a savior in the daughter who Irene hid from you. Irene gave our people the gift of peace as prophesied, so now many believe her daughter will rule one day."

"You will help my hunters bring in my niece's daughter just as they have brought back all the others," Amara says sharply. She pushes herself upright. "It is not my descendant who will save or rule us. I am the last immortal!" She slaps her own chest. "My gift has power beyond any other, and I have enough loyal hunters to bring every Atlantean to their knees!" She stands abruptly.

"Apologies, my queen." Helen lowers her eyes, staring at the cobbles beneath Amara's feet.

"When you find that child for me, Irene will finally know my wrath for trying to hide her in the first place."

Helen shifts from her bench and onto her knees, again bowing her head. She rises and walks to the framed map. "Are you ready?"

"Far beyond ready." Queen Amara points impatiently at the map. "Show me."

Helen takes one of the golden pins from her hair and presses it into the map. "My gift has directed me to this unmarked area, most certainly a Nymph village, in this large landmass of northern Earth. The region is called Alaska, and from what I can tell, there is not much there. The Gifted target will certainly stand out in such a small population."

Amara closes the distance between them and stands next to Helen, looking at the pin, pressing an index finger against the smooth head of it, a golden bump marking the map.

"Perhaps this would be a good hunt for Dagan," Helen says. "He is restless after so many months."

Queen Amara pulls her hand away from the pin and looks at Helen. "This will be my son's first hunt. It is isolated enough to hide his mistakes. Dagan can join him later when it is time to finish the job and show him how it is done."

"A wise plan, my queen."

"And Aric's presence may keep Dagan from getting too carried away. I do not mind his collateral damage with humans and Nymphs, but he has gone too far with some of our own kind recently." The queen kisses Helen on the cheek and turns to leave. "It would be a shame if I never got to experiment on the youngest of my line due to an overzealous hunter."

Chapter Six

I SAT UP AND read the clock on my bedside table. It was after three, and I gave myself a moment to panic as I realized my dreams were more active than ever. Mom's treatments clearly weren't working at all. When I thought about the things I'd seen and heard tonight, my skin broke into a cold sweat. I got up and walked across the hall.

"Hazel," I whispered loudly, shaking her awake. "The god freaks are coming for me. They know where I am. I'm pretty sure that Aric guy at Gale's is one of them, but he was a little boy in my dream, so I can't be sure."

"Wha..." Hazel sat up, blinking and attempting to focus on me. "What are you talking about?"

I briefly told her about my dreams, or whatever they were. "They put a pin in a map right in the middle of Alaska, right here," I finished.

"Get in my bed," she said, getting out of it herself. "I'm going to tell Mom and Dad."

I slid to the far edge of her bed, pressed my body against the cool wall, and pulled her blanket up to my chin. It felt like I hadn't slept at all, like I'd been in those places, doing those things. I tried to wait for Hazel to come back, but the exhaustion pulled me back under.

QUEEN AMARA

Queen Amara is sitting naked in a gigantic tub set into the floor of a massive bedroom. A series of high windows and skylights send square beams of golden sunshine across the room, and the black stone floor glints where the light touches it.

Sitting on a long silver bench just outside the tub is a woman who looks like a goddess even compared to Amara. Her hair is molten gold, falling in large, perfect waves halfway down her back. She has full, wine-red lips and pale, luminous blue eyes.

Her gown is made up of layered cords of shimmering blue fabric, braided and knotted skillfully about the bodice and waist to cover only the smallest portion of her glowing golden skin. Everything about her is long and slender, from her face and neck to her limbs and delicate fingers. Her long legs keep peeking out of skirt layers that move like water as she shifts her position. The power flowing from her radiates perfection.

"I will take your blood in here today, Agnes," Amara tells her. "My son is meeting me in the throne room shortly, and he loses intelligent thought in your presence."

"I am quite used to that response." Agnes's brow creases in disapproval.

Amara sits up in the tub and turns to face the far wall.

There, sitting on the floor is a small woman wearing a white linen top and shorts. Her light brown hair is held back in a ponytail, and her eyes look almost human with barely any light behind the hazel coloring.

"Girl, bring my robe," Amara says.

The young woman scurries over to the bench Agnes is sitting on. She picks up a shimmering emerald robe and carries it behind Amara, who stands and steps out of the tub, allowing the woman to wrap her in the silky cloth.

"Agnes, I will have your gown as well as your blood today," she says. "Now, come with me."

Agnes bows her head and follows Amara up three long steps that lead to a vanity table. Amara settles in front of the mirror, and her wet hair shines like the fine metal it's named for.

"Just look at me, Agnes. Do you see how drab I am? It is obvious your blood no longer flows in my veins."

She picks up an emerald-backed brush and hands it to the servant. The young woman immediately sets to work on Amara's wet strands.

"Queen Amara, you have always been beautiful and filled with more power than any other," Agnes says. "My gift only enhances what is there."

Queen Amara waves her words away with a hand. "I have one more requirement of you today, Agnes. Your mother has been one of my most loyal hunters, but she has been on Earth for so long now. I must admit, I have not seen her in my halls in almost a century. You are in contact, correct?"

"Yes." Agnes tilts her head curiously. "Mother currently runs hunter resources through a company called Atlantis Technology in a place called California United State."

"I need you to bring her here to set up a cover for Aric."

"She will be honored by a direct request from her queen," Agnes says. "She has never failed in her duties assisting your hunters. She will not fail you."

"Excellent. She will personally outfit Aric for his first hunt."

"It will be done, Queen Amara. Will I be permitted to use the arches to retrieve her?"

"Of course. I will send one of my guards and the Immortal Stallions to ensure your trip is a success."

"I assume you will want this taken care of promptly?" Agnes asks.

"Yes. I want the boy to have a chance to prove himself before I send Dagan."

Queen Amara pulls open a drawer in the vanity and removes the same silver and emerald knife that she used in the throne room.

An invisible energy takes hold of Agnes's hand and pulls at it until Amara can hold Agnes's fingers and stretch her palm wide. Amara puts a small slice there, which draws a quiet noise from Agnes. And after cutting her own palm, Amara presses the wounds together.

The woman looks slightly uncomfortable but doesn't seem to be in pain. After a few moments, Amara takes her hand from Agnes and turns back to the mirror.

"Ah! Lovely."

There's a noticeable difference in the perfection of Amara's every feature—skin smoother, radiating more power than ever, lips pink and full, and hair falling like thousands of silver filaments. Her eyes sparkle like the gem they mimic. She stands. "I will take that gown now."

ARIC

"Aric." The guard, Theron, steps up to Aric as he walks into the circular palace foyer. The room not only holds several high arched hallways and doors in every direction, but it also has a wide staircase leading to a second floor.

"Theron, sir, Queen Amara sent for me?" His young man's voice has a slight quaver.

Theron nods. "She is in the throne room." And he leads Aric to the set of doors nearest them and pulls one open.

Aric shuffles through the opening and faces the throne on the other end of the white floored room.

The space seems filled with Queen Amara in her shimmering blue gown. Her skin glows pale and bright, like the sun is contained just below the surface, and her green eyes do the same. It makes her extremely difficult to look at, and Aric drops his eyes. Even her silver hair is illuminated, her braided crown topped with a delicate tiara of twisted silver.

Her voice carries easily across the hollow room. "You may go, Theron."

He bows and exits the room, leaving Aric alone with Queen Amara.

"Come here," she says.

He hurries to obey, nearly tripping as he does so and stops at the steps leading up to her throne.

"It is time to finish your hunter training," she says.

His head snaps up and he looks her in those glowing green eyes, causing her to sit up a bit straighter and let her face go cold.

Aric drops his eyes again, fists balled up tight. "My queen, I am sure my gift will develop."

"I am aware of this, foolish child," she scoffs. "This is why you will prove yourself as a hunter. Even as one of the Giftless, the position will bring you the honor I deserve." She stands, the intensity of her overall glow picking up, ensuring his eyes stay low.

She notices how he's struggling to look at her and laughs. "You like?" And she slowly turns in a full circle, arms wide.

"You are radiant, my queen," he says quietly.

"Drop the formality, Aric," she says.

"Apologies, Mother. It is difficult to stand before you when you have so recently taken Agnes's gift."

"Theron reports that you are training well with the guard, but he has reservations about you completing your hunter training," she says. "He believes you should spend more time in study at the university instead. What do you say, Aric? What is it you want?"

His voice is slightly choked when he speaks next. "I want to make you proud, Mother. With no gift, that means proving myself as a hunter."

She nods her approval with the answer. "Come bond with me like a hunter, then."

She walks over to the small table near her throne and picks up the beautiful hand-slicing knife. After gliding down the steps, she stops in front of him, and he automatically goes to one knee.

When she speaks, her voice has just a hint of softness to it. "Are you ready to commit to this? To our people? To me?"

"My queen," he bows his head. "I am ready."

She reaches her free hand toward him and lifts her knife hand. "This is not a comfortable experience for the blood giver, but I will take care to minimize your discomfort." Another moment of gentleness enters her voice. "Give me your hand."

Hesitantly, he holds it up for her, and she takes it into her own cool palm. She makes a small, nearly painless slice in the meat near his thumb and presses the palm near the opening to help the blood flow. "These calluses on your hand tell me Theron has progressed your training."

She pricks her own palm now and presses her wound to his, but after just a moment, Amara jerks her hand from his.

"Oh!" Her eyes are wide with shock and hinted with fear.

"I apologize, Queen Amara." His voice shakes. "What did I do wrong?"

"I could not take your blood or give mine to you. I felt it beginning to work when I reached for you with my magic, but before our blood could merge..." She looks at him like he's a lab rat.

After an agonizing wait under her narrow-eyed gaze, she snaps back out of her thoughts. "Normally, I keep a blood bond with all members of my guard—especially my hunters, but you will have to wait. You will be at a disadvantage because I will not be able to sense or communicate with you, but I am sure you will adapt," she says. "And we will investigate bonding blood again after your return."

He nods at her but says nothing.

"I have arranged your first hunt," she says, and her lips press firmly together as she looks him up and down. "I am sending you ahead of Dagan to gather information. Report to him when he presents himself to you—follow his guidance after that. You will need to blend into the human world. Will that be a problem?"

He shakes his head. "No, I have studied current human cultures at the university."

"Well, you are going to get a practical course with them now. Your first hunt is in a small community in a place called Alaska. Do you know where it is?"

He nods at her. "I have studied Earth geography. Who am I looking for, my queen?"

"That, Son, is for you to figure out. Helen only sees the use of magic on this end."

"When will I go?"

"Tomorrow. Go to the training room for your credentials and supplies when you leave me. Any more questions?" Her voice has a curt edge that says he better not.

He shakes his head.

"You are excused." She returns to her throne and slumps into it.

He acknowledges her once more with a quick bow and wastes no time trying to escape the room, but she stops him when he's halfway to the door.

"Aric."

"Yes, Mother?"

"Do not disappoint me."

* * * * *

I woke for long enough to realize that biology student Aric probably wasn't what he'd been pretending, but I was so tired. I slipped back into my dreams before I could rouse myself enough to tell Hazel about what I'd just seen.

DAGAN

I stand—no—a man stands in Gale's front yard. He climbs the stairs up to the deck where Aric sits in a camp chair and Gale stands with his back turned, tending a grill. The smell of burgers is thick in the air.

"Dagan?" Aric looks surprised.

"Hello, Aric," Dagan says.

Gale turns to look as Dagan closes the distance between them.

Aric stands from his chair and steps into Dagan's path, but after a moment of staring, Aric lowers his eyes and steps aside again.

"Who is our host?" Dagan asks.

"This is Gale," Aric says obediently.

"Is this your house, Gale?" Dagan asks him.

"Yeah, but who...who are you?"

Dagan steps past Gale and pivots on one foot. His arm snakes around Gale's neck in a single motion, and he drags him back against his body with wiry arm muscles. Gale is shorter, giving Dagan's body leverage while his hands swiftly take hold of Gale's head, and he twists with a strong jerk. The feel of tearing muscle and tendons vibrates under his fingers. There's the barely audible sound of popping bone as it cuts across everything vital and Gale falls into a crumpled heap.

Dagan shoves Gale's form off his boots and looks at Aric again. "Is there anyone else living here?"

Aric shakes his head, mouth gaping. He steps away slightly as he replies, watching Dagan's eyes closely now.

"This will make a fine base of operations," Dagan says. "Go finish whatever that thing was cooking. You may make your report over our meal."

* * * * *

"Oh, no." I sat up in Hazel's bed. "Oh, no—oh, no!" There was a pounding coming from the front door at the bottom of the stairs, but I couldn't focus on that. The memories from Atlantis and from Gale's house flooded my mind. I felt ill as I remembered every moment of that man Dagan killing Gale.

Hazel sat up next to me. "What's happened?" Her eyes shifted from sleep to high alert in an instant.

"Someone's pounding on the door downstairs. What time is it?" I asked.

"Five. Who the hell is that?" She got up and went to her door, stepped into the hall. "Who is it?" I heard her asking before she came back in.

"We need to get dressed," I said. "Now!"

I went to my room to follow my own directions, pulling a hoodie over my T-shirt and slipping into some sweats before I laced up my hiking boots. I grabbed my phone on the way out of the bedroom and stopped across the hall again. Hazel was still in her matching pajama set.

"Seriously, hurry up. I'm going to find out what's going on downstairs."

In the kitchen, Mom and Dad—tired-eyed and also still in their pajamas—sat across the table from Aric. He looked up at me when I came into view, and I was shocked to see that his previously human brown eyes were the deep luminous blue of sapphires. I was certain he'd been in my dream, and that those dreams were real memories.

"Get away from him, Mom!" I yelled. "He's Queen Amara's son, and she sent him after me. His friend killed Gale!"

"We know," Dad said. "This is Prince Aric. He's betrayed the hunter who came here for you."

"What are you talking about?" Hazel asked, coming in behind me, still not dressed. "Nobody's killed Gale."

"We do not have time for this." Aric stood up. "We must go now! I lied about you, but he did not believe me. He could tell I was hiding something. I snuck away from the house as he slept, but he will not be long.

"Mother—Queen Amara sent Dagan after Alexa," Aric continued. "He did kill Gale, but he is no friend of mine. I was sent here to spy on her and assist him in returning her to my mother, to Atlantis, but I cannot do it. I have never wanted anyone to get hurt. Please, I have nowhere to go now that I have betrayed Mother's favorite hunter."

"I already left a message with the air service to reserve us seats for the morning flight." Mom glanced up at the clock on the wall. "It leaves in an hour." She stood and walked over to the kitchen counter, opening the drawer where she kept all her recipes and her journal.

She pulled out the leather book, reaching into a slim pocket in the back cover, and handed me a key and a bank card. "Get your bags from the shop and get to the runway before that flight. Use this card to get cash. I'm not sure how far the money in there will get you, but it is yours to use. Your names are on the account."

"I reached out to Lukas," Dad said. "Use that key to check the post office box until you hear from him."

"I emailed you both the banking and post office box information," Mom said.

"Wait, we're leaving now?" Hazel asked.

"Without you? Why?" I asked.

"We'll follow you after we make sure the rest of our community is safe," Mom said. "But you need to go today."

"I need someone to take care of Jane Goodall." My eyes found Mom's.

Right on cue, Dad said, "Who cares about the rodent?"

It was shocking that someone who was centuries old could play the cranky and unreasonable human parent so well, even in a crisis.

"Gale was going to watch her!" I said, tears bursting out with my words. Even as Hazel's overly eager ex-boyfriend, Gale had been one of my few life-long friends. He'd been excited to watch Jane for me, and now he was just gone.

"I'll find someone to watch her." Mom ran a hand over my hair.

A slow loud knock came from the front door.

"Dagan," Aric said, every bit of color draining out of him. "He must have followed me. Please, I cannot be here. He will punish me for betraying Mother."

"You will have to take this Godline youth with you, girls," Dad said, opening the hall closet and pulling a shotgun down from its wall-mounted storage. He took out a box of shells and loaded the gun. "We can vet his honesty later, but I trust his words and his fear."

The knocking stopped. We all stood a moment, in frightened silence, until the sound of shattering glass replaced the knocks.

Dad moved into the front of the hall, between us and the sound. "Get out now," he whispered. "I'm not inclined to become a murderer this late in my life, but I can buy you time."

"Aric," Dagan's voice called from somewhere inside our living room, just beyond the hall. "It seems you left some details out of your report. Tell me now, young prince, and all will be forgiven."

Hazel grabbed me by the arm and pulled me toward the back door, snatching her hiking boots from the mudroom floor as we went. "Come with us, Aric," she whispered.

Aric, who now had a large duffel bag over his shoulder, followed us without hesitation.

"Go to the shop, Fern," Dad said. "I love you, girls." Then he disappeared through the hall.

We crossed the distance between the house and our detached garage at a run, Hazel still carrying her shoes. When we got into the shop, I shoved my phone in my bag and threw it over my shoulder.

Suddenly the sharp boom of Dad's shotgun sounded through the walls. A second later it sounded again. And again.

"Go now, girls." Mom hugged me tightly. She repeated the ritual with Hazel, pressing her leather journal into my sister's hands. "Go!"

And so, we slipped into the woods behind the shop, picking our way between the trees, headed in the general direction of the airstrip. We'd connect with the main trail after we crossed our front yard, but the going was tortuous.

Hazel grabbed for my hand and pulled me along, supporting my weight whenever I stumbled. I could hear Aric crashing his way behind us, struggling to keep up. I had every reason to be afraid of him. If he couldn't keep up, I wasn't helping him out. That said, it had been Dagan not Aric, who had killed Gale. A knot formed inside of me as I thought about my parents staying behind with a murderer.

When we got onto Main Street, we ran to the far end of the empty road, pausing only long enough to catch our breath. Aric kept up without issue once we were on the wide flat gravel.

The only person at the airstrip when we got there was Robin, who owned the plane. Hazel gave him some excuse about the change in passengers, but he didn't really care. He was a family friend and we flew to town with him often. We didn't even have to convince him to take off early since we were the only ones scheduled to fly out.

I took a breath of momentary relief as the plane lifted off with the three of us safely aboard, taking us away from Oread Basin, away from the killer who'd been sent to capture me. When I looked down over our village, bright orange flames and billowing gray smoke obscured my view of our house.

I gasped involuntarily. "Hazel, he's burning our house."

She grabbed my hand from the seat next to me and squeezed it a little too hard.

Chapter Seven

DAGAN

I'M IN MY OWN living room, but I'm in Dagan's body, gasping on hands and knees as he watches my dad disappear through the hall, toward the kitchen. Dagan tries to get up and pursue, but when he attempts to draw in breath for the effort, the pain doubles him over and he falls back to his knees.

He recovers enough to stand again and turns toward the still open front door with its broken pocket window. Glass crunches under his feet as he approaches the mirror hung on the wall there.

Dagan pulls apart the fabric of his shirt at the chest, revealing an angry, fist-sized circle of torn flesh and partially coagulated blood near his heart. He pokes around the wound, carefully examining the damage before he turns away from the mirror.

He walks up the stairs, running a hand along the wall—touching the pictures that mark the way. Dagan stops at a close-up photo from my senior year of high school, staged in a field of white tundra flowers. Even in the picture, my too-bright eyes give me away.

Dagan grabs the picture off the wall and smashes the frame, stuffing the paper photo in a side pocket on his pants. He looks in the first room at the top of the stairs—Mom and Dad's room. It's empty except for the furnishings. He crosses toward the long dresser facing the foot of the bed. Instead of a mirror on top, there's the large TV Dad falls asleep to most nights.

Dagan pulls open drawers, throwing clothes all over the room as he goes, pausing momentarily when he encounters a drawer of Dad's shirts. Dagan replaces the remains of his old shirt with a plain black T-shirt.

He swipes a hand behind the TV and lets it topple off the dresser face first, coming to rest partially on the floor and partially suspended by its cords. Then he passes his way through the rest of the room, knocking everything over, pulling the papers out of the file drawer on the desk, flicking through them, and tossing them on the floor.

Dagan stops at a file filled with our family's passports and flips through each one of them with calloused hands. He stops to look at Hazel's, and then stuffs it into his pants pocket along with mine. After finding the IDs, he tosses the remainder of the file contents loosely on the bed. Then he walks into Mom and Dad's bathroom.

He searches the cabinets quickly, opening bottles and tossing them all over the room until he finds a bottle of nail polish remover and a hairspray. After adding their contents to the pile of papers on the bed, Dagan grabs one sheet of paper and pulls a lighter out of another pocket.

Once the paper is burning, he tosses it on the bed and walks out of the room—an instant surge of heat and light flaring behind his back.

* * * * *

I woke exactly where I'd collapsed after arriving at our hotel room—on top of the clean white bedding, face down in my pillows, and fully dressed. I turned over with a groan. Hazel sat right next to me, reading a book. How normal. Aric had fallen asleep on the other bed and the sight of him brought the world of Atlantis and hunters and Dagan burning down my house right back to the surface, fueling both anger and fear inside of me.

I picked my phone up off the nightstand. It was late afternoon, which explained my hunger. Then I opened the group text from my mom again.

Dad and I are safe.
The community is evacuating into the
mountains until fall.
We can't risk more Nymph lives and
we're needed here.

Also, we have Gale.
We have to skip the Prothesis for his
funeral but we will do the Ekphora
as we leave the village and
Interment when we set up camp.

His death is a great loss, and
I'm sorry I can't be there for you two now.

You girls should know that in Atlantis
Prothesis at a Nymph funeral is one
last party with loved ones rather than a
gathering to mourn over the dead. Ekphora
becomes a festive group walk to the

Nymph's chosen place. And in Interment,
instead of cremation and burial, we simply
merge our magic with nature. This is an important
part of our culture that you should know.

Stick together.
Find Lukas.
He will help Alexa stay hidden.
We love you.
(I'll text when we get home.)

That text was on my phone when we touched down in Fairbanks. Of course, everyone in my hometown could drop their lives to hide from a killer in the inhospitable mountains. The least my parents would expect is that Hazel and I could manage to hide out in hotels on their dime.

"Welcome back," Hazel said.

"Still tired." I yawned. "Did you see Mom's text? We have to find that Lukas guy. He's my only shot at learning to stop my dreams so I can hide from those magical psychos and finally have a normal life."

She nodded. "It's our only goal right now. Stay hidden. Get Lukas to help you control your magic so no one gets kidnapped."

I didn't want to think about my possible kidnapping, or what might happen to Hazel as a Nymph. That hunter murdered Gale. I couldn't let him get to my sister.

"I'm so pissed at Mom and Dad, Lex. For all the lies," she said. "And then I also feel terrible about how things ended with me and Gale and sad about missing his funeral."

I put an arm around her and leaned in for a half hug. "Everything sucks."

"Not everything," she said. "I ordered a bunch of stuff from room service. I'm starved and didn't want to wake you, so I got one of everything."

"Hazel, you know that is going to be super expensive—"

"We nearly died today. Dad shot someone in our living room. Our house burned down. Someone wants to kidnap you. And my ex was murdered! So, you're going to have to live with my frivolous use of our parents' secret fortune."

"Fortune?"

She'd changed out her pajama set for a pair of black fitted hiking pants and a zipper hoodie, and her hair was neatly braided. Hazel always managed to look so put together. Meanwhile, I was covered in a layer of sweat from having real-life nightmares or memories or whatever.

"Anyway," she ranted, holding her phone screen up to me. "I used the directions in Mom's email to log into the account she told us about. There's over eight hundred thousand dollars in their secret family expense account, and it's linked to several others that I couldn't access."

"Really?" I asked.

We didn't use money in Oread Basin, but Mom's products sold out at farmers' markets, she supplied a few stores year-round, and she sent out mail orders constantly. It made sense that money would add up over a couple of lifetimes, but it was still a strange twist.

My anger flared as I thought about all the times they refused to buy me nice clothes and talked about the large expenses of the far-away schools I'd wanted to attend. They'd purposely made it harder for me to find the life where I belonged. My anger quickly turned to worry as I thought about what I'd just seen.

"I just had another crap dream where that Dagan asshole burned down our house after Dad shot him right in the chest, so bring on the comfort food," I said, as a knot formed in my throat and my chest tightened painfully. "And...and...he murdered Jane!" I ended in tears, already missing that little hairball. Mom had sent me a separate text to break the news—Jane Goodall had died in the house fire.

Hazel leaned her head against mine and wrapped my arm in hers so she could hold me from her spot beside me. "I'm so sorry," she whispered.

"He scares me, Hazel." I sniffed, trying to focus on what I'd just seen in my dream. "I saw his chest wound, but instead of dying, he walked around stealing our passports and lighting our house on fire."

"You have my condolences about Gale." Aric joined in. "I do not know this...Jane, but I see you feel the loss and you have my sympathies." He sat up in his bed. "Did you just say you saw Dagan in your dream? What is your gift?"

"I still don't know if I trust you, Aric. Even if I knew what my so-called gift was, I don't know that I should tell you."

"Why would that man kill Gale?" Hazel asked him.

"Dagan is Mother's most depraved hunter. He killed Gale because he felt like it."

Hazel's shoulders sagged.

Aric's eyes met mine. "If you used your gift here, we must leave. My mother's advisor, Helen, uses her Artemis-given gift to track Godline magic. She tracked you to Oread Basin."

"And she sent you to scout out my kidnapping." I snapped.

"I never wanted to become a hunter!" He almost whined it. "I am Giftless. Mother only placed me in hunter training to save her the shame of a useless son."

Room service knocked at the door before I could grill him further, and my hunger temporarily buried my mistrust of Aric. There was no ignoring the spectacle that came with ordering everything on the menu. Three servers brought us a mountain of food packed onto overstuffed carts.

Conversation halted as we sorted through and tasted everything this hotel had to offer—the hotel we needed to leave because of my stupid dreams. We were going to burn through all the hotels in Fairbanks in no time at the rate I was going.

Aric started back in on me while my mouth was full of burger. "What exactly is happening in these dreams of yours?"

I thought about his question as I chewed, thinking back through what I'd just experienced while I slept. I'd been Dagan. I'd been Aric before, too—and others.

All these memories from all these different lives were suddenly mine too, joining those of my lived experiences. My heart raced as I realized this magic was changing me, and I tried to bury the out of control feeling.

Without Jane there to comfort me, I tried to keep my mind on other things—like how I wasn't going to let anything get in the way of my plans. I was still going to build a better life with college degrees, trips to Europe, amazing girlfriends, and everything else I'd dreamed up. My well-planned life had nothing to do with the Godline.

But maybe Aric could help me understand my dreams enough to stop them. To get the Godline problems out of my life.

"Did your mom try to like...push her blood into you, but it didn't work for some reason?" I asked.

"Did you..." A deep crease formed between his brows. "Did you see that?"

"No. I experienced it. As you." I gave him a humorless smile. "Thanks for the memories."

"You must desist at once!" he said sharply. "I cannot return to Atlantis, and my resources were all compromised when I saved you. There are Godline all over Earth who support our hunters with human assets, but they will have cut me off from the royal purse and be tracking my false identification by now."

Nothing like a little guilt to distract me from the major trust issues I had with this guy, but from what I'd seen of his mother, he had every reason to be afraid of betraying her as he had.

Hazel walked to the closet where our bags were, and I could hear her digging around. "Here, Aric. Take this key to the post office." She tapped on her phone for a few moments and then handed that to him too. "I've set up the Ryde app with my parents' bank account and just ordered a car to take you to check the mail."

"Please tutor me on this device," he said. "I never learned the features of my assigned phone before I had to discard it."

Hazel took Aric through the basic features of her phone and made sure that he knew how to get back after his errand. Then she climbed into bed next to me.

"What if he, like...hides the message from Lukas or something?" I whispered into her ear while Aric put his shoes on across the room.

"Dad said we have to keep him," she murmured. "Plus, I'm pretty sure he needs Lukas's help as much as you do."

"I will see you both upon my return." Aric headed for the hotel door.

"See you soon, Aric," Hazel replied as he stepped out.

"Hazel, I'm nervous about him living with us. What if this is all part of some plan? We're just going to listen because Dad said to trust him?"

"Well, to be fair, I saw Aric's face when the other guy showed up at our house. He was terrified. I would be too if I'd betrayed a killer."

Poor Gale. "Hazel, I'm so sorry about Gale."

My sister let out a gasping sob. "I feel so guilty, Lex. I...I led him on for over a year. I let him set his house up, thinking he was waiting for me. Then I just dumped him out like trash, and that's the way he died!"

"Hazel, he made you break up with him twice. You were a good friend. He just got that all confused." I sighed, not sure what to say to make it better. "You were a good friend. And when it happened, it was fast. He didn't suffer."

She leaned her head against my shoulder and sniffled quietly.

After she calmed down some, I asked her the question that had been burning at the back of my mind from the moment our plane took off that morning. "What now?"

"Well, we keep checking the post office until we hear from Lukas. That was the plan with Mom and Dad, so I think we stick with it for now."

"We should rent a car," I said. "Since we're on the run, you know?"

All I really wanted was to sign up for fall classes and get back on track with my life, but I knew that was impossible while a killer hunted me, and I had no control over my dreams. I touched my index finger to the soft skinned tattoo behind my ear. The girlfriend part of my plan was also off to a terrible start. I was pretty sure I was never going to hear from Claire again, which was probably best since I was on the run. Getting a car was the only smart call that came to mind.

"We could use a rental," Hazel grumbled. "I need to get outside of town to resupply for some essential remedies. I would pick up where Mom left off with your experimental dream-blocking tonics, but she never bothered to teach me to understand the magic I was using."

"Yep." I nodded. "I guess we need to find a new hotel now that I've puked magic all over this one, but I don't know how long we can keep up with hotel hopping to hide from these people. They have some lady running a tech company. She's the one who created Aric's cover. What if they find us because we're booking these rooms on cards in our names? I mean, Dagan has our passports." Dad had insisted the whole family get passports when Hazel and I had graduated even though not one of them had been used so far. Until now. Now they were in the hands of a murderer.

"If we could get your dreams to stop, we could rent an apartment in cash or something. One problem at a time, though. I was thinking Aric and I could take turns watching you sleep—"

I cringed at the thought of anyone watching me sleep, but especially the literal stranger who was deep in my life.

"I know." She continued. "It's not ideal, but we're desperate."

"Fine," I sighed. "But his fake name is Aric Hunt. If he kidnaps me, I deserve it."

She chuckled at my lame humor. "We have to do something, and it's the only idea I've got until help arrives."

I thought about Aric watching me sleep with his stupid glowing sapphire eyes—eyes he'd hidden with contacts to spy on me. He'd had a lifetime of training in who knows what horrors before beginning his hunter career to come after me. And I was supposed to just trust him to watch me sleep, something I didn't want anyone doing. It was certainly one way to find out his true intentions quickly.

"I'm taking a nap before we go," I said. Whatever magic was happening in my dream-riddled sleep, rest was not in the equation.

Hesitation crept over Hazel's face.

"I know sleeping is, like the worst thing I can do with my time, but I've already screwed this location anyway."

She took a long, silent moment to contemplate. "Yeah, why not." She patted my pillow and grabbed her book.

When I gave in to it, the exhaustion engulfed me in under a minute.

Chapter Eight

PRINCESS AMARA

AMARA SITS AGAINST THE trunk of an oak, shaded by its leafy canopy while she watches a black horse wade chest-deep into a lake just outside the tree line. The horse splashes his front hoof in and out of the water until the saddle-shaped sweat pattern on his back has been rinsed away. When he's thoroughly soaked, he turns and gallops up to Amara.

"Better?" she smiles.

"Praise the gods, yes," the horse responds. "Why does Earth have so many places that are sweltering? The humans have been very entertaining, but this heat! And sweat!" His head is bobbing up and down. "I want my pristine stall and our perfect Atlantean temperature."

"It was good we found this lovely lake then," Amara tells him. "I am hungry. Did you see that orchard just before we landed? It could be dinner."

"Might I suggest we find a kindly human farmer to put us up instead?"

"I would rather we stuff ourselves in the orchard and sleep under the stars." She sighs. "I abhor walls."

"I know you were sheltered, but you were not exactly kept in a dungeon," he snorts, spraying a fine mist all over Amara.

"You try living betrothed to Markos through a prophecy and say that again. I have lived only two decades, and Mother has spent half that time reminding me of my important role in the prophecy."

"To make babies with Markos," the horse said. "And that is why I support your freedom adventure, but I have gone far too long without a prepared meal and soft bed."

"We stayed with that lovely nomadic community just days ago. They fed us and let us sleep amongst them."

"Those horses were so aggressive, I barely slept."

"They were half your size," she says with a grin.

"Yes, and they used that to their advantage, attacking down low with razor teeth and slashing hooves." He opens his mouth wide and gnashes his teeth, acting it out. His ears are pinned flat as he erratically tosses his head, assaulting the air a final time before he continues. "No. If we are to continue this adventure, you will find me a stall tonight.

Sleep outside if you wish." He turns away, lifts his tail to release a large pile of manure at her feet, and trots back toward the water.

"Fine, Xanthus!" Amara calls. "We will do it your—"

A rope flies around his neck and pulls tight, its source blocked from view by the trees. It catches Xanthus off guard, and he stumbles, landing on a knee before righting himself and thrusting straight up into the air. He fights violently against the line holding him close to the earth, like an angry balloon on a string. "Unhand me, foe!" he shouts toward the ground just before a coughing fit. "What is the meaning of this?"

Amara is on her feet and running toward whatever's just out of view.

And then she sees him.

Up against the tree line, just down the shore is a blond man on a massive draft horse. The rope is wrapped tight against the horn of his saddle and his eyes are wide as he stares at Xanthus flying above him. He's trying to release the line, but it's stuck somehow, pulling at his saddle and causing his chestnut horse to shift uneasily from foot to foot.

"Stop!" Amara yells at the man as she runs toward him, still too far away. "Let him loose! Xanthus, come down!" She raises one hand like she's grabbing his rope and gestures at the man with the other. A warm energy bursts suddenly from her center and out both hands.

In the next instant, her energy takes hold of the rope and pulls Xanthus nearly back to the earth. At the same time, her other hand sends a massive force into the man's chest, knocking him off his horse.

Amara runs over to Xanthus, who's now being held to the earth by the magic flowing from her fingers. "Let me get it off," she yells.

He may be able to talk and fly, but at this moment, his fear-filled white eyes give the appearance of just another frightened horse. At Amara's voice though, he focuses and looks at her. She pulls the rope from Xanthus and runs toward the groaning man. He's trying to catch his breath next to his bewildered but loyal horse. The nervous animal sniffs its fallen rider.

She stops when she's standing directly over him. "What do you think you are doing?"

He holds his hand up to her and coughs. When the fit ends and he's drawing breath normally, he pushes himself to his feet. Her hand begins lifting in his direction, but it pauses, waiting.

"That horse was flying!" he stammers. "It can talk...it yelled at me. And how did you do that thing with your hands?"

She points at him with delicate fingers and energy flows between them, bumping his chest so that he stumbles back into his horse. "I asked you what you were doing. I am the daughter of a queen and both myself and that horse are perfectly trained to destroy you if necessary."

The man laughs and then just as quickly stifles his smile. He gives Amara genuine brown eyes. "Please accept my apology...Princess? That...talking and flying horse is a fine animal. I wanted to bring him into the safety of my barn while I searched for his owner, but I see you are right here. On my honor, I meant no harm."

"I do not own Xanthus," she says reflexively. "He is my friend—a friend who you nearly scared to death."

"You exaggerate, Amara," Xanthus says, walking up beside her. He chomps his teeth menacingly a few times. "Anyone would take offense to being strangled about the neck."

"He really does talk," the man says.

"I am right here." Xanthus snorts.

"Apologies. I am Dante. My family has a farm just through these trees. Allow me to host you tonight."

Amara turns to Xanthus. "Well?"

"I asked for a stall. He has a stall. I will forgive the offense this once, but I want oats with dinner!"

"Of course." Dante replies. "Anything for such a magnificent creature."

He locks his eyes with Amara. "And you are exquisite and powerful. And those eyes! Please, accept my offer. You can stay in the barn with your friend. There is a hayloft above the stalls, or if you are feeling social, my sister would happily share her bed with you. I warn you though. She is thirteen and very talkative."

"I will stay with Xanthus, in your hayloft. Thank you."

"Come then. Follow me." He holds a hand toward Amara, and she reaches back. She lets him wrap her fingers in his warm grip. He takes hold of his horse's rein and begins leading them toward the trees. A wide path leading away from the lake becomes visible as they walk.

"Perhaps you would be willing to tell me your story," he says. "It's as if I have been in a lovely dream since the moment I saw you, and I wish to experience as much of it as possible. May I bring my dinner out to join you in the loft?"

Amara smiles as heat rises into her cheeks. "I think I would like that."

He beams at her as they make their way through the well-worn trail. "I cannot wait to hear about a world of magic princesses and flying horses. I have not seen much myself, growing up stuck on this farm, but I always dreamed there had to be more. You are like a dream come true."

Amara's blush deepens, but her voice is firm. "If you prove a pleasant host tonight, perhaps I will bring you along on my travels."

"Do not volunteer my back to this human stranger." Xanthus snorts and then launches up over their heads, pacing from above.

"I had not realized you were feeling so old that you would have to worry about a little extra weight on your back, Friend," Amara yells up at him with a grin.

"Oats!" he yells back down.

* * * * *

"Nap's over!"

Hazel yanked the pillow out from under my head, jarring me fully awake.

"Okay, yes! I was having another dream." I sat up. "Amara, you know the queen." I gestured vaguely at the air. "When she was our age—a princess—she was like this headstrong feminist or whatever. How the hell did she become the woman who is now trying to hunt me down for her creepy torture dungeon?"

"What are you talking about?" Her eyebrows wrinkled at me.

"Young Amara hung out with flying horses and traveled the world to escape her mother's obsession with prophecies." The part about world travel made me a bit jealous of the evil queen. "But I need to stop calling these things dreams. I'm not sleeping when they happen. My mind is somewhere else, experiencing someone else's memory, feeling the sensations their bodies feel—along for the ride, no matter what they do. I'm sure of at least that much."

"In-body experiences?" Hazel suggested lightly.

"Bit of a mouthful," I laughed. "I wish I could pull some Atlantean clothes straight out of these in-body-experiences I've been having, though. They're fabulous, Hazel, the fabrics have to be magic somehow and the designs are all so intricate."

"Well, pretty dresses aside, if you really are living the memories of others, I wish I understood my magic enough to try a memory blocker for you, but that tonic was complicated even when I had Mom's help

66

and still thought I knew what I was doing." She was getting a faraway stare that I was sure had to do with magical tonic plans. "Once we have a kitchen, I'll check Mom's journal to see which recipes she thought worked best for you."

"They are visions," Aric's voice said from the doorway.

I jumped. I'd missed him coming in. "What do you mean? What do you know about it?"

"Visions are an Apollo-given gift, though I have never heard of visions like yours. I have only heard of those gifted with flashes—clues of a future to come, for example." He walked into the room and handed Hazel her phone before sitting on his bed.

"So, you don't know anything practical about my gift then? Like, you know, how I can stop it?"

"I am your age and Giftless," he said. "I am not fit to tutor you on your gift. I can tell you that after your visions today, Dagan most certainly knows where we are. He will likely go back to Atlantis to have Mother's healer remove the wound your father inflicted, but he could be there and back in less than a day. One of the arches opens to Mount Denali in Alaska, United States."

"Denali!" I suddenly felt exposed knowing there was some weird magical connection to Atlantis so close. "It's barely a hundred miles south of us. And you can drive there or even take a train if you wanted to get all touristy. It's close, Aric."

"I know. It is how I arrived."

I quickly changed the subject to something less terrifying. "I've never heard anyone refer to Denali or Alaska that way." I chuckled a little. "It's kind of subtle, but it's funny when I notice that you didn't grow up here. Where is Atlantis, anyway?"

Aric's forehead creased as he contemplated my question. "I am not sure where to tell you, on your map. Our maps have Atlantis and Earth shown as separate systems, with the arches as the connection."

"People have theories about where the lost city of Atlantis is buried underwater," Hazel said. "Some people think it's in the South Atlantic. Some think somewhere in or near the Mediterranean.

"No. Atlantis is connected to Earth, but it is not part of Earth," Aric sighed. "I am unsure about how else to explain it. It is no lost city—it is far vaster than that."

"I have so many questions." Hazel obviously wanted to geek out about this.

But it felt like Dagan might barge through the door at any moment. I really shouldn't have taken that second nap. At least now we knew we could stall him by inflicting what should be deadly wounds. Force him to go to their healer.

"We're probably safe here for a while, right?" I looked at Aric hopefully. "I mean, there's no flight out of Oread Basin until tomorrow and then it'll take him a half day to get to Denali and back."

"Do you want to gamble all our lives on my guess that he will see the healer? Or that he even has to wait for tomorrow's flight? He could choose to mend more slowly on his own or he could have other means of travel. He is Mother's most successful hunter—the only one she does not send as part of a team. We should not count on his incompetence."

"Okay, okay. We'll go tonight. What happened to that healer woman, anyway? In one of my dreams...visions she was this happy and gorgeous redhead helping my birth parents whisk me away. Then I saw her healing you, and she was completely destroyed."

Aric's forehead crinkled as he drew his eyebrows together. "Ivy is a very unappealing woman. She lives in the palace with us. She spends most of her time in the cells but constantly frightens me, lurking around the main living space. I have often felt as if she were following me, suddenly just there watching me, mute as a mouse. I guess she had a tongue before you were born, though."

"What does that mean?" I asked, a sick feeling rising in my gut.

"I always knew her missing tongue was a punishment. I just did not know what she had done. It must have been for helping you escape."

The sick feeling rose in my throat but stopped at my tightened airway.

"Let's not unpack that now," Hazel jumped in.

In need of a distraction, I recalled the image of the other woman who helped me. "Someone else...Penelope, I think, helped with my escape too."

I remembered the graceful arch of her neck and shoulder, brown skin radiating power, and was suddenly struck with an intense desire. I tucked that unexpected response away quickly.

"I have heard stories of how she made the two of you invisible to get through the arches. She got in a lot of trouble for that, but Mother loves Penelope like a daughter. So she was given grace. Mother made her my nursemaid. Penelope cared for me during the long days while the queen fulfilled her sacred duties downstairs."

"You mean in her dungeons, don't you?" It suddenly became difficult to draw in a full breath, hearing Aric speak so reverently about Amara. How could we be sure he wouldn't decide to follow her completely again?

"The queen is duty-bound to many kinds of work, and there are facilities for all of it downstairs," he recited.

"I've heard about some of her work." I made sure my last word dripped with sarcasm. "Breeding people like animals, right? That's how your people do things?"

"We are your people as well!" He spat. His sudden anger only reinforced my fears.

"Woah. Okay," Hazel interjected. "How about we circle back to—what was her name? The invisible woman who raised Aric. It sounds like neither of you have an issue with her."

"Penelope," I said. "She's funny. I don't know, just her whole tone was carefree, which was welcome while I experienced my birth mother's pregnant and crying body."

"She is amusing." Aric appeared happier than I'd seen since meeting him. "She was always so kind to me. She took me on adventures all over Atlantis, and she made me laugh."

"Do her powers make her...I mean, do people tend to like her a lot because of her powers or something?" I asked, wondering about the pull I felt when I remembered her.

"Well, maybe some of her illusions, her Apollo given gift, have that kind of effect, but mostly, I think it is her," he replied. "It is why I was so happy when our mothers had us married four years ago."

"What the hell?" I yelled, and then self-corrected with a whisper. "I mean, you're my age. You would have been sixteen."

"Yes," he said.

"Why?" I groaned.

"We were to be the first couple to produce the new line of Gifted Immortals when my mother's work downstairs came to fruition." He gave a long, soft sigh. "That was the plan, anyway. But then, I never came into my gift, Penelope snuck away from Atlantis before we could even consummate our marriage, and mother forced me to begin training in her hunter program."

"I see why my parents smuggled me out," I muttered.

Hazel stared at Aric, lips slightly parted, silent.

"You realize," he retorted, "if you had been raised in Atlantis, where you belong, we would have grown up together. Perhaps there are some issues, but you do not know the life you have missed."

"My dreams gave me the impression my upbringing would have been pretty different than yours."

Aric just didn't seem to understand how terrifying it was to hear how close he still felt to the woman trying to torture and breed me. As hard as it was to hear the way he talked sometimes, Aric was like a living dream translator. I really hated needing his help.

"I think we've processed dreams enough for today," Hazel said. "Was there anything at the post office?" She turned to Aric.

"There was not." He pulled the key from his pants pocket and handed it to her. "We need a new hotel room. And a plan for when Alexa sleeps."

"I hope Lukas comes soon," I said, walking over to the closet for my bag. "Let's go."

Chapter Nine

ONCE WE'D SETTLED INTO our second hotel, there was a lengthy debate about how to best prevent my dreams. In the end, it had been decided that Aric would stay up that night and wake me every few minutes. Once again, giving me help I wish I didn't need.

Aric spent the night with one hand gripped on my shoulder. He used his free hand to explore the features of my phone and shook me awake almost instantly every time I fell asleep. It was torture, but it also worked. I didn't dream once.

When I finally woke from the cycle of sleep stupor to jarring wakefulness, it was early afternoon. Hazel and I left Aric to sleep while we picked up the rental car.

"You're pouting at your phone again," she told me when we started the drive back to the hotel.

It wasn't surprising she'd noticed, given how often I'd looked hopefully for a reply from my more and more distant ex-girlfriend, but this time was different because I was secretly downloading the MXR dating app. I figured if I was going to move on, meeting some new girls was the best way to help with that. I knew I couldn't date anyone in person at the moment, but what harm could a little online chatting do?

"Screw Claire," Hazel said, assuming I was pining. "You're a damned goddess."

"If I were a goddess, I'd bring my ass to Atlantis and make my great auntie Amara behave less like a psycho." I laughed because sometimes you just have to laugh when things are shit. I figured laughing was better than curling up in fear.

Aric slept the day away and we only woke him when take-out for dinner got there. Once we'd all eaten, Aric started griping. "I tire of hiding in one small room, my only purpose to keep your unskilled magic at bay."

"Well thanks, your highness." I was sure my sarcasm was clear, but he gave me a solemn nod in response.

"You are welcome, but I am not some Giftless sleep servant!" he said.

"Well, I don't want you waking me all night again, anyway," I snapped back.

"I'm taking tonight's shift," Hazel said. "So you can both settle your asses down."

"But I will have to be her sleep servant again on the following night?" Aric asked. "I do not wish to stand guard over Alexa's sleep again."

"Aric, we'll get you some magazines or teach you how to use the TV. Alexa, hopefully Lukas shows up soon. I'll see what tonics I can make to help in the meantime."

"Sorry for my whining," I muttered. Hazel was less than a year older than me, but it just felt like I'd been lectured by Mom, if Mom swore casually.

Aric sighed. "I accept the task."

That night, Hazel sat in the bed beside me instead of Aric, who was stretched across his own bed. I fell asleep to the sound of him shifting channels as he explored the hotel TV stations.

PRINCESS AMARA

Dante holds Amara close, his hand around her waist as they watch a barn and farmhouse across a field of half-grown corn. Xanthus stands grazing a few hundred yards away, black coat glistening under the setting sun.

"Now you see for yourself," Amara says. "Your family farm has prospered in the year we have traveled your Earth together. Please tell me you will return to Atlantis with me. We can visit here any time. You can help with the harvest each year. Our children can learn their human trade. And we can continue to explore the world. I want everything with you, Dante."

Dante steps around so that he can meet her gaze with his human-brown eyes. "I would follow you anywhere. Though, perhaps we should start our own life somewhere new together."

"Xanthus's brother is due back any moment. He will certainly come with an order to bring me home. Also, I do wish for you to meet Candace and Irene. My twin and her baby are my favorite people back home." Amara squeezes Dante's shoulder as he pulls her in closer to him. "No one will stop me from bringing you back with me."

"And what happens when your mother insists you marry Markos, have his children, and complete your part of the prophecy?"

"No one can make me do that. I do not desire conflict with my family, but I will fight for my love. I love you, Dante. Never Markos."

"I am only human, Amara. Are you truly willing to fight your mother and the prophecy of your people? To be with me?"

"You are the only one for me, Dante. Ever. And my baby niece with her gift of peace was the prophecy our people truly waited for. She will rule as the prophesied queen in less than two decades. The fertility prophecy with Markos and me means nothing to our people. Only my mother cares." Amara presses her lips to Dante's. "I am sure you can give my mother the many grandchildren she is always on about. Let Markos give children to someone who desires him."

"I've thanked your gods and mine every day for a year that you landed at my lake."

A second black horse suddenly drops out of the sky and lands before them. He's massive and sleek, but he's slightly shorter and stockier than Xanthus, who trots up to meet them.

"Balius." Amara greets the new horse. "We will be bringing back a guest."

Chapter Ten

"WAKE UP!" ARIC HISSED, shaking me hard. When our eyes met, proving I was awake, he walked to the foot of the hotel bed so that he could glare at me more easily.

"What?" I rubbed my eyes.

Right. I'd had another vision. Lived another memory that wasn't mine. Given away our location again.

Hazel sat up beside me. "I...I must have dozed off."

"Shit," I groaned. "I guess this means we have to move again."

"It does," he said. "And I need better reading. I used all the power on your phone to study humans on your Instant Grams."

"I'll teach you how to use a phone charger. And I'll find us a new place to live—one with a kitchen for Hazel's tonics."

"I must sleep now if I am to continue in my servitude to you at night," he said with a deep sigh.

"Don't be such a drama queen," I said. "We'll do some online shopping with my new fortune tonight. You can pick out some books. Then I'll set it up so you can stream shows and movies, too."

"That sounds of interest. I agree to your terms." He yawned and plopped back on his bed.

I spent the next half hour under the hot water of the hotel shower, thinking about Amara again. I'd been shown another piece of her life where she was young and falling in love. She'd been filled with love from what I'd seen. Sure, her people were obsessed with prophecies, but she seemed to love her niece—my birth mother. I still didn't understand what could have turned Amara into today's version of herself.

Just as I was opening my laptop to search for a new hotel, Hazel walked back into our room holding foil wrapped food. I hadn't even noticed her leaving, which felt like a bad sign for my Atlantean hunter evasion skills.

"Breakfast sandwiches for everyone," she said. "Why don't you come with me today, Alexa? It would be good to have you gather some of your own plants."

"Sounds better than watching him sleep, but I need to find a new hotel first." I walked one of the two breakfasts Hazel had given me over to Aric.

"Show me how, and I will find and secure us a new place," Aric said.

"I already did it. We'll be back before check-out here," Hazel said. "Now let's go."

She walked back out of our hotel room and left me to scramble in my bag for some clothes. Once dressed, I threw on some sunglasses to avoid my contacts and headed after my sister.

"I'm driving us to a spot on the Chena River," Hazel said, as she pulled the car onto the highway, and I munched away on the remains of my breakfast burrito.

"What do you think it takes to become someone like Amara?" I asked Hazel.

"What do you mean? A queen? Evil?"

"The evil part. It seems like she has enough power to be any kind of queen she wants, but she chooses to hunt people down and torture them instead. What caused that?"

"Not my area of expertise," Hazel said. "Maybe you should study psychology—if you're still undecided on your major."

"Of course I'm undecided. I failed out of my last semester and can't register for fall classes," I sighed.

When we got to the spot Hazel had chosen, we parked on the side of the road and hiked into a hillside filled with low brush and tundra plants. Hazel spent the hours efficiently filling her leather bag with all sorts of plants and yelling about how I didn't know the difference between anything she was trying to direct me to pick.

"You'd know fireweed if I ever needed that, at least." Hazel grinned.

"Too soon!" I touched behind my ear. "I can't believe I got a couple's tattoo with my first girlfriend."

"At least it's small and tucked away." Hazel offered.

"Yes. And it's not like I hate fireweed."

Chapter Eleven

THAT NIGHT, ARIC WATCHED me sleep and Hazel made me some sort of bedtime concoction. We came to an agreement that he would keep a hand on me but wouldn't shake me awake unless he saw signs of me talking or moving in my sleep. I thought my visions probably made my sleep look restless, so I convinced them both it was worth testing. I needed rest and we could move again if the test failed.

Through our teamwork, or some freak miracle, I made it through the entire night without a vision or Aric having to wake me. I hadn't felt so well rested since before my first vision flashes back in April, and I got to remember what it was like to have normal, senseless dreams that are hazy and slip away as you try to remember the details.

I spent the next day in our hotel room chatting with a few girls I'd matched with on MXR, trying not to think about the fact that I'd probably have to give them up when they finally wanted to meet in person.

Hazel went out to gather more plants while Aric slept off his night of watching me.

That night when Hazel took over, I dreamed again. She and I were just so used to sharing a bed, she fell asleep for most of the night. I dreamed more about Amara falling in love with Dante, traveling the world with him on Xanthus. I saw Amara's betrothed, that guy Markos, harassing her to marry him. Then I saw the more recent Amara again, forcing some woman to give her blood.

We were forced to hop hotels again.

After a few more days of the same pattern—success one night and failure the next—I realized that I was going to have to try something for myself. We couldn't just wait around for word from Lukas forever. There were only so many hotels in Fairbanks.

With Aric often sleeping while Hazel and I were awake, it didn't take long before he complained about having not eaten in over twenty-four hours. The next day, Hazel picked him up his own phone and set it up with the Ryde app and a food ordering app. I was just thankful that Aric would quit using my phone all night to entertain himself.

Aric was happy to pick up the daily chore of checking the post office for word from Lukas because he and I had both started making online orders for ourselves. He shopped with me as I added to my growing wardrobe of stylish and professional clothes—items my parents would certainly call a waste of money.

Aric's shopping tendencies quickly veered away from books when he discovered gossip magazines. He read them cover to cover during the nights and bought the clothes and items advertised inside. His purchases ranged from random gadgets like digital picture frames to cologne to clothes he saw on famous people.

"Dressing like the human rich will help me feel more at home here," he said. "So many of you humans are drab with your garment choices." He eyed my sweats and ratty T-shirt as he said it.

Hazel noticed the packages after our first large order came in. "I'm not sure this was how Mom intended us to spend the money," she said, holding up my new pale pink, wrap coat. "And I don't think it's the best idea to have so many packages delivered through the post office."

"We're cut off from the world and on the run, Hazel. Can't we have this small thing?" I asked.

She threw her hands in the air and walked back into our little hotel kitchen. "I've been spending hours a day blending tonics for you. Hours more than I'm used to because the stupid plants around Fairbanks don't act like the same damn plants in Oread Basin. I know it has something to do with the magic, so I've been forced to experiment with basic mixes I've known since childhood." Her voice was raised, and she pointed to a corner of the counter overflowing with bottled liquids, tins of lotions, and herb mixes. "All of these work just not in the way they were supposed to. It took all this to get the one mix you've been using for sleep. What am I even going to do with it all?"

"Sorry, Hazel," I said. "I didn't know you were having such a hard time. I just thought you were...I don't know..." I trailed off, gesturing at the counter. "But there's no reason for Dagan to go reading packages at all the post offices in town."

"I sure hope you're right," she said, before walking out of the room.

After that brief tiff, Hazel resigned herself to rolling her eyes at the packages flowing in, and I slowed down on the purchases.

We'd had a week of mixed success with stopping my dreams before I decided I was done waiting for Lukas. I was going to try to have a vision on purpose to try and learn to control and stop them.

The morning after we'd moved to yet another hotel, Aric was sleeping, and Hazel was off gathering plants, so I ordered a car with my Ryde app.

"Just drive around town while I take a nap," I told the driver who picked me up at the hotel.

The driver glanced at me skeptically, but then he nodded and took off down the road. I leaned back and closed my eyes, ready to sleep and have a vision on purpose. I was ready to take control.

I fell asleep to the vibrations of the road and the low playing radio.

MARKOS

A young man walks through a well-tended orchard, filled with fully mature, purple-leaved trees. They are plump with golden apples, and he grabs one from a low branch and takes a bite. It's the perfect combination of sweet and tart and juicy.

After he passes through the final trees, he comes up to a small house of white brick. The front yard is filled with an overflowing herb garden, and he follows a path through it and around the side of the house.

His eyes fall on a woman—Helen—who's standing in front of a fence made with closely spaced black metal rods.

"Thank you for coming, Markos!" Helen's luminous golden eyes and hair match her off-the-shoulder dress. She seems highly aware that the color complements her almond skin perfectly.

"You told me you have something I need," Markos says, "in exchange for the use of my gift. What is it, Helen?"

"I do." She reaches down into a basket sitting at her feet and pulls out a dark glass bottle. "Every time we make love, it begins with you lamenting your failure to gain the affections of Princess Amara, who is yours according to prophecy. You complain that she has returned home with a human lover. And then we make love to soothe your pain."

"You bring me here to ridicule my weaknesses?" he asks, aggression seeping from every word.

"You misunderstand," she says. "I can help you. This elixir tastes like nothing more than a sweet and delicious drink, but it is an ancient Nymph recipe I learned in the time of the gods."

"You are from the time of the gods?"

"I am. And old friends with Queen Kyra. Only, I have been away for a time. The night we met last month was my first night back."

"And what is it this Nymph potion does?" Markos gestures at the bottle in her hands.

"I mixed it this morning," she says. "When it is freshly made, it opens the mind of she who drinks it. Shall I say, makes her more receptive to things such as realizing the wisdom of marrying her betrothed? It removes the nerves, helps her see the value of your suggestions. Humans have stories of love potions that are referencing this very elixir. It must be ingested within six hours, but it has a long history of success when used properly."

"Why would you do this for me?" he asks. "If the princess accepts me, I will no longer be your lover."

"You seem like a fine young man, but I do not seek more time with you in my bed. As I told you, Queen Kyra is an old friend who I am always happy to help. I have a more mundane problem with which you can assist me."

"What is that?"

She gestures beside her at the gate section of the tall metal fence, which closes in a large area around a chicken coop. "A phoenix has learned how to get through my gate here and into my hen house. He has developed a taste for eggs, and now nothing I do will keep him out."

"You expect me to hunt down a phoenix for you?" Markos scoffs. "Will it not just be reborn?"

"I do hope you can help me thoroughly eliminate it. It will be reborn as a new phoenix—one without a working knowledge of my fencing. I can relocate the chick somewhere it will not be such a nuisance. You get your bride, I get my eggs and the knowledge I have helped an old friend, and the bird gets a new start. All win with my proposal."

"And how shall I hunt this bird?"

"I have locked the chickens inside their house. Now I simply need you to use your Zeus-given lightning to set a charge in my fence. I am told you can do that—charge items and remove the charge later?"

"Easily."

"I am happy to hear that. Then for one easy chore, you may have this." She lifts the dark bottle. "Only remember it will be of no use to you after six hours, though it should still make a fine tasting drink."

Markos steps toward her with his hand out, but she puts the bottle back in the basket, stepping in front of it. "The fence first, please. That terror comes every night. Set the trap."

As Markos walks to the gate, an energy forms in his center. In the next instant, it jumps into his hands, which begin crackling with white pops of electricity. The miniature lightning dances across his palms in tiny arcs and when it builds up so there are two white balls of light in his hands, he touches the fence and allows the charge to enter the metal. "Do not use this gate until I return in the morning—unless you wish to test the strength of your eternal life. I will pull the lightning from it when I return."

"I am grateful. And I look forward to hearing the news of your princess when we meet again."

Most of the electricity has left his hands to take residence in the fence, though it's a hardly visible flickering of light within the metal at this point. His fingers seem to be playing with the remaining power, letting it jump from hand to hand and along his fingertips. The tickling buzz of it feels interesting on his skin as he reaches toward Helen who is holding out the bottle again.

"I fear it a hopeless cause if this does not work," Markos says. "Amara has always been headstrong and determined to do things her way. It is why I am so fond of her. If only she could see how much I care, maybe then she will see why the gods chose us for each other."

* * * * *

I woke from the vision. Amara's advisor, Helen, had once meddled in her love life. I had one more clue to the Dante, Markos, Amara love triangle and the origins of evil Amara. I gripped the seat with my hands only to feel a shock at the touch.

"Ouch," I yelled.

"Is everything all right?" asked the driver.

No, everything wasn't alright. Just like when I woke up on fire, my magic was flowing from somewhere in the center of me, and there was an electric build up in my hands that I didn't know how to make go away. So much for trying to take control of myself.

"I'm fine." I gritted. "Take me home now, please."

I balled my fists the whole drive home, but still, I felt the buzzing and tingling as the lightning zipped along my palms.

Chapter Twelve

"HELP, HAZEL!" I YELLED as I came into our hotel, shocking myself on the doorknob. "Are you home?"

"I just got back," Hazel said from the kitchenette counter.

"Where have you been?" Aric murmured from his bed.

"I tried to go practice my visions on my own, but now..." I held out my palms. "Look at me!" A light tingling sensation jumped across my hands. After they both saw my palms, I balled them into fists again, trying not to get shocked.

"You have a gift from Zeus? How do you have gifts from different Olympians?" Aric moved to the foot of the bed for a better view. "Stop at once!"

"I don't know how!" I whisper-screamed.

"Sit," Hazel said, patting the spot beside her on the foot of the bed. "Calming down can't hurt."

I sat down, closed fists hovering just over my thighs.

Hazel went to the kitchen counter and began sifting through her growing supply of herbs. When she had two small jars in each hand, she set to work on some sort of drink, referencing Mom's journal frequently. "Don't worry. I perfected the Fairbanks calming tonic first." She gave me a wry look. "I needed it to keep from freaking out when my recipes kept coming out bad."

How had I been so oblivious? "I'm sorry, Hazel."

"We've got bigger problems now." She shrugged. "Give me a minute—I need to focus to get this right."

She stared intently at the work in front of her.

I turned toward Aric. "What do you mean, gifts from different Olympians?"

"I mean, that you have a gift from the prophecy family—your Apollo-given visions, but you are currently using one of the many gifts from Zeus—it appears to be some version of his lightning. I have never heard of anyone with more than one gift, though my mother is searching for a way. Already, she has achieved temporary results."

I ignored the topic of Amara's freaky experiments. "Well, I can't control either of them," I said through gritted teeth. "And I don't think what's happening now is actually my gift. This happened once before, with fire. Both times, I woke from a dream where I was in the body of someone else using a power."

"I have never heard of a gift doing that."

"Distract me," I said. "Tell me about the prophecies all you people are obsessed with." Amara had been pretty opposed to her prophecy arranged marriage, and the guy prophesied to marry her was willing to try a love potion to make it happen. It seemed people either hated the prophecies or were completely devoted to them.

"I assume you are referring to the latest in the series of prophecies that started shortly before my mother's birth, about three hundred years ago."

He pulled a chair over to the bed and sat facing me. "Prophecies from the gods dictated marriages, births, and rulers for our people in exchange for an end to the curses they put upon us. The Olympians treat us like their playthings and Mother has been the first to stand up to them. She created the Queen's Laws to help our people prosper without following the prophecies.

"What are the Queen's Laws?" I had my permanent memory of Aric reporting to Amara about who Godline people were and weren't allowed to breed with, but I wanted to know what he had to say when she wasn't standing right over him.

"We must work together to provide offspring, and we must give ourselves to our queen so she has every resource at her disposal. Every law supports one of these necessities with the understanding that she will find a way to bring us back to a thriving population of Gifted and Immortal Godline."

His indoctrination sounded thorough.

"I saw how Amara disliked having a prophecy control her life, but you aren't going to convince me what she's doing to people with these laws is better. How do you even find out about the prophecies, anyway?"

"The prophetess Cassandra is the only one with the Apollo-given gift of prophecy. Through her, the absent gods try to keep people in the old ways, to follow their whims, but Mother has locked the prophetess up to prevent her words from causing further harm."

"So, what's the latest prophecy?"

"It is treason to repeat Cassandra's words, but I suppose it is too late to worry about such things," he sighed. "Prophecy says one from the ruling line will use a gift from every Olympian to restore the Godline to its original glory."

"So, your mom created laws that let her use her own people to find a workaround?" I asked. "To manufacture the results of the prophecy in her own way? Somehow steal the gifts for herself? I've seen Amara take a gift from someone in one of my visions. She took the woman's blood into her body and the gift came along with it, causing her to literally glow with beauty."

"That was Agnes with the Aphrodite-given gift of beauty," Aric said. "Mother takes that one regularly. She takes blood from her people and uses her gift of telekinetic control—a powerful Zeus-given gift—to harness the gifts in the blood of others. The effects are temporary, a few months at most, but yes, she is working to save the Immortal line through the Queen's Laws."

Hazel walked over and sat beside me with a warm mug of cure in her hand.

My fingers touched hers as I grabbed the drink, sending a shock into her body. "Sorry!" I glanced at the palm of my free hand. The jumping white lines had grown faint, but I was suddenly aware of the energy inside me that continued to flow toward my fingers.

"Drink up," Hazel said. "It's good stuff."

My heart sped at the awareness of my out-of-control power and caused miniature lightning storms to erupt where I held the mug and inside of my now fisted, free hand. I swallowed the hot tea in four panicked gulps, burning my throat.

"Tell me about Cassandra," I asked Aric, seeking another distraction. "How long has she been the prophet?"

"Cassandra is the oldest of the Godline," he said. "She was a child on Earth a thousand years before the Olympians left. She has been on Atlantis for most of her time, a celebrated prophetess until my mother exposed how she has helped the old gods manipulate our history."

"If it's the gods sending messages through Cassandra, it doesn't seem fair for her to get the blame." The warm tonic inside me began reaching out, filling every part of me with a growing calm.

"Whether or not she is to blame, her prophecies cause great harm. Fanatics will do anything to make or avoid a prophecy, and they do not care who is hurt in the process."

"So, Cassandra's like three thousand years old and your mom's only three hundred," I said. "Weird it's not Queen Cassandra."

"Mother is the last Immortal—and more powerful than any other. There is no questioning her right to rule. Age is no factor."

I grunted, annoyed at his glorifying Amara, but calm enough from the tonic to recognize she was his mother.

"Most of our people are between three and five hundred years old because of the curses," he said. "Helen is the only other really old one that I know. She was a young woman when the Olympians left—"

"Wait," Hazel said. "Is she the Helen? Like Helen of Troy, Helen?"

"No," he said. "Cassandra was raised by the king and queen of Troy, but that was a thousand years before the time of Mother's advisor. Our Helen is a daughter of Dionysus, though her gift was given by Artemis. She is the last of our kind with an Olympian parent—though her Nymph mother kept her from being Immortal."

"What do curses have to do with Godline ages?" Hazel asked.

"The Olympians created the curses for their immortal children and grandchildren. Unlike the Godline who had been diluted by Nymphs, making us slightly mortal, the immortal descendants could not die. When the Olympians decided that Earth and Atlantis were to be left to the mortals, they forbade the Immortal Godline from staying behind, fearing they would claim the roles of gods."

"But they did stay behind," Hazel said, enjoying the story a little too much for my taste.

"Yes," he said. "When many Godline and Immortals refused to leave, the gods wove a story for the humans about a single, all-powerful and fearsome god. Hephaestus armed human zealots of this new religion with the blades he designed especially for killing Immortals, creating the Death Curse. The Strife Curse from Ares did the rest of their work."

"But why aren't there many Godline younger than Queen Amara?" Hazel asked.

"On that, I am less certain. With Cassandra contained in the cells, those prophecies have not spread widely," he said. "It has something to do with Hera cursing most of the remaining Godline with childlessness over the last few centuries," he said.

"Aric..." I said, the warm calm of Hazel's tonic washing over me, "Your world confuses me. I mean, I'm sorry you've been raised to expect that your body will be bred and experimented on all in the name of making new Immortals. Your...our kind basically live forever anyway. Isn't that enough?"

"Atlantis is dying!" He snapped. "In simple terms, breeding with humans and Nymphs dilutes our lines, making us more likely to remain Giftless. We do not blame humans for being so mortal or Nymphs for having no gifts. We simply cannot survive as a people if we mix with them. We no longer have a well of immortal lines to draw from. Perhaps when Mother has restored our immortality, we could live in harmony with lesser beings agai—"

"Enough!" I yelled, as my heart rate picked up speed. Not once in my life had I felt superior to a single person in my Nymph village. How could he dismiss them so easily? "Don't insult my family."

I flopped on the bed, covering my eyes with my arm and letting the calming tonic embrace me again.

"This conversation has become absurd," Hazel said. "Alexa and I were raised as humans, and honestly, it seems like Nymph-kind views things differently than the Godline."

"Indeed, they do," he said. "Nymphs love humans and do not mind dying in obscurity for that love."

"The lesson from all this..." I changed the subject. "Is that I can't have a normal life. You know I've already been ghosted by one of the girls I've been chatting with because I couldn't meet for a hook-up," I muttered.

"What is this...hook...up?" Aric asked.

"Well, Aric..." I began, using my most sarcastic voice. "These days, people have these wonderful apps on their phones, allowing them to match up for a night of hot sex without the tiresome details of a relationship. At least, that's what the girl who already dumped me thinks."

"I am interested. How do I navigate this...sex app?" he asked. "Atlantean breeding chambers have a similar function."

"Aren't you concerned about breaking your breeding law?" I mocked. "You know it's going to be humans on an app like that."

"I am schooled in how to prevent human offspring."

Hazel grabbed my empty mug and stood up. "I'm sorry about the dating fail, Lex. And the whole lightning hands fiasco." She smiled and grabbed my hand. There was no shock between us as she held my palm open for inspection. "But no more lightning."

"Oh good," I said lazily, the warm fuzzy calm lulling my mind. "Another near crisis averted."

"The good news," Aric said, "is that you did not have visions here."

"Don't forget Alexa came in with lightning hands," Hazel said.

"That gift will not be recognized as hers. I panicked when I first saw it, but I should not have worried over a first-time gift use. If Helen does not miss it entirely, she will pin the city at most. She only pulls out detailed maps after a gift has had multiple uses somewhere."

I sighed with tentative relief, though I was more anxious than ever for Lukas to arrive after my failed attempt to help myself.

Chapter Thirteen

AFTER THE FIRST WEEK in Fairbanks, we'd realized that Aric was much better at staying awake and keeping me from dreaming, so we decided to have him take over the job while Hazel focused on her tonics. I was feeling useless, my life suddenly reduced to hiding out all day in a hotel and messaging girls on MXR. The few times Hazel asked me along over the next week to pick plants, I found myself jumping at the opportunity to get out and do anything productive.

Under Aric's watch, I made it a whole week without a vision. Enough time to enjoy not running from hotel to hotel and just long enough to make a stupid choice in bored desperation. While Aric slept and Hazel was out, I took a Ryde to a coffee shop to meet up with one of the girls I'd hit it off with on MXR. Even though I paid in cash and had the Ryde drop me off away from the coffee shop, I knew I was taking an unnecessary risk. At the same time, I needed it. I needed something normal.

The date was nice because I got to talk with another human being for a while, but it was clear there was no chemistry between us. We parted with a friendly hug, and I headed home, hopefully before anyone was aware I'd even left.

But when my Ryde dropped me off, Aric was pacing outside the hotel lobby. He was decked out in the three-piece suit he'd ordered to match his eyes. The pre-ordered size didn't fit his bony body well, sagging at his shoulder joints and swallowing the rest of his shape in the layers of fabric.

"You're finally wearing some of those nice clothes you ordered," I said. "You look sharp." Even with the poor fit, it was true, although I should probably tell him that formal wear like that would seem odd among the Carhart and flannel clad population of Fairbanks. "How was your day? Why are you out here?"

"An inspiring day, as always," he said dryly. His sarcasm had improved in our time together. "Lukas has made contact." He held up a paper.

"Why didn't you call me to come home sooner?"

Aric shrugged and handed me an envelope with only the name Delmon written on the outside. Our parents had told us Lukas also had a key to the box and checked it periodically for messages from them or a handful of others who might need to get in touch. I opened the envelope, which had already been torn along the adhesive portion.

Greetings Delmons,

I would be honored to assist you however I can.

Let us meet in three days' time—at noon on Monday, the twenty-second day of August. I will wait for you at a gravel pit just past the mile four marker on Murphy Dome Road. Climb over the hill you see from the road. I will be there.

I look forward to making your acquaintance,

Regards,

Lukas

Finally. "We meet him tomorrow," I said.

"I am aware." Aric's irritation was clear in his deadpan response.

"What's up? I thought you'd be relieved, not having to babysit me anymore."

"I have kept your gift in check for a full week. And now you are ready to reject my help for perfect Lukas. Did you know his Artemis-given gift is animal transformation? How useful do you imagine the ability to become a squirrel will be in controlling your visions?"

"What're you talking about?" I asked. "I thought you hated watching me sleep."

"I assumed he would never make contact," Aric yelled. "Lukas abandoned the palace over a century ago and pulled his younger sister into his betrayal just before I was born."

"You waited long enough to share this."

"It is not a topic I am fond of," he snapped.

"Just tell me what I should know."

"Fine," he sighed heavily, crossing his arms. "Lukas and his younger sister, Penelope, were born to Helen, and they grew up with both Mother and Helen fawning over them because of their gifts and their prophesied sire, Markos."

"I thought Markos was in love with Amara."

"I was getting to that," he said. "When Mother rejected Markos, he retaliated. He somehow found an Immortal Death Blade and murdered Mother's family for rejecting him and the prophecy."

"Shit," I mumbled.

"Markos was jailed immediately, but he had already conceived Lukas with Helen." Aric scowled. "It shows that all he cared about was his fertility prophecy—not my mother. Now you see how prophecy destroyed our family."

So, not only did Helen mess with Amara's love life, it somehow ended with Markos killing her family. I remembered Amara talking about her love for her twin and wondered if she was one of those killed by Markos. Amara's fall from loving girl to evil queen was making more sense as the pieces came together.

"It sounds like it was that guy Markos who destroyed your family, not prophecy," I said.

"You learn nothing." Aric shook his head slowly.

"Well, maybe Lukas will get through to me." I joked.

Aric missed the sarcasm. "Maybe."

"So, you hate Lukas and Penelope because they have gifts and your mom showed them favoritism?"

"You try being compared to those far more talented than you for a lifetime."

He obviously had no understanding of my own insecurities after growing up with the Nymphs, but I kept the focus on Aric's palace drama. "Where did Penelope come from if Markos was jailed for murder before her older brother was even born?"

"A decade after his capture, Penelope became the first successful offspring of the breeding program when Helen coupled with Markos a second time. That success determined a basic rule for the punishment of criminals that has been used for over two centuries—Gifted Godline criminals with proven fertility serve their sentence in the breeding chambers and the rest serve in the cells." Aric sighed. "I wish Penelope was coming instead of Lukas."

"Why?"

"Her brother may have led her astray and helped her flee Atlantis, but Penelope was captured and successfully reeducated when I was young. It was a painful betrayal when she ran from Atlantis just after our marriage, and still, I would be happy to see her again."

"I still can't believe your people would marry off a sixteen-year-old child," I said.

"So?"

"It's wrong, Aric. You weren't old enough for that and you didn't even get to decide for yourself."

"Penelope cared for me through most of my life and there is no other person with whom I feel closer. I was overjoyed when Mother told me I was to marry her."

"I think it's a good thing she ran away," I said.

"Facilitated by Lukas, no doubt," he muttered.

"Can you just try to be positive about meeting him?"

"I will be civil."

"Where's Hazel?"

"She called to say she would be back shortly," he said. "She went to deliver another supply of her extra remedies."

Hazel had used our family connections to the local farmers' market to make deals with a couple of vendors to sell her extra tonics and lotions on commission. Her botched remedies seemed to be particularly popular with human buyers despite the fact that they were basically just natural lotions and herbal teas.

I wondered how she felt about her magic still not working. Evidenced by the constantly overflowing pile on her 'failure' counter, but I was hopeful she'd find success in the large stack of books and journals about the local plant life that were due to arrive any day. I'd gone in search of anything that might help her after she first told me what was wrong.

Just then, an unfamiliar car pulled up and Aric stepped past me, toward it.

"Where are you going?"

He stopped and turned to glare at me. "I know where you went today," Aric said through gritted teeth. "I have read your MXR messages."

"Invasive much?" I glared at him. "Why'd we even get you your own phone?"

He ignored my questions. "Your sex habits did give me the idea to download that fascinating app for myself. Lukas is here to save the day now, so it is time I indulge."

He walked the rest of the way to the waiting car but locked eyes with me before getting inside. "I have my first hook-up tonight, so do not wait up."

"How am I going to sleep?" I asked, shocked by the sudden end to his cooperativeness.

"That is not my problem tonight." He got in the car and it pulled away.

AMARA

Amara stands in a dim room of stone walls and metal bars, a cowering woman at her feet. Even though the woman's dark curls are hanging in limp tangles and she's wearing a filthy tunic made of something like burlap, her luminous blue eyes glow with power.

The source of energy within Amara flashes to life and rushes into her mind. "Helen told me your gift was active last night. You will tell me what the gods have shared, Cassandra."

When the energy suddenly releases from Amara's mind, Cassandra sits up in a jerk, back against the wall, and squeezes her neck with her hands. She's trying to gasp, but there's no sound to indicate she's taking in air. Her legs thrash in a feeble attempt to bring oxygen to her lungs.

The energy flow seems to ebb, and Cassandra's fingers release their crushing grip, allowing her to finally take a breath, broken by spasmodic coughing.

"I would pull the prophecy from your head myself, but that is not a gift of mine...yet," Amara says.

Then more energy flares up from that endless source somewhere within Amara and it flows freely again.

Suddenly, Cassandra grabs her own index finger and snaps it sharply to the side, screaming from the moment the bone breaks. Amara's gaze shifts to Cassandra's middle finger and the same occurs. The screaming is continuous until a tendril of the energy connecting them travels inside of Cassandra's throat, clenching the airway closed.

Amara's eyes move from one finger to the next as she forces Cassandra to snap them, mouth gasping for air. Only after forcing Cassandra to break her good fingers with the broken does Amara allow Cassandra to breathe again. Now she's too weak and short of air to scream her pain.

"This is rather entertaining for me, and though I would love to play all night, I have dinner guests. Do not force me to stand them up."

Her eyes beg Amara desperately, still gasping and unable to speak.

"Cassandra!" This time her energy slams Cassandra's face into the stone, and she starts laughing as the blood begins to pour.

Cassandra whimpers, almost inaudibly, "The gods spoke a message."

Her next words are hollow, free of emotion. "Children of the ruling line, only together will their gifts renew the Gifted."

Amara clenches her fists until there's a sharp pain followed by the warm release of blood in her palms.

"Come here." The line of magic is still stretched between them, and Cassandra stands like a puppet on a string.

Amara embraces her. "See how simple that was? Why do you always speak in riddles though?" She takes Cassandra's bloody face in her hands and stares into her eyes.

One of Amara's hands moves to Cassandra's hair and grips it hard enough to make her gasp. Then Amara slams Cassandra's head into the wall and starts laughing as she watches Cassandra fall into a lifeless heap on top of her ivory skirts.

"Dagan!" Amara calls, using one of her feet to shove Cassandra off the pale fabric of her dress.

Almost instantly, the cell door opens, and Amara steps out past Dagan.

His black hair flows loosely in soft waves over the shoulders of his guard uniform.

She turns and starts walking down the hall. Dagan's footsteps echo quietly on the floor just behind her as they pass countless cells on either side. Few are empty.

When she reaches the end, she passes through a door into a small room of doorways and through the far door again. They've entered a hall leading to an ascending staircase and Amara stops just inside.

"You should have stopped me sooner," she tells Dagan. "Now my dinner gown is soiled."

Dagan stares at her with a cold smile that doesn't reach his eyes. "I enjoy watching you work far too much."

She reaches out and brushes the tips of her long red nails along his cheek, causing him to visibly shiver as she leaves a line of Cassandra's still moist blood behind.

He steps closer and grabs both of Amara's hands firmly. He turns her bloody palms toward herself and gently presses them at her throat, smearing blood down her skin and streaking her fabrics.

Her body fills with excited tension, and she takes him in an aggressive kiss, arms holding him against her while her nails dig into his back. She pulls herself away with one last nip on his lower lip.

"When will you take one of these women I have gathered as a pet of your own?" Amara asks, gesturing back toward the halls they'd just left. "You know you have earned your pick of the litter. I would even give you Ivy." She presses her fingers to her lips. "What fun that would be—no matter how much you hurt her, she can heal herself quickly—a fresh canvas for your violent art over and over again."

"I serve your needs alone, my queen. These women are nothing after having you."

"My loyal pet, I would have no other lead my hunters or..." Her fingers trail toward the embroidered collar of his shirt and pull open the top buttons. "To entertain my physical needs, but I will never be yours." She sighs. "One of these women on the other hand, would be utterly and completely yours."

Amara walks to the end of the hall with Dagan just behind her again, and they stop in front of a mirror set at the base of the stairs. Red smears cover the pale skin and gown in Amara's reflection, and through the glass behind her, the cream shoulders of Dagan's shirt are also stained with blood.

"We will have to change before dinner," she says.

He takes her shoulders in his palms and turns her to face him. He looks down her body slowly. "I would enjoy attending dinner with the region leaders like this. They could use a visual reminder of what it means to break the Queen's Laws."

"They can be quite...trying," she says. "If I had time to collect taxes and breeding reports from the Distant Regions without them, I would let my temper run free at their thinly veiled questions about my rule."

"Perhaps you should take them for your experiments, replace them with younger, more loyal Godline." His lips brush against her ear.

She presses her hands, fingers spread wide, across his chest before running them down the front of him, stopping at his belt. "Do not tempt me."

He covers her hands with his own and shifts their fingers over the buckle, "I heard Cassandra's prophecy." He leaves her fingers to work at his belt while he reaches up and begins unpinning her hair so it splashes down over the skin of her shoulders.

Amara pulls at the bottom of his shirt, yanking it away from the loosened fastenings of his pants. "It assures me that I must rely on the gifts of others in my experiments." She begins unbuttoning his shirt.

He reaches behind her back and starts unlacing the strings that hold her corset in place.

"I will free our people from the empty words of gods who have all but forgotten us." She finishes with his lowest button and pulls his shirt wide, pressing her hands against the skin of his chest. "I will harness their abilities to give gifts and immortality to the Godline."

"You are the only goddess I will ever worship, my queen." He's worked the back of Amara's dress loose and pulls at it in earnest to open up the fabric clinging to her skin.

She reaches back and pulls his hands away from her bindings. Then turns and begins leading the way up the narrow stairs, lifting her skirts clear of each step.

When she stops one stair above and turns back to him, it makes them almost eye level, though he's still taller. "I need something, Dagan."

"Anything, my queen," he says.

"When my niece delivers her daughter, I want you to take the child and bring her to me," she says. "It is to be Irene's punishment for hiding the father. And I will raise the child protected from the harms of prophecy, serving my work instead."

Dagan drops to one knee on the stair below her, bowing deeply with his upper body. His open shirt drapes like curtains along each of his sides. "I will die before failing you, my queen."

"Do whatever it takes short of harming Irene." Amara grabs both sides of his head as he turns his face up. Leaning down, she kisses his forehead softly and runs her fingers through his long hair before he stands and presses close again.

He kisses her and pushes her against the wall, then takes his mouth from hers so that he can speak.

"Why did you insist on interrogating Cassandra right before a dinner party? You know we will have to leave this unsatisfied if we are to get changed in time."

"Yes...I feel your point..." She kisses him deeply again. "...and I am regretting my impatience regarding Cassandra. I envy the way you toy with your quarry for weeks on hunts." Her arms and chest are suddenly covered in goosebumps, and she pulls Dagan in so she can kiss her way up his neck. "Denying yourself what you truly want...such sweet anticipation." She reaches his mouth, and the heat rises between them.

"Your guests, my queen?" he breathes.

"Exactly," she whispers. "I am Queen. My guests can wait."

* * * * *

And I'm suddenly, jarringly aware of who I really am and the body I'm in. This is not a sexual experience I've ever had, and I have no intention of starting now, even if it's not my own body. And then I realize I have a body of my own, and I think about it lying asleep in our hotel.

Chapter Fourteen

"SHIT! NO...NO..." I jumped up in bed.

Hazel groaned and pushed herself upright next to me. "Sorry, Lex. I don't even remember falling asleep."

"I just tortured a woman and nearly had sex with the jerk who's trying to kidnap me." My gut twisted as I recalled my new memory, another ugly and permanent part of who I was becoming because of my horrible gift.

Hazel cringed. "That's awful. I'm sorry I fell asleep."

"Well, I'm sorry we have to move again." I frowned. "I'll find us a new place."

"Thanks," Hazel said. "I need to run out for some new plants this morning. I know enough to guess the magic is changed by the season each plant is gathered, but everything is still all trial and error." She sighed. "I don't get why this is suddenly so hard, Lex."

"Don't worry. When Mom gets here, she'll help you and explain whatever she kept secret because of me," I said. "In the meantime, you're just making us richer." I grinned.

"Speaking of money..." She gestured at our one small closet, bursting with the clothes Aric and I had ordered over the last month. "Your shopping is getting excessive. What happened to traveling light because you're, you know...on the run?"

"You can blame all the time I spend wearing Atlantean finery. It's only gotten me more obsessed with nice things," I joked. "But for real, I'm pretty happy with my wardrobe at the moment, so I promise to stop the online orders."

Hazel left on her plant gathering errand while I found us a new place to live. With Lukas on the way and my sleep success over most of the last week, I took a chance on an actual apartment that rented by the month, cash up front and no paperwork.

Our new studio apartment was part of a larger complex. It had a ground level entrance into the blue building and two neighbors on either side of us. The setting was more private than any hotel we'd been in so far, with forest lining the roads around it. I wasn't sure if that was a good or a bad thing in helping us hide from Dagan, but it seemed smart to change the pattern and get away from the hotels for a bit.

After we got moved over to the new place, Aric grudgingly went back to watching me sleep, saying it was so I wouldn't, "Ruin everything with my total lack of skill and control."

Aric seemed to be getting more irritable by the hour, and by the time we were all driving to meet Lukas the next day, he had reduced most of our conversation to grunts, nods, or headshakes while generally ignoring me for his phone screen.

When Lukas's designated gravel pit came into view, Hazel pulled well away from the road, right up to the base of the massive hill of gravel.

"There's no vehicle here," Hazel said. "Maybe we're ahead of him."

"I am sure he spends a lot of his time as an animal," Aric said. "He probably came as one."

"Well, let's go then," I said, and started climbing the hill. It was easier to ignore my nerves about the meeting if I didn't stop too long to think.

The loose gravel slipped under my feet as I climbed. It was easiest to lean forward and use my hands to help me pass through the shifting material. I could hear Aric panting and scrambling through the rocks below me, but only a slight crunching of Hazel's steps as she climbed up to and then ahead of me. She disappeared over the top half a minute before I reached it. After I crested the hill, I collapsed to catch my breath, and Aric slumped down next to me soon after.

We both watched Hazel walk around the top of the gravel pile, which was about a hundred meters wide and completely free of other people...and animals.

"It's noon," Hazel said, flopping down beside me.

Aric sighed heavily as he sat up on my other side. "How inconsiderate."

We all stared across the empty plateau. And that was when we noticed the red-tailed hawk circling above. It was circling closer with each revolution until it was flapping down to land on the gravel a few feet in front of us. Its hawk eyes flashed, glowing amber, and then it was blurring, growing, shifting. In seconds, he'd become a fully clothed man, only the glow behind his eyes unchanged.

"Woah," Hazel said.

He was wearing worn jeans, a black T-shirt, and a pair of running shoes. His black hair was braided into neat locks that ended at the base of his head. His skin was a rich brown, and just like his outfit, perfectly clean. It made no sense for someone who lived as an animal, so I figured it was part of his gift.

With the sun behind him, his body seemed to glow along with his amber eyes. He was skeletal and formidable and graceful all at once.

I finally found my voice. "Hi Lukas." I held out my hand. "I'm Alexa."

He shied ever so slightly, like a wary animal, when my hand reached toward him. He didn't seem like he wanted to touch me at all, let alone shake my hand.

I lowered the gesture. "This is Hazel." I pointed at my sister. "And Aric." I indicated Aric on my other side.

Lukas was watching my hand movements closely but remained silent.

"Hello, Lukas," Hazel said.

"Hazel." He gave her a nod. "A beautiful name. Your parents and I had a friend in Old Atlantis with that name." He watched Hazel closely and even took a step in her direction.

"What's Old Atlantis?" I asked.

"The Nymphs were exiled when I was young...that was when Old Atlantis died," he replied, very little expression in his voice. He was still looking at Hazel, his hawk gaze softening.

"Right," I said. "My dad mentioned something about that."

Lukas shifted his gaze to me, which was good. Striking as he was, it would have gotten uncomfortable if he'd stared at Hazel any longer.

"My history lessons never spoke of an Old Atlantis," Aric muttered loudly enough for everyone to hear.

"So, Lukas," Hazel said. "What is it like to fly? I'm so jealous."

"I could take the form of Pegasus so that you might experience it for yourself."

She actually giggled. "Maybe some other time?"

He nodded.

"I'd love to learn what I can about Atlantis and my family and whatever else I can from you," I told him. "But right now, I desperately need help controlling my powe...my gift."

"I will help however I can," he said. "But my sister, Penelope, will fly here from her home in Seattle tomorrow. She is more experienced assisting Godline in hid—"

"How have you avoided hunters for two hundred years while using your gift, anyway?" Aric asked, a little aggressively.

Lukas ignored him, but I was curious too. "Would you mind sharing? Maybe it will help me stay hidden too?" I asked tentatively.

"My shifts happen too fast for Mother to get her maps out, so as long as I don't shift over and over in one place, her gift is too slow to find me," he said. "Even so, I do not linger anywhere and spend most of my time among the animals."

"That sounds a little lonely," Hazel said.

"I enjoy spending my time with the earth and its creatures," he told her gently. "I visit my loved ones when I get lonely. It is a better life than I would live on Atlantis." He turned to me. "Tell me about your gift."

"Well, the visions come in my sleep. I have no control of what I see. Aric's been watching me at night to keep me from having them." I paused, trying to think of all the highlights. "They show me memories. Oh, and recently, when I have a vision in someone's body while they're using a gift, I wake up with that gift stuck in the on position."

After almost a minute of silence, Lukas just shook his head.

"What?" I asked, voice clipped.

"I am sorry," he said. "Prophecy line gifts are nothing like my own."

"No," I groaned. "I can't keep living this way." My jaw tightened and my body vibrated with tension. Lukas had failed to bring my promised solutions.

"There must be something she can do to control her gift," Hazel said softly.

Lukas shifted closer to Hazel again. "I have never heard of a gift like she describes, especially the use of gifts that belong to others." He paused for several long seconds. "She cannot help but have visions in her sleep because her magic demands attention. Perhaps, if she could have visions while awake, she might release some of the unused magic."

"So, I could control where I do it then?" I asked. "Yes, please."

"I will try to help you now." He turned around, examining the plateau. "Let us sit down for this. You will need a topic to focus on."

"Why don't you try to learn more about your birth mother, Lex?" Hazel wove her legs into each other on the gravel next to me.

"Okay. Now what?" I asked Lukas.

"Try to focus on your breath. Then focus on your body. Find the magic within you and call it forth."

Eyes closed, I tried to do what he said, but I only got as far as focusing on my breathing and my body. There was no sign of magic. I spent several minutes trying anyway. I could hear an occasional deep breath of one of the others, but otherwise, I was left to focus in silence.

"I can't find any magic," I yelled into the quiet day and opened my eyes.

Aric and Hazel were sitting on either side of me, still. Hazel gave me a small smile while Aric stared at his hands, folded in front of him.

Lukas sat facing me and again waited a painfully long time before finally speaking. "We will try another way. Focus on your breath again, but then, once you feel lost in the patterns of your own breathing, I want you to focus all your thoughts on your topic of choice."

"So, focus on my breath. Then focus on Irene. Alright."

"Try to reach a sleep-like state before thinking about your mother."

"Here, Lex," Hazel said. "Put your head in my lap and lie on your back. That's more sleep-like, right?"

"A sound idea." Lukas told her warmly.

"Okay." I shifted down into Hazel's lap and realized quickly that I was good at falling asleep. In just a few moments, I'd settled into a hazy and lulling consciousness. And that's when I started thinking about Irene. I tried to imagine her right now, wondering what she would be doing. I stayed in my lull and filled it with thoughts of my birth mother.

IRENE

A scene fills most of my consciousness, but I also know I'm lying on a pile of rocks, trying to make this happen. The sensation of the gravel under my back is replaced by the rocking motion of a horse beneath me and a narrow waist gripped in my arms. Before the vision pulls me all the way in, I realize that I recognize the feel of my mind in Irene's body.

The rider in front, who Irene holds a little too tightly, guides them through the night sky next to another horse and rider, galloping just in front of them. The wind roars past and distant fires speck the earth far below.

A blinding panic consumes my waking mind when I first realize I'm on a flying horse with no means of control, but I settle into the sensations as the minutes pass and soon we're descending.

The horses land gently in front of a mansion of white stone with a matching stable beside it. They ride through the open doors of the barn and stop in front of a teenage girl wearing a clean beige tunic and matching breeches.

Irene slides off the horse just before her companion, who turns once landing on her feet. Penelope. She's wearing a blue dress with deep pleats in the skirt that seem to be styled for riding. Her hair is woven into several dark braids that come together at the base of her neck and flow into a thick cloud of curls, exposing the long curves of her neck on either side.

Penelope takes Irene's pale hand in hers and leads them toward the woman still on her tall black horse.

Her dress also seems designed for riding, its long black skirt made with hundreds of small braids spilling around her legs, and it shows off her light brown skin with its golden glow smoothing over her angular body. Her dark golden hair is pulled into a ponytail on one side and the bundle of hair stops just shy of the corset that matches her bright jade eyes.

Her horse bends at the knees and lowers itself to the ground next to an elegant golden wheelchair. When the animal is settled, the woman efficiently shifts herself from her perch of flesh to the cushioned metal.

Then Penelope pulls Irene along as they follow the other woman back toward the house. "It'll be okay, Irene." She squeezes Irene's hand as they make their way up a long stone ramp and through the front doors.

The space inside is filled with low benches and cushioned seats. On the far side of the room, Agnes—the woman who Amara takes blood and beauty from—is sharing a low backed couch with a man whose dark brown skin glows warm with power. The pair of them are dressed in silky black fabrics.

Agnes smiles warmly, and she and the man stand when they see Penelope and Irene's riding companion.

"Chloe!" Agnes says.

Chloe closes the distance between them and Agnes leans in to embrace her.

"Mother." Chloe turns to hug the man. "Father."

She turns to face Penelope and Irene. "Come sit."

Penelope, hand still in Irene's tight grip, pulls Irene toward the couch facing the couple and they settle there.

"Thank you for hosting us, Agnes, Terrance," Penelope says. "Chloe is here on official business, but the queen will be expecting Irene back soon."

"She does not like me to have free time," Irene says.

"Let us begin, then," Agnes says. "When Queen Amara started making the Queen's Laws nearly half a century ago, only Markos and a few other criminals were in the breeding chambers, available to those wanting children."

"But now," Terrance says. "Her laws have gone too far. She took my daughter." His voice becomes louder, rigid. "And exploits her gift!"

"It is not fair, Chloe!" Agnes says. "You run her stables. You are the official rider for all royal business. How dare she pull you from your studies at the university to treat you like a common prostitute." She sighs heavily and slumps against Terrance.

"Mother, I still make time for my studies," Chloe says. "And I highly doubt I am privy to all royal business. I am only trusted to collect taxes and now..." She pulls a scroll from a pouch concealed at her waist. "Spread word of her new laws."

Terrance takes the papers and reads them over, the crease between his brows deepening as he reads. "It requires us, as region leaders, to keep a census and develop a rotation for all our eligible people to participate in the breeding chambers. This requires that we report Gifted status and keep detailed records of all attempted breeding, for everyone over a century. Marriage is only allowed for proven producers and must be approved by the queen." He tightens his grip on the paper, crumpling it in his fist. "The queen is writing laws that allow her to take our Gifted babies to use however she pleases and—"

"She is forcing all of us to take part in this breeding program now," Agnes interrupts. "And she forces my daughter of twenty years to breed for her and use her gift in support of those shameful laws." Agnes closes her eyes and buries her face into Terrance's shoulder.

He strokes her hair, attempting to calm her.

"I'm right here, Mother," Chloe says, patting the other side of her hair along with her father. "I use my gift to serve a daily shift in her breeding chambers, but even she realizes my value in the stables. She trusts me, Mother. She trusts Penelope. And she hates Irene. Let us use all of that, however we can, to fight her laws."

"You are simply brilliant," Agnes wails and buries her face back into Terrance's shoulder.

Chloe continues with her idea. "We can hide Gifted children who come to us, give them lives among the Giftless, teach them to go undetected."

"What happens when breeding reports start coming back with too few Gifted?" Irene asks. "She will punish whoever she catches severely."

"I can use my gift to convince all involved there is nothing to be concerned about," Terrance says.

"That is a great risk," Irene says.

"I will face the consequences, if it comes to that," he says. "I cannot stand by and let another parent lose their child to these repulsive laws."

"What will the rest of us do?" Penelope asks.

"Whatever you can," he says. "Gather information, seek allies, don't get caught by the queen's hunters, and resist these laws whenever you get the opportunity."

Chloe moves to Terrance's side. "I am proud to call you Father." She leans sideways to rest her head on his free shoulder. "And you, Mother." She grabs Agnes's hand and squeezes it. "I miss you both, but the pride I hold in my heart for you will carry me as we resist."

"That is what we will be," he says. "The resistance."

"To the resistance, then," Penelope says with a nod of her chin.

"The resistance," their voices echo.

PENELOPE

And then, in a single blink, my eyes open to a new scene. A young man drifts up, weightless, weaving through the closely spaced branches of a tree above me.

"Catch up, Penelope," he yells at me from above, now obscured by the bright teal leaves and golden blooms that sprout from every limb.

"You have an unfair advantage, Sebastian." Penelope starts climbing up between the branches of the odd tree.

When she reaches the higher branches, she has a distant view of the landscape, which slopes downhill from the tree and into a wide valley. The center is made up of a large orchard of purple trees next to a huge garden, speckled with a maze of bright plants that create a series of walking paths. Next to the garden, there's a wide road hosting an open-air market with a row of colorful fabric roofs on either side. There's a circle of homes, both large and small, separating the inner community from the forests and fields of crops that form the outer parts of the valley.

Penelope settles in on a branch next to Sebastian, a sandy blond with extremely pale and glowing blue eyes. The glow of his own power reaches his angular shoulder bones and his too thin body, glossing it over until he's the perfect prince charming type, including his embroidered cream top, dark breeches, and shiny black boots.

They look over the landscape for a few minutes, neither of them speaking.

Sebastian breaks the silence. "Did you ask Queen Amara for permission to marry me yet?"

"It is not as easy as you always seem to think. She is in no mood to indulge my whims right now."

"The queen has always preferred you over her own niece. She will be more likely to give you what you want if she is still having fits about Irene."

Penelope shoves a hand against his ribs, hard. It throws him off balance enough that he tumbles forward off his perch and begins to fall out away from the tree. Before he can hit the ground and start rolling downhill, he catches himself in midair and flies back up to settle next to Penelope again.

"Careful!" He's laughing. "You could have killed me."

A crease forms between Penelope's eyes and her lips tighten into a scowl. "It is not a game, Sebastian!"

His jovial demeanor slips at her tone.

"She sent Irene to the breeding chambers less than an hour ago," she adds.

"I do not understand why that is so upsetting, Penny. She is well over the age of obligation. Queen Amara has been particularly generous, and you must admit, Irene has not even attempted to follow the Queen's Laws."

"Nor have I!" Penelope says. "If we are not approved to marry, Mother plans to finally convince Queen Amara I should go to the breeding chambers too."

"You know I have been to the chambers regularly since I lived my first century. There are far worse fates than taking Chloe to bed," he says.

"Do not talk about my friend that way," she says. "Chloe does not use her gift like that by choice."

He drifts through the air and branches between them and sits beside her. "Just ask the queen. A marriage buys us both ten child-free years."

HELEN

After a few moments, the scene in front of me blurs, darkens, and refocuses, but the surroundings are different again: the jungle-like palace courtyard with its spiral of flowers.

This body—Helen's body—is standing beside the large, mounted map, but there's a small table I hadn't noticed before, and on top of it Helen's hands are spread across a map of Fairbanks.

Helen's body is pulling energy for her gift, the power radiating from somewhere within her, causing a tingling warmth. The energy isn't building up or trying to escape though.

She reaches back into her firmly pinned hair, brushing fingers over several round bumps before gripping and pulling one. Helen holds the tiny golden spike over the map and then the gift leaks from her fingertips into the point, causing it to shift itself at an angle toward the top of the map. As she moves her hand across the paper, the pin repositions itself a few times, narrowing down the location.

The magic finds the location and she marks it. Without turning, she speaks. "Theron, I need the queen to contact Dagan. The gift we have been tracking is being used presently." She pulls paper and a golden pen from a drawer. "Take this to her."

Murphy Dome Road, mile four

And in this moment, the shock of the vision pushes me out. I can feel the rocks under my back, Hazel's lap under my head, my slow and steady breaths.

Chapter Fifteen

"SHIT!" I GASPED, BACK in my own body. "Helen just pinned this location."

"I didn't think there was technology on Atlantis," Hazel said.

"No. I mean, she literally stuck a golden pin in a map, showing this." I swept my arms around me in the air as I sat up. "How long have I been lying here?"

"Twenty minutes have passed," Aric said, glancing up from the screen of his phone.

"We should leave now," I said.

The others all stood up quickly at my urgent tone.

We slid carefully down the giant rock hill toward our parked car. Every time a vehicle passed, the group of us would slow our movement instinctively, watching until it moved out of sight.

As we closed the distance to the car, Lukas walked up beside me.

"Penelope's gift is from Apollo like yours. She will be much better at helping you," he said. "She is also much better at being human than I."

"You've helped me more than you could know already," I said, stopping beside the car. "You helped me choose where I have a vision for the first time, and I got to see my birth mother and her friends today. It's one of the few gentle memories I've accumulated."

He acknowledged me with a quiet nod.

Aric made his way toward the front passenger seat.

"Shotgun!" I yelled at him.

The next moment was a blur of Lukas disappearing and his hawk form shooting up into the sky and out of sight.

I stood there with my mouth partially open, staring at the empty air. And then Lukas flew back over my head from somewhere behind me and landed before shifting into a man once again.

"I apologize for leaving you to fend without me," Lukas said. "My instincts to flee shotguns have become very strong. Though I see no weapon."

"I didn't mean to spook you." I pressed my lips flat so he wouldn't think I was laughing at him. "I just meant to tell Aric I wanted the front seat. It's a saying I taught him the other day.

Hazel was grinning as she got into the driver's seat.

"Would you like the front seat?" I asked Lukas.

"I will follow from above," he said a moment before he shifted into a hawk again. The shift came so easily, it was as if the bird was his natural form, and his body couldn't leave the man behind fast enough.

"Let's get out of here." Aric nervously swept the area with his eyes.

* * * * *

When we got back to our apartment, we invited Lukas in to talk through our plans. All of us settled around the coffee table. Hazel sat on the couch with Lukas while Aric and I pulled stools from the counter over to form a circle.

It occurred to me that Lukas might be able to help explain part of my latest vision. "Do you know how Amara uses shared blood to communicate with her hunters?"

"I do not know how she could do this," Lukas said. "I have spent little time as a human and almost no time on Atlantis in the last two centuries. Penelope will know more. Her first escape was only two decades ago."

"You should have asked me, Alexa. I was a hunter, remember." Aric said this like it was something to strive for.

"I'm so overwhelmed with new information and scattered visions," I said. "I haven't even known what to ask. Please tell me what you know." I didn't mention the trust issues I was still getting over with Aric, the hunter.

Aric continued. "She uses telepathy, a gift she keeps in her blood at all times. It works for simple messages, even over long distances for those who have shared her blood."

"That's what she tried to do to you before you came here, right?" I asked.

"Yes," he said, and his face dropped. "But her gift would not work in my blood. She is normally connected to her hunters as long as the blood they have shared lives."

"What else can she do?" I asked.

"I do not know the extent of her talents, but they scare me and every other member of the Godline," Aric answered.

"Why did her gift not work in your blood?" Lukas asked.

"I do not know," Aric said, voice bitter. "It must not be too vital since she sent me anyway even without the bond."

"Why are you being defensive about your ability to be a hunter?" I asked. "I thought you left that role when you saved us."

"I am not," he sputtered. "I did. Leave it behind, I mean." His shoulders sagged as he looked at his feet.

"It sounds as if your gift might manipulate the powers of others," Lukas said. "Alexa said that you keep her from having visions at night. How do you do that?"

"I would wake her if I saw signs of her visions, but her sleep is peaceful when I watch," Aric said. "Of course, her sister fell asleep literally every time she tried to do the same thing."

"I do not believe it has to do with watching for dreams," Lukas said. "I believe your proximity or touch can dampen the gifts of others."

"Wait, you are telling me that my gift makes it so other people's gifts do not work?" he groaned. "That is worse than no gift at all."

Lukas shrugged. "My grandfather had the same gift, and he could also amplify the powers of others. He amplified the fire that destroyed Hephaestus's swords, saving our people," he said. "Your gift has been useful to Alexa as well. These assistive gifts are honorable."

"Well, praise Alexa then," Aric yelled. "Thank the gods I am a convenience to one of our people's most notorious traitors!" He gave me a mock bow and then stormed out of the apartment.

"That was unexpected," Hazel said. "I'll go after him."

* * * * *

At bedtime that night, Lukas was perched on a nearby tree in his hawk form and Aric was still gone. We decided it would be safest for me to stay at a hotel room for the night, so I didn't lead Dagan to our apartment—if I even had a vision. We hoped I wouldn't since I'd used my gift earlier in the day.

After a long hot shower in my hotel room, I went to sleep thinking about how Lukas had identified Aric's gift in a single interaction. And about how that somehow hurt Aric's feelings enough that he took off on me again. I didn't understand how he could be so selfish sometimes.

HAZEL

I'm walking out the front door of our apartment, holding a warm mug in each of my hands—hands that aren't mine. They're Hazel's hands.

She brings the drinks past the parking spaces and turns down the road. After a couple of blocks, the area around the road becomes undeveloped, surrounded by giant spruce trees that block out the sharpest lights in the dusky sky. Hazel follows the road, watching the forest on both sides as she goes.

"Lukas," she whispers, and continues at a steady pace, searching deep into the shade of the trees. She repeats her call for Lukas every few seconds.

Finally, as building structures begin to appear in the distance, a shadow moves through the forest toward her, and she becomes still, watching. As it gets closer, Hazel finds herself staring at a brown bear.

"Lukas?" she asks quietly.

The bear steps toward her slowly and then lies down just off the road, curled around itself.

"You are beautiful." She sets the mugs down on the gravel and climbing into the ditch next to him. She tentatively reaches a hand forward as the bear postures like a friendly dog. Finally, her fingers meet fur, and she trails them along his neck.

He leans into the touch and nudges her shoulder with his muzzle.

"I brought you some tea," she says.

A few moments later, Lukas is in his man form, Hazel's hand now touching his shoulder. "It is a pleasure to see you again. I would love some of your tea."

"Would you like to come into our apartment and visit for a while?"

"It would be an honor to spend time with you," he said.

She smiles as heat rises into her cheeks. After handing Lukas a warm mug, she takes his other hand and begins walking back toward our home.

And I'm suddenly extremely aware that I'm prying into my sister's private life. I think about my true body until I can feel myself twisted in the hotel sheets. I wake myself up.

* * * * *

After I was awake, I ordered a car back to our apartment. During my short Ryde home, I thought about the vision I'd just had. The good news was that I'd made it until five in the morning before having just one small vision. It felt promising, like I might be able to control at least one aspect of my gift. The bad news was that I felt extra guilty about spying on my sister.

When I got inside our apartment, Hazel was still asleep on the couch and Aric was back, sleeping face down on the bed. He was dressed in the same hoodie and jeans he'd been wearing when we met Lukas.

I walked up to the bed and kicked his leg as it dangled in the air. "Thanks for last night. Ass," I said.

He turned over, grumbling indistinctly before twisting the other way and burying his face in a pillow. As he shifted, a strong smell of booze wafted off him.

"He came in loud and drunk a few hours ago," Hazel murmured from behind me.

I jumped at her sudden wakefulness, but channeled the movement, turning so we could talk. I saw the two mugs from my vision sitting on the small table near the couch and I flushed with guilt. "I only had a random little vision. I think using my gift yesterday helped."

"Did you see anything we should know about?"

"No!" I said too quickly, and instantly started searching my memories of Atlantis for a change in subject. "You know, I wish Atlantis wasn't run by a mad woman. The more visions I have of that place the more I wish I could go there."

Hazel arched an eyebrow at me. "Because you like their fancy clothes?"

I laughed. "Maybe. But also because it only seems to be Amara doing awful things. I'd like to see a society of people like me and where I came from. The whole place is magic, Hazel, you'd go nuts for the plant life there."

"Let's see if I can get the hang of non-magical plant life first," she grinned. "I guess if nothing else, your visions have given us a lot of inside information."

A single loud snore came from the bed where Aric had fallen back asleep.

"Do you think we should try cheering him up about his gift?" I asked.

"I don't think he's ready to talk about it. Maybe just let him sleep while I'm gone. I'm gathering some plants and then taking Lukas to the airport to pick up Penelope."

"I can't wait. I almost have this vision control figured out. If I can control where and when, I can hide from Dagan and Amara. Just thinking about it makes me impatient. Hurry, change the subject!"

"Lukas told me Penelope uses her illusions to act in supporting roles for various TV shows. It makes me wonder how many people are out there using magic to excel at human things...even unknowingly, like me." Her eyes narrowed and one side of her lips turned down in a thoughtful frown, no doubt feeling renewed annoyance at her life of secret magic.

"I wonder how she can use her gift for her job and still avoid getting hunted," I said.

"I guess her personal illusions use almost as little magic as passive gifts like Aric's. Lukas told me she got caught the first time because she hadn't yet worked out how much magic she could use before showing up on their mother's radar," Hazel said.

"I kind of understand," I said. "I can sometimes feel energy differences in people's gifts when I share their memories. Maybe Helen can only see magic that puts a certain amount of power into the world."

"Well, aren't we lucky that your visions are a shining beacon for Atlantean hunters," she joked.

"Yeah, sorry about that," I said. "The scary part is that the more visions I have, the more I think my gift is kind of like Amara's. I looked up telekinesis, and she has some form of it, using her mind to control people's bodies. There's a physical part to my gift as well, where it feels like I could almost control the gifts in people's memories. If I had Amara's control…"

"I don't think you want to be modeling after that woman," she said.

"I know." I sighed. "I just mean…well, she is my family. It'd be silly to ignore the connection…if I can learn from it."

"This sounds like a really good conversation to save for Penelope," she said. "Lukas assures me that she's the social sibling." Her eyes were unfocused as if in a memory of their time together.

"I can't believe an actress is going to become my Godline teacher," I said. "You haven't seen her yet, Hazel. She's gorgeous."

"If she looks anything like her brother, I already see. And I don't mind that he'd rather spend his time as an animal. He's still good company." She was staring off at nothing again.

I rolled my eyes and grinned. "Personally, I like to know my animal friends are really animals."

That said, if Hazel was going to grow fond of someone after what happened to Gale, I didn't care if he wanted to spend his time traipsing around as a bear or that he was two hundred something years old.

* * * * *

Hazel decided to go on a morning trip for some new plants while we waited for Penelope's afternoon arrival, and of course, Lukas went with her. I realized that I couldn't just sit there watching Aric snore and waiting on Penelope. Lukas had shown me how to have my own visions and I had time to practice again. I'd just hike off into the woods this time instead of taking a Ryde somewhere. I didn't want to wake up around some stranger full of electricity again.

And so, I left Aric to sleep off his drinks and crossed the road from our apartment where a large forest started. I hiked straight into the woods for a half hour, knowing for the first time in my life that it was okay to stumble and trip over the bumpy tree roots that covered the ground.

When I finally stopped, I sat back against the trunk of a wide birch tree and closed my eyes. I pulled back the memory of what I'd done the day before with Lukas, and I let my mind relax until I was almost asleep. And then I felt my mind slip into a vision, into another body at another time, into a memory.

Chapter Sixteen

HELEN

MY EYES OPEN, BUT they're Helen's. I recognize the feel of Helen now. She stands in the lush herb garden that fills the yard in front of her small, white-brick house. Dagan is stepping out of the purple tree line with the neck of a sandy blond man in his grip.

"Sebastian, my dear son-in-law," Helen says as they stop in front of her. "Why has my most loyal guard brought you to me today? Has he finally found cause for my daughter's annulment?"

She meets Dagan's eyes and he nods. "I caught him aiding the resistance. Tried to fly right through one of the arches with a child under his cloak."

"But the guards at the arches are quite loyal to me," Helen says, lips forming a wide smile. "Now, Sebastian will go into the cells for reeducation, the queen will insist on your annulment, and my daughter will finally be forced to continue the family line."

"I cannot go into the cells!" Sebastian yells. "Send me to serve in the breeding chambers!"

"You produced no children with Penelope in your provided decade," Helen says. "Only known producers serve their time in the chambers."

"What if I could give you something that would soften Queen Amara's bond with your daughter?" Sebastian rushes to get the words out. "I have noticed your resentment."

"I do not resent the queen. I merely wish my daughter would set an example by following the Queen's Laws. And I wish Queen Amara would not be so indulgent with her. That is all."

"Then let me give you something that will force the queen to finally see Penelope as a citizen avoiding the laws instead of a wild-spirited daughter. Just agree to send me to the chambers instead of the cells. Surely, I am here so you can decide my fate before presenting me as a traitor to the queen." His voice is filled with panic.

"Your marriage will be annulled, you will present yourself for regular breeding in the chambers, and you will leave the merchant trade to become the queen's royal messenger. You will train under Dagan and report directly to me," Helen says. "If you make good on your promise."

"Agreed," Sebastian says, casting his blue eyes at his feet. "It was Penelope who asked me to move the child. Penelope has been assisting the resistance."

PENELOPE

In the next instant, I'm in a dim room with gray stone floors and walls. A woman stands behind a white stone desk across the room from me, near an oversized door to my left—a door reinforced with iron bars.

I'm in Penelope's body.

"Your procreation paperwork, please," the woman behind the counter calls. Her skin is the same warm brown as Penelope's, but her hair is long and black. She has the glowing Godline eyes, like brown diamonds. Her pale blue dress, every hemline a tiny braid, exposes her narrow shoulders as she reaches forward.

Penelope reaches into a pocket of her skirt and hands the woman a small book with a leather cover. "Please, do not do this." Her voice is thick from crying. "Do not force me into the chambers like my father, your own brother!"

"The Queen's Laws will save us," the woman recites, as she flips open the book without taking her eyes off it. "Only one name? How did you expect to get anywhere with only one name?" She's muttering it to herself as she turns toward a floor-to-ceiling bookshelf that stretches the length of the wall behind her.

"Only one name that counts in that horrid breeding book," Penelope says under her breath.

There are at least a thousand small books that all closely resemble the one from Penelope's pocket. The other woman only has to go halfway down the wall, running her finger along the books on the shelves before she finds the one she wants.

"I will reconcile your procreation records and set your next several appointments while you are in the chambers," she says. "Do you prefer mornings or evenings?"

"Aunt Melody, I do not want to breed someone at any time of day," Penelope says.

"Child, you had your ten years. You were given special privileges to get married even before you proved you two could produce a child. Just be thankful for that. If the queen did not love you so, you would have been in the chambers over a century ago."

"Then let me go find my own...appointment. Do not send me down there." Penelope's voice is weak.

The woman Penelope had called Aunt Melody stops reading the two notebooks and focuses her eyes on Penelope, like she's about to finally see reason, but after a very long pause she returns to business. "I will make sure to have your annulment paperwork ready for when you come out. Now, let me call you an escort." She doesn't speak aloud or move at all, but after a few seconds of silence, she says, "He will be here shortly. Have a seat while you wait."

Penelope turns around and walks toward one of the stone benches that line the wall opposite the reinforced door, but before she can sit, a guard comes through the wood and iron door.

"Please escort Penelope to her assigned bed chamber," Melody says.

"Gods, I hate this place!" Penelope says as the guard takes her by the arm.

"Shall we, Penelope?" the guard asks.

"Can I say no?" But she allows him to lead her through the heavy door.

As they walk, they come upon intricately woven, black iron fences on either side. They're carved into designs of leaves and flowers, birds and other wildlife, stretching from floor to ceiling. On the other side of each fence are stone dividers. The lighting in the room is soft and glowing from torches inside the enclosures as well as in the passage itself. The first two spaces are empty, except for beautifully made beds and delicate washbasins. These are just pretty cages.

In the next cage on the right, there's a woman in a sheer nightdress, reading on a sofa beside her bed.

"Well, this is you," the guard says, when they stop in front of one of the pretty iron gates looking in at a man in dark silken pants. His bare chest is smooth and well sculpted, though still thin in the Godline way. His glowing brown eyes flicker up at them, giving Penelope a dismissive glance before a heavy sigh.

The guard inserts a key into the latch and walks Penelope inside, then uses his fingers to peel himself free of her before exiting the cage and locking the gate.

"Someone will come for you in a few hours." He turns and disappears back down the passage.

Penelope shakes all over and her heart pounds painfully in her chest. Her muscles are tensed to fight or to run, but neither seems possible. Her back is still to the man locked in here with her.

Then his light footsteps touch the stones as he moves around her. He reaches out and takes Penelope's hand in his. His thumb wipes the tears from under her eyes and he leans in close, until his lips brush her earlobe. "Is Melody in your head as well?" he whispers.

Penelope nods.

"My gift will make this better for you," he says loudly.

Then he reaches around her waist and whispers in her ear again. "Then you know I am with the resistance too. We will need to do a little acting, but worry not. I never breed the unwilling."

His hand trails up her back, and her dress loosens as he pulls on the strings. Gently, he works at it until the dress is so loose, she can walk out of it.

"My gift creates a feeling of ecstasy," he whispers. "Would you like to experience it while we fool those in the chambers into believing we are dutiful breeders?"

Penelope nods again.

* * * * *

I remembered my true body then and felt the solid tree at my back. I wasn't Penelope trying to fake her way through the breeding chambers. I wasn't Helen getting Penelope's husband to betray her to the queen—Helen, who seemed to be collecting followers of her own. I was me, Alexa, and I suddenly felt guilty.

Penelope's memories were now mine and I felt like a stalker knowing so much about her before we'd even met. While I mostly felt guilty about the invasive nature of my gift, I also had an instant of deep gratefulness to know that the Godline resistance had saved me from being raised in Atlantis.

My mind kept trying to sort through all the new memories and feelings as I walked. Memories about the importance of new babies in Atlantis. A resistance forming. Memories of the resistance hiding important babies. Resistance members getting caught and the consequences. Memories of laws that force blood sharing and baby making. And shame. Shame that I was grateful those memories were from bodies that weren't mine.

When I'd almost reached the road on the other side of the wooded section, I came upon a small brown bear, sitting upright, studying me.

Because brown bears aren't a common encounter in town, I assumed it was Lukas, especially being so near our house.

I felt stupid, but I waved at the bear and actually said, "Hi."

Then I started second guessing myself because it began to snarl and stalk toward me.

Before I had time to plan an escape, it sped up to a full-on run, which may have been slower due to the uneven ground, but he was on top of me in seconds.

I felt steam-rolled. The young bear must have still weighed at least six hundred pounds. He'd plowed through me with his body like I was a leaf, sending me face first into the dirt.

To my short-lived delight, he had apparently forgotten to use his knife-sized claws on me and while he regained his balance and stalked back toward me, I gasped for air and tried to get up on all fours. I crawled into the fetal position to protect my vital parts and tried to lie very still, hoping that might discourage it from attacking further.

He stalked up to me, still snarling. He pummeled my body as if he were backhanding me, still not using his razor claws or teeth. This bear wasn't acting very bear-like. Had Lukas lost his mind? Was this what rabies did to animals?

I went to all fours again, hoping he'd stick to not using his claws, and tried to start crawling toward a dense group of trees. He used his gigantic forepaw to knock me onto my back. Being hit with the lean muscle and dense bone felt like being knocked around with a tree stump.

He walked over me while I lay on my back and lowered his face to mine, snapped twice, and dripped spittle on my face. With his dark eyes so close to me, I thought I saw a faint glow, but maybe it was just reflecting the evening light.

Then, as suddenly as he'd appeared, the bear turned and disappeared through the trees.

I shook and shivered. I was on my back, not quite sure if I could get up. I felt bruised from head to foot, and though the bear hadn't used claws on me, I had a bleeding lip, and could feel a couple of spots on my face and neck where exposed skin had been scratched up from being used as a human bowling ball across the forest floor. Those scratches felt like they were trickling warm blood across my skin. My right shoulder felt like it might have taken the most damage, maybe trying to catch myself when he initially ran me over. I could move it slightly, but the muscles in my shoulder didn't want to work without severe pain.

After a few more minutes of lying splayed on the ground, I scooted up against the wide trunk of a nearby spruce tree. I closed my eyes and tried to focus on what was happening with my body, besides agony. Supposedly, I should have special abilities to heal. Maybe I could feel the magic inside of me. I slowed my breathing and tried to ignore all the pains to notice anything else, but everything just hurt. There was no magic happening that I could tell.

I hobbled the last couple of blocks to our apartment. Aric was gone when I got inside, but I didn't have the energy to wonder about where he was. I crawled on the bed to rest. The aches were screaming at me angrily, but I settled onto my back and closed my eyes. If I couldn't help myself heal faster, I could at least have a vision and get out of my body. I didn't care if we had to move again.

I started focusing on my breath, keeping it deep and steady. And I thought about Penelope. I really liked her, even if I shouldn't admit that before meeting her. Later, she could train me, and with any luck help me figure out my magic healing, but now I just wanted to see her again.

Chapter Seventeen

DAGAN

"WAKE UP, LUKAS," PENELOPE'S voice calls to me.

I'm staring at a white ceiling as I lie on a small bed. Even lying still, I can tell I'm in the body of a large man. I remember being in Dagan's body and know that's who I am, but then I hear myself speak. "Good morning, Penelope." I recognize Lukas's voice in my words.

I don't know what to think. I sound like Lukas and feel like Dagan.

"Morning, Brother," she says.

If Penelope is talking to Lukas, I must be Lukas.

Lukas rolls up onto an elbow so he can look at her. She's wearing worn jeans and a plain white T-shirt. Her curly hair is wrapped up in a bright blue scarf. It's cute. I'd call her fragile if not for that Godline glow, that special magic that somehow tells the brain to see her frailty as strength and health instead. With Penelope, there's also warmth and gentleness and joy. At least that's what I feel when I think about all I've seen her do.

I have a moment to feel my own body, hidden somewhere beneath this vision, with the tickle of butterflies amongst the torn and aching muscles.

"How long have I been staying with you sister?" my Lukas voice asks.

She laughs. "Almost three weeks...long enough for me to worry about when you're going to shift into a kangaroo and hop off for half a decade again."

"I have enjoyed our visit, except for the issue with Terry."

"What issue?" she asks. "Terry likes you."

"I do not know how you could mix with a human," he says.

"Since when are you so judgmental about humans? She is a good person, and I love her," she says.

"I only wish to understand. You did not even give the breeding program six months before you quit and ran away. You could have put another Godline child in the palace by now had you fulfilled your required breeding plan."

"Lukas, I have no idea why you are suddenly promoting the Queen's Laws." Her eyes are wide with shock. "You left Atlantis before your first century because even the earliest laws disgusted you." She folds her arms across her chest. "I've loved Terry for over two years now, and you need to accept her. Also, my body doesn't exist to make babies for Mother or the queen, and I thought we agreed on that point."

Lukas stands up from the little bed and crosses the room so he can put his hands on her shoulders. "Well, Penelope, I finally find myself growing tired of our game this morning. I am ready to take you home."

Her eyebrows knit together in confusion. "What are you talking about Lukas? What game? I am home."

"Oh, never mind. Do I smell bacon?"

"Terry made breakfast. Come have some," she says. "And why don't you put a shirt on." She pats his bare stomach.

"I do not think I will. I like letting my skin breathe."

The sensation of being a half-naked man feels strange.

Lukas follows her down a skinny white hallway with two other doors. The hall opens to a living room filled with plush couches and an open kitchen.

A woman sits, eating at a small table near the kitchen. She stands when she sees Penelope and Lukas. Her well-toned muscles show under sunbaked skin, covered by a loose T-shirt with cuffed sleeves. Her soft round face is topped by a head of shortly cropped hair.

"Morning, Lukas. Come, take whatever you want," she says.

"That is why I am here," Lukas says as he approaches the table.

Confusion covers her face, but she doesn't question him.

Lukas is smiling, and it grows the longer he stares at Penelope and Terry. "Oh, you two. I am so happy right now. This is my favorite part. All that build up. All the waiting." Lukas's muscles tense, in preparation for something.

This version of Lukas, who I possess now, has me feeling on edge.

"Terry, come over here for a moment." Lukas's smile has reached a near comical level. "Do not worry. It will all be clear in a moment."

Terry walks over to him.

"Watch, Penelope," he says. "This is what humans are good for."

Before either can process his statement, he snatches the wrist on Terry's far arm, pulling her in front of him. In nearly the same movement, he coils his arm around her from behind until her throat rests in the crook of his elbow. He uses his free hand to help press the offending arm in deeper. His back arches as he lifts her and squeezes her throat, audibly cutting off her air.

Terry begins frantically trying to free herself, trying to pull his arms away from her throat, fingernails tearing his skin. When she can't free her neck, her legs start flailing, trying to wriggle out of the hold. She strikes his shins several times with painful hits from her heels, but nothing stops him.

Even as I feel my own terror at the actions of this body, I can't seem to leave the vision, and I already know there's nothing I can do to stop it. This is a vision from the past. This happened. Unfortunately, now I'm the one doing it. Committing murder and not for the first time. The fact that it's happening in my head won't make the memory of it any less real.

Penelope's been screaming at Lukas from the moment he grabbed Terry, and she runs up when she sees that he's not going to stop. She tries to help Terry pull his arms away. She claws at him too and starts hitting him in the face. There isn't a lot of force behind the punches, but her small hands make sharp blows.

All I can do is hope that Penelope can somehow stop this, but even as I think it, I feel his arm muscles press harder against Terry's neck until something inside of her throat collapses under the pressure.

She goes limp in his hands, but he keeps holding her by the neck.

"Here is your human, Penelope. I just saved you from crying over her decrepit body a mere fifty years from now."

"No! Lukas! What did you do? No. Gods. Terry! Wake up. Please, wake up!" She starts grabbing at his arms again. "It might not be too late. Let her go!"

He releases Terry, and she falls to the floor. "Oh, Penelope. I assure you it is too late. I have done this many, many times."

"What? No, you haven't. This isn't you, Lukas. Why are you doing this?" Penelope pulls Terry onto her lap, holds her face and sobs.

"Yes. I was getting to that," Lukas says in a gleeful voice that makes me want to gag, but I don't control this body.

I feel the energy begin rolling from somewhere inside Lukas's body. When it reaches his skin, it starts rippling across the surface, and he pushes from within to increase that ripple to waves of vibrating energy. Warm power is buzzing pleasantly all over him.

Penelope's face is horror stricken as she watches. "No...no!" She doesn't wait for the rippling to stop before she runs down the hallway.

He catches her before she can get inside the first room, pinning her arms down as he pulls her body against his.

She gives a pitiful wail before sobbing again. She tries to wiggle away, but is so petite, her efforts are useless against his solid form.

"Dagan please, let me go," she cries, eyes desperate.

Clarity crashes over me as I realize I've been Dagan this whole time and that Dagan can change his appearance. I feel a terror creep inside of me. Can he become anyone?

I speak, this time using Dagan's voice—Dagan's mouth and body. "You left Atlantis against the Queen's Laws." I feel Dagan smile at her. "And you married and bedded a filthy human. Thank the gods there was no risk of you having a child by that beast."

Tears pour from her eyes as Dagan leads her by the nape of her neck, down the hallway toward the front of the house. As they pass Terry's body, Penelope collapses over her, sobbing. "Why? Why would you do this?" She pleads at Dagan.

He gestures at the dead woman on the floor. "There is no value in a human."

"They don't force each other to breed like cattle for the good of the race." She grits. Her face becomes hard, and she sets her glare on him. "I swear that someday, you will pay for this. For everything you have done."

Dagan just laughs, but he's suddenly quiet when the room disappears, all light obliterated. Penelope fades into the blackness, but Dagan reacts instantly, leaning down and swinging the back of his hand in the direction where she'd just been sitting. He restrains his arm muscles, lessening the force, but there's still a loud smacking sound as he contacts the side of her face.

The light comes back into the room, and everything is back as it was. Penelope glares up at Dagan, holding her hand against her face.

"Foolish girl. You will not play illusion games with me the whole way home. Our queen asked me to give you special consideration because she favors you, but I assure you that she will forgive me taking my breeding rights without a second thought."

Dagan walks forward so that his legs straddle her body. "If you need to be taught your place in our relationship, I am happy to do so."

He's suddenly on his knees above her, one hand pinning her flower-stem throat to the floor and moving his lips toward her ear. "Do I need to teach you your place?" he whispers.

"No," she breathes.

I still can't find a way out of the vision—back to myself—but I think about Penelope, at a different time, any other time.

PENELOPE

I'm pulled into Penelope's body as she kneels on the white marble floor of the throne room, currently glowing in candlelight as a dark sky fills the high windows all around the room. Three long steps lead to the golden throne in front of Penelope.

Penelope is staring right at Amara as she sits in the throne, her green skirt, made of many lengths of silken fabric, moving like seaweed around her legs.

Helen stands next to Amara in a golden gown of similar style. Her hair isn't up in pins this time, but running down her back in soft, dark-honey waves.

"I gave you everything you ever wanted," Amara yells. "You betrayed me by joining the resistance. I was soft with your punishment, and you broke more laws by leaving Atlantis and marrying a human!" She ends in a shrill, barely controlled voice.

"Remember, my queen," Helen says. "If she were anyone but my daughter—your daughter, really—she would serve time in the cells for what she has done."

"She should be in a cell," Amara says. "Because she certainly cannot be trusted." She yells wordlessly and descends the steps to pace just before Penelope, fists clenched at her sides. She stops, bends down, and brings her face close to Penelope's. "I have this inexplicable soft spot when it comes to you, and I always regret letting it color my decisions. Yet here I go again. I cannot put you through reeducation in the cells. You will live in the breeding chambers until you are with child, instead."

"Gods no!" Penelope yells. "Do not send me there." She collapses forward so her face is between her hands on the floor. "Gods. Please. Queen Mother. Please, just kill me instead."

"Penelope. Do not make a fool of yourself in front of your queen. Sit up!" Helen hisses.

Penelope doesn't respond to her demand, but her body is suddenly jerked back into the sitting position by what feels like a warm tingling cord around her neck.

"You will respect your mother, Penelope. Do you understand?" Amara asks.

Penelope can't speak as her neck remains tightly constricted in the invisible coil, so she nods instead.

Amara releases Penelope's neck and starts pacing again. "I know what you did when you left, Penelope. When you helped my niece hide her child from me." She stops and smiles at Penelope, the warm gesture mutated into something disturbing by her anger. "I might consider letting you stay out of the breeding chambers and put you under guard in the palace instead. If you tell me where Irene's child is."

"My queen, I do not know where she is. I only helped them get through the arches."

"You only helped them get through the arches?" Amara mocks. "Only? Ivy only told a few lies and it the cost of her freedom and her tongue."

"My queen, I am sorry I failed to raise a faithful daughter," Helen says. "Perhaps if you give her some reeducation, bond blood for instance, you will reveal some of her secrets at last?"

"Perhaps," she says, and she strides up to the small table behind her throne. She pulls a slender knife from its surface and approaches Penelope. Her heartbeat increases until its rapid pumps feel painful in her throat and head.

Amara holds her free hand out to Penelope, and before she can even think about whether she's going to comply, her left hand raises and is held around the wrist by the rope of energy that had circled her neck. Her palm is stretched open for the knife, tiny tendrils of invisible energy tugging at each finger. When she tries to take her arm back, it's held firm.

Amara slashes into Penelope's palm.

Penelope cries out as the knife bites into her skin. A scarlet pool forms along the cut from her little finger to her thumb. A dull throbbing pain replaces the initial sting as blood continues to rush to the surface.

Amara makes a small prick on her own palm, releasing a single drop of blood. She clasps her hand to Penelope's, forcing another cry from her as the ragged skin is aggravated.

I can feel everything happening to Penelope as if it's happening to me.

A small heat forms at her palm seconds before her blood is pulled through her hand. An invisible gravity pulls at the energy within, coaxing it toward the bleeding wound.

At the same time, Amara's foreign energy tracks into every part of Penelope. The process is turning her body into a scalding bath as her own energy reacts angrily at being pulled from its home by force, and it tries to defend itself by gripping her insides with white-hot claws. In the end though, Amara's energy is so strong that I know nothing will stop her, and Penelope screams as some of the magic that belongs to her body is pulled away.

When Amara finally releases her, she collapses, panting and burning, weak on the floor. Amara isn't pulling anymore but Penelope's energy doesn't want to risk being caught off guard in another assault, so it continues to burn and stab her insides. Or maybe, it's attacking the invading energy in her blood. Either way, it's the same result. Penelope lies on the cold floor, breathing in labored gasps.

The pain in this body makes me think about the pain in my true body and I start searching for that with my senses. Soon the throbbing magical pain is replaced by a throbbing pain of a body that's been mauled by a bear.

* * * * *

Finally free of the hell visions I'd gotten myself stuck in, the pain in my body was joined by an anxious tension as I thought about how I'd violated yet another person's privacy. I really hated that this was becoming a thing I did, and I couldn't even blame my lack of skill because I'd gone searching for these visions. I didn't deserve Penelope's help.

"I'm here, Alexa." Hazel's soft and hesitant voice came from over by the couch. "Lukas is with me, and there is a pain relief tea on the table next to you."

Bless her. I opened my eyes and sat up gingerly. I was still in pain all over my body and my muscles felt like they were pulled or torn in several places, but the pain no longer made me feel like I was going to pass out. Apparently, I did have magic healing.

Hazel was sitting on the couch next to Lukas, who was wearing the same jeans and T-shirt as always. I guess when you're an animal ninety percent of your time, your clothes don't get dirty fast. How did the clothes always come back?

"You were having visions." Lukas said. He wasn't asking.

I reached for the mug and took a drink of Hazel's cure. Seconds after the first gulp, I could feel the herb magic begin taking effect.

"I was tired." I took another gulp. "Oh, and I got beat to hell by a bear. I saw him become a different person, but can Dagan shift into animals too?" I asked.

"I do not know his gift." Lukas became unnaturally still. "But such a thing is possible."

"Have you been a bear recently?" I asked.

"Lexa!" Hazel said sharply.

"I'm sorry," I said, and meant it. "My head is scrambled. I don't know how many people I've been in the last twenty-four hours. And I hurt. And I'm scared. And confused," I whimpered.

"No bear form today," Lukas said. "I spent my day with Hazel in human and dog form."

Hazel laced her fingers into his, holding his hand quietly. How cute. My sister was dating a two hundred-something-year-old—not that he looked it. Weirdly, they made sense to me. Maybe it was their affinities for nature.

"Thank you." I finished the mug and rested back on the bed. "It could have been a bear today, but it didn't act like a normal bear. Maybe Dagan's toying with me. That's part of how he hunts."

"You know how Dagan hunts?" Hazel asked.

"Yes. You don't want to know any details, but yes."

"If there's a chance Dagan's found us, we need to run again," Hazel said. "Before he moves out of the toying with phase."

"A wise course," Lukas said. "We can leave as soon as Penelope arrives."

I groaned, "I don't want to leave everything behind again."

"Yeah, Lex, I know," Hazel said.

Chapter Eighteen

LUKAS AND HAZEL LEFT me to rest and heal while they went to get Penelope from the airport.

"I'll wait for Aric to respond to our messages and get home," I said. "And I'll try to keep him here long enough to tell him we're moving."

Once I was alone, Penelope's impending arrival brought out my nerves. Would she still help me if she knew how I'd spied on her life on purpose?

I distracted myself with packing finishing with my things and starting on Hazel's. Only when Hazel called to tell me they were on the way with Penelope did I stop for a shower and a fresh set of clothes.

The front door opened just as I was putting my wet hair into a braid and Lukas walked in with Penelope.

She was laughing as she came through the door, and just like in my memories, her skin had the Godline glow across every part of the surface, looking far more like a goddess than a human. Her dark hair was cut short, curls up close against her head, and she was wearing expensive athleisure—a loose, off the shoulder sweater with yoga pants.

I was lucky she was busy talking to Lukas because I was momentarily struck wordless at just how stunning she was in person.

"I'm serious, Brother," she said. "I didn't use even the slightest glamour. The flight attendant at the ticket counter gave me a free first-class upgrade without me requesting it." Her voice was high and sleek.

"Lies, Sister," he said with a grin. "I can see you have glamoured your gift-magic visible."

She'd moved on already, looking at me. "Alexa! You have become a lovely woman." She smiled and then walked up to hug me without warning.

"Hi," I said, shocked by how forward she was. My visions hadn't told me everything about her, which made me feel better somehow.

"My brother caught me up on the basics, and the most pressing issue is escaping Dagan," she said, jumping right in. "We want to be long gone when he decides he's finished hunting."

"Where should we go?" I asked.

Lukas sat on the couch, quietly smiling while Penelope led me by the hand to sit next to her on the foot of my bed. "Based on your current appearance, we don't have long." She brushed her thumb along a bruise on my cheek.

I shivered at her touch and tried to play it off as a wince, even though she hadn't hurt my bruise at all.

"Sorry about that." She grinned, her luminous eyes less than a foot from my own. "I forget about personal space sometimes."

"I don't mind," I said, and then immediately felt weird about saying it. "I mean, the bruise. It doesn't hurt much anymore. I could barely move a couple hours ago. That magic healing is no joke." I realized I was starting to ramble. "Do we need to leave Fairbanks?" I asked.

"This city should work for now," she said. "It wouldn't do any good to rush off somewhere new without any planning."

"Aric's going to be a problem. He's sort of gone on a bender and isn't talking to any of us," I said. "He's even started spending nights away."

"Let me worry about Aric," Penelope said. "He'll be okay. He's just a sensitive soul raised by a couple of abusive manipulators."

"Speaking of abuse," I said, "Do you have any idea why Dagan would turn into a bear just to beat me up?"

"Lukas told me about that. I think he was trying to figure out your gift," she answered. "He likes to already know everything about his victims before he reveals himself. I assume he became a bear to make you question Lukas or to let you know that he has seen you with Lukas."

"So, he's found me and is toying with me. How do we escape someone who can be any living thing? I don't want him to kill anyone else I know, and I've seen him kill others in my visions," I rambled. "Well, I actually was him when he did it."

Her eyes widened. "Right! I keep thinking everything about our people is brand new to you. Your mother begged Fern and Reed to keep your identity a secret, even from you, but Lukas told me about your visions. Talk about a crash course."

She talked to me as easily as if we were old friends.

"Well, I should start by telling you I've had a number of visions with you in them," I admitted while staring down at my hands. "It was your human wife that I saw Dagan kill."

"Oh. I wish you hadn't had to see that," she said quietly. "It still hurts to think about that day."

"I'm sorry." I could feel myself turning red in my shame.

"It certainly isn't your fault. That man is a monster who works for monsters." She pressed her lips together. "Gods know, the resistance saved me from becoming just like them. The least I can do is help keep you free."

"I actually saw the night you formed the resistance," I said.

"What a night! I would love to relive that. Since then, our resistance has become a whole network of Godline and Nymphs working together to save people from the cruelty of the Queen's Laws. You would be surprised at how many Godline live in hiding among Nymph villages and human cities. It is completely possible for us to live full lives on Earth now."

"I'm glad to hear that," I said. "All I've ever wanted was to get out of my Nymph village and into a human city where I could feel adequate for once. Even if I didn't know about the Nymph part until a few weeks ago."

Penelope kicked off her ballet flats and crossed her legs on the bed. Then she turned to better face me with a sly smile on her lips. "I know the feeling. No matter the village, the Nymphs tease me when I visit. They think it's hilarious how I stumble around like a no-magic fool in the lands saturated with eons of Nymph magic."

"That pretty much sums up my life so far." I grinned. "Can you tell me about Helen and Queen Amara? Like what's their deal? All I've ever seen Helen do is push golden hair pins into a map. Amara's given me more than enough memories of her torturing people. Why is it that the queen asks your mother's advice when she's deciding on her evil deeds?"

Penelope's perpetual happiness faded, and she pursed her lips. "My mother's hairpins are quite deadly if you think about what they represent. About Dagan. And, Helen likes to keep her hands clean. She whispers ideas and watches Amara act them out."

"Our mother lacks humanity," Lukas said from the couch. "The quest for immortality and giftedness has been the ruin of Atlantis, and my mother is at the head of it all, being one of the old ones."

"Only, she lets the people believe Amara is solely responsible for the evil ideas behind the Queen's Laws," Penelope said. "And you are a funny one to speak of humanity, Brother." She added with a light laugh.

"Spending my time as an animal gives me a better view of humanity." Lukas stood up. "I will be back. I must escort Hazel home from the farmers' market. She is making a large delivery to her vendor in case she doesn't get to return for a while."

"And you've had enough human time." Penelope smiled. "It is good to be with you again."

With the most subtle lift of his lip, Lukas walked out of our apartment to become some kind of critter.

I turned back to Penelope. "I have to ask you...do you glamour yourself to glow with power on purpose? Lukas and Aric don't glow like you, even though everyone I've seen in Atlantis does. And why do Aric and I look like bags of bones while you and your brother make the same frame sexy somehow?" I pressed my hand over my mouth and groaned. "I'm sorry if that was rude. Was it rude? It's just...you look, well, you look amazing, but like inhumanly amazing, you know? Shit. I'm sorry. I can't shut up."

Penelope threw her head back and laughed. "It's okay! Yes, I tend to glamour my magic visual. All it does is make the humans see my magic the way it is seen in Atlantis as the glowing power that rolls over us after years of gift use. But because human minds can't actually see it, they just keep trying to figure out why they get so tongue tied or why they battle with themselves over a sudden obsession with me. Since they can see the glow within our eyes, that's usually where people focus their obsession, despite me keeping them subdued with contacts or illusion." She grins. "It is kind of funny and it's genuinely helpful in the acting industry."

"I don't really understand most of what you just said." Though I embarrassingly understood the obsession part.

"It's a sort of gift side effect that messes with humans all the time. You will get used to it, but a human will always just feel an urgent and inexplicable attraction or affection toward Gifted Godline. The longer the gift has been in use, the more powerful the effect. I glamour myself so that other Godline can see the glow of my magic like they would back home. It is a perk of my gift and I admit, a sign of my vanity...or loneliness for our kind." Her eyes were suddenly far away in her thoughts.

"I'm not at all used to it." I tried to keep my tone light. "I feel that urgent attraction when I look at you." I knew my cheeks were red, but I was determined to push past it since the reaction was all just some side effect of her magic. "Maybe I'm human after all," I joked.

"It tells me a lot about your tastes that you didn't notice the same about Lukas." She raised an eyebrow at me. "It may not be visible to you like mine is, but his magic is there. Part of why he spends so much time as an animal is to avoid the humans fawning over him."

Her eyes met mine again. "And you are certainly no human."

More blushing. Maybe pink cheeks were just going to be my default around Penelope. "I noticed how beautiful Lukas was too, but yes, I'm drawn to...uh...beautiful women." I put my face down into both palms. "I'm really trying not to sound like an idiot and I'm failing like one of the tongue-tied humans you were talking about." I gestured at myself. "Whatever you and Lukas have, I don't have that effect on people."

"First, you are exquisite. Second, Lukas and I have more of the Godline effect because we have active gifts that we use often. The effect is cumulative as well, so we have a couple of centuries on you."

"You're just so beautiful and I'm humiliating myself right now and I'm really happy you're going to help me control my gift. I really hate being a murderer and torturer."

"It will get better. Most of our people are quite wonderful, so we just need to figure out how to help you see more of that instead. You'll come to love your gift. I promise."

"Thanks for being so cool about me snooping around your memories, by the way. I never chose what I saw, but I know my curiosity about you pulled me into your memories."

"Honestly, the idea of you sharing in my memories excites me. And I cannot wait to know you as well."

Fresh heat filled my face. "I only saw you in a handful of visions, but I admit I was excited to know you too. You were always so passionate and funny and confident."

She laughed again. "I do appreciate humor and a good cause to throw myself into, but with a gift for illusion, acting, including acting confident, has become second nature."

Penelope stood up. "Okay. We need to find somewhere new to live and a way to get there without Dagan following. I assume these are not your furnishings."

"How can we move without Dagan following?" I asked. "He can shift into anything, so we can't exactly tell if we've lost him."

She smiled dramatically and stretched her fingers wide. "I'm going to illusion his ass so hard he'll be watching the empty apartment hours after we leave."

"You seem excited." I smiled.

"I have only been able to use glamour level illusion for years. Pulling big magic from my gift is like greeting my oldest friend. I miss it so much. Also, I really hate Dagan, that murderous asshole.

* * * * *

By the time Hazel and Lukas were back, we'd found a new place to live. Penelope had insisted we only consider places with at least two rooms, so our new house ended up about fifteen miles down the highway from Fairbanks. It was surrounded by trees with no neighbors nearby and would be a good place to hide from Dagan if we could keep him from following us there.

"Okay," Penelope said before leaving to exchange our rental car for something bigger. "I have an idea about your gift. Alexa, come get the SUV with me?"

Penelope had somehow managed to talk Aric into coming home, and he was listening to her talk, his face and hair scruffy and smelling of liquor. "I should just let Dagan take me home now," he muttered. "I am not needed anymore, anyway."

"If you go back to Atlantis, Aric, you will need to do so away from the rest of us," Penelope said. "How would you feel if you were responsible for the torture, or worse, of all of us?"

Either they were the right words, or she was just as enthralling to Aric as she was to me. He nodded silently, raising no further argument.

Penelope cast an illusion around the two of us as we walked out and got into the car. "If he is watching us, Dagan will see Hazel getting into the car and driving it away. He should be least interested in following her, but just in case, I will make our car invisible when we reach an empty stretch of road. He won't be able to track us on this errand."

I could tell her gift was working when I saw just an empty passenger seat instead of Penelope, but then she took my hand, and I could see her again. Her skin was soft, but her grip was reassuringly firm.

"One of the ways to protect you from my illusion is through touch."

We drove for a few miles in the disguise of her magic before she let the illusion slip away. Penelope exchanged our car for a minivan, claiming it was the best deal for its size. The drive back to the apartment was quick, and when we were nearly there, Penelope pulled over in a bank parking lot.

"Lukas told me you have decent control for a beginner. I want you to try to have a vision of me right now, and experience me using my gift. If you get the wrong vision, just keep trying to find it. If you come back to reality, I want you to try to find it again. Keep it up until we are packed and well away from the apartment."

"I'll try. I need to lie back and close my eyes," I said. "Just shake me out of it if you want me to stop."

"Let's see what you can do."

I relaxed back and tried to just think about Penelope, her gift, and this moment.

* * * * *

I find myself in a new body moments later, but this one's walking around our apartment on long skinny legs—Aric. I'm picking up articles of clothing and stuffing them in a kitchen trash bag. Well, Aric is doing it, but being in the moment and in our apartment makes separating myself from him more difficult.

When I—he looks up from his work, he stares at Lukas standing next to Hazel by the small counter. They're smiling at each other as they pack the various bottles of herbs and plants, placing them carefully in several sturdy tote bags.

"Ugh," my Aric voice says. "You have known that animal-man for days. Do not look at him like that."

Hazel frowns up at me. At Aric. "Please don't be mean. I haven't ever hurt you. Nor has Lukas."

"You two can run off together for all I care." He points at Lukas. "But Penelope and I belong to each other according to our laws. Help me convince her to come back with me. All will be forgiven if I bring Penelope home."

"My sister does not belong to you," Lukas said, enunciating each word.

"And what about my sister?" Hazel asks.

"If Alexa came willingly, my mother would welcome her. The queen would find great value in a gift like hers. The Gifted live good lives on Atlantis. Probably even someone with a gift as poor as mine," he mutters the last part almost inaudibly.

"Good lives do not include being experimented on in a dungeon. If you didn't already know where we were moving, I'd say it was time to leave you behind, Aric," Hazel snaps. "Your anger and bitterness are going to get one of us hurt."

He reaches into a large side pocket in his slacks and pulls out a flask of whiskey. Then he twists off the cap and takes a large gulp, feeling a hot burn follow the sharp liquor down his throat. "Well, if Penelope is going to keep treating me like her child and all the rest of you are going to keep acting like my home is so evil, just leave me to stay with my human companion, Bridget."

"Wait," Hazel says. "Is Bridget the girl you've been spending all your time with lately?"

"So?" Aric's voice is defensive. "She thinks I am handsome and superior in bed. And she likes to drink without asking too many questions."

"Well, I'm glad you've been having a good time." Hazel suppresses a grin. "But if you're coming with us, it won't be safe to see her for a while."

He flops back onto the couch and takes another large drink of the booze. I can feel his head getting lighter and the room getting fuzzier.

Not only am I not having a vision of Penelope, but being in buzzed Aric feels especially useless. I refocus, thinking about Penelope using her illusions right now.

* * * * *

I'm suddenly backing the van up to the front door of our apartment, but it's Penelope's hands guiding the steering wheel.

Once parked, I check the passenger seat, and see my real body lying back, eyes closed. "Stay here," my Penelope voice says. So weird.

As I walk into the apartment, I notice the gift at work inside me— inside Penelope. The magic courses through her blood and fills her mind. Then it radiates in all directions. Once she gets inside, the radiating magic shifts behind her, reaching out and around the van. None of the magic is going into the apartment.

"Listen up, everyone. I am brilliant," Penelope says. "But I'm out of practice, so focus. The minivan is here, I'm hiding it in an illusion. I'll sit on the bumper and open up pockets in my magic so you three can see where you're loading things. We cannot risk even a moment of dropped illusion out there, so I won't be talking much until we've driven off." Penelope tosses the keys to Hazel. "You can get us to the new place, right?"

"Yes," Hazel replies. "I think we can be out of here in a few minutes. We don't have much."

Penelope settles onto the corner of the van as Lukas, Aric, and Hazel load bags and bedding into the cargo space.

As I focus on Penelope's body, I can feel her core pushing out a steady flow of energy. The energy mingles with her blood and rushes to her mind before pushing it out around the van and apartment entry.

Each time one of the others approaches with a supply, I can feel her create a small opening in the illusion just around their minds.

In less than ten minutes, we're ready to leave, the illusion surrounding the entire van like a bubble, anyone outside seeing only the landscape and road around us. With Hazel in the driver's seat, my Penelope hand gestures Aric toward the back row.

"We have to be careful not to touch until we're far enough away for me to drop my illusion," she tells Aric as he settles in behind her. "Lukas told me about your gift to dampen other gifts."

Lukas sits beside her as Hazel slides into the driver's seat.

Once we're on the road, I turn to look at Aric with my Penelope eyes. "I've missed you, Aric. And I'm proud of the choices you've been making to help Alexa. The kind-hearted child that I raised has certainly grown into a good man."

I feel for the magic again. The energy leaving Penelope's center begins to slow, filtering down the amount of magic coursing into her blood. In a single instant, when the truck is on a stretch of road without other vehicles, the bubble of illusion pops away, the magic all contained within her body now. I...she leans back and takes Aric's hand in hers.

* * * * *

I opened my eyes, in the passenger seat again, and turned to Penelope. "That was amazing!"

"Were you able to see me?" Penelope asked.

"Yeah. I really got to study your gift. It was great."

"You have excellent control," she told me. "You had exactly the vision you were trying for. You've only been experiencing your gift a few months?"

I nodded.

"I figured it would be easier for you to visualize and find someone actually with you in the moment," Penelope said. "My gift is all about visualization as well. It works in a similar way. You will probably master gifts like mine before gifts from other gods."

"Honestly, I don't even care about the other gifts," I said. "Just learning how to control these visions and being able to sleep normally again would be enough."

"I would guess your gift to be undetectable when you enter the mind of someone near you, in the present rather than a memory. Based on my own experiences, I would also bet that if you did that regularly enough, it would keep your magic from bursting out in your sleep."

"Wait. Meaning, I could essentially funnel off my magic and become invisible to Helen?"

"Yes. My illusions used to burst from me in sleep when they first began. I gave a number of palace servants quite a scare, I'm sorry to say."

"I imagine dreams coming alive might be horrifying," I said, thinking about how freaky that would be. "I love that you understand my gift so well."

"Well, your secondary gift is still a bit mysterious. It seems tied to your visions, but also that you can replicate the magic of others."

"We're here," Hazel said.

She pulled the van up to a white, two-story house. The entire property was surrounded by a forest of massive spruce trees and tall, now golden and yellow, birch trees. The ground was covered in thick, thorny patches of wild rose plants with no view of the road or any other sign of civilization from this house. It was a good hideaway.

The small furnished house was a luxury after all the single room living. There was a tiny bedroom with a twin bed next to the kitchen and a large open loft overlooking a small living room. The loft had a queen bed that Penelope suggested Aric and I share with her. She wanted to be closer to us both as we went through 'active gift development,' as she called it. The bed size wasn't really a problem since we were three twig people. Hazel seemed content to take the small bed downstairs.

"Lukas can always become a cuddly kitten if it gets too crowded," I'd said, thinking I was hilarious. Hazel had punched me squarely in the shoulder for saying it, but she did laugh.

On our first night at the new place, I got a sense of how warm Penelope's heart was toward Aric. "I'm going to sleep in the middle." She patted the bed on either side of her. "This way I can check on either of you in the night."

I suddenly felt very badly about how judgmental I'd been toward Aric's recent childish behaviors. He was going through a hard time too. He had a new gift that he didn't like, just like me. He was scared about what was going to happen to him, just like me.

By lying in the middle, it also felt like Penelope was telling Aric that he didn't exist only to keep me from dreaming. I'd been using him and resenting him for a long time. I hoped Penelope would never fully realize how I'd treated Aric up until the time she came.

I sat on the bed and wrapped my blanket around me before plopping down on my pillow on one side of Penelope. In my periphery,

Aric was still standing next to the bed on her other side. I shifted so I could see them both better.

Penelope reached out and took Aric by the hand. "Come lie next to me, Aric. We have so much to catch up on. You are grown now!"

He stood still, crossing his arms and staring anywhere but at her.

"I'll stroke your hair like the old days," she said.

"I am not a child!" he yelled.

"Of course, you aren't!" She matched his volume but somehow still sounded calm. "It will still feel nice!" I could hear the smile in her voice.

Aric finally got into the bed and Penelope took a bottle of vodka from him when he tried pulling it out for some goodnight glugs. Then, without any of the talking I'd expected, I could feel Penelope and Aric falling asleep beside me, their breathing beginning to come in the slow regular pattern of sleep.

Just when I thought they might both have been sleeping, I heard Aric's whisper, meant for Penelope. "You left me."

"And I have felt torment about that choice every day," she breathed back at him. "But Aric, you were my child from the time you were four. I was not going to let our mothers force us to live as husband and wife."

"You could have taken me with you," he mewled.

"I wish I had, but I barely escaped myself, and you seemed so pleased about what was happening. I was afraid you would not be convinced. And I'm ashamed to say, I thought you might have stopped me."

"Please do not leave me again."

"I won't," she said, and then all was quiet. Soon, the rhythmic breathing was back.

I glanced at them before drifting off myself, and saw that Aric was clinging to Penelope's arm with both of his. It was the image of a child snuggling tightly to someone who makes them feel safe. He could talk about them being married all he wanted, but Penelope was right. They had the relationship of a caregiver and their now grown child.

Chapter Nineteen

THE DAY AFTER OUR move, we started a new routine with most of my time scheduled to practice my gift. I no longer resented the detour from my original life plans. Instead, I was excited to learn about this new version of me, and to spend so much of my time with Penelope.

Now that we lived out of town, Hazel left the house on foot to gather plants and Lukas joined her as a large dog. He was clearly not comfortable spending a long time in his human form, but Hazel seemed content with all his variations.

Penelope, Aric, and I parked at a state trailhead near our old apartment. We'd decided to use that area for as long as possible in an attempt at magical misdirection. From the roadside lot, we hiked, off-trail, straight into the forest.

We used the half-hour car ride and brief hike to answer all of Penelope's questions about the short history of my visions. Aric helped me fill in details I'd forgotten. He was back to being kind and helpful, like when he first saved us. Penelope was clearly important to him and had a positive effect on his attitude.

"Do you know...I mean..." I stumbled through the words as my feet stumbled over roots and fallen branches. "Does my father have a gift?"

"Of course," Penelope said. "His is a gift of the mind like ours, though passive, meaning he doesn't have to do anything for his gift to do its thing."

"What's his thing?" I asked.

"He can sense when people are lying."

"Why is he not working for my mother?" Aric asked. "She would have so many uses for such a gift."

"It is no accident Amara doesn't know about Damian," Penelope said. "He was raised by members of the resistance, so he was taught to hide his gift. Of course, that was easier with a passive gift because Helen can't sense them. Damian has pretended to be one of the Giftless his entire life and as a result, has worked one of the farms at the far side of Atlantis."

"So, both of my parents have passive gifts. Maybe that's why they tried to have me raised to think I was human—maybe they thought I'd have a passive gift too."

"Maybe, but they had to know that was wishful thinking. The gods do not pay attention to such things when choosing a gift for a new child.

Consider your family. Your father's gift is from Athena, your mother's gift is from all of them—being the prophesied peace they promised with her birth, and you are showing a gift from at least Apollo."

"How did my mother even meet my father if he lived so far away?"

"While the queen hardly leaves the palace, Irene has spent her life trying to sneak away from it. We have a friend who runs the Royal Stables and uses the queen's flying horses for royal business. You saw her if you saw the first resistance meeting."

"Chloe, right?"

"That's her. Irene and I have tagged along on plenty of Chloe's trips to the Distant Regions, especially for resistance meetings. When we can fly with Chloe, it only takes a few minutes to get there instead of nearly a week by horse and cart. Irene met Damian at a meeting."

"Those horses talk, right? Didn't you worry about them reporting back to the queen? She seemed tight with them."

"You must have seen that from an earlier time. Amara has not visited the Immortal Stallions in the two hundred sixty years I've been alive. Their feeling of neglect by their queen is a big part of why they joined the resistance. She's so uninterested in leaving the palace that she has servants bring her whatever she needs from the Royal Market or the university. And she just sends for region leaders when she does want something or someone from one of the Distant Region communities on the far side of Atlantis.

"Aric tried explaining Atlantis to me before, and I got the impression it was its own little planet, but now I've heard you refer to a far side. Where and what is Atlantis, exactly?"

"It took me living in both places to even begin grasping the concept of Earth and its connection to Atlantis. They are fully separate, but connected through the magic of the arches, which allow passage between the two. Atlantis is a vast and singular landmass surrounded by ocean on all sides. You can travel by ship from Atlantis for several weeks, into nothingness, but without fail, there is a point, when reached, you suddenly see yourself traveling toward the part of Atlantis from which you departed. We don't have a planet like Earth. We have a magical plane. I'm not an expert of the magical or non-magical sciences, so that's the best I can describe it."

"Yeah, that's exactly what I thought about Atlantis," I joked.

"I'm sure you've seen the odd plant life in your visions," Penelope said. "The wild magic of Atlantis used to be tended by the Nymphs before Amara ran them out to enforce her breeding laws. They'd spent thousands of years shaping the nature of Atlantis according to their imaginations, but that all stopped when they disappeared. Since then, the wild magic has become a little wilder, or so I've been told. I was born right around the time of the exile, so I don't remember Old Atlantis like my brother."

"I wish I'd known all this twenty years ago," I said. "I spent my whole life feeling like a failure because I didn't know I was living with Nymphs."

I felt a little shy sharing my crappy feelings, but Penelope was easy to be around and easy to talk to.

"Your mother was so afraid you'd end up back there, but I can see that you've been living a different sort of pain than the one awaiting you on Atlantis."

"Don't get me wrong, I've seen the result of the Queen's Laws on Atlantis and I'll take feeling like a failure any day," I said. "How does the whole Gifted and Giftless thing work there? Seems like a status thing people really obsess over."

"It is the Atlantis class system under the Queen's Laws, though the two classes unofficially existed long before that. In addition to the breeding laws, it is the system that the resistance is fighting against. Even with compliance to Amara's breeding rules, few babies are born, and even fewer will grow into gifts. Some of that is just what's happening to our people as a result of Hera's curse against births. The latest Olympian curse I know about. Some of it is the gods forgetting about us, leaving most births without gifts."

"So, Giftless are a class of Godline people, and they don't have powers?"

"Yes. They are a servant class because the Queen's Laws officially describe them as less valuable. Collectively, they are the backbone of Atlantis, but individually, the queen cares nothing about them. The resistance has been relocating Giftless Godline to Nymph villages or Godline dense communities on Earth since our very beginning. The queen has never gone searching for any of them."

"What about the ones like me?"

"The Gifted are a lot harder to hide. The Royal Guard heavily enforces the Queen's Laws with the Gifted. The breeding laws are enforced and well documented. Gifts are reported and then used in services or in shared blood to the queen. That is how we pay taxes in Atlantis."

"I think I'd rather be Giftless."

"You say that, but they grow up being told their only value is the labor they provide. They are left with the single hope that they produce a Gifted child, their only way out of the servant class. Well, aside from leaving Atlantis."

"But there have to be Gifted people other than me to escape, right?"

"Yes. We help some hide in plain sight, like your father, and we assist others in the painstaking act of an escape. Unfortunately, even with a strong resistance network on both Atlantis and Earth, the long-term odds on Gifted escape are not good. Last time I had access to our records, we were at nearly a seventy-five percent recapture rate. Many, like myself, have escaped at least twice."

"So, what Dagan's doing to me? It's a common occurrence?"

"Unfortunately."

"And my mother refused to tell Amara about my father because it might reveal him as Gifted or reveal the resistance?" I asked. "Sorry I'm all over the place. I have so many questions."

"Amara knows about the resistance but hasn't been able to learn much beyond that because our network is very compartmentalized. Only a few of us have access to a larger scope of the resistance. People we help normally know almost nothing about us, for everyone's protection. You're a special kind of exception," she said with a chuckle. "Amara learning of Damian would potentially expose too many resistance members, especially if she tortured him, or took and used his gift."

"Why did you never tell me of any of this?" Aric asked Penelope, accusation in his voice.

"My sweet Aric." Penelope touches his cheek. "You were raised surrounded by the love of those in the resistance, but you were also under the constant gaze of our mothers. And you were just a child. And then, a well-groomed teen, faithfully reciting Amara's rules and philosophies. But now that you are grown, have made your own choices, and become an escaped Gifted yourself, I see that you are ready for the truth."

"I will never let you down, Penelope," Aric said. "I love you."

"And I love you, Aric. You are the closest thing I will ever have to a child of my own. Our mothers had me raise you as punishment for not wanting children and for running away. But caring for you was a gift they never realized they gave me." She walked around in front of Aric and stood on a downed tree so that she could wrap him in a tight hug.

"Okay!" Penelope said, hopping down from the log. "Time for practice. For both of you. And then I have an experiment in mind."

"What's that?" I asked.

"We'll pick a spot for you to practice mind-sharing with one of us every day. I believe it will take less magic for you to slip into a nearby mind in the present, like how my personal glamour takes less than my illusions. Helen can't pick anything up that puts out less energy than the magic of Atlantis itself."

"So, if I mind-share in one spot for a while and then use visions to go poking around Helen's maps, we can check to see if she's found that place or not," I finished. "Genius."

"Of course, I am." Penelope smiled confidently. "Your visions are quite an advantage. When I was first figuring out how much of my magic I could get away with, I spent almost two years in constant fear that I'd be found. Just like you, I was running all over the place, using my magic, because just like you, my gift cannot go long unused."

"I don't think I could survive two years of this," I said.

"Luckily you no longer have to. I'm going to spend a little time helping Aric practice first though."

Aric gave me a smug look.

"Alexa, I'd like you to mind-share with me while I work with him. The more you practice that small magic, the easier it will be for you. Let's stop here."

We'd reached a small open area in the forest, and I pulled out the large blanket I'd packed, allowing all of us a nice place to sit. Penelope shifted so that she and Aric were facing each other on one half of the blanket while I stretched out awkwardly on the other. I nearly squirmed knowing Penelope's gaze was on me. I wished she could see me as interesting in a more captivating way and not as some science experiment she needed to sort out.

To avoid the feeling, I closed my eyes, appreciating my lack of contacts for a moment, and then tried to visualize Penelope as she sat beside me. And as if my magic had some kind of muscle memory, it led my mind to hers in an instant.

* * * * *

Her head turns so she can look at my body draped across the blanket, as if asleep. "Are you sharing my mind?" I ask in Penelope's voice.

My body doesn't respond because my mind is with Penelope, and as far as I know, I don't have the ability to use her mind to voice an answer. It's a frustrating sensation, and it makes me curious about whether I could ever gain some level of control. Although that causes me to immediately ponder the moral gray areas with that kind of gift. It's too similar to how Amara uses her mind and blood to control other people's bodies. What might I be able to do if I took control of a gift while inside someone's mind?

"Well, she's somewhere," my Penelope voice says. "She'll tell us later." She turns to face Aric across the blanket. "So, let's talk about your gift."

"Some gift." He mopes. "Lukas told you. All I am good for is sapping the gifts of others. It is shameful. I might as well be one of the Giftless."

"Don't be silly, Aric. Your gift is not common, but it is well known, and highly coveted. You are at great risk of becoming a tool, or worse, one of your mother's experiments. If you'd been Giftless, she would have just made an exception for you and given you a job, like she was doing when you started hunter training."

"Why would my gift be wanted? Why would you think my own mother a risk to me?"

"Okay, love, I'm just going to be direct. There is no one else currently alive known to have your gift. You will eventually be able to use your mind to project your dampening on others."

"Well...it sounds alright when you say it like that," he mumbles.

"There's more. If this gift is like those before it, you will also be able to learn to use touch, and eventually your mind to amplify the powers of others. Do you see why this gift would be wanted? And Amara has been learning how to take people's gifts for over a century. Before I left last, she believed she was close to finding a way to take gifts permanently...and I don't think the outcome is good for those she takes them from." She reaches out and places her hands on Aric's knees as he sits there with his arms crossed. "Sweet boy, don't you see, you're in as much danger as Alexa."

"But I want to go home so badly," he says softly. "I do not like Earth. The humans dislike my appearance, even when I hide my eyes. I have heard them talking about how thin I am, in disgust. I think Bridget only likes me because she is quite intoxicated whenever we see each other."

"Please stay with us, Aric," Penelope says. "The more you practice your gift, the less humans will notice the differences in your form." She meets his worried blue eyes. "Plus, you have me, Alexa, Lukas, and Hazel."

"It does sound like there are more of us here on Earth than I used to believe," he says.

"I have been lonely for our kind as well." She holds his hands in hers. "Maybe we can build a new homeland for ourselves somewhere on Earth."

Aric joins in on the dream. "We could find a place where Godline already live, or we could build one of our own. Possibly near a Nymph community."

Penelope smiles at him. "It sounds like we have the makings of a new resistance member." She leans forward and wraps her arms around his neck, his unpadded shoulder bones pressing into her arms. Then she leans back, holding his face, and kisses his cheek. "Gods, I've missed you and your heart. Let's see what you can do now."

"What do I do?" he asks tentatively.

Penelope sits back so they're no longer touching. "I'll create a simple illusion. Once I do, take hold of one of my hands, but do it slowly, trying to stop my gift before you make contact."

"I will try."

She stares at a patch of weeds next to the blanket and I can feel Penelope's energy instantly surge through her blood and into her mind. A moment later, a chubby black cat is sitting next to Aric.

He jumps slightly when he first sees the animal, but then laughs. "It is like the games you played with me when I was young." He reaches over and pets the cat. It leans into the touch, curling around his hand with its body. "I don't really want it to go away. Your creatures always love me."

"They are only like that because I want you to feel their love." She laughs. "I could just as easily make them aloof. Concentrate on stopping my gift."

He reaches a hand toward Penelope's, stopping slightly shy of touching.

Penelope's gift is surging steadily, the cat rolling about on its back. "Stop my gift," she says.

Aric is quiet and completely still, but after several seconds, he rests his hand on her wrist.

Instantly, the source of Penelope's illusion, the magic in her blood, dissipates. The cat disappears in the next moment.

"Okay, that is a start, but you will learn to be much more precise. You should be able to pull the magic from me instead of just blotting it out."

"May we try again?" he asks excitedly. "I think I felt your gift for just a second."

"Yes. Focus on that. Reach for it sooner. Try to let it into yourself."

We repeat the cat illusion three more times, each ending the same. Aric balls a fist up in frustration as the cat disappears for the fourth time. "I can feel your magic, but I cannot seem to reach it without touching you."

"I have an idea," Penelope says. Then, slowly, she says, "Alexa, if you can hear me, try sharing Aric's mind instead of mine."

This would be new for me, but also the coolest thing I've used my gift for so far. I think about Aric's mind as I stare at him with Penelope's eyes. Between one blink and the next, my perspective shifts, and I see Penelope, gorgeous as always. She's dressed in athleisure again today, and again, she's too goddess-like for the outfit. My eyes shift from Penelope to her illusion cat, which sits beside me again.

"Okay, take my gift," she says.

I reach out toward her hand, looking down at her delicate fingers, noticing that her nails are painted a dark blue that matches her shirt. I wonder if the detail is an illusion or if she makes time to match her nails to her outfits. She does wear a lot of blue.

I realize I'm not doing what I'm supposed to and focus on Aric's body as he sits there, nearly touching Penelope. There is no gift energy, but there is something else. It feels like a sort of negative pressure where I normally feel energy. I can feel it throughout his body, but notice the vacuum increasing at his fingers, where they're about to touch her skin. Once he touches her, the buildup of emptiness transfers to Penelope, and I lose track of what it does from there. Within Aric's body, the anti-magic is still coursing in every part of his blood, continuing to rush additional emptiness to the tips of his fingers as they stop Penelope's illusion. Suddenly, he reaches over to my body lying on the blanket next to us and flicks my arm.

* * * * *

My eyes snapped open to a mix of blue sky and treetops. I sat up, blinking as I adjusted to being in so many minds in a short time. It took a moment to get a sense of self again.

"So." Aric turned to me. "Were you just in my head?"

Penelope looked at me too.

"Yes," I said. "It feels like the thing in your blood is sort of like the opposite of what most Godline have. Most people have a buildup of energy as they use gifts. Yours was like a buildup of emptiness. Anti-magic was how I was thinking about it. It spread into Penelope when you touched her. It seems similar to the way Hephaestus's swords worked. They sent something that ate magic into the bodies they cut."

"As I thought," Penelope said. "I believe Aric's gift is pulling magic from those he touches and storing it until he learns to use it to amplify gifts in others.

Aric practiced with his and Penelope's gift for the next half hour or so. He was never able to do anything without touch, but he was able to begin feeling his anti-magic where it gathered at his fingers. He got to a point where he felt it touch and suck up some of Penelope's gift magic.

He was able to feel the difference in the two energies as they interacted, but he couldn't yet do anything with it beyond that. And so he could turn off Penelope's gift without trying, but her magic never got farther into him than his fingertips, where he lost track of it and it dissipated in his body. Penelope assumed even those little bits of energy might accumulate in him and eventually allow him to use it to amplify someone later. When he's able to find it, anyway.

When I was in his head, it was hard to keep track of the foreign magic and his own anti-magic at the same time. Probably because we were both beginners. I still completely struggled with keeping track of my own magic, even with my advantage of seeing so many gifts used while I inhabited various minds.

When Aric started losing focus and showing more frustration at his lack of gains, Penelope shifted what we were doing.

"Alexa's turn. I do want to work on your secondary gift, but not until you have a bit more practice controlling your visions. You are mind-sharing with such ease that I'd bet the payout from my next acting gig you can do it without detection." She clapped her hands together lightly. "But again, we'll test that later. Time to have a vision. Why don't you focus on Amara and take advantage of your ability to spy on the enemy?"

"Okay," I said, lying back down, thinking of Amara. I imagined her glowing green eyes and her shining silver hair, and I said her name over and over in my head.

Chapter Twenty

AMARA

STEADILY, THE DARKNESS BEHIND my eyes fades and focuses until I'm looking out of new eyes, and I feel the subtle differences of my new body. I am Amara. She slips down a wide and dimly lit hallway, slippers scratching and torches flickering are hints of her presence. There's an arm-length sword in her hand, point dangling toward the cool stone and brushing around her nightgown as she walks. The blade reflects warm yellows from the flames lighting the way and silver from the moon slicing through high skylights.

As she comes to a set of heavy wooden doors on the right, her breath quiets and she pushes into a room so dark her eyes have to adjust from the dim hallway. The shadows of bookshelves and wardrobes and benches take shape as the moonlit sky comes through a large window over a bed.

A rug extends all the way around it and then covers the stone floors in a path through the room, stopping right in front of her. Amara creeps along the plush trail until she reaches the left side of the large bed frame, made entirely from densely braided and sculpted, willowy branches.

On the side closest to her lies a woman who is Amara's reflection—her twin, Candace. Amara's mirror image lies twisted in the sheets and her hair shines brightly as it wraps around her pale neck like a silver collar.

The movement of Amara drawing up the sword seems to rouse Candace. She startles at first with Amara looming directly over her, but relaxes, as recognition flickers in her phosphorescent green eyes. Relief turns to fear as her gaze moves from Amara's face to the sword, poised to pierce Candace through the heart.

Candace can only lift her head slightly and still avoid touching the blade. "Amara?" She gasps as Amara drives the blade down.

When she draws it back, the thirsty white of Candace's gown drinks up her blood and wicks it across her chest. She lies utterly still.

Amara wipes the blade on the sheets, leaving them smeared with blood. "Do not worry, I will care for Irene. Sleep in peace Candace, free from the prophecies."

She leaves the room, sword at her side again, and follows the hallway until it ends, facing one final pair of doors, larger than the others.

Amara wipes her now clammy hands dry on the skirt of her gown and squeezes into the room, pausing once the door closes, every muscle straining to keep still. Her eyes adjust to the single torchlight, and the queen's tub and benches, her vanity table and a set of French doors come into view. The doors have been left open, sheer curtains dancing in the breeze and letting a splash of moonlight cover the bed.

The cold creeps through Amara's slippers as she crosses the room toward the bed, breath slow and quiet again, even as her heart races.

Queen Kyra lies asleep, carefully tucked under her bedding. Her silver hair is draped neatly down the sides of her neck and her fingers are laced just under her chest. She looks like someone who's been staged for an open casket funeral, except for the beautiful glowing energy pouring from every part of her.

Four thick wooden posts hold a rippling canopy away from the bed and Amara uses a small stool on the floor where the canopy opens so that she can stand over Kyra, sword in hand. Kyra stirs at the sudden motions around her, and Amara leans forward to kiss her forehead. "You chose wrong, Mother," she whispers and draws the blade up with both hands.

Kyra blinks. "Amara, what—"

Amara drives the sword deep into Kyra's chest and watches the glow behind her shocked green eyes fade. Even as Kyra stills, frost climbs the blade so fast it bites painfully at Amara's fingers on the hilt before she finishes pulling the blade back out.

Amara steps down from the bed and strides past the open doors toward the vanity, catching a glimpse of a large balcony outside.

When Amara sits in front of the mirror, the moonlight reflects her face—Candace's face. It's horrifying to see Amara's murdered twin again right after killing her. Even worse though, are the green eyes that also belong to my true body, eyes I've seen in the mirror for my entire life.

Amara has somehow managed to keep all but a few specks of blood off her own white gown, which seems impossible considering the large amount of it she's spilled using the blade lying across the vanity table in front of her, still covered in wet streaks. She picks up the brush from that same table and begins running it through her pale hair, repeating the motion over and over until the first signs of daylight begin to creep above the horizon and through the open doors.

She finally gets up and brings the sword down to the tub in the floor to rinse it off. Swirls of scarlet spread away from the weapon, staining the water as the blade comes clean. When it gleams against the entering light, she wipes it dry on the robe draped across the bench before wrapping herself in that same robe.

With the morning light on the clean sword, I can see the familiar rows of alternating rubies and sapphires on the hilt, the floral tooling and the words Immortalis Excessum etched down the blade.

Amara walks to the bookshelf running the entire length of the far wall and pulls out the same burgundy book, Immortalis Populus—the one from the day Ambrose burned. The shelf is a little taller from her vantage point as she reaches into the space where the book had been and removes the loose stone. The sword slides into its custom-made hiding place and she returns the shelf to its normal state before walking back down the hall.

She passes several sets of doors on either side before reaching the top of the staircase, and I wonder who might be living behind all the doors where she didn't commit murder as she glides down the stairs into the circular entry room below.

A familiar guard, Theron, is standing in front of the main doors in the usual cream and black uniform. The sword strapped to his back triggers a memory of the other sword and the murders Amara committed while I wore her hands.

As he notices Amara approach, he bows formally. "Princess Amara. It is quite early. Is all well?"

"Markos just attacked me in my bed," she says. "Send guards after him."

His eyes widen and he steps toward the stairs. "I will secure the queen," he says.

"It is too late for that, Theron! Send the guards for Markos!" Her voice is loud and angry. "He murdered my mother and sister!"

"But how, Princess? You are all immortal."

"He found the missing Immortal Death Blade. I woke only an instant before he drove it through my heart, and I fought him off with my gift. He got away with that cursed weapon. Find him, Theron. For my family."

"What of Irene?" He speaks hesitantly, softly.

"The child lies safely in her bed. Secure her father from his bedchamber until we know his role in his brother's betrayal."

"Praise the gods, we have not lost our Peace." He sighs deeply. "Why would Markos do this?"

"Because I refused to marry him. Because he is hateful and vile. Send the guard, Theron. I am your queen now."

"But Irene is the prophesied—"

A spike of energy bursts from Amara's center and out through her palms squarely into his chest, causing him to brace against the force.

"It is time I rule Atlantis by the power of my gift and my sole remaining immortality. We are through with the random whims of gods who abandoned us two millennia ago. That is what killed the ones I loved. Now kneel before your queen, Theron."

The energy shoots through her body again, leaving her hands in an arc that lands on his shoulders, pressing him down until he stumbles to his knees.

"My queen," he grunts. "We will find Markos."

"And send word to all region leaders. They should make arrangements to witness my family being put to rest and my crowning tomorrow."

He gives a slight bow with his head, eyes averted. "It shall be done, Queen Amara."

"See that someone is sent to clean the queen's chamber. I wish to lie there tonight," Amara says. "I must go speak with Irene now, no doubt this will be hard news."

He bows again and turns to go. He doesn't make it two steps before she stops him.

"Theron. One more thing."

He turns toward her again, eyes politely cold.

"There is a woman living in a farmhouse on the far side of the orchard. Her name is Helen. Send for her immediately."

Theron bows and strides off through a set of doors on the far side of the room.

"She will know what to do now," Amara whispers to the empty room.

* * * * *

I found my own body again, fleecy blanket below me and a small circle of blue sky surrounded by trees above. I sat up.

Aric scrolled on his phone and Penelope weaved long strands of grass into a braid.

"Finally!" Aric said. "We just watched you sleep for over an hour." He fell onto his back dramatically. "And I have almost used all the power on this phone watching humor-filled videos of strangers."

"That was quite a long vision," Penelope said. "Is that usual?"

"I'm not sure. I've had so many in my sleep, without people waiting on me," I said. "But it seems like they run in real time, and a lot of time passed in the vision I just had."

"I believe you will be able to learn how to browse visions more quickly, eventually," she said. "But it makes sense that your default would be to follow things at the actual rate of their unfolding."

"What did you see?" Aric asked.

"Amara killed her twin and her mother to become queen," I said. They both stared at me.

A deep crease formed between Aric's brows and his lips parted slightly. "That is madness. The traitor, Markos, is the murderer."

"The murders were before my birth, but I've long suspected Amara and my mother were somehow involved despite the official rulings against Markos," Penelope said, setting the now circular grass braid down at her feet. "It may have been Amara's hands, but I still believe my mother played some role. She's involved with everything the queen does."

"I do not know," I said. "Helen was not there as I—Amara murdered two people."

Penelope took my hands in hers, and it was then that I realized I'd started shaking, sickened by the actions I'd participated in. I let her hold my hands while I closed my eyes, trying to make it stop.

"Do you normally speak in a more Atlantean style after your visions?" she asked me.

No? Or at least I hadn't noticed. Shit. What now?

"I do not know how to cope with all this." My chest was tight. "I have seen or committed or experienced so many atrocities in the last few months. And it all feels real. I can barely tell that I'm another person while they happen. I forget I'm not supposed to be all these other people. And I have all these memories that aren't mine," I whispered. "I'm so scared. And sick to my stomach. And I just want my life back." I couldn't believe I was letting myself become a complete emotional wreck in front of her.

"Things are grim with the Godline," Penelope said. "The immortals have passed trauma down like a family heirloom for thousands of years, but many of us are younger now, and we've seen other ways to live."

"It's a little funny you call yourself young." I smiled.

She smiled back and I felt a warm connection between us. One of shared history and shared memories and maybe a shared mind as well.

"Well, with fewer Godline born each year, I am of the youngest generation to make up a large part of our population. Aric's generation...your generation...anyone under a century...there are maybe a hundred people that young on Atlantis."

"Doesn't sound like Amara's terrible laws are increasing the population as intended," I said. "Too bad someone else wasn't put in charge."

"The rule should have gone to Irene," Penelope said. "But when Amara publicly declared the prophecies treasonous, that included the prophecy naming Irene the rightful ruler."

She had picked the braided grass circlet back up and now wove in the small white blooms of dwarf-dogwood that sprouted all over the forest floor. "If Irene had been raised to rule instead of what happened, everything could have been different," she sighed. "But our powerful and immortal queen has her own plans."

"I wonder if the murder sword is still in its hiding spot in Amara's room?" I mused. "I mean, she used it to kill off an Immortal ruler."

"The Immortal Death Blade?" Aric asked.

"You have seen Hephaestus's missing blade?" Penelope said at the same time.

"Yeah. I've seen it twice, actually," I replied. "Amara and her dad put it away in the same hidden recess, behind a bookshelf in the queen's room."

Penelope sat up straighter. "That could be a way to change everything."

"Are you two suggesting that someone should murder my mother?" Aric glared at me with his lips pressed flat in disapproval.

I was thankful when Penelope answered him and took the brunt of his scowl. "I hope not, Aric, but we need the option."

"You need to find another way!" he yelled and stood up. He started pacing next to the blanket, arms crossed over his chest. "I understand that some of the laws are harsh, but there has to be a solution that does not murder the only parent I know. Even if she was not often present enough to parent. I still owe her my loyalty." His final sentence sounded unsure.

"Of course, none of us want to resort to murder, Aric," Penelope said. "If Amara would just let the Godline choose how to live under her rule on Atlantis or with the humans on Earth, none of this would even be a conversation."

Aric mumbled inarticulately under his breath and sat down again. He turned his back to us and wrapped his arms around his knees, staring off into the trees.

Penelope let Aric brood on his own and turned her eyes to mine. She leaned in close to me, stopping with our mouths just inches apart. Her lip curled up on one side as she placed the flower crown she'd made on top of my head. Our closeness and the sensation of her touch sent a pleasant shiver down my back, like the magic rolling off her was tickling me.

She finished settling the crown of grass and flowers on my head and sat back on her part of the blanket again. I felt the absence of her closeness instantly, wishing she'd lean back in. And in the next moment, I internally kicked myself for pining after my two hundred and something year old...coach?

Penelope was still looking right at me from her spot, staring proudly at the adornment on my head. "You are suited for Atlantean braiding." She suddenly changed the subject. "I'd love to see you in a gown to match those eyes." She gave me another half-smile and arched an eyebrow at me. "Our weavers pride themselves on their ability to spin and braid fabrics imbued with their magic. I dated a weaver once who made fabrics capable of mimicking the exact color and glow of Godline eyes."

My face flushed hot at all the focused attention from Penelope, but it was easy to imagine myself dressed as she described, having seen it so often in my visions. "Well..." I hesitated. "Maybe one day we can get some smuggled clothing from Atlantis. I'd like trying it out on my real body for once. Although, I don't know where we'd wear clothes like that," I finished lamely.

"There's more than one reason I like making my living with small acting roles," Penelope said. "Not only does my work allow me to glamour myself into exciting new forms, but there are so many parties with that crowd. Atlantean gowns fit right in. I know this from experience. I'd love to have you as a guest some time."

I was too caught up staring at her to respond, and I paused for way too long, which caused the blood to run warm through my cheeks again. Finally, I found some words. "I've only ever dreamed of being a part of something like that. I don't exactly compare with that crowd when I stop dreaming, though." I grinned. Maybe it would seem less pathetic if I could laugh at myself.

"Trust me, Alexa, you are beyond comparison to even the most glamorous humans," Penelope responded. "But I'm not surprised you're blind to it. You're used to feeling very different, but to our people...to me, a single glance shows how special you are. You are quite lovely, and your magic is fascinating." She reached up and slid a finger along my cheek, brushing a hair from my face.

Another shiver ran down my spine.

"I'm happy we met and even happy to be sitting in a forest thousands of miles from my comfortable apartment and my parties," she said.

"Wait," Aric interrupted. "You seriously speak of parties and dresses as if you do not conspire to kill my mother?" His voice was sharp. "And...and...this!" He gestured at my head. Whether it meant the crown of flowers or Penelope's hand on my face, I didn't care to ask.

"It's not about who gives birth to you, Aric. It's about who's there for you and who shows you love and support when you most need it," Penelope said gently. "If I learned anything in human therapy about my mommy issues with Helen and Amara, it's that."

"Enough of this talk!" Aric yelled as he jumped up and stormed off into the trees.

"I am sorry for my careless words, Aric," she called after him. "Please come back soon, Love."

"Fine!" he hollered over his shoulder, as he disappeared between the branches.

"Well, I guess this means we have more time to practice," Penelope said.

"I think...part of why he's upset..." I trailed off. I didn't know why I'd suddenly decided to get into their business.

"What?" she asked. "He has acted this way since childhood. He gets upset or overwhelmed, and then he runs away, won't listen to reason. I've always had to just wait until he's calm enough to return."

"I mean, I think that's what upsets him," I said. "Before I met you. Before we knew you'd be coming, he proudly told me about your marriage. He really seems to want that with you."

"And then I treat him like my child," she finished my thought, which I was grateful for, feeling nosy enough talking about it at all. "I had not considered that he would see that marriage so traditionally. Amara was hardly ever present while I was raising him." Penelope's voice was quiet, hesitant. "I mean, sometimes he would repeat the rhetoric, but I always tried to help him find his moral compass at those times. Theron did too."

"Theron is one of the guards, right? What does he have to do with Aric?" I asked.

"He is resistance as well. Amara assigned Theron to prepare Aric for hunter training starting not long after I was assigned to be his surrogate mother. We both used our time with Aric to try and help him break free of Amara's warped ideals."

"I had a vision of him shortly before he came to Alaska, and I got the impression Amara had taken over at least some of his training in a sort of violent homeschool. And it just seems like the idea of being married to you was…is a defining thing for him."

"Oh," she said. "I do carry a deep guilt of leaving him behind, but he was nearly grown, and they would have forced us to breed like animals. He was the child I raised." Her voice was soft. "I had to escape."

"You don't owe me any kind of explanation. I've seen it there. It's scary as hell."

"Possibly scarier." She gave me a wistful half smile. "But your gift could be a powerful tool for the resistance. You can see everything, Alexa."

"I'm not sure if my gift is reliable enough to come up with information that's actually useful," I said. "But I do wish I could meet all the resistance members you seem to miss so deeply. People like Irene." I stare down at my hands, wishing I would just stop talking sometimes.

"Irene is very kind. And loyal," Penelope said. "I think her gift has allowed her to endure the great pains inflicted on her by Helen and Amara without becoming like them. She wasn't much older than you when she became a founding member of the resistance."

"I remember it." I recalled riding across Atlantis on a flying horse with Penelope in my arms. "Well, I know I wasn't there. I just mean…I remember seeing that memory. It's confusing." My embarrassed rambling finally ended.

My new life as one of the Godline brought me mostly confusion. Magic was real. I was born in a hidden and magical land, but it was as terrible as it was beautiful. If I kept running, learned how to hide, I could finally have the life I was trying to build. The life that had come at a cost to so many other people. Or, Penelope thought I had something to offer. Maybe a way to make up for some of the pain caused to get me here.

It was hard to even know what I wanted from life or valued anymore, and the confusion was overwhelming enough that I found myself fixating on a growing adoration for Penelope instead. "Can I change the subject?" I asked.

"Of course," she said. "I am here to serve. You, like your mother, are a princess, after all." She grinned. "It's true, but I understand it probably sounds a bit absurd from your current perspective." She pressed her fingers to her lips. "Sorry! I'm a talker. What did you want to ask?"

I paused for a moment and listened to the birds and rustling leaves of the forest as I built up the nerve for my question. "Well, am I reading you correctly? Have you been...flirting with me a little?" I felt myself flush as I asked it, directing my attention to my hands again.

I wasn't used to being so direct, but I'd felt safe with Penelope from the moment we'd met, and even though that had been barely twenty-four hours before, my mind had known her for weeks.

"I've been flirting." She smiled and said nothing more.

I thought maybe she wanted to watch me squirm, and I glanced around at the trunks of the spruce and birch trees surrounding us, searching for Aric.

"I know you see Aric differently because you helped raise him, but he and I are the same age. Don't I seem like a child to you as well?" I asked.

"Well, you are a young woman...new to your gifts. I know you will grow and change, but we all spend our lives changing, after all. That doesn't make you any less delightful or fascinating to be around, and you deserve to know that. Also, you're right. I didn't raise you." She took my hands again. "I should warn you though. Your mental age, in time, will not match your years on Earth."

"What does that mean?" I asked, a crease forming between my brows.

"I mean, the visions you have don't just give you information. I am not surprised you are already confusing them with memories and slipping in your language. You'll grow and learn from the experiences of others. Even now, you must feel a change in yourself since you started experiencing your gift."

"Other than sleep deprivation and constant anxiety and suddenly sharing too many of my feelings, no." I couldn't acknowledge the idea of my gift changing me so drastically.

"Well, I'm here if you need to talk about anything." She leaned in close to me and her magic whispered against my skin again. She held my eyes in her gaze.

Then she reached up and picked the crown off my head. "This isn't nearly elegant enough for a princess. Lie back for another vision, and I'll make a better one." She placed the crown on her own head as she sat back again.

I rolled my eyes. "I'm not a princess."

"Lie back," she repeated with a grin. "Why don't you see if you can learn more about your mother."

Once I was settled on my back again, eyes closed, I tried to focus on Irene. I wanted to know more about this resistance starting woman who also happened to be my Godline princess of a mother.

Chapter Twenty-One

IVY

THE WARM TINGLE OF power is coiled tight around my wrists, pulling my arms painfully in either direction, and my knees barely reach the white stone floor of the throne room. As I settle into the vision, I realize I'm screaming wordlessly, tears soaking my face. My body—that of an unfamiliar woman—trying to jerk one or both of my arms free.

Amara paces in front of two people who stand against the wall to my left, or to the left of whomever I am at the moment. Her back is to me, but I can tell it's her from the silver hair and elaborate green gown made in the Atlantean style, formed from braids. I can also see that she's holding something in her arms.

The body I'm in stops screaming when Amara speaks.

"You all realize by now why you are here," Amara says.

As she speaks, I realize it's Theron and Irene pinned against the wall. From my position in the middle of the room, I can see that Irene's hair isn't actually silver like Amara's, but she does have her eyes. Haunting green eyes must be a family trait.

Dagan is standing in front of Theron with the tip of his very large sword pressed against Theron's throat. A trickle of blood runs down his neck from the sword piercing it.

"You have all been involved in the most traitorous of acts against me." The words come out of her somewhere between a screech and a hiss. "You are traitors against your own people!"

Amara turns toward the throne in front of me then, and I notice Helen standing there in her golden suit of silk and braids. Despite their wildly different ways of presenting themselves, I suddenly see the resemblance between Penelope and her mother.

"Shall I bring your knife, my queen?" Helen asks.

"Yes. Bring my knife," Amara says.

"Shall I take the traitors' baby—I mean your baby while you work, my queen?" she asks.

Amara nods and exchanges a baby for a knife.

Amara is walking toward me now. "You!" She stops just over me, and I feel her invisible grip tighten and stretch my arms too far, pulling a fresh scream of agony between my lips. She continues, almost spitting her words at me. "You betrayed me, Ivy." She flicks the blade of her knife with her fingernail.

So, I'm Ivy, then.

"Please. Please. Don't hurt him," I whisper—Ivy whispers through a tight throat.

Amara turns to Helen, who is bouncing the baby in her arms as it begins to cry, and laughs. "That child is mine now."

She glares at Irene and Theron and then me as she turns between us. "You all know that my niece's child was supposed to be mine. This child will have to take her place." Amara's voice carries across the room in echoes.

Suddenly I feel my arms—Ivy's arms—jerk strong and fast, ripping from the coils long enough to jump up and begin sprinting toward Helen. I make it all the way to the foot of the steps below Helen before I feel my feet being yanked behind me, twisted together in the grip of Amara's power. The fall is so fast that my arms don't get out in front of me, and my face hits the marble step.

My forehead takes much of the impact and all I can do is roll on my back as the room fills with bright spots. The magic of Ivy's body radiates toward the bleeding part of my head—her head—and I can feel it becoming dense around the wound, working to mend the damage, but an opposing energy suddenly displaces the healing magic.

"Don't even think about healing yourself," Amara says. "You deserve to suffer."

"May I suggest she is given a lasting reminder of obedience, my queen?" The baby has gone quiet in Helen's arms.

"I think that will do well, Helen. Have you an idea in mind?"

"She cannot speak to anyone about your baby without a tongue," Helen says. "It would also serve as a reminder to the other two, to keep their mouths shut about this fine child of yours, or see him, too, suffer the consequences." Helen looks directly at Theron and Irene. Theron is stony faced, but Irene sobs violently.

Amara kneels next to me as I lie on my back, head throbbing. She brings the knife to my face, and though I struggle to move away from her, my entire body is pressed to the floor by the invisible weight of her power. "Open up Ivy."

* * * * *

I jerked out of the vision in a hurry, and it took a moment to adjust to the peaceful scene of Penelope weaving grass again, especially because I'd had such difficulty separating myself from Ivy in the vision this time. Maybe it was all the mind-sharing, but I was feeling more and more like the people I experienced, not less.

This time Penelope's grass work was thicker and had a series of small braids coming together. The woven grass wasn't that long, but given the detail in the small section she had finished, a long time must have passed. Aric was still gone, but my insides twisted as I remembered what I'd just learned.

"Welcome back," Penelope said.

I had to unclench my teeth in order to speak. "Uh..." I didn't know what to say.

"Were you able to get to know your mother?" she asked.

I could answer questions. "No. She was there, but...it...it was Ivy's story."

"Well, that makes sense, I guess. They are close friends, and both resistance members."

I lowered my voice even though we seemed alone. I didn't want to even risk Aric overhearing. "Aric's not actually Amara's son. He's Ivy and Theron's. He was raised by that psycho because I escaped." My lip started trembling.

"Wait," she said. "Slow down. What are you saying?"

I sniffed and wiped a tear off my cheek. "I just watched Amara take baby Aric from Ivy and threaten her, Theron, and my mother not to tell anyone. Ivy's missing tongue was meant as a reminder."

"Oh," Penelope said. She had a faraway look in her eyes.

"And it's my fault! All of that!" I whisper-screamed.

"What's all your fault?" Aric asked, walking out of the trees. "I mean, I am not surprised, but do share."

My eyes snapped up to meet his. I was too scared to talk, and Penelope seemed to be in a similar state because we both stared at him far too long.

My eyes finally landed on Penelope, and I lifted my hands and shoulders into a shrug. "I don't know what to say here."

"What's going on?" The smile had slipped from Aric's face. His brows were drawn close in confusion as he sat down on the blanket beside us again.

Penelope finally spoke. "Aric, you have to promise me that you won't leave. We just found something out about you, and...well, just promise me that you will try to stay calm and stay with us."

"Just tell me what has happened!" he shouted. "Why are you both acting so strange?"

"Say you'll stay," Penelope said again.

"Fine! I will stay! What could be so scary to talk about?" he replied.

Penelope repeated the facts of Aric's birth to him in a soft voice, as if she were trying to coax a stray animal not to run away. As she spoke, Aric's expression grew more distressed. He was shaking his head as she finished, disbelief written all over his face. Finally, predictably, he jumped to his feet and started to walk toward the trees again.

"Aric...you promised," Penelope called. "Talk to me."

He walked back toward us and started pacing the edge of our blanket instead. "We cannot be sure that is true!" he shouted. Then he pointed accusingly at me. "We cannot trust what she says! Who knows if her visions are even true?" He sounded desperate.

"You know her visions are true, Aric. I'm sorry," Penelope said.

"So, my mother is not my mother, but the palace crazy is?" he exclaimed the question, not seeming to actually want a response. "The woman I have feared my whole life. The one always hunched and filthy in the corners of rooms. The mad healer with no tongue. That is my mother?" he yelled. "How could both of my parents let me be raised right in front of them and say nothing? I trusted Theron, and he never even hinted at it. He acted like I was just one of his duties!"

"Amara threatened them with your torture, if you ever found out," I said.

"You stay out of my life!" he screamed, not even looking at me. "This is your fault."

"Aric, calm down please. She didn't ask for this any more than you did."

"It is her fault. Just like I am on the run now because of her!" he yelled, but with a little less commitment.

"You're on the run now because you've always been a decent person despite the suffering Amara caused for you. Those who truly love you have been in your life all along, and you always chose to let them into your heart instead of becoming cruel and cold like Amara," she said. "This truth doesn't change any of that."

"Can we please just go?" he muttered.

We left without further conversation and dropped Aric off at the house before going back to an empty lot near our old apartment. I sat in the car with Penelope while I slipped into her mind. She spent the time uncharacteristically quiet, although, once I was mind-sharing with her, she really didn't have anyone to talk to. I had half expected her to just chat aloud to herself, but then again, I had just dropped a huge bomb on everyone. For me, it hadn't been much more disturbing than any of my other visions, but for Aric and Penelope, I'd basically told them they'd been living a lie for twenty years. I knew how that part felt.

Chapter Twenty-Two

TWO WEEKS PASSED. TWO weeks of practice with Penelope in various forests around Fairbanks on what I'd begun to call my vision blanket. Two weeks of Aric spiraling, making his own practice ineffective.

"Did you see the stallions at their first resistance meeting?" Penelope asked me as I sat up after another vision, guided by a memory of Penelope's. She was working on one of her ever more complicated grass crowns to pass the time, getting more intricate every day we went. She'd been incorporating the fall flowers, leaves, and even berries of the different places we visited, and there was a growing collection of dried crowns lining the front windows of our house.

"Yes, and being in conversation with two giant black stallions is still one of my stranger experiences," I said.

"Those horses are snobs," Aric groaned, sitting up from what had become his daily hangover nap. "They will hardly let anyone ride them."

Aric had started going out at night again, relying heavily on the dating app he'd learned about from me to facilitate his daily hook-ups. I'd take that back if I could, especially since I'd never even cared about that stupid app.

His nightly activities left him too tired to stay awake for long around any of us. He'd been aloof and fragile ever since my vision about his real parents, and none of us had been able to bring him around.

So, with a wary concern, Penelope convinced Aric to follow some basic safety practices to keep off Dagan's radar. I was skeptical that he'd be able to effectively combine his heavy drinking with going incognito, especially when Dagan had access to magical tracking as well as whatever human resources the hunters had with the Godline businesses on Earth, but there was nothing to do about it for the time being. Aric may have been terrible at coping, but he was a victim too.

The worst part about Aric's recent cascade into depression was his inability to make gains with his own gift. He stopped our gifts through touch every day during practice. This action came to him naturally. Unfortunately, that is where the skill advancement ended. Despite Penelope's coaching and my mind-sharing, Aric couldn't use his gift without touch. It wasn't really a surprise in his constantly hungover state.

"I think I found exactly the memory you told me about," I said, lying back on the blanket with my arms behind my head.

Ever since my vision about Aric's parents, Penelope had been describing her own memories in detail before I entered my visions. It had significantly improved my precision. In fact, I'd even learned to effectively fast forward through visions by taking a series of jumps through an event. I'd mostly done it with visions that I'd already seen because it helped me know what I was skipping as I rode them through time, though there was one new vision where I successfully skipped ahead when I came upon Penelope making out with Chloe.

Penelope and Chloe seemed to be very, very close friends. The thought made me sit back up and scoot closer to Penelope. I realized I was being possessive about her without any right and shifted my attention to how much I also liked Chloe. She was a talented horsewoman who also happened to need a wheelchair in a world with magical healing. The curiosity prompted me to finally ask Penelope about it.

"Hey..." I started, unsure how to ask the question. "I hope this is okay to ask. Chloe is amazing as she is, but I'm curious, why wouldn't Ivy just heal her legs?"

"There's nothing to be healed," Penelope said. "Chloe is as Aphrodite made her. Sometimes the gods play a more personal role in forming the Godline they are gifting. Aphrodite made Chloe the way she is as a tribute to her husband, Hephaestus, who's own mobility is impacted by clubbed feet."

"Do the gods often play such a personal role when they give their gifts?" I felt uncomfortable as I thought about Apollo forming me with his own ideas in mind.

"They do it occasionally...you usually see it in things like golden skin and silver hair and even the brightness of the emerald eyes in the royal line." She held my gaze as she said it. "But remember that time moves more slowly with the Godline. The gods forget about us for long periods, but you can see the influence of their vanity in a handful of people each generation."

"This gives me so many ideas for future vision practice," I said.

"Pretty soon you'll be ready to learn those secondary gifts of yours too."

"If I learn enough control of my visions, I might not need to mess with any of the side effect gifts."

"You'll get curious eventually."

I was curious already, but nearly catching on fire and turning into a lightning rod were scary side effects to have no control over. Plus, I feared what I would become if I did learn to control the other gifts. Was I bound to become another Amara?

Penelope shifted her attention to Aric. "Are you feeling better?"

Aric stared down at his lap and shrugged. "I am fine."

"How about after we finish up for the day, you and I go out for dinner together?" She placed her hand on his forearm. "I can answer questions you might have about your parents."

"If it is just the two of us."

"Of course."

"So, what do you want me to try?" he asked.

"I've been thinking, maybe the nuance of using your gift without touch will just take time. As you know, gifts develop over years— sometimes decades."

"Okay, then what do you want me to do?" His words were brittle, at risk of shattering.

"I want to see if you can amplify my gift," she said. "Just do like you normally do, but when you feel the magic this time, hold back the void part of your magic. Let the rest through."

"I can try," he said. "I can recognize the emptiness as it captures magic now. I will try."

Penelope created the illusion of her little black cat, and Aric reached toward her without touching. He stared at his fingers for a long time before finally closing the gap between them. When he touched her, the cat flickered in and out of existence in two flashes.

"Wait," Aric yelled, still staring at his hand.

And then something new happened. The cat turned into a black jaguar. The forest around us became jungle, blotting out the sky above with a massive canopy of leaves. The earth shifted and rippled beneath us until it was a rich, vine-covered jungle floor. The smell of soil and thick detritus filled my senses. Sounds of birds singing and various animals scratching about their nests and caves filled our space. After a few seconds, the illusion snapped back with a sharp shifting of light and reality. We were back in the boreal forest of Fairbanks again.

Aric was wide eyed and smiling. "Did I do that?"

Penelope was smiling back at him, also shocked. "Yes..." she began. "I was only using the energy to make the cat. That illusion rivals my very best work, which usually leaves me exhausted." She leaned toward him for a hug. "Incredible work, Aric!"

It was a relief to finally see him have some success. The pride was written all over his face, a feeling that had been in short supply for him, maybe always.

* * * * *

That night, while Penelope and Aric were away for dinner and Lukas was out frolicking with animals, Hazel and I took advantage of the sister time. We spent the night snuggled together on the couch, drinking one of Hazel's experimental tea failures. I'm not sure what she had been attempting to make, but the result was a drink that tasted like raspberry tea and acted like a strong alcohol. It was definitely some magic at work because the pleasant lightheadedness and giddiness only lasted as the sip was still wet on the tongue.

"Lex," Hazel said. "I was thinking that I might go back home soon since you're sleeping normally and in control of your visions now." She giggled as she took a swallow of tea.

"Oh?" The thought of being without Hazel made my breath catch. I took a sip. Laughed to myself. Another sip. If I kept sipping, the selfish angst would stay away. I giggled.

"Yeah." Hazel smiled lazily, pulling her cup from her lips. "Mom and Dad should be coming in from the mountains soon. With the house burned down, they might need some help."

"The whole village will be helping them out," I said. I took another sip and let my head flop back against the couch, enjoying the warm and fuzzy feeling. "I mean...yeah—such a good daughter! Such a good sister!" I took a long sip, grinning at my mug.

"I know they don't need me, but I'm tired of my malfunctioning magic. I need Mom to teach me whatever she left out of my training." Hazel stared at the wall dreamily. "Lukas said he'd come help with rebuilding. Then he makes a sort of migration through a bunch of Nymph villages. I thought it would be fun to tag along."

"You two sure have gotten really close in just a few weeks." I winked meaningfully and then snorted because I was so funny. And I took another long shallow slurp to make sure everything stayed hilarious.

"He's very easy to be around." She took a quick sip and giggled. "And he's very kind and thoughtful and so handsome." Her eyes lost focus. She was probably imagining him. "I feel like I've known Lukas for like...forever. And he's so...so...handsome."

"You don't say."

"I know you don't know about handsome guys...you need to know he's a really handsome guy."

"Yeah, okay. Anyway, you two seem great together...like since the moment you met." I bumped her side lightly with my elbow. "I approve, even if he is like two hundred million years old."

She rolled her eyes. "Oh, you approve, do you? Well, don't think I don't see you and Penelope flirting every time you talk to or look at each other, so don't be too judgmental about age gaps among the mortally challenged." She glanced away quickly and sipped her tea.

"Is Penelope the most gorgeous woman I've ever seen? Yes. Is she funny and smart and brave as hell? Yes. Is she way too good for me? Seems that way." I took a long sip and felt the smile come back. Sipped again. The giddy feeling returned.

Hazel took two quick sips, and her smile grew as she stared me right in the eyes. "Is Alexa allowed to have a crush on her pretty goddess friend? Yes. Does goddess friend flirt like she wants more? Hazel thinks so." She took a big sip. "Wow! My failure tea is the best!" she yelled at the room.

That pushed me into a fit of laughter, which sucked Hazel right in. It took us several moments to regain any sort of composure.

"It's all talk and she's just a natural flirt." I wiped the laughter tears from my eyes. "She never actually acts on any of it."

"Lex, you're killing me!" She drained the rest of her mug. "That woman has had you traipsing through her memories every day since she's arrived. She wants you."

"Oh, those visions are just for practice." I finished my mug as well. I held it out to Hazel and she took them both over to the stove and refilled them from the kettle. "Yeah, I'm sure the only way to practice was to build a heap of shared memories together. And then you sleep right up next to her body every night." She winked at me this time.

"With Aric on the other side of her." I bit the side of my lip to stop a nervous smile. "Plus, she talks about Aric like he's a child and he's my age!"

"She asks me all about you every time we talk, and she doesn't seem to be asking with motherly interest." Hazel brought our mugs back and sat beside me. "And really, you need to start thinking about age differently because...magic. Plus, remember the whole mental aging thing? From all those memories?" She took a small sip of the still very hot tea.

"Alright, knock it off." I try to sound serious, but then I'm sipping my tea carefully, giggling. "Penelope's not here to date me. She's here to train me and then get back to her much better life."

"At least tell her you're into her." Hazel took too large of a sip, burned her mouth, sprayed her drink everywhere and then fell into another fit of laughter. When it passed, she added, "Maybe you should think about transferring to a community school or something in Seattle with Penelope for next semester. I mean, it would be good to start somewhere that Dagan has not actually found you."

She was right. It didn't seem likely that I'd be able to stay here if I wanted to go to school and work and live a normal life. In a new, bigger city, I could get a fresh start, but I didn't want to lose Hazel again. "I hate the idea of being so far from you."

"I hate it too, but we can visit each other. And we can talk every day.

"We better." I sipped, felt the happiness return, sipped again.

"Well, none of this will happen before next semester, so let's just enjoy our time together." She grabbed me around the shoulders into a one-armed hug and smacked a kiss right on my cheek. "Love you!"

"Ugh. Yes! I love you, too!" I groaned. "I don't love your drool!"

And that was when Penelope and Aric got back.

"I need this!" Aric said with an actual smile as he snatched my phone off the coffee table on his way toward the stairs. "I have an idea for a post on the Gram, as some of us say, but my battery failed."

"Do I want to know?" I asked him.

"Unlikely." He grinned.

"Just remember not to post anything related to locations!" I held the mug to my lips.

"You can stop reminding me. It was I who first told you of hunter access to technology resources."

"Well...technically, I remember Amara talking about one of your tech savvy troglodytes in one of my visions...right before you brought Dagan to my front door." Another long sip and it was all too funny. It probably seemed as if I was laughing at Aric then, which was not the case. The word "troglodytes" was just hilarious.

Aric ignored me, striding upstairs and out of sight before I could say anything else.

"You ready to do this, Lovely?" Penelope said, smiling down at me. "Maybe leave the tea."

Hazel coughed in the kitchen and arched her eyebrows at me. I ignored her and followed Penelope with a blush. We were finally going to test out the whole mind share, undetectable power leaching theory.

We drove away from Fairbanks on a highway that wouldn't meet another town for over a hundred miles, in search of a quiet rest-stop.

"So, Aric seems better," I mentioned.

"Yes, he is hopeful," Penelope said, eyes on the road. "He was already close to Theron, but I told him about his mother from the time before he knew her."

"I remember her from before," I said. "She seemed so close to Irene. She has this fabulous red hair and blue eyes much lighter than Aric's, I think?"

Penelope was nodding. "I told him about the funny and gentle person she is below the surface of what Amara has turned her into. That was when he really started getting happier, but…" She hesitated. It was strange to see Penelope nervous. "He wants us to plan a rescue. He wants us to bring at least Ivy into hiding."

"Well, that is something the resistance has experience with, right? Could we make that happen?"

She sighed in one long exhale. "Aric's idea is definitely in the right spirit, but your birth was the most difficult removal from Atlantis that we ever did, and as you know, we were partially caught and severely punished. We were caught because you were someone Amara was aware of. Ivy, Theron, Irene, and many others we love are right under her eyes. It would not likely succeed. It could end very badly." Her final words tumbled out.

"You escaped while under Amara's watch." I pointed out.

"I chose to take that risk, and I paid the consequences almost as often as I got lucky. Ivy is more than twice my age and has never wanted to leave Atlantis."

"Does Aric know that?"

"I told him she would not leave, but he couldn't let go of hope in the idea, and he is right that she might be convinced now. If she could reunite with her stolen child, she might try to escape. I told him I would try to make it happen."

"Well, that sounds okay," I said.

"He was very excited about it. I fear his hopes are too high."

"I hope they aren't. The guy needs a win."

"He does," she said grimly. "We are here."

She parked the car in an empty pullout and turned to face me. "You are advancing your gift with ease, Alexa. If we find out your mind-sharing is safe, it would be best to start planning where you will move next." Her speech was more formal than usual. "You will not be able to go back to the Fairbanks campus, not when Dagan will be lurking around town until he finds you."

"Hazel talked to me about that tonight too," I said. "She thought I should go to Seattle so you could keep helping me with Godline stuff. She's planning to go back home when it's safe."

"Lukas told me he planned to go with her." Penelope smiled warmly. "Hazel seems to be someone Lukas has been searching for his entire life. He's not spent as much time with another person since he and I were children together in the palace."

"I've noticed." I grinned. "But really, I'm happy they both have someone to feel so close to."

Penelope reached out and slid the tips of her fingers lightly over the skin on my hand until she was able to wrap it in her gentle grip. "Please come to Seattle. I have the space for you, and Aric if he will come. I don't want to go back to being alone."

My heart fluttered at the invitation, even if it was just so Penelope could avoid her own loneliness. I'd always assumed my time with her had a fast-approaching expiration date, so the idea of following Penelope—of living with her—filled my body with anticipation. I finally squeaked out a response. "I'd love that."

"Hazel mentioned that you like to dance," she said. "Let me take you out in Seattle."

"I'm guessing she told you about my obsession with ballroom dance, then?" My face filled with heat.

"How you were obsessed with a reality dance show, so your mom took online dance classes with you. And how she made you share what you'd learned with everyone in town and give dance lessons. Adorable."

"I spent a lot of time dancing as a high school student." I groaned. "I'm so embarrassed you know all that."

"I've learned a lot of dances in my time with humans, but I'm sure you could teach me a move or two." Penelope arched an eyebrow at me as just one side of her lip tugged into a crooked grin. "But I was thinking more about dancing at a club."

"Well, I won't be old enough for most clubs until next April."

"I forget about that strange age limit for passage into some buildings."

"I suppose that gets hard to keep track of after a couple hundred years." I smiled.

"It really does. And it doesn't help that you and I spend every day talking about my old memories. I've started forgetting you haven't been with me all along."

"I'm starting to have similar issues," I said. "Half the time I wake up thinking we just left the palace or the stables together...at least I can talk to you about your memories now, which I much prefer to the torture memories featuring Amara. It feels a hair less creepy."

"It's not creepy if I like it," Penelope scoffed. "But we should probably get started."

"I'm ready," I said, reclining the passenger seat. I closed my eyes and focused on Helen's mind. This was a vision that I had practiced for since I knew we'd do this. The practice seemed to pay off because it was almost as easy as mind-sharing with Penelope.

HELEN

Helen isn't in the garden with the maps this time. She's in one of the lavish bedrooms in the palace, a moonlit sky shining through the window as she lies in the soft bedding. She's getting ready to sleep, which won't do me any good. I have an idea about how to fix it though.

With a split in focus, I keep my mind in Helen's body, while thinking back to her day and her time with her maps in the palace garden. My mind flickers on a few flashes of the palace, the stables, the throne room, and then I see the garden. And I see Dagan. I stop there.

"This is taking a while, even for you, Dagan." Helen's voice is silky like Penelope's, but deeper. Weird. "Over a month now, on a single hunt?"

"Take care with your judgment, Helen," he replies. "Your son is there helping her. Your daughter is there as well. How did you manage to raise such traitorous children?"

"My children are still young. They will come around," Helen says.

"This hunt will bring four home instead of one...due to idiotic choices by the young prince."

"At least I can be proud of raising you, Dagan. Have you determined her gift?"

"I have observed no sign yet," he says. "If I fail to discover her gift, our queen will get much joy learning what it is while the girl rots in a cell. Either way, it will not be long before they are all back where they belong."

"Then I suppose you want to see the latest mapping of her gifts? She has been very active, but all over the place. I am not sure how much use this will be."

"Do not worry, Helen. I have a plan to capture them all. Just show me the map."

Helen walks up to a tall stone table and pulls a loosely folded map, bumpy with location markers, out of a drawer. When she spreads it out, Dagan comes over.

There are at least a couple dozen bumps. They aren't the golden pins like Helen uses on the framed maps. Instead, it's marked with tiny shimmering golden spheres that seem to be affixed to their location through either strong glue or magic. The little markers form a circle of random places all around Fairbanks. I wish I were in my own body to sigh with relief because the parking lot we've been using for my mind-sharing doesn't have a single golden dot. Helen's magic doesn't detect my mind-sharing.

"Well, this is not at all helpful." Dagan says. "No matter. My plan will still work."

"I have no doubt." Helen reaches over and sweeps a loose strand of long dark hair out of his eye. "Come, now. Amara has requested your assistance with an experiment downstairs."

This is enough information and I have no desire to see Amara doing anything downstairs. I search for my own mind, my own body, and settle back in where I belong.

* * * * *

I sat up and wrapped Penelope in a giant hug before I could think too much of it. I further surprised myself when I leaned back slightly, shifted my hands to her shoulders, and smacked a loud kiss on her cheek. "It worked!"

She didn't seem fazed by anything I'd just done. In fact, she returned the favor by touching my cheeks with her fingertips and leaning in to press her lips gently against mine.

"I like you, Penelope," I blurted, the second she pulled her lips away.

"In that case…" She leaned in and pressed her lips to mine again, a little longer this time.

Just as my whole body filled up with heat, she pulled away, smiling at me.

"I do not mind you in my memories, but why don't you tell me about some of yours tonight?" She wove her fingers into mine.

Chapter Twenty-Three

I WAS NERVOUS AFTER my vision of Dagan so confidently stating he had a plan to capture me, but another week passed without any signs of trouble.

Aric's mood had improved, though he started asking daily about when Penelope could get his mother out of Atlantis. He hadn't gone out drinking since his dinner with Penelope, but there was an irritable edge to his mood that made his positivity seem fragile.

I'd begun taking steps to move to Seattle at the end of the semester. I was going to apply for a transfer and start taking classes in the spring. My life was starting to feel exciting for the first time in almost six months, and I'd even started to see some of the perks to being a descendant of gods—like new friends and magical powers I could control. And though she returned to casual flirting after our brief kiss, I hoped Penelope might like more than friendship.

Aric and I continued our daily lessons all over town even as temperatures began hovering just above freezing and the trees started dropping their gold and yellow leaves. I didn't mind it as much as Aric or Penelope, who were used to a milder climate, and I never felt myself getting cold while I did vision practice anyway. Based on the large number of complaints from my friends, I could tell we'd have to start practicing in the van soon. In the meantime, I was glad for the excuse to finally be wearing my expensive wool wrap coat, which I hadn't had many opportunities to do while living in hiding.

Penelope had been right about my curiosity, but I still hadn't successfully used the gifts of anyone else. I had gotten close a couple times. Penelope figured it was probably a part of my gift that would take time to develop. If it ever did.

I'd started using our car rides every day to practice mind-sharing. I didn't need to do it because we were still practicing with my visions so often, but I wanted to. I wanted to make the habit something natural, reflexive. I had no intention of letting the dangers of my gift follow me to Seattle.

We were deep in the woods for practice today, miles from town, away from anyone or anything except the wildlife.

"So, I have an idea." Penelope turned to face Aric and me.

We both waited. It wouldn't be long before she continued, unprompted.

Sure enough, she did. "I think Aric should use his amplification to give you the power you need to use the other gifts."

"Uh...okay?" I said, hesitantly.

Aric shrugged. "I will try."

After some debate about who should start first and when and where we should touch, Aric and I had a plan. I sat on the blanket and focused on a time when Penelope used her gift. The specific memory didn't matter. I just needed a reminder of the blueprint of her gift in order for it to come to life within me. Maybe Aric's gift could finally give me the control of the foreign gift that had eluded me so far.

In a matter of seconds, I'd flashed on a vision and brought her gift into my body. Without me being able to turn it into something, it would just linger inside me until finally dissipating. "I'm ready," I whispered.

Aric reached out and touched me, and in that instant, I felt all of the magic inside me grow. I would have thought that increasing the magic would make it harder to wield, but it somehow made it tangible to me for the first time. I was able to coax the illusion from my center, through my mind, and in just a few moments, the gold and yellow bed of leaves around us turned into my bedroom back in Oread Basin, just as I'd envisioned it in my mind. Aric and Penelope gasped in the background, so I was pretty sure they were seeing the illusion.

Suddenly, I realized the power Aric had given me was continuing to grow even as I channeled it into the illusion. More magic flared within, throwing me wildly back into a vision.

In the next second, I was out of the vision with another gift growing inside me.

The illusion of my bedroom was expanding, becoming warped, images twisting and changing, no longer in my control, probably reacting to some part of my subconscious. I felt the new magic come to my skin and set every part of it aglow.

I could hear Penelope's voice, but the mental chaos blotted out her words. Aric had only touched me for a few seconds, but the magic just kept growing.

I was snapped into yet another vision, and back in an instant, aware long enough to watch Aric fly backward into a tree and flop to the ground in a heap.

Another vision pulled me in even as the magic from each of the others flooded out into the world around me. I was in my bedroom again, and I was standing. The carpet at my feet caught fire, and fall leaves were set aflame replacing the illusion for a moment.

For an instant I was back in my own head—fire, distorted images, groaning Aric—everything around me was in disarray and then another vision took me.

When I came back to myself, with the magic of yet another gift, I tried to focus on the tight grip of Penelope's fingers on my shoulders, tried to figure out what words she was shouting, but then she was jerking her hands away from me.

My skin felt cool and tingly. My muscles and bones suddenly ached and then the tingling became tearing. Just as my voice opened up to scream at the ripping and shifting of muscle and bone, a roar escaped my mouth instead.

The pain had snapped the magic of the illusion like a rubber band, the remains recoiling inside of me. There were still a few small fires that Penelope had stomped out, but I felt that magic retract as well. Before I had time to process what was happening with the remaining gifts inside me, I felt a shocking hot impact barrel into my furred shoulder. My muscles and bones ripped and shifted again, leaving me back in tingling skin, my shoulder throbbing and shooting waves of pain out through my body.

Aric and Penelope looked down at me, talking again. I saw both of their mouths moving, but the words couldn't reach me through some high-pitched screeching sound. And then, like a reflex, my mind moved into Penelope's.

* * * * *

I'm staring down at my body now. It's lying in a pile of leaves, blood soaking all the way through the shoulder of my pink coat. Aric stands across from me. I guess I'm in Penelope's body. The high-pitched sound has stopped, and my true body is limp on the ground, no longer being inhabited by my conscious self.

"We need to carry her out of here...get her home," my Penelope voice says.

"Fuck!" Aric responds, rubbing gingerly at a swollen bump on his head. "What the fuck just happened?"

"I don't know, Aric." My voice is a bare wire at the edge of panic. "I can keep us hidden, but we need to get away from here now," I say, glancing out into the trees around us. There's a black circle enclosed around us where the trees fade into nothingness. We're in some sort of illusion Penelope's using. I can feel it now that I am aware of it. In fact, I find that I can seize the magic. I can feel the tug of it now, pulsing through her blood, running up through the mind we're sharing, and radiating out of us into whatever I want to create. I look down at my own body and it's suddenly lying on a hospital gurney. We're in a white walled corridor, Aric and Penelope rushing along with the gurney and the bleeding body on top of it.

I realize with horror that I've just hijacked Penelope's gift. Worse than that, what I'm doing with it isn't helpful.

I ripped myself out of Penelope's head, and the screeching sound started up again. I looked up at Penelope and Aric, who both reached down, sliding their arms under me. A haze cut across my vision, I couldn't hear over the screeching. I was being stabbed in the shoulder with hot electricity, and as my body shifted from the ground, the throbbing heat redoubled. My vision went black and the sound finally cut out.

* * * * *

When I next became conscious, I was in the downstairs bedroom of our house, tucked into the small bed Hazel and Lukas had been sharing. I was stripped down to my bra and panties under the blanket.

The memory of the magic disaster came back to me all at once, and I sucked in a deep breath of dismay as I remembered the chaos I'd somehow caused. The movement in my chest from the deep inhale brought a sharp pain from my shoulder. I tried to look over at the source of the ache, but that just caused the deep stabbing to also begin throbbing.

"Be careful there," Penelope's voice came from behind me. She scooted the chair she was sitting in over until we could see each other without me having to move.

"What happened?" I croaked, voice hoarse and painful.

"What did not happen?" Aric asked, walking into the room. "You threw me into a tree," he said, pointing to the long scratches across his face and a bandage on the back of his head. "Then you tried to set fire to the forest before you turned into a bear, tried to eat Penny, and got shot by some random hunter."

"She didn't try to eat me, Aric," she reproached, giving him an exasperated look before turning her pretty goddess eyes back to me. "The entire ordeal happened in under a minute, and you were shot almost instantly after turning into a bear. The spectacle of it all must have caught the hunter's attention, and I think he saw me standing in front of a bear and thought I was getting attacked. You'd started screaming right before you shifted."

"What happened to the hunter?" I whispered. How could I have forgotten about hunting season?

"I surrounded us in illusion to hide from him, and then we carried you back to the van and took off. I lost control of my magic for a few moments before we carried you out. I don't know why, but we still escaped the situation."

I felt a knot form in my throat as I remembered why Penelope lost control of her gift. "I'm sorry," I whispered, fighting back the sting of tears trying to escape my eyes. "I took control of your gift. I was out of my mind in pain, and I didn't even realize what I'd done at first." I caught my breath, feeling fatigue just from the small amount of talk. "I stopped as soon as I realized."

"I will get you some water." Aric turned and walked out of the room.

Penelope's face was hard to read. She seemed to be guarding her emotions. "Well..." She started. "I guess that is a side to your gift nobody anticipated. I doubt you need amplifying to use it, seeing how you did it after Aric's magic finally left you." Her neutral expression broke, and a few tears leaked from her eyes. "I am so sorry I had you try that." Her lips quivered. "I did not think it through at all, and I had no idea that would happen. I am so sorry."

"None of us realized that would happen," I breathed. "And I don't like that new side of my gift. It felt so intrusive and...violating. I'm the sorry one."

"Yes, it was scary having control of my gift seized away from me for the first time in hundreds of years, but you were acting on instinct," she said. "The entire thing is my fault. I am supposed to be the experienced one...the one who helps you stay safe!"

She paused and took a long breath. "I should have known Aric wasn't ready to amplify gifts. He does not know how to regulate his power yet. I should not have had you try using gifts you don't understand. I knew you had not practiced channeling and managing excess magic. Why did I throw extra power at you?" She pressed her hand over her eyes and shook her head.

Aric came back in with the water, handing it to Penelope. "I am going to go wait on the porch for Lukas and Hazel. They should be back any minute."

Penelope helped me prop myself into a seated position. No matter how carefully I shifted, my shoulder stabbed and throbbed, causing a wave of nausea. Once I was finally settled, she held the cup up to my mouth and helped me drink.

Then I felt myself fading again, exhausted from the entire ordeal. "How long was I out? I asked.

"We've been back a couple hours," she replied. "The bullet came out of you when you shifted, but that thing was like two inches long, so you were still bleeding and torn up." She pointed at the bandage taped to my shoulder. "I pulled off your bloody clothes and cleaned you up the best I could. Now you just need time to let your healing magic work. Sleep will help."

"You know I saw Dagan walk around with a chest full of buckshot like it was nothing right after my dad shot him," I told her. "It didn't really seem to faze him."

"I'm not sure what would kill that monster," Penelope said. "By the way, I called Hazel, and she has a tonic that will cut your healing time in half."

"My sister has the best magic. Hopefully she can make me a painkiller tea too." At that, my energy was fully spent, and after Penelope helped me shift onto my back, again the blackness took me.

HELEN

Helen comes upon a boy who can't be more than eight years old crying against the front door of a hut. When she stops in front of him, I can see that he'd had a bloody nose that has since dried, leaving crusts of red behind. He's also covered in dark red and purple bruises and deep cuts all over his bare arms and neck.

"What is your name, child?" Helen says, as she walks up to him. "What is the matter?"

He sniffs and wipes the tears from under his dark brown eyes. "My...mother," he says in whimpering sobs.

"Is she inside?" she asks.

He nods and stands, taking hold of the handle on the door. He pushes inside and Helen follows him. The hut is dark, ragged curtains covering the windows, and the place is just generally cluttered and filthy. There's just the one room with a bed on one side and a tiny kitchen on the other. And on the floor between those two places, is the body of a dark-haired woman lying pale on the floor, a deep cut in her thigh and an Immortal Death Blade next to her.

The boy sobs again as they look down at the dead woman, and he leans in against Helen, hugging at her waist.

"What happened?" she asks.

"She brought the sword back after she was with one of her human men." He begins. "She was hurting me, and I grabbed it, and pointed it at her. I didn't want to hurt her, but she ran toward me. It cut her there." He points at the wound. "She fell down and shook for a long time. I could not stop the blood." There are discarded bloody rags around her injury. "And then she just stopped. I ran out for help, but I got scared. I killed her. What if the queen locks me up?"

"How about you come with me, child?" Helen asks him. "I will not tell a soul what you did here, and I have goals I believe you will be able to help me with. What do you say?"

"Really?" he asks.

"Of course, but do tell me your name."

He takes Helen's hand and follows her out of the little shack. "I am Dagan."

* * * * *

I woke long enough to realize that Helen had likely raised Dagan, the monster trying to hunt me down, but then I fell back under the stupor of medicine and pain.

* * * * *

HAZEL

I'm sitting on the same little bed in our downstairs room, but now Lukas is beside me and I'm in Hazel's body. I'm no longer feeling pain, but her heart races as she turns to face him.

"I heard back from my friend, Rose," he says softly.

"The one from the Nymph village in Nepal?"

He nodded. "She had an answer about why your tonics are not working. It is because the land here is like most land on Earth, void of Nymph magic. But the land around your village has been walked and explored by generations of Nymphs." He brushes Hazel's hair behind her ear and kisses her cheek. "Rose told me that you share your magic with the lands you interact with. So, the land around your home has been filled with magic for ages."

"All my recipes are off because there's no magic in the plants here. The magical measurements are off." She sighs. "Thank you for learning this for me."

He leans down and cups her chin in his hand gently, placing a soft kiss on her lips. "You are welcome." He kisses her again. Again, her heart picks up pace, and she presses closer to him, turning the kiss into something deeper.

"The house is empty." She stands and walks to the bedroom door, closing it and turning the lock. "And I love you, Lukas. I told my sister I was going to travel to the Nymph villages with you after we check in on Mom and Dad."

He crosses the room to meet her. His fingers lace into hers and he presses her back against the door with the front of his body. He pushes Hazel's hands against the door just above her shoulders. And then he kisses her again.

"I love you, Hazel," he whispers before picking her up as they continue kissing and he carries her to the bed.

He breaks the kiss long enough to pull off his shirt, and I can suddenly feel my real heart pounding, and not in a good way.

I realize way too late that I'm not my sister, and that I not only don't want to experience sex with Lukas, but I really, really don't want to spy on my sister with her new boyfriend. I guess I've already partially blown it on both accounts. I focus on my real body, lying in bed, healing. It doesn't help that I'm mostly undressed and in the exact same bed.

* * * * *

My eyes stayed closed as I processed my panic, but I was awake again, and Penelope must have realized that.

"Are you okay?"

I opened my eyes to find hers staring back at me from the same place she'd been before my stupid visions. "I guess, I accidentally had a couple of visions."

"It'll be okay. Try not to worry." She took my hand, the one connected to my good shoulder. Even moving the other hand still hurt me.

"Hazel might be able to make a tea for the visions." Oh gods, Hazel. I was embarrassed for myself. Best to bury the whole vision and its related feelings.

"Are you sure you can't convince your sister to come with us instead of going back to your family home?" Penelope asked.

"Oh, I'm sure." I smiled. "She's pretty set on her plans to travel the world with your brother. We'll just have to mail order our potions in the future."

Penelope smiled down at me, but there was hesitation in her eyes. "Alexa, I know I've already said it, but I am sorry for getting you hurt. We have an eternity to practice, and I thought a shortcut was a good idea. I approached this like a human, trying to get you answers fast, to avoid wasting too many years. It was silly."

"Trust me, I was right there with you," I said. "I was raised as a human, so that's the only way I know how to think."

"But I should have known better." She squeezed my hand in hers. "I have lived among humans for barely a decade in total. I lived over two hundred years on Atlantis where no one rushes around in that way, but I got so caught up." She hesitated. "I guess in my feelings for you? I had some foolish need to impress you."

My heart was racing in my own body now. I wasn't sure how to respond, I never was. She flirted and hinted and said nice things, but that was always where it stopped. Given my current pain level, I decided to just smile at her.

Besides, I was probably very interesting to her right now because of all the new magic, but the novelty would wear off and she'd be left with someone else she saw like Aric, someone else to care for. "I must just seem like a child fumbling over my gift to you."

She looked stunned, eyebrows wrinkling as her head tilted to one side. "I know I have told you this before, but I will happily reassure you. Yes, you are young. Yes, you have a lot of gift development ahead of you and will surely grow and change for a very long time. And, our people do not see age or years in the same way as humans. Age difference between adults is never a consideration for friendship or romance or love or even the resistance."

I flushed all the way into my cheeks. "What do you mean when you say your feelings for me?"

She met me with her luminous brown eyes. "I feel drawn to you. I enjoy getting to know you. I enjoy our time together. I'm excited for you to come back to Seattle with me. I find you beautiful, inside and out. And, for a few moments in the forest today, I was very frightened of losing you."

"Oh," I said. The lame reply was all that would come to me as I processed her words.

"Though you don't need to feel pressure to feel any sort of way," she said in a rush. "Time is the one thing we have plenty of to find out what kind of 'we' we're meant to be." She leaned forward and gently kissed my forehead. "Your sister should be here soon. I'm going to go check on things. Rest."

She walked out, and I nearly instantly faded right back into the darkness, feeling at peace as I eased away from my pain.

* * * * *

THERON

I'm standing. A man is standing with the metal bars of a cell gripped in large, unfamiliar hands as he gazes across the cave shaped chamber under the palace where Ambrose burned the swords. His cell is new though. As is the large portion of floor that's covered in silver metal and sapphires and rubies, the remnants of Hephaestus's murder blades.

Dagan is lifting someone up off a stone table across the room—also new. On the other side of the table in a flowing silver gown, Amara stands watch, and then follows Dagan toward me as he carries the limp pile of rags and arms and legs and tangles of matted red hair.

A tight knot takes hold in my throat—the man's throat, but he's otherwise silent and staring as they approach. Dagan shifts the bundle to free one of his hands and insert a key into the lock on the cage. When the mechanism clicks, Amara pushes the door open.

"Throw her in," she says.

Dagan complies with a smile, stepping forward and unceremoniously dropping the body to the floor. She's limp and broken, but I recognize Ivy.

I can feel the man try to swallow a sob, but it escapes in a low harsh groan through the knot in his throat. He sets his lips tight, trying for control, but his hands shake at his sides, and he has to press them against the rough fabric of his pants to steady them.

"Well, Theron," Amara says, "I have decided to overlook the annulment rules as a gift to Ivy for helping me finally learn how to fulfill those incessant prophecies in my own way. Enjoy this time together. I want you to remember that all of this…" she sweeps her hand down at Ivy "…is because you betrayed me to hide my niece's daughter. Because you thought your resistance could best me." She laughs. "And it was for nothing. The girl will be sitting where you are any day now." She turns to Dagan.

Dagan is still wearing a terrifying grin. "It is true. I have found her, and I know now how I will take her. And we will also fill the cells on either side of you with Lukas and Penelope." His grin broadens at what he's about to say. "...and Aric."

Theron's fists clench, but the rest of him stands as if made of stone, not giving anything away with his expression.

"And every one of you will pay," Amara breaks in. "But you will serve me as well." Her eyes are wide and wild. "For so long, I only borrowed gifts like Ivy's for mere months at a time, but now, I have finally discovered I simply had not gone far enough. I need only take the life magic along with one's gift to make it mine. And now, I am a healer," she says, voice shrill and manic. "And soon it will be me giving divine gifts to the children born from my chambers."

She turns and walks out of the cell. "See you soon, Theron. You will give me a gift from Poseidon's line after I have rested." She glides toward the door in the far wall and exits the chamber without another glance in his direction.

Dagan closes and locks the cell door so he can follow her out.

The room is quiet now, and Theron falls to his knees in front of Ivy, burying his face at her throat as he holds her. His chest burns, and he sobs and cries and murmurs the word 'no' over and over again.

He eventually sits up and pulls Ivy into his arms, carrying her to the back of the cell before he sinks to the floor in the corner and adjusts her so that she's lying on his lap.

Her skin is translucently pale under her dirty linens, but there's no blood or bruising or weirdly angled bones. Theron picks up Ivy's hand. There's a massive hole in her palm, still open and dripping with blood.

Theron's sobbing intensifies as he presses his face against hers.

"Ivy, please forgive me. I failed you. Gods, please forgive me." For a long time, the sobbing is too severe for words.

When it finally stops, he rubs his palms over his eyes, attempting to dry them. Then he starts to move Ivy's hair away from her face, setting it so that it falls softly onto each shoulder.

"Aric is free of his false mother at last, and you are finally free of her too, my love," he says. "I will be with you soon."

Chapter Twenty-Four

I GROANED AWAKE IN Hazel's small bed to find her sitting where Penelope had been before. She'd set three mugs on the small bedside table.

"Welcome back." She glanced at my shoulder with worried eyes. "They filled me in on your day," she sighed. "What a mess. I don't know if I can move back home if this is how you're going to spend your time. And really, Alexa, turning into a bear in a forest during hunting season?" She was trying to be funny, but I wasn't ready to see the humor in it.

"I'll be alright," I whispered. "But I need to tell you something now, before I pass out from pain or from those mugs of cure I see you've brought me. Tell Penelope for me. I don't know what to do with the information. And it's bad, Hazel."

She touched my forehead with her cool hand. "Calm down. What's going on?"

"My body seems to like having visions when I'm in pain. I guess I'm a real baby."

"What did you see?"

"Do you remember a little over a week ago when I told everyone that Dagan was making a pit stop in Atlantis with some master plan to capture us all?"

"Yeah," she said. "That hasn't seemed to amount to much though. I think he was just talking shit."

"I just had a vision from later that same day in Atlantis, and Amara killed Aric's mom...and I think his dad by now, too." I whispered as quietly as possible. "They had cells picked out for me and Aric, Penelope, Lukas. They were so confident, Hazel."

"They live essentially forever with magic from the gods. I don't think they know how to do anything except act confident. We're making it work, Lexa. We have a long-term plan that'll keep us all safe, as long as you promise not to practice nuclear magic again without proper training." She grinned at me.

"Believe me, I don't want to relive any part of that," I said. "I wish we didn't have to tell Aric what we know."

"He'll inevitably find out one way or another and we don't want him to learn that we kept it a secret. If we think he reacts poorly to bad news, think how he would react to bad news and betrayal from the people he's risked everything for."

I groaned because she was right. "Can I have my magic teas now? I'm tired of pain...and just tired." I had a moment of panic as I realized that I'd had two visions in our home, giving away our location.

I asked Hazel to pass those worries along to Penelope as well, and then she helped me drink down a swallow of healing, a swallow of dreamless-sleep, and a whole mug of pain relief. She also re-dressed the bandages covering my wound, and pressed some gauze soaked in some sort of other healing liquid between my wound and the outer bandaging. After all that was finished, I faded out, and this time, I slept in blissful nothingness.

* * * * *

By the evening of the third day after my magical explosion, I woke up feeling almost completely healed. I pulled the bandage off my shoulder to find a dark purple bruise the size of my palm, with an even darker, quarter sized bruise at the center where the bullet had gone in. I had a moment to marvel at my ability to heal a bullet wound in days. Then, with a sudden pang of sadness, I realized that Ivy could have healed it instantly. Aric's dead mother had been a healer, a resistance member, and one of my saviors. And now she was gone.

Penelope had come in soon after I'd gotten myself cleaned up and dressed. She first reassured me of her confidence that two stray visions were not going to give us away after the random map around town that we had made with my gift. She also reminded me that my intel indicated Dagan's plan for capturing us had nothing to do with Helen's maps, and that in fact, he'd hardly given the map any attention on his last visit.

"I remember. He basically called it useless," I said.

"Yes, let's just try not to let it happen again, and we should have nothing to worry about," Penelope replied.

"Did you tell him?" I shifted the conversation to Aric. "About Ivy and Theron?"

She groaned softly. "Yes." She was uncharacteristically quiet for a long moment. "He has not reacted well. In fact, he's just woken up and is planning to leave again shortly."

I stood up from the bed and stretched my arms toward the sky, feeling relief to have full range of motion again. There was no residual pain unless I pressed on the bruise. "I need to talk to him before he goes."

Penelope shrugged. "Go for it. I don't think it could get much worse."

I walked out through the kitchen and up the stairs to the room we'd shared until my shooting. Aric was fully dressed and grabbing his phone off the bedside table.

"You are alive," he said to me, eyes never leaving his screen. He didn't sound at all excited about the fact that I was okay.

"Hey, Aric…" I began lamely. "I'm really sorry—"

"Stop," he yelled, finally looking at me with his dark blue, shining eyes. "Do not say it!" He tapped on the phone screen and then held it in my face, showing me a profile picture of a pretty, dark-haired girl. "I met a new companion on this sex matcher app you showed me, and the only thing I want to think about is what she and I will do later and how much alcohol I can consume."

He turned his back on me and walked down the stairs. I followed at his heels but didn't really know what to say to him after his outburst. I hoped he just needed some time and space.

"Aric, you can't take the car again," Penelope said, as he neared the front door, car keys in hand. "You didn't get back until mid-afternoon today, and we can't be stuck out here without transportation,"

"Oh, come on!" he yelled. "Just use Ryde or rent another car. It is Friday night! I already have a sex date!"

"No, Aric," she said firmly, holding her hand out for the keys. "You can take a Ryde, and please remember the safety rules we talked about to keep Dagan from finding you."

"Ugh!" He threw the keys on the floor at Penelope's feet and walked out the front door.

"I'm sorry for that," I said.

"You didn't kill his parents," Penelope said. She was right. I wasn't sure why I'd apologized, except that I'd spent a substantial amount of time in the mind of the woman who had killed his parents. I couldn't shake the guilty feeling that came with Amara's memories.

* * * * *

That night, I went upstairs about an hour after Penelope, and when I got into our bedroom, only the bedside lamp was on. Penelope was reading, wearing a slip-like nightgown I'd never seen on her before.

"Is Aric coming back tonight?" I asked, pulling my sweats off and sliding into the bed next to her.

Penelope set her book aside. "He's sleeping over with...gods, I don't even remember the name," she sighed. "Regardless, he confirmed that he safely arrived at the house of...his date."

I hated that it was me who'd delivered the news of Aric's parents, sending him into this downward spiral. And I realized I'd been avoiding using my gift because of that fact.

As if she'd read my thoughts, Penelope asked, "When was the last time you mind shared?" She turned to face me, and I was suddenly distracted by the fact that I was alone in bed with Penelope. My heart picked up pace as the nest of butterflies inside of me stirred.

"Yesterday?" I answered, unsure because of how my recent days had blended together.

"So, you're overdue. Please, share my mind." She looked into my eyes and held my hands in hers.

I moved into her mind as we sat facing each other on the bed. I'd learned to move in and out of minds quickly, so when Penelope asked me if she could kiss me, I slipped right back into myself.

I nodded and Penelope leaned into me, brushing her fingers along my cheek as her lips touched mine. The kiss spread warmth from my lips down through the rest of my body.

"I'll mind share later," I said. Now that I was touching her again—kissing her again—I didn't want to stop and I didn't want to leave my mind while it was happening. "I want you, Penelope. I've wanted you for a long time."

She closed the distance between our lips and kissed me a second time. "And I want you, too," she whispered in a soft breath, pulling me up against her. "Can I undress you?"

I nodded.

She gripped my shirt in her fingers, and I lifted my arms so she could slip it off over my head. Then she repeated the action with her nightgown.

For a moment, her hands rested on my shoulders as she took me in. Then they trailed down the front of me and she hooked her fingers into my panties, started slipping them off of me.

I shifted so she could keep tugging the fabric down my body. My pulse racing, I felt the rhythmic beat of it between my thighs as she continued to travel over my flesh. She helped me shift my legs out of the final material between us before tossing it behind her, and then pulled the length of my upper body close against hers. Every new detail I noticed just pushed me further into ecstasy and caused my breath to catch in the pleasure of our bodies together.

Later, when she brought me to my peak, my head went fuzzy, the blood rushing through me was hot and tingling, and my body spasmed as I cried out, my mouth muffled into her shoulder.

And then we were flopped back together on the pillows, naked arms and legs twined together, breathing hard.

We passed most of the night that way, alternating between moments of bliss and blissful exhaustion. I never wanted it to end.

Eventually though, the sky began to lighten, and we reluctantly got under the blankets and held each other, falling asleep for the remainder of the early morning.

* * * * *

I was alone in bed when Hazel's call woke me up on Saturday.

"Where are you?" I asked. I knew she'd planned an early morning plant gathering outing, but it was nearly ten.

"I'm in the driveway waiting for Lukas."

It felt strange to have her calling me from just outside my window. Why hadn't she just come upstairs?

"Okay," I said. "Enjoy hiking around in close to freezing temperatures," I teased.

"I will, Alexa, because you need my help." Even through the phone, I could hear her annoyance.

"What's with you?"

"It's just..." She paused for so long that I didn't think she'd finish her sentence.

"Just what?"

"Just let me think, Alexa!" she yelled, loud enough I had to hold my phone at a distance. "I'm out here gathering shit tons of plants because I have to figure out how to make a bunch of tonics to leave with you before I can go, but my recipes still come out wrong all the time. The tea I gave you the other night was just a calming tea because I still don't even know how to make the one for dreamless sleep! And I'm still fucking up so much that I'm oversupplying every vendor contact I have." When she spoke next, her frantic tone shifted, grew a sharp edge instead. "And my sister kept the whole house up all night, so the weekend is already off to a shit start."

I felt a heat instantly roll up through me and I knew I'd turned red even though there was no one there to enjoy my embarrassment. No wonder she hadn't come upstairs.

"I'm sorry, Hazel!" I yelled back, focusing on anything but my sister overhearing my first night with Penelope. "I didn't know you were still having so many magic problems! Anyway, Lukas told you why your magic was acting up. As soon as you go back home...and to the other Nymph villages, you'll be surrounded by all that land saturated with Nymph magic again."

The line was silent.

"Hazel?"

"You weren't there..." she began, and I realized my mistake. "You spied on my private conversation? What else did you watch me do that night? Fuck, Alexa! You weren't getting enough of your own sex, so you had to steal my memories too? Stay out of my head!"

"I didn't mean to, and I left as quick as I could!" I said in a rush.

"You never mean anything, but my life is on hold so you can have your perfect fucking life, like those of us who grew up loving you were never enough."

"It's not like that! You've spent a few months feeling slightly less adequate because for once, you don't just do everything perfect the first time. That was my whole life! And it didn't matter how many times I tried. I was always inferior. Forgive me for wanting to feel like I belong for once!"

Silence again.

Finally, "I never acted like you didn't belong. That was a fucked-up thing to say."

"I'm sorry, Hazel. I know you've always been a good sister, but you'll never understand what it was like for me to grow up like that."

"I'm tired of hearing about this," she sighed. "I need to go." And she hung up.

I instantly regretted making Hazel feel like she was somehow a part of my suffering and desperately hoped she'd be willing to talk after she got back. I wasn't used to us fighting and it didn't feel good.

* * * * *

Penelope came back to bed shortly after Lukas left and we slept cuddled up together into the late afternoon. When we woke to a still empty house, we cleaned up and fed ourselves before falling back into bed together. Penelope had laughed when she learned about us waking

Hazel and told me we should take advantage of our alone time then. I wasn't about to argue.

Later that evening, we were just settling in on the couch to watch a movie together when Aric called Penelope, begging her to come pick him up from North Pole. He'd somehow gotten himself stranded in the small town thirty minutes south of Fairbanks and he couldn't get a Ryde to pick him up.

"A disappointing interruption..." Penelope said. "But I'm relieved to hear from him."

"Yeah, me too. I feel terrible for him. Maybe we can all have movie night together when you get home."

"I'll ask." She stopped to give me a kiss that left me wishing for more alone time, and then she headed for the door. "Watch something while you wait. We'll be at least an hour."

I browsed through the available options on our TV and decided to watch my favorite romantic comedy while I waited. The opening credits hadn't even finished when Penelope was back, standing in the open front door, looking at me.

"That was fast," I said, pausing the movie.

"Aric called back and told me to go home. He just scheduled another date."

"It kills me to see him self-destructing like this," I said. "Come sit with me." I patted the couch. "We can watch this or find something else."

Penelope sat down next to me and reached a hand over to pull at my shoulder, encouraging me to turn toward her, so I did. She smiled and brushed at my hair before taking hold of the back of my neck, pulling me toward her, firmly pressing our lips together.

Something felt off with her.

She reached her hands around me and pulled my body up against hers, grabbing at my legs, trying to shift me onto her lap.

Her touch was wrong. Her movements had become less fluid. She kissed me again, too aggressively. She smelled different. Her blue nail polish was gone.

And it finally hit me.

I froze, not quite settled on her lap, but she tightened her arms around me and started kissing my neck just before shifting me to my back, suddenly putting her on top of me.

This wasn't Penelope, but that meant...had Dagan finally come for me?

Before I could think of a way out of this, my attacker shoved her—his hands up under my shirt so he could play his fingers eagerly over my breasts even as I tried moving out from under him.

"Stop," I breathed.

He'd already shoved my shirt up over my stomach so he could kiss along my bare skin with Penelope's lips. He started opening the buttons on the front of my jeans and began shifting them down over my hips.

"Stop!" It came out as a yell this time.

"I've waited long enough," he growled, and then continued his efforts on my pants.

"Let me up!" I yelled and grabbed at my waistband. I tried to squirm up and out from under Penelope's form.

She—he abruptly sat up, as if he finally heard me, but then I watched in horror as Penelope's skin started to ripple.

His hands had shifted from my pants up to my shoulders, and he was gripping me painfully. Penelope's short brown curls became long and black and wispy. Her warm brown eyes darkened just as her skin lightened into a rich tan.

I finally processed how truly fucked I was just before Dagan retracted one of his hands and brought it down hard and fast on the side of my head. Everything went black.

* * * * *

DAGAN

I'm in an unfamiliar body, but it feels wrong. It's like the time Dagan had shifted into Lukas to trick Penelope. I'm mostly sure this is Dagan's body as I walk. He walks through a crowded bar with his arm around someone's waist and that someone's arm over his shoulder, leaning heavily. They pass by a laughing group of people near the building's exit, and then Dagan turns toward his companion, lips curving up into a smile.

I'm looking at Aric. I'm in a vision with Dagan and Aric. And it's recent. It's cold and dark outside.

"Hand me your phone, handsome. You said you use the Ryde app?"

I'm sure it's Dagan, but his voice is soft and high, more like a young woman's. Dagan isn't normally so short compared to Aric either, but this is why his body feels wrong. He's shifted into some woman to trick Aric.

"Yup," he says, eyes closing as he reaches into his pocket and hands over his phone.

"Thumb print please," Dagan says, pressing Aric's print against the lock on his phone. Dagan pulls up Aric's Ryde app and clicks on his last trip. It shows our address and the map leading to this bar. "Change of plans, sexy," Dagan says. "I want to bring you over to my place."

"Jur place?" he asks.

"Absolutely," Dagan continues to smile as they walk, Aric's weight still partially supported on his shoulder.

Dagan takes Aric through the parking lot to a black SUV parked off by itself. When they get to the car, he helps Aric maneuver into the passenger seat and get buckled in. Then he leans down toward Aric's feet and pulls a heavy plastic zip tie out of his jacket pocket before securing Aric's ankles together in the car. He doesn't seem to notice. Dagan stands and pulls out a second tie.

Dagan presses Aric's hands together. "Hold still," he says.

Aric complies lazily as his hands are secured together. "Kinky." He smiles before closing his eyes and rolling his head back.

Dagan walks around to the other side of the vehicle, and I feel an instant flare of magic erupting from his center and blasting out instantly through every part of his body, ending with his skin. I feel the short burst of tingling, a dull and nagging pain of shifting muscle and bone, and then it's over.

Dagan—for sure Dagan—gets into the driver's seat. "Give me just a moment to report back to your mother. She will be pleased to know you are coming home."

"Tha cow issn my m...mother," Aric says.

Dagan snaps his palm up against Aric's jaw in one quick motion. It slams his head against his window with a hard smack.

"Shut up!" Dagan says.

So, Aric has already been taken. Dagan found Aric through the MXR app, which he only had because of me. He found our house using another app on Aric's phone. Panic drives my mind, and I go searching for Hazel.

* * * * *

DAGAN

I'm Dagan in a wrong body again. He's standing in the road, watching Hazel walk toward him in the morning light, loaded up with her large camp pack and decked out in her hiking pants, cold weather shirt, and jacket layers.

"How'd you get out here already?" Hazel stops in front of Dagan. "I thought you were going to catch up after you finished talking to Penelope." She groans suddenly. "You didn't just hear me yelling at my sister for forcing us to hear her sex with your sister all night, did you?" She gestures toward our driveway, where she'd just emerged. All but the entrance is obscured by trees.

"I heard," Dagan says in Lukas's voice. And then, in one motion, he steps around her and pulls her against his body by the neck. Dagan pulls a knife off his belt and brings it to her throat with his free hand. "Stay quiet or die." He presses the knife against her skin.

Her body is trembling slightly, but she complies.

Lukas comes up the road a few minutes later. I can see the instant he processes Hazel's situation in the shock and fear and desperation rolling over his expression, but it's almost instantly washed away as his face becomes stony and unreadable.

"Stand in front of your Nymph bitch. Put your hands together behind you. You are going to let her tie you up now." Dagan hands a plastic tie to Hazel. "Do it." He presses the knife a little harder into her neck, piercing her skin and freeing a rivulet of blood.

I frantically move forward in the vision. I can't feel the panic in my own body right now, but the back of my mind is just repeating, *No...no...no...no.*

I focus on what happened next and the vision shifts until I'm driving Dagan's black SUV down the highway. I can see Denali on the horizon, and I know they're headed there, headed to the portal. To Atlantis. I glance in the rearview mirror. Lukas is in the back, lying on his face, arms and legs zip-tied behind him.

"If you shift, I kill her," Dagan says. "You hear me?"

Lukas doesn't say or do anything.

Hazel is in the passenger seat next to me, knees on the floor, face on the seat. She's tied the same way as Lukas.

Dagan's hand slides off the wheel before pulling the knife back out, and he presses the blade point straight into Hazel's shoulder, tearing a sharp cry of shock and pain from her. All this is happening while he keeps one eye on the road ahead.

"I will not shift." Lukas says.

Dagan grins and returns the knife to his belt. Then he tussles Hazel's hair with his free hand. "You are good for something, after all."

* * * * *

When my eyes opened, my arms were torqued behind me, crushed under my own weight and bound tightly in the plastic cuffs. I shifted in an attempt to stop squashing my hands, and I noticed that he hadn't bound my feet. I tried to sit up, but my head throbbed hard where he'd hit me. The pain caused me to slump back onto my hands again, squinting tightly.

"Good. You are finally awake," Dagan's voice called at me from somewhere behind my head. I could hear his shoes as he walked toward my feet.

I opened my eyes to find him staring hungrily just before he jumped back on top of me, straddling my hips, pressing my legs down easily with his weight. "You were a hard-won prize. Perhaps I will keep you when we return." He shoved a hand painfully into my hair. "You have her eyes."

I tried to buck underneath him, to get him off me, but he just reached up and slapped me hard across the face. The stinging pain of it made my breath catch.

"Be still," he hissed. "This is my right." He slapped me again before he pulled both hands back down to my still partially opened jeans.

He finished opening my buttons with one violent yank and began jerking the snug fabric toward my knees. He worked with one hand as he lowered the other over my neck and squeezed. "You are breeding age under the Queen's Laws. If I choose it, you will mother my offspring."

Bile ran up the back of my throat. This wasn't happening. This couldn't happen. I couldn't be here with him on top of me. I closed my eyes.

* * * * *

And suddenly, I'm in Dagan's body, looking down at myself. He's grabbed the waistband of my pants in both hands and has partially exposed my panties, my hips, but then I think of the shifting magic in this body. I remember the pattern of it, and it ignites inside of him as I think about it.

I can feel the shock in Dagan's body as I fuel and take hold of the magic, pressing it through every part of us, toward our skin. I don't know how to shift, but I keep thinking, "small, harmless...small and harmless..." as I pull forth more of his magic.

And then I feel muscles and bones crushing in on themselves, skin crumpling. The pain is tremendous, and my mind pulls away to avoid any more of it.

* * * * *

When I opened my eyes again, I scooted as upright as possible and brought my legs up close to me so that I could have held my knees in my hands, if they hadn't still been pinned behind me.

Dagan was now howling in pain on the floor next to me, his body twisting and writhing. His skin wasn't just shimmering or rippling, it was ripping and bleeding. Bones were shifting and ejecting themselves all over his body just to come back together and fuse in some indiscernible pattern. After just a few horrifying seconds, his howling stopped because his face had melted into the rest of his body. The ripping, bleeding, and shifting continued for a few seconds more before the surface fused together in a squelchy pink lump the size of a Labrador...minus the legs...and head.

The room became still and quiet as I stared at the Dagan lump, panting, disgusted and terrified...and sick. I leaned to the side just before I wretched up the bile that had threatened earlier. I leaned my side against the back of the couch to take the pressure off my arms and stared at the wall as I shivered, unsure what to do.

When I finally forced myself into action, fixing my pants became the top priority. I left the couch and the pile of Dagan to find something in the kitchen to free myself. I managed to get my hands on a steak knife and a pair of kitchen shears.

I cut my hands several times in my frantic attempts to work the serrated side of the knife up through the plastic tie before giving the kitchen shears a try, my breathing becoming more panicked with every passing moment. I couldn't grip the scissors right but tried to make them cut anyway.

I alternated tools, cutting my hands and back more with each attempt, all while keeping my eyes on what was left of Dagan, terrified he'd somehow repair himself again. Finally, after cutting myself more than the plastic binding, the tie had become weak enough to pry the binding apart until it snapped. I collapsed to the floor in relief, new cuts welling blood where the binding had cut in at my final push for freedom.

That was when Penelope walked back into the house. She saw me sitting on the kitchen floor, too shocked to do anything but avoid the

Dagan lump. She glanced from me to the lump and back a few times before asking, "What has happened, Alexa?"

I pointed to Dagan, looking like a giant wad of chewed gum covered in hair and other debris. "Dagan attacked me. I panicked. I mind shared and used his gift," I said dully, thinking idly that it was good I hadn't accidentally shifted into a blob when I'd done it in my own body. "I didn't mean to do that, though." I gestured at the Dagan ball again. "Is he dead? I know we're hard to kill, but..."

"I don't see how anyone could heal from such a state," Penelope said, closing the distance between us, pulling her attention away from my monstrous creation. "Are you okay?" She held a hand toward me, not touching. She knew what Dagan was like. She probably had a good idea what had happened, taking in my cut-up wrists, my throbbing face, and my generally rumpled appearance.

"I'm not." I took her reaching hand and stepped up against her, pressed my face into her shoulder and started bawling.

When the tears finally slowed enough that I could speak, I told her about my visions. Her face went still as I talked, likely coming to the same conclusion I had. We had to go to Atlantis. We had to try and save them.

Chapter Twenty-Five

AMARA

AMARA STANDS IN THE palace courtyard under the light of a full moon as it reflects off the framed map in front of her. Helen is studying a paper version spread across the tall table before them.

"We renewed our blood bond yesterday, but I no longer feel our connection. Find him!" she screams.

Helen meets Amara with stricken eyes. "I cannot sense his magic anywhere."

"He is not answering my calls through our telepathic bond." Amara's voice trembles. "What has happened to him?"

"Perhaps you should question Aric," Helen suggests.

"Perhaps," Amara mutters, and storms away from Helen, back into the palace. The vine covered doors open with a flick of her wrist, and she walks across the circular palace entry room. The front door sentry bows silently as she passes, and swings open a large iron and mahogany door before starting down a dimly lit stone stairway.

* * * * *

I woke up in Hazel's bed in the downstairs room of our house. I'd asked to sleep alone last night, unable to sleep next to Penelope after what Dagan did to me in her likeness. A sickness rose inside of me as the events of the previous evening came flooding back.

Being tied up. Him on top of me and hurting me. My terror and the horrible thing I did.

I'd thought back to that moment over and over, with no idea how I'd manipulated Dagan's gift. I could track as far as sharing his mind and tapping into his gift, but the rest of what happened seemed to be a horrid side effect of me using a gift incorrectly. It terrified me to think that I could make a gift go so wrong, and I cringed at the thought of doing that with Penelope's mind. A single dread-filled night left me completely anxious about my magic.

I sat up and stretched. Afraid or not, Penelope and I had started planning our way to Atlantis, and that plan included me using my gift to check in on Aric, Lukas, and Hazel.

After Penelope and I had processed the initial shock of what I'd done to Dagan and all our loved ones being kidnapped, Penelope put the Dagan lump into a kitchen trash bag, trying not to gag as she did so. She dragged the bag out of the house, and the whole time she worked, I was just thankful she didn't ask for my help.

In the light of a new day, I was becoming increasingly anxious about Hazel, a Nymph in the hands of those racist psychos. My gut twisted as guilt rushed in to join the anxiety; my last words to Hazel were about me feeling sorry for myself. All I cared about now was getting her back.

I needed to check on her, to see that she was still okay, but I couldn't use my gift like that again. What if I twisted someone else's magic, someone I love? I went to find Penelope, to tell her I couldn't do it. She was making toast for breakfast in the kitchen.

"I need to see Hazel, but I can't go into someone's head again," I said shakily, still feeling slightly removed from myself.

"Okay," she said softly. "But you need to eat a little first."

I sat down at the table with Penelope. I couldn't bring myself to talk as I forced down a slice of plain toast and a glass of water.

"I've eaten," I said after my last bite. "I don't want to kill anyone else with my mind."

I hated that I was a murderer now. And I hated that I couldn't look at Penelope without seeing Dagan.

"Why don't you start with some visions, to get a better sense of what has happened so far," she suggested. "Those don't have any impact on the person you see."

She was right. How hadn't I thought of something so simple?

We spent the morning recalling moments from the last couple of days. I tried to use the heads of people I didn't care about in case I struck again and turned someone else into a dead monster.

* * * * *

DAGAN

Dagan is in the silver floored cavern where Amara experiments on people, and he's staring into my sister's frightened face as she stands strapped into an X on the wall. Lukas is in an identical position next to her.

They both look haggard, but Hazel is more damaged, with a swollen eye and split lip. She's terrified and is staring into Lukas's face. I can tell, even without words, he's soothing her fear or maybe just making her feel less alone in it.

Suddenly Dagan reaches out and slaps Hazel hard across the face.

My nausea wells up again as the action strikes a memory of Dagan from last night.

"Use this one to keep Lukas in line. That is why I brought it here." Dagan squeezes Hazel's mouth hard in his grip before he turns to Amara beside him. Aric sits in a cage along the wall behind her. Across the room, he's harder to see, but he seems okay.

"You never cease to delight me, Dagan," Amara says. "You really built up to this one." She closes the distance between them and slides her bare arms up around his neck.

And then I pull myself out of the vision to avoid reliving anything sexual with Dagan ever again.

* * * * *

When I reentered my body after that vision, it took me a while to settle the queasy feeling and calm down enough to go into another.

* * * * *

DAGAN

Dagan stands on top of a huge hillside, facing two uniformed Atlantean guards. Behind them are many door-sized stone arches. All but one have mirrored surfaces. The one closest to Dagan is filled with black spruce and tundra.

Dagan twists his body around, away from the portals, and comes face to face with the light blue eyes and sandy hair of Penelope's former husband. Below them, sitting woozily, is Aric. His legs are no longer bound.

The man lifts Aric to his feet by his bound arm and attaches a small sort of body harness to Aric's lanky frame.

"Being a royal messenger suits your talents, Sebastian," says my Dagan voice with an approving tone. "You were wasted as a community merchant."

"I aim to please," Sebastian says before taking off, holding two loop handles connected to the harness on Aric.

They fly up into the sky, and in half a minute, they look like little more than a distant bird, headed toward the tallest of the hillsides on the horizon, across the valley filled with the colors of farmland and forest, market and community. Toward the palace.

Dagan turns and walks back through the arch leading to the tundra.

* * * * *

"I admit that part of me had hoped Sebastian had stopped working for Amara," Penelope had said when I'd told her about how he was part of Aric's capture. "But he always did take the path of least resistance. He only married me because I made it easy. He followed our annulment just as easily." She tried to hide it, but she seemed bothered.

"At least they're all still alive," I remarked, not feeling at all relieved. "But we need to hurry. I don't know how long they'll stay that way."

"We're leaving on the train to Denali tomorrow morning." She reached into a handbag on the table beside her and pulled out her phone. "I have our tickets." She wiggled the sleeping phone. "So, we just need to pack up the place and drop the van back at the agency."

"You're organized."

"And when we get through the portal, we will stay at the stables with Chloe." She continued. "We can plan our next move from there."

I gave a long sigh. It was the small relief of moving forward after something bad has happened. It wasn't guaranteed to make things better. Things could get worse in a hundred ways, but at least there was a small hope in having a plan.

Penelope put her hand flat on the table and reached across the space between us. She slid her fingertips toward me, stopping just before touching my folded arm. "Do you want to talk about anything?" she asked carefully.

I didn't take her offered hand and instead pulled my own tighter against myself, curling in at the shoulders. I felt ill again as I thought about everything I'd done up to this point, leading to my sister's kidnapping. How I'd been having sex as Dagan took Hazel. How Dagan had used my infatuation with Penelope to hurt me. To hurt the people I cared about.

"I can't," was all I said, eyes never meeting hers.

"Can we talk about how you used your gift?" she asked.

My mind flashed back to Dagan on top of me. My stomach twisted painfully, and I flashed to memories of Dagan's muscles and bones ripping and twisting, his blood flowing on the wrong side, his screams of pain and surprise. "I can't do that again," I breathed, my heart beating harder. "I told you I don't know how it happened. I can't risk trying anything like that again."

"Alexa, Dagan deserved whatever happened to him." She was speaking carefully again, aware she was treading on dangerous ground. "Your gift is an asset against enemies."

"He could have become a fire breathing dragon, fried me crispy and eaten me for all the control I had," I said in a rush. "That's not an asset. And I shouldn't be able to make someone's mind do that. It's wrong. It's more wrong than Amara using her gifts to torment people."

Penelope held her hands up in a sort of surrender gesture. "Okay. Okay. We don't have to go there. Just know that at least for me, I see a difference between you using a gift like that for self-defense and Amara using it to control and harm people, but we can figure something else out."

"You're worried we won't be able to save them," I said. It wasn't a question. "You think me controlling people's gifts could help, but please believe me, Penelope. It isn't the right way. It's dangerous. It's...a violation."

"I am worried, but as I said, we'll meet with the resistance and figure out what to do. Maybe we can get our hands on the Immortal Death Blade and use that somehow. Please don't feel pressured."

I laid my head down on the table and wrapped my arms around it so Penelope wouldn't see the tears leaking out of my eyes. I kept flashing on the events from my night. I kept seeing Dagan's face. Feeling his hands on me. Feeling my terror erupt fresh over and over. The horrifying memories of Dagan's death just made me afraid of myself as well. And of course, I then felt so guilty for daring to be afraid for myself when so many others had paid a greater price.

Penelope touched my forearm lightly. "I am sorry you suffer. I realized last night that I will do anything for you, and you make me feel like I can overcome anything if I am with you. You've reminded me of a bravery I thought I had lost. We can fix this, Alexa."

I sat up a little. Hearing her faith in me, her words of devotion for a total fool filled me with dread. "All I've managed to do so far is make a total mess."

"You didn't do any of what's happened."

I got up and pulled my backpack out from the closet under the stairs. "I may not have done anything yet, but I'll do whatever it takes to get our family back."

* * * * *

It took Penelope and I a few hours to get the house cleaned up and our things packed. Penelope found a small storage unit for us to keep most of our stuff since things like our technology wouldn't be functional and my extensive new wardrobe wouldn't be practical. Plus, we had to pack up all of Aric and Hazel's stuff too. Penelope prepaid the storage facility for a year.

"This can't take a year, Penelope," I'd said at that revelation. "I don't care if your people move at a slower pace or whatever."

"I promise we will rescue them at human, not Godline speed," Penelope assured me.

We packed light, each carrying some dried food and water as well as a couple changes of clothes for our hike to the portal on Denali and our walk across Atlantis.

"The weather in Atlantis is always a fairly comfortable temperature," Penelope said, as we picked clothing for the trip. "Not too hot or cold for light clothing."

"Is that just the climate or is there magic to it?"

"Magic," she said. "Speaking of magic, there will be a point on Atlantis where I can't use my illusion to hide us. Do you still have those contacts of yours?"

"Yeah, I'll pack them." I grabbed sunglasses and a baseball hat as well. I wasn't sure how helpful they'd be for a disguise in Atlantis, but they'd still be useful on our hike, if nothing else.

"I know this is a dangerous trip, but I look forward to reuniting with old friends. I've missed them," Penelope said.

"I can't believe I'm going to finally meet them," I said nervously.

"It never ceases to shock me when you talk about them as if you've never met. After talking to you about all the memories you've lived—all of my memories—it feels like you've been in my life all this time. They'll get a kick out of you."

"Great. I'm the strange girl with an entertaining gift," I muttered.

"Your gift is splendid, Alexa, but you are so much more. They will love you for your determination and loyalty." She grinned at me. "And for your wonderful sarcasm."

Chapter Twenty-Six

AFTER WE GOT TO the train station in the morning, Penelope revealed that she didn't actually have train tickets. Instead, she illusioned us onto a car full of some sort of science equipment headed for the mountain. We spent the four-hour trip to Denali balanced on seats made amongst the stacks of plastic cases and carefully wrapped equipment.

I distracted myself for a portion of the ride by checking in on Hazel, Lukas, and Aric. Not much had changed, but Hazel and Lukas were now each in their own cells next to Aric. They filled three of six cages along the side wall of the experimentation cavern. Aric's face and shirt were covered in dried blood, but he didn't have any visibly fresh wounds. Amara must have healed him. Lukas and Hazel both seem untouched since leaving Dagan's care.

I'd decided to only allow myself to check on them once a day so that I didn't drive myself mad with worry. Amara could kill any one of them at any time, and there was nothing I could do. The problem was that there would be nothing I could do once I got there either, unless we came up with a plan to overthrow an immortal queen with seemingly limitless abilities. I was hoping the resistance would have a brilliant idea of what to do, but I was skeptical. I doubted a person existed who could match and best Queen Amara in violence and power.

I also sent a carefully worded text to Mom, knowing she'd be home any day. I couldn't keep the truth from Mom and Dad, no matter how much I wanted to protect them. So, after I told them Penelope and I were going to Atlantis to save Hazel and the others, I invested just as much text begging them to stay away. The last thing I needed was to be responsible for my parents running off to die in Atlantis.

We hit a snag as we began our hike in search of the Denali portal.

"Where do we go now?" I asked Penelope, as we walked toward the mountain, away from the structures marking the train station.

"I have no idea," she said. "I never came through this portal."

"What?" I asked, panicking. "Where did you come through?"

"There is a portal in the Black Hills in the mid-west United States."

"Okay. How are we going to find this thing?"

"Follow where Dagan went, Alexa."

Of course, I could do that. I didn't want to, so I conveniently forgot that for a moment. "Fine."

The portal was hidden in some foothills, buried in the entrance to a thick stand of spruce trees. It was probably less than an hour from where we'd left the train, but trying to follow Dagan through visions with only natural landmarks proved extremely difficult. Everything looked the same, and we went in a lot of circles before we found it just after dusk, shimmering slightly in the darkening sky, like heat ripples in the air.

"This is so close to the train station," I said. "It's not even near the actual mountain. Seems like it would be easy to stumble into."

"Humans can't see or pass through a portal unassisted," Penelope said.

"Alright," I reflected. "I guess there needs to be some level of convenience."

We found ourselves preparing to enter Atlantis just after dark. Penelope had let me do most of the leg work today, so I gladly handed the responsibility baton off, letting her plan how to get us through the next steps.

"Let's do this," she said, reaching out toward me with her hand.

I'd still been avoiding her touch before this moment. I had to swallow the knot in my throat and remind myself that Penelope had never hurt me—that someone else wasn't wearing her face again, waiting to hurt me. My heart was pounding as I took her hand, but the instant our fingers touched, something inside of me eased and I settled into the comfort and connection between us.

Penelope pushed out her illusion, hiding us in her bubble of magic, and she stepped through the shimmering air, pulling me along behind her.

We came out of the portal on the top of the same hillside Dagan had been on in my vision. It was the bright daylight of late morning here in Atlantis, and I had a sneaking suspicion that Earth science didn't apply when it came to the whole day-night cycle. Now that I was in Atlantis in person, I noticed a massive mountain range filling the entire left side of the landscape. I wasn't sure how I'd missed that in all my visions.

Penelope held a finger up to her lips as she pointed toward the two guards standing on the hill with us. The closest one was only a few steps away. She gestured to the two of us and then pointed down the hillside. Then she made a motion pointing across the valley and up the hillside on the far horizon. She stabbed at the air to indicate some spot there in the distance.

I shrugged and nodded before following her as she headed for the crest of the hill. There was a wide dirt path that wandered into the valley below. We followed that for about half an hour before she said anything aloud, and we were still only about halfway down at that point. There was not another person anywhere in sight now that the guards were out of view.

Atlantis was beautiful with magic. I hadn't been able to appreciate it in my visions because I'd always been more focused on what people were doing, but now, walking with my hand in Penelope's, I saw it for the first time.

The magic was growing and twining through nearly everything around us and I suddenly understood why my parents missed working their magic here. I hoped Hazel would get a chance to see this.

"This path will converge with the wide cobbled road connecting all of Atlantis," Penelope said, breaking our long silence. "We'll follow that to the Royal Stables."

I gazed across the expanse in front of us again. "How long will that take us?"

"If our rests are short, we should arrive by tomorrow evening," she said. "The riskiest part will be passing through the Royal Community. My mother is region leader there and most of the Gifted on this side of the mountains are loyal to Amara. Even a majority of Giftless servants are loyal followers of the Queen's Laws because to get royal jobs, they need to have produced Gifted children, giving them higher status under the laws."

"Can we go around the community?"

"We could, but I am hoping to connect with what few resistance members are on this side."

I searched ahead of us for signs of the upcoming community, but the cobbled road was the lone sign of civilization on this side of the valley. We'd just entered a section of trees that were tall and branchy with teal leaves and golden flowers, but there were also a few oddly formed amber-colored trees rooted along our path. The strange smaller trees created the form of a human out of many intertwined, translucent vines.

When we passed closely by one, I reached out to touch the shiny surface and rich yellow tendrils reached out like a hand, fingers sliding up my arm.

Penelope pulled me away from the moving plant. "Be wary of nature here."

"Really?" I asked, unsure if she was joking.

She nodded. "It is mostly charming, but without the Nymphs here tending the natural elements, they have become unpredictable over time." Even though she was giving me a warning, she was smiling peacefully. It was easy to see she'd missed this place, and I could understand why.

"I can see the magic all around us," I told her.

"You can see the wild magic?"

"Well...and I can see your magic, too."

She was quiet for long enough that my skin started to flush. Maybe there was something wrong with me.

"It seems you have twin gifts...magical perception from Artemis in addition to your Apollo-given visions. Your ability to use other people's gifts makes sense now, though having more than one gift to begin with has still never happened before...it's hard not to think there is some connection to prophecy."

Hearing Penelope talk about my special gifts and that damned prophecy just made me squirm on the inside. I wanted to go back to talking about the pretty wild magic. "I thought everyone could see the magic here."

She shook her head. "I can feel my own magic, but I can't see it or anyone else's. You really are quite remarkable."

I learned that even the air here was filled with magic when I started to stumble, and a gust of wind wrapped itself around me to keep me on my feet. After that, the wind stuck with me, supporting my body so that moving took almost no effort. It was subtle enough that Penelope didn't notice anything even as she held my hand. Or maybe the wind just helped everyone here...or it was part of my Godline magic. I didn't ask.

Instead, I just enjoyed the sudden surety that the magical air would keep me from falling on my face. It was a new experience for me in nature, and I suddenly understood why Hazel had always been so confident with her own nature magic protecting her.

* * * * *

We spent the next several hours making our way down the cobbled road as it wound through the strange forest. It would have been wide enough for two cars to pass by each other, though I was fairly certain we wouldn't be seeing those around here.

As we continued through the wilds of Atlantis, the sporadic, humanoid trees of amber showed up more frequently and were joined by those of emerald and onyx and ruby and sapphire. They all were translucent and glowing with daylight–or magic.

We spotted a few very skittish silver deer grazing at bushy purple trees that had become common after we'd stopped walking downhill. Even though we were illusioned invisible, the animals skittered away any time we got within a few strides of them.

"Can they hear us?" I asked.

She nodded. "I'm only using visual illusion right now, and actually..." She took in the quiet forest around us. "I need to rein in my magic now that we're getting closer to the community. Mother can detect my illusions, which doesn't do her much good when we're invisible, but she can track our movement."

"And we don't want her to see where we're going," I finished.

Penelope broke the illusion but kept her gentle hold on my hand. Our visibility left me feeling exposed, even as the sky darkened, but Penelope's warm hand over mine was reassuring.

After another couple of hours, the night was so black, I could hardly see the forest. In my lifetime of hiking experience, that meant it was dangerous to continue, but not here, and not for me. Even without daylight to guide me, I could see the pattern of magic woven through everything around me. The trees and shrubs and earth formed with infinite tiny lights.

I suddenly understood the delight of knowing the earth wouldn't let me fall when I saw the bright lights defining the ground below my feet. As I passed over them, they shifted into stable footing to support every step I took. Plus, the little gust of wind was still there, dancing around me, eager to walk together again. It was unbelievable, even as I experienced it.

When I glanced over at Penelope, I could see the pattern of her magic as well. It wasn't active, but I could see it waiting there, see the route it would take when it was at work. Each gift had its own unique little road map inside the body, and Penelope's had become familiar, but seeing it like this—shaped with infinite specks of bright white light in my mind—was new.

Finally, when the forest began to thin and I could see the magical lights forming the shapes of fields not far in the distance, Penelope found us a lush tree to lean against for a rest.

"Let's just close our eyes a couple hours." She gave a tired sigh.

I sat against the tree next to her. "You can use my lap as a pillow if you want."

"I do want," she said with another sleepy, but happy sigh. "Thank you."

She settled her head on my legs and reached for my hand. I gave it to her again, and again it felt right. With the flashing images of Dagan no longer assaulting me in response to Penelope, my butterflies were back, fluttering contentedly inside of me.

I could feel Penelope relax and her breathing become regular as I held her there in the dark. As tired as I was, I couldn't fall asleep that fast. Instead, I looked out at the wild magic of the forest again.

I noticed that it only differed from Penelope's magic in shape and in the bright yellow-green specks that formed them. This side of my gift was perfect. It felt easy, as if I were being welcomed home, and the magic was like pulling on a familiar comfy sweater.

And finally, I forced myself out of the pleasant thoughts of my new gift and shifted my attention to the reason we were here. Hazel. I needed to know how she was. And I needed to drain off some of my excess magic to avoid an accidental vision. Apparently, Helen's magic sensing gift was amplified here. I could totally believe this after my own magical awakening.

But even knowing all that, Hazel's words echoed in my memory. "Stay out of my head!" Some of her last words to me.

I could respect my sister's wishes. And I didn't want to risk mind-sharing with anyone I cared about, anyway. I searched for Amara's mind instead.

* * * * *

In the next moment, I recognize the familiar sensation of losing touch with my true body and settling into the shape and feel of the body connected to the mind I'm now sharing. I instantly recognize the feel of Amara's body, and even the feel of her perpetually intricate garments, layered and braided, but still light and revealing, baring my shoulders—her shoulders. The entire forest green skirt is made of thousands of floor length, yarn thin, silk braids, shifting around her movements. And she is moving, stepping forward to stand over a trembling and screaming Aric, reaching one heeled foot and leg through the tendrils of her skirt to kick him over so that he's on his back, staring up at her—at me, eyes filled with terror.

"Tell me." Amara spits the words at him. "How did she kill my best hunter?"

"I told you...I do not know." He's cringing as he speaks.

The magic in this body roars to life, and I realize it's been active this whole time. I feel the pattern of it, feel the unique path that it travels, making it like a fingerprint for Amara's gift. I don't know how, but I know I could take over this magic right now if I were willing to risk it. I could make it do what I tell it to do instead of letting Amara use it to punish and torture. The problem is that I have no idea how to use Amara's magic, and me taking it over could result in killing Aric.

I continue to study the magic instead of reaching out to control it. As I do, I realize I can see many magical patterns inside Amara. They're all the same bright white as Penelope's when I visualize them, but one pattern after another is layered within Amara's body. I can't tell them apart, except for her own gift, which is brighter than the rest, and flowing along its routes, but I know these other patterns are the gifts she's stolen. Ivy and Theron's gifts are in here somewhere. Others too, all lives lost so that Amara can hoard power until she has every Olympian line inside of her.

I realize with horror that while I'm mesmerizing myself with the pretty lights of magic inside Amara, the gift she's using, her gift, is slashing out of this body and down into Aric. I can feel it slice into him and take hold, making him rise, making him grab the bars on his cell wall, making him slam his face into the metal rods.

"Please, Mother," he gasps. "Please stop. I do not know how she killed him. I do not know her gift."

"Do not call me Mother," she hisses at him. "You are just the unwanted orphan of two dead traitors. You proved you were a born traitor when you betrayed my hunter and hid that pathetic girl from me. You forsake me still, as you sit there lying to me. I know you did not spend months with that girl without learning what she can do."

She pauses until her heart rate slows, and her throat softens before she next speaks, making the words come out gentler. "Now tell me what her gift does...Son. Prove to me that you deserve my forgiveness. As my son, you will never want for a thing. You will have only the best jobs. Penny will finally be the bride you have waited for."

Amara closes the distance between them in a stride but doesn't touch him. Instead, her magic reaches out and very gently coils around his wrists. It tugs at him, encouraging him to turn toward her. "I know your gift now, Son. Your beautiful, perfect gift. You will carry my blood for a few months, so I can make you feel better after these punishments, but I will not share blood with you again if you remain uncooperative. I do not like using those human needles and tubes to give my blood. I cannot heal you through touch, so without my blood, your punishments go unhealed," she says. "You have as long as this blood lasts to come to your senses. In fact..." She turns and walks out of the cell, slamming the gate behind her, magic reaching out and turning the lock until a loud clack echoes in the silent room. "You can go unhealed now. A taste of what will come if you do not tell me everything I want to know."

She watches him through the gate as he slides down to the floor and wraps his arms around his knees. Hazel reaches through the bars separating their cells and rests her hand on his shoulder.

"One more thing, Aric," Amara says, voice tight and angry again. "If you are not my loyal son, I might as well stop my search for another gift of your line. If you are not my son...if you are indeed a traitor...you are more use to me dead."

Amara shifts to the front of Hazel's cell, and her magic lashes out, slamming into Hazel's chest so that she's knocked away from Aric. She smacks hard into the back wall of her cell, and groans as she sits back up.

"And you!" Amara yells. "As soon as I get the final Olympian line gifts, you will serve as my first test subject. You will help me learn how to use my new gifts as one. You will be the first sacrifice for the science of bringing back our immortality." Amara wraps her magic around Hazel's throat and drags her to her knees before hauling her across the ground to crash into the bars between us—between them. "And keep your filthy hands off my son. Lukas will be the last of our people that you spoil." Without a glance at Lukas in his cell next to Hazel, Amara walks toward the exit of the cavern.

* * * * *

I pulled myself back into my own mind, my own body. I shuddered as I remembered dragging Hazel into the metal bars, hurting her just for being kind.

And even after crossing through a magical portal, my guilt found me. Hazel had been nothing but kind and loving my entire life, but she was right. I had acted selfishly.

I'd been so selfish, trying to chase my life, no matter the cost. I'd ignored Hazel's magical problems while expecting her to drop her life and help me with mine. And even when she did all that for me, I'd insisted on trying online dating to lick my ex-girlfriend wounds. Aric had downloaded that stupid MXR app and been caught because of me. Hazel and Lukas had been taken because of me.

Now the evil queen had my sister and planned to murder her for science, and I might never get a chance to tell her and show her how much I love her.

* * * * *

Penelope and I woke with the sun on the next day, and though I'd barely slept, we were walking hand in hand again in time to finish watching it pop over the horizon.

"Amara is torturing Aric for information about me," I told her. "She's threatened to stop healing him...actually she threatened to kill him for his gift like his parents. What is his gift line?"

"Theron is gone as well, then." Penelope's hand became tense in mine. "Aric's is an Athena-given gift," she said quietly. "We need to get him out before she kills him."

"We need to save them all."

"But I worry about losing you just as much."

"Why? If anyone, it should be me in Amara's cells. No one else would be at risk if I had just let Dagan take me in Oread Basin."

"I cannot agree with that." She bit her lip. "We need to save them without putting you in danger."

"I told you I'd risk anything to get them back. If that means risking my life, I'm okay with that."

"But we can find a better way," she said.

"Whatever we do, we need to hurry."

Chapter Twenty-Seven

WE REACHED THE OUTSKIRTS of Helen's community after a few hours of walking, making our way along the cobbled path that led between well-tended crop lands. As we approached the heart of the Royal Community, I started seeing the magical patterns of more and more people in the distance. They were so far away that I only saw the outlines of bright light forming the basic shapes of people, and I added them to the magical landscape.

Before we got close enough to actually see other people, Penelope pulled us into a small livestock barn.

"I can glamour myself unrecognizable, but I can't extend my magic to you without Helen sensing it." She'd set her pack on the straw at her feet and was digging through her clothing. "Your clothes draw too much attention. Human clothes here are either considered bold fashion or trashy. Either way, you don't wear them if you don't want everyone staring."

She handed me a small bundle of silky blue fabric. "It's the only Atlantean clothing I have with me."

I stripped down and changed into the dress, a simple blue gown that clung lightly through my middle, but otherwise fell airily to my feet. It was the nicest thing I'd ever worn on this body.

"You're beautiful. But you'll need to put in your contacts to appear Giftless. No one outside the royal family has eyes quite like yours."

I blushed, and having so much of my emotion warmed skin exposed caused me to feel even more uncomfortable, but I set to work on the task of my contacts. The sunglasses and hat suddenly made no sense with my disguise.

When I finally succeeded in turning my eyes brown, they were so dry I needed to close them for a few minutes.

"I'm going to check on Hazel," I said, as I carefully sat down against the barn wall, straw poking through the thin fabric of my dress.

* * * * *

When I slip into Amara's mind, I'm standing beside Helen, examining the map of Atlantis, the road from the Arches. It is the path Penelope and I have been taking.

"They are in Atlantis, my queen. Soon you will have access to whatever gifts are hidden in Alexa and the ultimate leverage over Irene."

My chest...Amara's chest, tightens as her pulse picks up, but when she speaks, the words give none of it away—cold as ever. "Alexa has already murdered my lover. My best hunter. I will not risk anyone else before I know more, and I cannot make sense of our prisoners' thoughts when I try to listen in."

"That gift would be easier for you to master if you were willing to take it from Melody permanently. If you remain unwilling to do that, then torture the false prince again," Helen says. "I only ever advised you take him in the first place to help control the resistance encroaching on this palace, but you have eliminated Ivy and Theron. The boy is disposable now, my queen."

"I did not like doing that, Helen," Amara says, heart still racing. "I claimed that child as mine."

"I warned you about getting too close with the boy."

"There must be an alternative!" Amara yells. "I should not be wasting my time on these children when I am so close with my experiments." Her voice softens. "Thanks to your faithful mentorship these past few centuries."

"Then trust my advice now, my queen. These children have become dangerous. Alexa is dangerous. Remember that Cassandra's prophecies seem to refer to that child. Remember what prophecies have done to you before."

"I will never forget that, Helen." Her voice is dangerously quiet, but then Amara lowers her eyes from Helen's in a minute bow. "Advise my actions."

* * * * *

I pulled out of Amara's mind, more anxious to see Hazel than ever after hearing so much talk about torturing and killing the people I cared about.

I couldn't make Amara go check on my sister, and frankly, I'd rather she just forgot about them all together. So, I decided to mindshare with Hazel.

"Stay out of my head!" Her words haunted me.

But she was the only one without a Godline gift, which meant I couldn't accidentally kill her. I had to trust she'd forgive me this time.

When I found Hazel's mind, she was sitting in her cell. Through her eyes, I was able to spot Aric and Lukas, but they weren't talking. For the first time, I noticed the magic inside of Hazel. It wasn't bright white or moving in a unique pattern like in the Gifted. It was a luminous yellow-green like the wild magic in the plants, the earth, the air. It made up her essence in the same way it did in nature. It was beautiful, and I wondered if Hazel could feel her magic here in Atlantis.

* * * * *

When I opened my eyes, Penelope was holding a golden apple out for me. Even from a foot away, the smell was irresistible.

"I'm tired of sustaining myself on tiny, wrapped energy bars," she said. "These are magic apples designed by Nymphs long ago. You could live off of nothing else." She bit into her own apple.

"Did you just get this from the purple tree orchard?" I asked, biting into mine. It was sweet and flavorful and the most perfect food I'd ever tasted.

She nodded and then dug into her bag again, handing me a soft leather satchel and her ballet flats. "You can't carry your backpack or wear those hiking boots with that gown." She smiled. "Pack what you can in the shoulder bag, and I'll take the rest of your stuff."

After I changed shoes and transferred everything but my hiking boots to my new bag, I stood up to give my extras to Penelope. She'd become a male version of herself, glamoured to wear a navy-blue button up shirt tucked into brown pants. The fabrics weren't the shimmering silks often seen in the palace, but they still appeared to be high quality. They are a good match for my dress.

She offered her elbow to me, and I hooked my arm through it so that we could walk holding each other.

"People will see a Gifted merchant and his beautiful Giftless wife," Penelope said. "But stay near me. Giftless dressed like you are typically attached to a Gifted spouse."

We followed the road through the orchard and then took the left fork when it split at the community garden.

"We'll go through the market," Penelope said. "It'll give us a chance to find resistance members."

To enter the market, we passed through an expansive building constructed in the ancient Greek style with circular columns forming the perimeter. People milled around inside or sat on the many available benches, chatting happily and drinking from golden cups.

Penelope noticed me looking around curiously. "Every community has a service exchange building like this at the entrance to their market. It's run by someone Gifted who can enforce contracts, but it's the many Giftless assistants that keep it all running."

"I have no idea what any of that means."

"We don't use money," she told me. "People who want to go to market register their gift and other talents or skills with the community gift exchange and are given a magical card that tracks what they trade for in market. The cards adjust what they will allow you to trade for based on what you have to offer, but vendors are usually willing to haggle on side deals as well."

After we exited the back of the building, we walked down several steps to reach the road. The market sprawled before us.

On the side of the road that ran along the community garden, the vendor stalls were all made of permanent stone beams and shaded with those shimmering Atlantean fabrics. Most of the vendors wore clothing made from the high quality, richly colored material that seemed common on anyone who wasn't a ruler or a servant. They were the same type Penelope and I were wearing.

The vendors on the opposite side used homemade portable tents and metal framed pop-ups with green or blue canvas roofs. They looked like the kind that could be found at stores on Earth. Some of the vendors were also dressed in the simple, well-made fabrics, but many others were in a strange mixture of clothes that might be found on Earth.

Penelope told me that the garden side of the market was reserved for local residents of the Royal Community and the other side was left open for Godline traveling from the Distant Regions.

I did notice the numerous black and white clad guards peppered through the crowd, and it reminded me how tight Amara's grip was on these people. And also, that I'd better be careful not to get noticed.

"We can only window shop since we can't register at the exchange," Penelope said, leading me deeper into the market.

Between the human clothing being worn and the sampling of Earth products being sold by the visiting vendors, the market represented a curious blend of human fads and magic. And though Penelope told me that the ruling members of the Godline looked down on everything human, I saw more than one royally clad person surreptitiously talking to a visiting vendor in a Hawaiian shirt, before tucking a polaroid camera into their bag and hurrying away.

I watched the saleswoman from a tent filled with fine fabrics approach the vendor of a corn-like food and haggle with him for a set of rubber boots and an umbrella.

"I will imbue one garment's worth of fabric with sizing magic in exchange for these trinkets." she said. She looked strange standing there in her flowing red silks, holding a pair of teal boots covered in unicorns.

"You ask for two of my treasures. I want two self-sizing garments, already made," he told her.

We walked on before I could hear their agreed upon terms, but they must have settled on something because the next time I glanced over at the fabric tent, the woman was sitting under the shade of her new rainbow umbrella.

"How do they get all this stuff from Earth?" I asked, as I watched someone buy a plastic kayak from a man in a cowboy hat and poodle skirt.

"I'm pretty sure every merchant or farmer who's been given a pass to Earth for work purposes has loaded up on any human merchandise they can get their hands on." Then Penelope lowered her already low voice. "But there are rumors that some of the region leaders who travel have created a black market for certain high end human items."

"What counts as high end?" I asked.

"Good question," she laughed. "I heard one region leader had someone with a sizing gift bring a BMW through one of the arches for her. They basically spend their time one-upping each other and then hiding their bounty so they don't have to admit they would ever own human stuff."

I gave her an amused smile. "How do these idiots even afford a game like that without using money?"

"Rumor also says Queen Amara has Godline CEOs running major companies all over the world. I guess there's money to be had by those in the right circles." The Atlantean tech company in California was only one of many human assets in Amara's control.

Penelope suddenly gasped her illusioned low voice and then an exuberant smile spread across her face. She pulled me through the crowd a little faster until we were walking right behind two people dressed in palace guard uniforms.

I studied the magic inside of them. One had the bright white gift magic patterned throughout his body, the gift's route mapped in its unique path, constantly flowing. The other man's magic was also bright white, but it didn't travel in any sort of pattern. Like Hazel, it simply filled his entire form, made up his essence. Somehow, I knew he was Giftless, but still filled with some sort of magic. Maybe it was the life magic that keeps us all ageless until someone turns us into a gory meatball.

"Hello, boys," she said to the back of their heads. The short style of their dark hair was identical.

Both guards turned around and looked at us. The Gifted one met me with confused, glowing brown eyes. He almost seemed apologetic because he clearly couldn't place us. The one without the gift pattern gave off a feeling of annoyance with his amber eyes, which were pretty, but without much of the unnatural light behind them.

As I watched her, Penelope's face rippled from the male version of herself to her true form and then quickly back again.

"Penelope?" the Gifted one whispered, delighted.

"What in Hades are you doing here, Pen?" The Giftless one's face was covered in worried shock.

"You rebel." The Gifted one was shaking his head and smiling. "But Matthew is correct. What are you doing here, Penny?"

She took a few moments to make sure the crowd was still ignoring us for more interesting things. "We're here to save my brother, my adopted son, and her sister," she said, aiming her thumb in my direction.

They both just stared at us, eyebrows raised.

"By the way," Penelope said. "Meet our missing princess."

She pulled me closer with the arm I was holding and placed a gentle kiss on my cheek, which sent a wave of warm pleasure through my nest of butterflies. "This is Alexa. She's Irene and Damian's daughter."

The Gifted guard reached out and offered me a hand. When I took it, he shocked me by kissing it rather than the handshake I'd been expecting. I tried to adjust my reaction, but I'd already made the whole exchange awkward.

"I am Mica," he said. "And this is Matthew." He gestured toward his companion.

"They are resistance," Penelope whispered into my ear before pressing another soft kiss onto my cheek.

Even in the middle of a magical market, Penelope's careful kisses had made my skin flush, and I focused on the scene around me for a minute, trying to find my head again and checking to make sure nobody was too interested in the four of us.

"We should move amongst the stalls more," Matthew said, reading my action. "We want to blend in."

We walked over to a stall with a vendor dressed in hardy brown fabrics, sunglasses, and a fanny pack. She was talking to a customer for a moment before she went into a small pen behind her tent and trotted out a plump pig. She then gave a silver tray to the customer to hold and pressed a hand to the animal. I watched in shock as the pig became fit and lean while the tray filled with fresh cuts of meat. The vendor led the animal back into its enclosure and gave it a few affectionate pats on the rump before returning to wrap up the customer's purchase.

"We're headed to the stables." Penelope's voice pulled me back. "I'm getting word to who I can—we gather tomorrow to come up with a plan." Her voice lowered, and she leaned toward the men. "We need to save our family from the experimentation room in the palace."

"Penny," Mica said under his breath. "No one outside of the queen, Helen, and Dagan knows a thing about what happens in there...but what we do know is that nobody leaves that room alive."

"Amara is killing Gifted Godline to take their gifts," Penelope told them. "So, we are in something of a hurry."

"That is news," Matthew said carefully, enunciating each word through gritted teeth. He reflexively grabbed at Mica's hand.

Mica jumped and took a step away from Matthew. Matthew curled his hand into a fist and rested it at his side. A crease gathered his brows together as he looked intently into Mica's eyes, and the two of them exchanged something silent.

"I will be okay," Mica reassured.

"You two must still hide your love, then?" Penelope asked, glancing between them.

"We do not want to give her an excuse to be cruel," Mica replied. "We still follow all of her laws, but her moods often do not consider reason."

"What is your gift line?" I asked Mica.

"My speed is a Poseidon-given gift," he said.

"She already has your line." Penelope lowered her voice yet again. "She killed Theron for his gift."

Mica and Matthew's eyes met silently, again participating in some unspoken exchange.

"He is gone, then," Mica said finally. "We have not seen him in weeks, but the queen has announced no deaths. Just as she has not revealed herself to have any new gifts."

"I believe she is waiting until she has all twelve so that she can say her work is meant to fulfill the prophecy and save us all. It would justify everything she's been doing in her eyes," Penelope said.

"That sounds likely," Matthew said. "What of Ivy?" His words were hesitant.

Penelope had clearly been devastated when I'd revealed that news, but she'd been distracted trying to help Aric through it. Now, in the presence of longtime friends, I could tell she was struggling with her composure.

I leaned in toward her ear and whispered, "I'll give you a moment with your friends. I promise to stay close—window shop right over there." I gestured at the booths nearest us.

I did want to give her space, but the seedling of a plan had also started forming in my mind. What if I could somehow save our loved ones without risking Penelope or anyone else? Maybe browsing the market would help me come up with an idea of how to make that happen.

"Thank you," she said. And since I was already turned toward her, she kissed me on the lips. "I'll just be a minute."

I walked a few booths down until I saw a large painting of one of the humanoid shaped amber trees that I'd seen on our walk here.

When I moved closer, a vendor in a white tuxedo stepped up to me with a smile. "I see the Modern Ambrosia has caught your eye." He gestured at several bottles in front of the sign.

"What is it?" I asked, hoping my ignorance wasn't giving me away.

Luckily the vendor seemed delighted at the chance to launch into a speech heavy sale, not that I had a way to purchase his wares.

"Modern Ambrosia is tapped from Gem trees." He pointed at the painting. "Which only form when the magic of many Nymphs have primed the earth. With the Nymphs all gone now, this treasure is in short supply."

"But what does it do?"

"What doesn't it do?" he yelled happily. "It is pure, wild magic after all!" He looked up at my eyes and then did a slow check of my dress from top to bottom before catching sight of Penelope, still talking to

Mica and Matthew in the middle of the wide road. "Someone like you could use it to fit in at the Gifted events your husband surely brings you to. With your beauty, all you need is a little magic."

Even though I wasn't really Giftless, his condescending sales tactic ruffled me, and I moved on, browsing the other booths in the area until I saw a sign reading, "Imported Nymph Potions." I stepped over and read the labels on the small dark bottles, which revealed a wide variety of magic, some that my own mother had done for me and some new.

All this magic could be the extra help I needed to keep Penelope out of danger and rescue our family on my own. Then I felt stupid because if these Nymph potions for sale at the market could stop Amara, we wouldn't be in this mess.

Just as I was walking away, the vendor spoke up. "My Nymph potions do work, if you were in need of something."

She was wearing a beige tunic dress and smiling placidly. Most of her booth was filled with a fruit that looked a lot like grapes, except for their star shape.

"I don't..." Maybe I could keep Penelope safe. "I don't have one of those cards, but I have things to trade."

I reached into my bag and pulled out my sunglasses, happy to see the vendor's light blue eyes fill with delight.

"Would you trade me for those two?" I pointed at bottles labeled Healing and Invisibility and then waggled the sunglasses in the air.

"Healing is my most popular potion since Ivy has stopped leaving the palace. The dark spectacles will only get you the healing potion."

I didn't have the heart to tell her Ivy was never coming back and pulled out my black hat instead.

"That will get you the other bottle," she said.

I handed over the glasses and hat and tucked the bottles into my bag.

"If you do not wish to be nude in order to be invisible, you will need this." She pulled a small plastic wrapped poncho out from under the shelf. "You can dip it in the potion and cover your clothing with it. I hear it is used in a popular game among the younger generation."

I reached for the poncho, but she pulled it out of my reach.

"What else do you have to trade?"

"Nothing. Well, actually..." I reached in and pulled out a few sets of contacts. "These change your eye color."

She scrutinized the little foil packets suspiciously and started shaking her head. "What is that nonsense?"

I leaned in close to her and shifted my own contact slightly, so it slipped off my glowing green iris for a moment. She stood back, eyes wide and her smile growing until there was no hiding her excitement. She handed the poncho over for the lenses and I headed back toward Penelope.

She'd just been looking around for me when I reached her.

"Mica and Matthew had to leave for their shift at the palace." Penelope hooked our arms together again. She returned to the task of escorting me through the crowd while keeping a lookout for resistance members, but we didn't meet anyone else before reaching the end of the market.

We followed the cobbled road again, which continued uphill toward the palace in the distance, but after another half hour of walking, we left the road to pass through a carved cedar gate into a pasture. The grassy expanse around the barn was filled with horses. Some were grazing, others dozing, and a few young ones running their hearts out, zipping in front of us in an effort to claim some extra attention. We reached the stables and walked through the double doors at the center of the building.

Chapter Twenty-Eight

WE STEPPED INTO A familiar wide hall filled with rooms and stalls, except this time there was a woman halfway down sitting on a white horse.

Penelope called to her across the barn. "Chloe!"

She was *the* Chloe. The one from my vision practice. The one who I had witnessed kissing Penelope. I suddenly felt self-conscious. Who was I compared to this beautiful and talented longtime lover of Penelope?

Chloe turned and clopped over, looking down at us from the horse's back, godlike in the glow of her gift. Her bright white pattern moved in a series of swirls throughout her body, perfecting the well-defined muscles of her slender brown arms and giving her a golden hue. Everything from the sleeveless green blouse tucked into her breeches to the dark golden bun pinned under her helmet was flawless.

"Penelope!" she said, delightedly. "And who is this?" she asked me.

"This is Alexa, Irene's daughter, and we're hoping you can hide us here while we work on a rescue."

"Oh? Let me put Goldie away, and we can talk upstairs. I will warn the stallions that we are harboring fugitives so they can...peel their eyes."

Penelope burst out laughing. "It's 'keep their eyes peeled.' Still butchering human idioms, I see." She paused. "Actually, do you think I could ask them to bring Damian here for a meeting tomorrow after sunset? And Irene?" Penelope asked.

"They can get word to Damian, for sure," Chloe said. "Amara is keeping Irene close these days, but I can tell her when I go to work at the palace."

She turned around, returning to the place in the barn she'd been when we entered. "Alexa can help me put Goldie away while you talk to the boys," she told Penelope.

I stopped next to Chloe and her horse, unsure of what she wanted me to do as Penelope walked toward the back of the barn.

Chloe leaned forward and clucked twice as she tapped her finger on Goldie's shoulder. Her horse drew her hooves together and folded at the knees, lowering to the floor on her front half, and then settled down with her hind end. Then Chloe pulled her wheelchair next to her and unclipped a belt from around each of her thighs before shifting from her horse into her chair.

"Up, Goldie," Chloe told the horse, who got back to her feet, standing just as quietly as she'd lain on the floor. "Brushes are over there." She pointed into an alcove behind me. Then she began unbuckling the girth from the saddle so she could slide it off the horse.

I pulled a bumpy rubber curry comb and began working on the horse's sides in soft circles, loosening dirt and sweat from the hair. Chloe had replaced the animal's bridle with a soft halter before joining me with a stiff bristled brush of her own. She worked behind me to remove the hair that I'd loosened.

A few minutes later, she led Goldie into a nearby stall and headed toward the end where Penelope had disappeared. "She's been wrapped up into some ridiculous conversation with Xanthus, no doubt," she said affectionately.

Again, I had a moment of insecurity. Would Chloe expect to pick back up some sort of relationship with Penelope? What was I to Penelope anyway? I pushed the thoughts away as we moved toward the back of the barn.

Penelope smiled at us as we approached her and the black stallions. "Balius reminded me that there are cliffside windows that access the breeding chambers," she said. "It could be a way in."

"I reminded him of those windows just the other day," Xanthus piped in.

"Of course, you did, brother," Balius replied, pinning his ears in annoyance. "Xanthus will go find Damian. I could certainly use some quiet."

"And I finally get a real mission!" Xanthus nickered, shaking his head excitedly.

"Do not act conspicuously, Xanthus," Chloe said. "Remember that Damian lives in hiding from the queen."

"Of course, Love." He shook his head and reared slightly. Then he jumped over the half-door of his stall, hovered over our heads for a moment, galloped back through the barn, reared up and kicked the double doors open, breaking the latch, before he jumped up into the sky and out of sight.

"I could have opened that for you!" Chloe called after him, but then she turned back to us with a shrug. "More to keep the stable hands busy."

Balius closed his eyes and lowered his head. "Just humiliating," he groaned.

Chloe laughed and turned toward the center of the barn again. "Get some rest, old man," she said. Then she led us through a hallway just past the section filled with horse stalls. It led to a wide stone ramp that stretched the length of the barn once in each direction. It was a beautiful white stone, like marble or something. It ended at an oversized door that opened as she approached. When she got to the threshold, she pressed a hand against the door frame. "Press your hand here," she said. "I will tell the door to recognize you."

That was fascinating. Penelope and I did as she asked before following her into a wide-open room. It was a large version of what you'd find in a family home, except everything in the room was richly adorned, intricate, and made from expensive materials. "My room is through there." She pointed to French doors on the far side of the living space. "There are four spare rooms to choose from back there." She pointed to a wide hall behind us.

"This place is huge," I said before I could stop myself.

"It is." Chloe smiled. "There are even more rooms downstairs with bunks for stable workers, but the rooms up here are reserved for visiting region leaders...occasionally, if they are not invited to stay in the palace." She sucked in a quick breath. "I am sorry. You are from Earth, this is probably overwhelming. Come in. Let us sit." She led us into a sitting area with four long couches facing each other. The floors were the same stone as the ramp, but there was a large rug in the space between the couches. Chloe shifted onto the end of one couch and patted the corner on its neighbor.

Penelope took my hand, and pulled me over to sit with her, facing Chloe. "Alexa is actually more familiar with our world than you'd expect." She grinned and bumped her shoulder into mine lightly. "Isn't that right?" She'd kept my hand in hers between us and gently squeezed my fingers.

"I have visions," I told Chloe. "And can do some other stuff."

"Intriguing. Tell me everything. But first, are you hungry?"

"Starving," I said, and at that moment I realized just how famished I was. As nutritious as that apple supposedly was, I hadn't eaten since.

Chloe made a variety of finger foods for us to eat while we talked. I'd had to ask about the kitchen that spanned a full wall of the room first, though. There was a stone sink with water that came out when you reached under it, which turned out to be magic, not technology, in that case.

Most of the buildings in Atlantis, Penelope told me, had been made by people with gifts for creating things. The homes cleaned themselves and they responded to the occupants' needs. Supposedly the buildings on this side of the mountains had all incorporated some technology, though it was hidden with magic so no one had to admit to using anything human.

At that revelation, Chloe had pulled out a blender and plugged it into an outlet on the counter that only appeared when she held the cord up to it. She pulled a variety of unrecognizable fruits from a bowl on her table including the star shaped grapes, making us all the most delicious smoothies I'd ever tasted.

We spent the afternoon snacking and telling Chloe what we knew, and what we were trying to do. It turned out that she hadn't known any more about what was going on under the palace than Mica and Matthew had...outside of the breeding chambers, anyway. It seemed that even the resistance members didn't know the extent of how horrible their queen was. I'd begun to understand the value of my being able to see what Amara was doing.

Finally, after the sun had set and darkness was pressed against the tall windows spaced around the room, Chloe had to get ready for work in the breeding chambers. The idea made me cringe, but I tried not to show that since I knew she didn't do that job voluntarily.

"I usually get home after midnight, so don't worry about waiting up. We can have breakfast together," she said before heading into her bedroom.

"Would you like to share a room?" Penelope stood up from the couch.

The idea of sharing a bed with Penelope here caused a flurry of unwanted butterflies. I needed to stay focused on Hazel right now. Not on Penelope, who even now caused goosebumps to raise on my arms as her fingers brushed down the skin of my shoulder. It didn't help that I had so much skin exposed in Penelope's dress. I tensed in the confusion of my feelings. First, I was jealous of Chloe. Now, I was afraid to be with Penelope.

"Would it be okay if we stayed in our own rooms?" I asked, taking her hand. "I feel so guilty about the idea of lying with you when my sister is in a cage."

"I will miss you." She stepped in and slid her arms around my waist, the thin layer of silk barely separating our skin. "But I understand."

I shivered and kissed her softly. "Thank you."

She held the kiss for a moment longer before gently pulling my bottom lip between hers. It was nearly too much for me and I almost followed her to bed right then.

"Goodnight, Alexa." She headed into the first room on the left in the hall of guest rooms.

After Penelope disappeared into her room, I peeked into the others. They all had giant beds with soft, clean linens and large stone tubs built into the floor, already filled with hot water. I was also surprised to learn that each room had its own uncharacteristically modern bathroom.

There were even massive wardrobes in every room, filled with clothing of all styles. The clothing was bright with the white magic I'd noticed embedded into all the other parts of the house. I slipped out of Penelope's silk and into a tunic when I was exploring the last room. The top had been quite large, but it rippled and adjusted to fit me comfortably as I pulled it on. Convenient.

The only difference in the rooms was the color scheme. I was currently in a room done in shades of green. Green stones covered the floor, green clothing inside the wardrobe, the bedding was green, and even the art on the wall featured the color. The other rooms had been red and yellow in their coloring. I decided to stay in the green room, dropping my backpack and Penelope's leather bag on a bench next to the wardrobe.

I headed back out for a snack before calling it a night. I wanted to talk those flying stallions into taking me to the palace right now, to storm in and break out my sister, but I knew that was a terrible idea formed from desperation. I filled another glass from the smoothie blender instead, noticing most of the dishes we'd used earlier were already back on their shelves, clean.

"It is good, right?" Chloe said, coming back out of her room.

I almost dropped my glass on the floor when I looked at her.

She'd redone her makeup so that her eyes were bold and decorated and her full lips were deep red. She was wearing green and black again, but now she was in a green corset and a black skirt. The corset was made of many stiff vertical braids, creating an accentuated hourglass figure with her upper body. It was hooked together up the front with shiny black fasteners and left her skin bare above her well supported cleavage. The long black skirt was a glittering silk with several cuts that went to her upper thighs. It completely bared her legs and sandal-clad feet as they rested on the carved footrests of her chair.

I'd seen plenty of outfits like hers in my visions, but never at the same time that I could see their magic. Her gift was moving through its pattern, brighter now. It moved within her and formed a bubble of white light around her, somehow deepening the golden color that radiated from her skin. It pushed out waves of pleasure and ecstasy and lust. It rolled away from her and filled the space we were sharing.

I certainly wasn't immune to her gift, and found myself moving toward her, my blood flowing hot through my body. My throat was tight and my stomach filled with a whole swarm of butterflies. I wanted to wrap my arms around her, wanted to kiss her, shit. "Woah," I said shakily.

"Sorry about that," she said, suddenly clamping down her gift, pulling her magic back into herself. "Just getting prepared for work, between my work uniform and my gift, things can get heated fast."

"Does it work on you as well?" I asked.

"Sort of. If I fully embrace it, but that is not always easy to do."

"For sure," I said, still a little weak in the knees at the sight of her, hearing her velvety voice. Crap, I bet that gift could be dangerous.

"Help yourself to the kitchen, and as I said, do not wait up. I am very happy you are here, Alexa. I will try to get word to your mother."

"Thank you," I said.

And at that, she headed out the main door, off to use that gift on someone else.

Chapter Twenty-Nine

I SLEPT LATE INTO the next day, recovering from our long walk across Atlantis, and by the time I came into the kitchen to find breakfast, or maybe it was lunch, Penelope was snacking on fruit at the table. I joined her, pouring myself a smoothie from the full pitcher.

"Chloe's already downstairs, hard at work on her day job," Penelope said.

She reached over and held her palm open to me, offering. I slipped my fingers into hers and let her close them in her grip. The touch gave me a pleasant tingle where my butterflies lived, and it gave me a moment of regret for taking my own room here. But then the image of Hazel in a cage flashed through my mind, reminding me that we weren't here for my hormones.

"Damian will be here tonight," Penelope said. "And Chloe told me your grandfather, Henry, will try to come too. He's Irene's father."

"He's not locked up like Markos?" I asked.

"He was made a region leader in one of the communities on the far side in exchange for publicly testifying against Markos and giving Irene to Amara."

"He gave up my mother?"

"We know how Amara took Aric. She did the same to Henry. Amara had already killed the rest of Irene's family. I'm sure his choices were to comply or die," she said. "He's our highest-ranking resistance member now. Chloe confirmed that her parents were discovered and are now living in the breeding chambers, and that Amara has appointed a new leader for their region."

"Oh no," I said.

"But hopefully tonight's meeting will help us figure out how to get that sword and maybe find a way to save everyone." She smiled sadly and I could tell she didn't believe her own words.

The hours waiting for the meeting passed slowly for me. After days of making forward progress, literally, being confined to Chloe's house only increased my fear for Hazel. Despite how badly I wanted to go out and do something, it was safest for us to hide away from the potential royal hunters, guards, or Gifted region leaders who might stop by the stables to rest or borrow a horse.

I wasn't sure how long my anxiety would allow me to wait up here without doing something though. I just hoped we came out of the meeting with a good plan.

I spent some time reading the instructions on my new Nymph potions and was disappointed to learn that the invisibility potion would only work for five minutes. That didn't seem like enough time to do much of anything.

When it was getting closer to our resistance meeting, I finally changed out of the soft tunic I'd fallen asleep in the night before and dressed back in my own clothes. After walking halfway across Atlantis the day before in Penelope's skimpy gown, I wanted the comfort of feeling fully dressed when I met with a bunch of Godline strangers.

Amara's face flashed back at me in my little bathroom mirror as I got ready. It had started happening so often after all my visions that I didn't even jump at the unpleasant image anymore. I was just happy that my flashes of Dagan had completely stopped being associated with Penelope and usually only occurred now when I was thinking about Hazel.

When I was clean and dressed, I went out to find Penelope, wanting to be near her while I did a mind share to check on our family. So far, she hadn't been on my case about using my gifts for anything but checking on our families, which was reassuring. I was still completely opposed to messing around with other people's magic while inside their heads. It would only lead to disaster.

Penelope was sitting on one of the couches, and I sat down beside her.

"I want to check on everyone," I told her. "Can you stay with me?"

She laced her fingers into mine, and I rested my head on her shoulder before closing my eyes. I felt for my sister's mind. It was easy to find now, easy to recognize, and her magic remained safe from my influence even if she had told me to stay out. I continued to believe that she'd be okay with the violation given current circumstances.

* * * * *

When I look out of my sister's eyes, I'm looking through the bars at Aric, reaching for him. Most of his body is too far away, lying limp on the floor, but Hazel gets ahold of his ankle and tugs at it, shakes it side to side.

"Aric," she says softly, "Please be okay." Her throat is tight, and tears burn at the back of her eyes. "Aric?"

"She hit him pretty hard in the head this time," Lukas says from behind Hazel.

"And she didn't heal him...again," she says, letting out an involuntary sob before she sucks her breath back in to stop any more from escaping.

Suddenly, Aric groans quietly and presses his palms to the floor so that he can sit up on his side a little. "I am okay," he says, voice raspy.

"Maybe we should just tell her about Lex's powers," Hazel says. "The queen wants to know what Alexa did to Dagan, but her visions couldn't have done anything, and she can't even use the other gifts without your help. Maybe she shot him or something."

"He would have recovered from such a wound days ago," he says. "She would have to do much more damage. Perhaps she has learned to use the other gifts without me."

"It doesn't matter what you tell the queen," Hazel replies. "Alexa isn't here, and hopefully it'll stay that way. However it happened, it sounds like Dagan might be dead. They got away."

He grunts quietly as he sits up and looks more directly at me—at Hazel. His face is covered in a mixture of dried blood, tears, and dirt. All his bones seem to still be pointing the right way, at least. I study the pattern of his gift, but I don't just see the form of his magic. It's as if each of the bright specks of his gift pattern have a mirror image connected to them. The queen's magic—her blood.

"Just tell her. Maybe she'll release you and treat you like the prince again. You'd be more help in that scenario."

Relief crosses his face. "Do you think she is telling the truth?"

"You know her better than me," she says. "But at this point it doesn't hurt to try."

"I do not know her at all," he says solemnly. "But I cannot take much more. Lukas?" he calls past Hazel hesitantly.

She looks at the other side of the cell. Lukas is sitting on the floor, his black hair braided neatly against his head, and wearing his typical outfit. I wonder if he's missing his animal forms. I'm sure Amara has shared blood with him, giving her the ability to stop his gift, but I also just know in my gut that he's not going anywhere without Hazel.

His amber eyes have a more vivid glow here, and sure enough, when I check his bright white pattern, it too has a mirror image. I bet Aric's gift acts in a similar way, but without the hand slicing and the blood like when Amara does it. It seems she's always got to do things the violent way.

"Penelope will keep Alexa safe on Earth," Lukas says. "Escape the fate of this room, Aric. And do not come back for us."

I feel Hazel stop another sob. "He's right, Aric. Just get out if you can. Find them and get away."

* * * * *

I pulled back into my own mind and focused my eyes on Penelope, across from me still. "Ugh," I groaned.

"What is it?" she asked, tensing.

"She's tortured Aric without healing him again, and he can't hold out much longer. Aric's going to trade information about my gift in exchange for his freedom."

"Well, they don't know everything you can do anyway and maybe it'll give Aric some relief from her torment," Penelope said. Then she added, "I don't understand why she's torturing anyone for information, anyway. She's been using my aunt Melody's gift of telepathy to communicate with her blood bonded hunters for a few years now. Why not just take the information?"

"Amara recently told Helen that she can't understand people's thoughts coherently. Maybe she developed a special form of shorthand or something with her hunters," I said.

"And I suppose even if she could read his thoughts, she'd still make Aric betray you as part of her sick game for control," Penelope said.

After that, people started arriving. Chloe got upstairs first and set to work on several dishes because apparently our meeting was going to be over a late dinner. Penelope and I helped out, cutting and rinsing and plating food as Chloe directed.

Mica and Matthew arrived next and settled in on a couch while we worked on the meal. And just as we were moving all the dishes to the table, which had grown to accommodate more guests, Xanthus and Balius ducked in through the door, oversized as it was, the stallions were taller still.

Damian came in last. He was wearing the beige work clothes of a Giftless farmer, but his brown eyes had a Gifted glow to them. It wasn't as bright as most of the Gifted I'd seen though. It was probably how he'd gotten away with pretending to be without a gift all this time. I wondered if he was just lucky or if he was intentionally suppressing the glow somehow. Either way, his body was still filled with the pattern of white magic that was unique to the Gifted.

Damian saw me and rushed my way, stopping just in front of me with an excited smile and staring with his warm brown eyes. "Alexa?"

The moment I nodded, he pulled me into a tight hug.

"So, you're my birth father?" I asked the obvious because I didn't know what else to say. The level of his joy at seeing me was uncomfortable—he was a stranger.

He nodded happily. "I have missed you every day. Your mother and I only hoped to give you a chance at a life."

"It's been a good life. My mom and dad… I mean…you know, your grandparents. Fern and Reed? They're great parents."

"Let us all gather around the table," Chloe interjected.

I took Penelope's hand, not wanting to be separated from her when we sat down. Damian stayed right with me as well, so when we were all settled in, I sat between the two of them, across from Chloe, Mica, and Matthew. Xanthus and Balius each took an end of the table, and I noticed that Xanthus had a large bowl of golden apples in front of him.

He saw me staring and bobbed his head up and down with a laugh that came out as a nicker. "These apples are what the humans refer to as my guilted pleasure," he said.

"Close." Penelope grinned at him. "It's a guilty pleasure."

"Eat away," I said. "Those things are delicious."

Penelope held a tray of cooked steaks up to me, one of the few familiar foods on the table. "I know you do not eat animals, but would you like to try some since you saw how we harvest our meat at the market?"

"I know it's technically different since the animals aren't killed, but I still don't think I'm ready to develop a taste for their flesh."

I'd said it quietly, but Xanthus piped in. "That is much appreciated. I like this one, Penny!"

She took my hand and kissed it with a smile. "Me too."

"So…" I glanced around the table, ready to start planning, ready to take action. "I don't know how much you've been told, but I'm hoping there's someone in the resistance who can steal the murder sword and free all the people Amara's keeping captive."

"Murder sword?" Mica asked.

"The Immortal Death Blade," Penelope provided.

"Those have been gone. Burned for centuries," Matthew said.

"Except the one Amara's dad saved for their family. I saw Amara use it to murder her mom and sister, and then I saw where she hid it," I said. "The only issue is, that was a few hundred years ago. I haven't seen her move it, but that doesn't mean it's there."

"What is the meaning of your statement?" Matthew asked. "If you are Irene's child, you are new in the world. Certainly, you were not present to view The Immortal Death three centuries ago."

I flushed with embarrassment. I hadn't meant to phrase my words that way. I knew I hadn't actually been here in Atlantis even days ago, but with all my visions...all my memories...damnit! It was hard to keep all my lives straight.

"She has visions, Matthew," Penelope said dryly, as if he should have assumed as much. It made me feel less foolish.

"Oh," he said.

"That is convenient," Mica said. "How much control do you have?"

I explained not only the basics of my gifts to the table, but also had to answer a lot of questions about my statement revealing Amara's role in the deaths of her family as well as what she was currently up to.

"She has been killing anyone who might resist her and stealing their gifts?" Xanthus asked.

I nodded.

"To create her own version of a prophecy?" Balius asked. "She thinks all twelve Olympian gifts will give her the ability to pass on immortality?" His nostrils flared.

"And to create Gifted babies," I said. "In some messed up way, she thinks she's saving Atlantis."

The same general questions continued from various members of the group, no one seeming quite able to grasp the full picture of what Amara was up to. Only Damian was able to move to other topics, slipping in a whole lot of questions about my childhood, apparently desperate to make up for lost time.

"Poor Markos," Chloe said, after I'd finally finished answering questions. "He hates being one of Amara's breeders more than I do. And he never gets to leave like me." She finished with a sigh.

"How are you away from work right now, anyway?" Matthew asked her.

She grinned. "Xanthus and Balius created a stable emergency only I could solve. Amara has had enough experience with their protests to know it is easiest to give me a night off from time to time."

"Now, how do we use all of this information," Balius redirected the conversation.

"We need to do something as soon as possible," I said. "She's murdering people. Also, who knows what damage she's planning to do with all those gifts."

"If we could get the Immortal Death," Chloe said, "we could risk it all and attempt to defeat her. It is high risk, but could mean a lot of people getting their lives back. Including me."

"None of us can exactly walk right into the living quarters of the palace," Xanthus said. "Plus, some of us lack thumbs."

"I do not think retrieving the sword is in your house of wheels," Chloe told Xanthus.

"Wheelhouse," Penelope corrected her absentmindedly.

"I could use my visions to somehow sneak into Amara's room and—" I began.

"No!" Damian stood up suddenly. "We cannot risk you, Alexa."

"He has a point," Penelope said. "Who knows what Amara would do if she could get her hands on you?"

"Irene might be able to slip into—" Chloe was saying.

"Not Irene!" Damian yelled. "She is not made for such things."

"Well, that's not giving her much credit," I said. "She seems plenty capable."

"He's not totally off base," Penelope murmured in my ear. "She hasn't handled the traumas in her life well. She struggles with panic attacks pretty regularly."

"Irene was nearly three when she and her father walked hand-in-hand into her mother's room to find her dead and covered in blood," Damian said. "She lost so much that day, and all she had was the hateful queen after that."

"If she is caught and the queen overreacts, and decides to harm the princess, all of us would pay the price," Matthew said. "Irene is not a viable option."

"Well, someone has to go get it!" I raised my voice. "She's going to kill my sister. She's torturing Ivy and Theron's son. She's threatened Penelope's brother. I'm not more important than any of them."

"With Penelope's illusions and Alexa's ability to see through Amara's eyes, they probably have the best chance of getting the sword," Mica said.

"My daughter is not risking capture by that madwoman." Damian had jumped up again. "I just got her back!"

"My mother knows I'm here already, since we used my illusions to get across Atlantis," Penelope said. "If I use them in the palace, we need to make sure she's nowhere near the queen when it happens, and we have to be in and out before she could tell her."

"I can provide a fast exit," Xanthus offered.

"Slow down!" Damian said. "You do not have to do this, Alexa. You have learned to hide your gift. You could stay here with me. You could go back to Earth. You cannot give yourself up to the queen. You cannot go there."

"Damian—"

"Call me Father or Dad. Call me Dad, please!"

"Uh...Dad? I'm doing this."

Balius interjected. "We cannot rush off with a half-formed plan. What do we do with the Immortal Death?"

"Always the voice of reason, Handsome." Chloe patted his neck as he stood next to her place at the table.

"Alexa and I can do this." Penelope squeezed my hand.

"Because it means freeing them," I said.

"You are so brave, Alexa, but please do not go into that palace. I cannot lose my child a second time." His eyes were panicked.

"I'm twenty years old," I said.

"Exactly. Still a child."

"She's not a child, Damian," Penelope said. "She's a grown woman in the human world and according to the Queen's Laws. Not to mention, you heard about her experiences these last months. She has the memories of scores of people over hundreds of years. Soon enough, she will be wiser than anyone in this room."

"Almost anyone," Xanthus said.

"You do not always have to talk, Brother," Balius said.

"The Queen's Laws are why we sent Alexa away in the first place," Damian said. "I will do it. I will steal the blade."

"Yes, because nobody will care about a Giftless farmer traipsing around the palace," Chloe scoffed.

"We aren't debating this anymore," I said. These people were supposed to be the resistance but if this was how their meetings usually went, how did they ever accomplish anything? "I'm getting the sword. I'm not going to keep doing nothing."

"And then who attacks the queen with the Immortal Death?" Damian asked. "None of us are exactly murderers, and that is the only way the weapon serves our needs."

"I will do it," Mica said.

Matthew looked at him, wide-eyed, but didn't speak. He took Mica's hand in his instead.

"Remember, we will never have the life we want together if we do nothing," Mica said, stroking Matthew on the cheek before leaving a soft kiss on his temple. "I will replace the sword in my uniform with the Immortal Death. I can wear it into the breeding chambers. If we can lure her in close, I will use my speed to end her in one strike."

"With Melody's blood, there is a strong chance Amara will hear your unspoken intentions before you can strike," Penelope said. "Even if she's not good at making sense of thoughts, it seems possible that murderous intentions might come through for her."

"What if we gathered enough resisters to confront her at a single moment?" Balius asked. "She could not sort all those thoughts at once, and Mica could get close enough to strike under the guise of protecting her from the angry mob."

"That is a serviceable idea," Mica said. "But where?"

"I was thinking about those cliffside windows into the breeding chambers," Penelope said. "What if we could fill the halls with our people and crowd up into the reception area, lure Amara there, and then stab?"

"Between us, only Mica and Penelope have gifts that would allow them to fight or distract the queen and the guards loyal to her," Matthew said. "That will not work."

"We could release people from the breeding chambers to join us if we are going through there anyway," Chloe said.

"We need more people," Matthew said. "If Mica is going to risk his life, we need the full resistance behind us."

"Matthew and I can stay in the Distant Regions during our off time the next two days to recruit for this plan. When we have enough people willing, we can make our move."

"Alexa and Penelope will wait until our army is ready before getting the weapon," Matthew said. "We should be ready to act as soon as we have it."

"And perhaps we will find someone better suited for the theft as well," Damian said, hopefully.

"My sister doesn't have that kind of time!" I yelled. "And I don't want to see you in Amara's hands again," I told Penelope, gripping her hand tightly. And fuck, crying in front of a table full of godlike strangers.

"We're working as fast as we can, Lexa," Penelope said gently. "And I'm not leaving you to face what's coming alone. You won't talk me out of that."

The group of us went round and round for nearly another hour, trying to find a better way to do what needed to happen. I stopped participating in conversation after it was clear that nobody except maybe Xanthus, who was always rearing to jump into action, was willing to talk about moving before the painstaking task of gathering a crowd of Gifted people to fight Amara.

When everyone was finally leaving for the night, Damian tried to talk me into coming home with him. "I would feel better if you were farther from Amara."

"Well, I'm not going any farther from Hazel until she's free," I asserted stubbornly.

"It sounds like Alexa could use some fresh air as much as me," Xanthus suggested to the room. "She and I will go make sure those cliffside windows are a viable option for our plan."

He looked intently at Penelope and then Damian. "We will stay out of sight," he promised. "This is an easy mission, and she needs it."

He was right. I guessed he'd picked up on my desperation to do something, anything to get Hazel back faster.

When there were no arguments, Balius added, "I will take Damian home while you two do that."

After everyone said their goodbyes and headed downstairs, I stopped into my room to change into a set of forest green riding breeches, a lighter green shirt, tall black boots and a helmet. They all fit themselves to me as I dressed.

When I got down into the barn, Chloe had already saddled Xanthus for me and Balius had taken off on his second trip for the Distant Regions, dropping Mica and Matthew off on their recruitment mission.

"Thanks," I told her. "And thank you for this, Xanthus."

I gave Penelope a warm smile before mounting the tall stallion. "We'll report back soon."

She blew me a kiss. "I'll miss you the whole time."

We clopped out of the barn, and the moment we stepped outside, Xanthus rocked back onto his haunches and launched into the sky. The weightless feeling combined with our upward trajectory and incredible speed made the ascent both terrifying and exhilarating. It was nothing like riding a regular horse, but then I remembered that I'd flown like this in my visions. The memories flooded me, and the fear was replaced by a simple joy.

We flew up until the stable was a barely visible square and rode out and over the water to approach the cliffside palace windows. We dove down the side of the cliff until the openings came into view, pushing a glowing light into the black night. It illuminated two towering openings large enough that we could have ridden right into the passages.

"This will work," Xanthus said. "If we wait for Mica and Matthew to be on duty in the chambers, we could get our army down there in a matter of minutes. Then we just have to somehow lure the queen into the crowd."

"She loves violence," I said. "I'm sure the potential conflict will draw her in. I doubt she could resist testing out her new gifts on people who are asking for it."

"Now let us talk about why I really brought you up into the stars tonight," Xanthus said. "I know you are unhappy with the lack of action, and I want to offer my services for a mission of our own. One only we know about. If you can figure out what to do once inside, I will get you into the palace."

"Yes!" I said, feeling my heart rate pick up at the idea of finally acting, and knowing I could keep Penelope safe. "I have a way to get invisible for a few minutes if you can get me in the palace door. I'm ninety-nine percent sure I know where the sword is and how to get to it. I've had enough visions of that damn place, anyways," I grumbled. "I'll get the sword and meet you on Amara's balcony. I think we can be in and out before I become visible again."

"I will gladly help with that plan."

"I'll use my gift to make sure Amara's busy, but let's plan on tomorrow morning. I'll sneak away when I can and meet you at your stall. Thank you, Xanthus!"

When we landed back inside the barn, we were surprised to see Irene, my real live mother, standing next to Chloe.

I slid down off Xanthus and walked toward her.

Irene pulled her arms around herself in a protective hug as I stared into her luminous green eyes—my eyes. Her pattern was bright with activity and her pale skin was filled with the now familiar godlike luster. It was a passive gift. Just by existing, she brought peace, or maybe sanity, to a people that had lost theirs after the source of their gifts had left them. After their immortality started fading.

"Alexa..." Irene said softly.

"Hey," I said lamely.

"Shall we find a quiet place to sit and talk?" she murmured.

I nodded and then followed her to an empty bunk room near the front doors. There were two sets of bunk beds inside. Irene sat on one of the lower bunks, and I sat across from her so we could face each other.

She looked like an extremely well-dressed farm girl. The brown fabric of her dress seemed both extremely fine and functional with a neckline just over her collarbone and not a hint of braiding in the outfit. She wore her clothes as if they were a uniform, armor even, separating her from the world with a protective layer.

"So, you are my mother..." I said nervously. I really loved to state the obvious. "Nice to meet you?" I felt stupid.

"Chloe told me you have come to save Fern and Reed's daughter—"

"She's my sister," I corrected, trying not to feel annoyed.

"Apologies. Your sister and Penelope's family."

"Yes."

"I have seen them," she said. "I clean up wounds and deliver food in the cells."

"You have?" I asked. "Can you tell Hazel I'm here?"

She unwrapped her arms and placed her palms on her thighs for a moment, but then she pulled them back into another self-hug. It seemed like a posture she'd spent a lot of time with. "Alexa..." she began. "Your father and I...we sent you away twenty years ago so you would never end up in my aunt's grasp."

"I know that, but stuff happened." This wasn't exactly how I'd envisioned reuniting with my birth mother. I wasn't about to tell her what we were planning.

"I do understand. And please know my heart aches for you. Seeing you now grown and stunning and very brave...hearing of your incredible gifts. It is a dream seeing what you have become, but..."

"What?" I asked through gritted teeth.

"You need to go now, before you are discovered," she said firmly, hands back on her legs long enough for her to finish her declaration. Then she pulled them around herself again.

"I'm not leaving my sister." I couldn't believe this. Everyone in this supposed resistance seemed to have given up.

"They are as good as dead, Alexa. I am sorry for your loss, but you must save yourself."

"She's alive! I saw her this morning. There's still time to save her. And don't act like I'm safe. Amara will be after me no matter where I go now."

"Listen to me! Amara cannot be defeated." Her words shook. "She is consuming our gifts and bringing death upon us. Please run from this place."

"You listen. I appreciate that you got me away from Amara so I could grow up happy or whatever, but that's just it. I'm literally grown up now. You don't get a say in what I do. I'd rather fight to be free of Amara than spend my life running. And I'm going to save my sister!"

I ran out of the bunk room and kept going until I was outside in the pasture. There was a dimly glowing light coming from the direction of the palace. I folded my arms over my chest and gazed into the blackened sky, filled with abnormally bright stars.

Suddenly, long and powerful arms wrapped around my middle, shoving my own arms out of the way and clamping tight over my sternum. Before I could even try to break the grip on me, we were rising straight up into the sky.

Chapter Thirty

IT ALL SEEMED TO happen in slow motion. Panic flooded through me as the earth pulled away from my feet and the horses below me started growing smaller. By the time I jumped into the mind connected to the overpowering arms, we were nearly a couple stories above the earth.

* * * * *

I don't bother trying to look at the external world instead I search for this mind's pattern. I can sense it, feel it pressing out through its body, manipulating the air around us. I tear at it with my mind, trying to get it to stop...trying to shut it down before we climb too high. Ripping at it turns out to be a bad idea. It pulls apart where I've struck it and snaps back inside of the body. I can feel the magic breaking into pieces as it flows back into the dormant white pattern it came from. And we fall.

* * * * *

I pulled back into my own mind in time to experience the breathless pain of landing hard in the grassy field, not far from where I'd started. The arms had released me the moment we'd begun falling. I had enough experience with falls during the hiking trips of my youth that after my feet hit, I instinctively bent my knees and sort of rolled into the landing. It only helped a little. My breath slammed out of me on impact, and I hit my head hard enough to see flashes of light before everything went briefly black.

I gasped soundlessly until I was able to draw a ragged breath. And then another. Then I felt the burning pain in my left ankle and the throbbing agony throughout much of my body, but especially my arm, ribs, and head. My focus faded and a painful ringing filled my head, blocking out the world around me.

It was Sebastian who'd done this to me. How many people could fly like that? He sat up a few feet away and fear consumed me. I couldn't fight him off again. But just as he stood, a massive black horse dropped down from the sky and landed in front of him. Chloe was astride the horse, shouting something. They reared up and slammed two metal clad hooves into Sebastian's chest, smacking him back into the ground.

Things went fuzzy for another moment and when my vision cleared again, Chloe uncoiled a rope from somewhere on her saddle and threw it to Penelope, who was just running up with Irene. The women squatted down together and went to work with the ropes.

At some point Irene left Penelope to finish tying Sebastian. She came over to me, getting down close to my face. She was saying something, but I couldn't process it. I did have a sudden feeling of calm when her hand held mine.

* * * * *

I woke up on one of Chloe's couches, minus my boots and helmet, which I suddenly realized I'd still been wearing when I fell, that was lucky. I ached all over with a dull bruising pain, but the burning and throbbing and loss of sense was all gone. The bright light of morning poured in the windows to land all around me, and I sat up gingerly.

"Oh, thank the gods!" Penelope's voice called from the kitchen area behind me.

"Welcome back." Chloe came into my view holding a smoothie. "Hungry?"

I was not. Not even for the best smoothies ever. I shook my head. "Where is Sebastian? Where's Irene?"

"Your mother wanted you to know she will come back as soon as she can," Penelope said.

"Sebastian is tied up and gagged in Xanthus's stall," Chloe added. "He claimed the job since Balius got to capture him."

That made me grin slightly, despite the pain. But shit. Xanthus. We were supposed to be sneaking off to the palace about now, but my aching body demanded otherwise. If I could get to my room and drink some of that Nymph tonic for healing, we could try again tomorrow morning. My fear for Hazel moved in next to my pains. This was taking too long.

"How did Sebastian know I was here?" I asked.

Penelope sat down next to me and lifted an arm over the back of the couch, offering to let me lean against her side. I shifted into her, wincing whenever I discovered a new torn or bruised muscle, and all I could be was thankful that I hadn't broken bones.

"He followed your mother here and realized who you were when you went outside," Penelope said.

Shit. My bad.

"Did you take control of his gift?" Penelope asked quietly, treading lightly on the touchy subject.

I nodded. Yes, damn it! I took control of his gift in desperation. It was way too instinctive, which scared me. Not to mention, I still didn't know how to control the gifts I took over. "Did he say anything about what I did?" I asked, nervous about the answer.

"He wanted to know what you had done to him," Chloe said. "He tried to take off as we were tying him up, but it seemed to cause extreme suffering."

"I think I temporarily damaged his gift." I'd felt the harm as well as the instant repairs taking place; I knew the truth of my words. "I took control of it too forcefully and I sort of...it felt like I tore it apart when I tried to stop him."

"Well, that stopped it," Penelope said. "I can't believe what he's become, trying to take you for the queen. Gods! I always knew he was an opportunist, but I swear I never dreamed he could take it so far."

"To be fair," Chloe cut in. "With his new job, he probably knows Amara is killing people to take their gifts. He is likely after her favor so she will spare him."

"I get it," I said. "It's super cowardly, but I get being afraid of that monster."

"Are you ready to talk about using your gift defensively?" Penelope asked me. "I know you hate it, but you seem to be using it reactively anyway. It would be good if you had a little control over it."

"And who should I practice on?" I asked, pulling away from her so that I could look her in the eyes. "Who wants to volunteer to let me accidentally break their magic or turn them inside out?" My voice got shrill as I approached a full panic.

"Okay, maybe don't practice, but be open to using it, maybe mentally prepare for it?" Penelope suggested.

"Yeah," I muttered. "If it's to save one of us, I'll use my stupid gift."

"We learned that Sebastian was set to have today off, but his absence will be noticed soon," she said. "Balius and I are going to bring Sebastian to a friend with a gift for memory alteration first thing in the morning. After I know you're feeling better. And then we will let him wake in the stables, thinking he drank a little too much Ambrosia and lost a day. It would not be a first for him."

"The memory person better make Sebastian think he did something painful while he was wasted because based on how I'm feeling, he's going to have questions." I winced involuntarily as if my body were trying to prove my point.

Penelope gestured me closer with her open arm. "Come back over here."

I leaned against her, feeling comfort at the touch, knowing I would do anything to keep her safe from Amara, including sneaking off with Xanthus while she was dealing with Sebastian. I memorized the feel of her body against mine in that moment, just in case I didn't make it back.

"Well, I have horses to ride and grooms to yell at." Chloe said, heading toward the door. "Rest up, Alexa."

"How are you feeling?" Penelope asked me suddenly. "Hungry?"

"Still no. And I feel bruised and achy, but a lot better than last night. Falling from a couple of stories up really doesn't feel great, magical healing or not." I rambled on, suddenly anxious. "Actually, I think I just need to have a nap and get cleaned up." And drink my Nymph potion so I could steal a sword in the morning.

"Sure, Lexa," Penelope said. "Do you want a hand to your room?" she asked, the concern clear in her voice.

"I've got it," I said. I barely had it, but I was going to hide that if I could help it. I shifted away from Penelope and began pushing up from the couch. The bruises and aches throbbed and burned again as I moved my body to stand for the first time since last night. I kept the back of my head to Penelope as the pain danced across my expression. Despite my attempts to muffle the cries, a few whimpers escaped.

"Are you sure?"

I nodded and gave a thumbs up without looking back. I couldn't bear it. Then I began a slow shuffle toward my room. Somehow, amidst all the pain, my brain had the bandwidth to flush with humiliation as I imagined her watching my back, hunched over, as I limped away.

The exhaustion began filling my body and mind again, and things started going fuzzy around the edges. I was going to get to my damn room before I passed out. By sheer will alone, I covered the final distance and slumped into the quiet dark of my room. I made it to the bed, downed my entire healing potion, and passed out on my pillows before getting a chance to change or clean up.

* * * * *

When I came to, my body ached with a soreness of mostly healed injuries, and my head was clear. The wall clock, a carving of vines twisting into the twelve positions, told me Chloe would be getting ready for her palace shift soon.

I peeled myself out of the day old riding clothes and stepped into the always warm tub. After a long soak, I cleaned away the dirt, combed my hair, and pulled on a plush white robe before heading for the wardrobe.

I thought about Penelope as I browsed the clothing provided by my room. She'd shifted to wearing Atlantean clothing as soon as we got to Chloe's. They were mostly airy pants or riding breeches, but I remembered the blue sundress she'd been wearing this morning. I'd been too out of it as I'd slumped against her to appreciate it, which was too bad.

I decided to give the fancy gowns another chance and I pulled out a silky green dress with a deep V-neck and a full skirt that stopped just above the knee. The hems were all covered in a braided white stitching and when I slipped into it, the dress instantly shrunk down to fit my body. I weaved my hair into one long side braid, slipped on a pair of white sandals, and went to find Penelope.

She and Chloe were sitting at the dining table, eating something that smelled delicious. I was finally hungry.

"Finally, you have taken out one of the dresses," Chloe smiled. "After seeing you in Penelope's gown when you arrived, I have been waiting to see you in one to match those eyes."

"Come sit, beautiful," Penelope said.

My skin ran warm all the way up into my cheeks. Chloe was decked out for work and Penelope was still wearing her blue dress, both gorgeous as always, and I suddenly felt like a child playing dress-up. I wished I'd just put my jeans and T-shirt back on. At least then I wouldn't feel like I was being indulged for my efforts. Too late for that. I pushed away my embarrassment and sat down to pacify my growling stomach.

"Sadly, I was just headed out for my shift at the palace," Chloe told me as I filled my plate. She was out the front door before I started eating, and I realized I missed her already. She was a good friend. I'd been wrong to worry about her and Penelope romantically.

Penelope and I eventually shifted over to the couch so I could snuggle up with her while I checked on the hostages. My anxiety bubbled up as I realized over a day had gone by since I'd seen that my sister was alive. What if I was too late because of that stupid flying jerk?

"Do you want to lay your head on my lap?" Penelope offered.

"Sure." I leaned back and rested on her legs. Once again, I regretted trying to be fancy because I had to keep my legs awkwardly

together in the dress while trying to lie down. Finally, I got into a
position that mostly worked.

* * * * *

I find Hazel's mind instantly and can feel her body sitting on the
floor, leaning up against the bars. I feel Lukas's fingers laced into hers as
we sit next to him. Hazel's arm is between the bars so they can touch.

"I wonder what she'll do with him now," I say–Hazel says.

"Anywhere is better than this room," Lukas says gravely.

"Do you think we did the right thing? Having Aric tell Amara about
my sister. I mean, he told her all of it."

"Learning of Alexa's gifts certainly did not please Amara, but I do
not see how she would use the information to cause any more harm
than she already inflicts," Lukas says. "Especially if your sister stays
away."

Well, too late for that, but I agree with him. So what if she knows I
have visions of people's memories and can spy on anyone anytime...and
can almost kill myself when I accidentally pull other gifts into my body?
She was after me before and she'd be after me still.

My sister seems okay, so I shift into Aric's mind, which is easy to
find, even though I have no idea where he's at. After living with him for
months and mind-sharing with him almost as much as Penelope, our
connection feels like a well-used trail.

What's new is my ability to see the bright white pattern of his gift. I
always had a slight sense of it when I shared his mind before, but now I
can see the paths it takes, see how it's capable of capturing and storing
gift energy, and see how to access the stolen energy, even pull it into
my own body through our magical connection rather than touch.

I suddenly feel fairly certain in my ability to take the energy, but
again, I have no practical experience in doing so. I could just as easily kill
him as use his magic. A fresh guilt wells up as I realize how I've been
thinking about controlling Aric's gift for myself, and what would be the
point of that, anyway?

When I focus on my surroundings through Aric's eyes, I see myself
coming face to face with Chloe. Amara is in front of me—Aric—and a
guard walks at his side.

"Aric will be staying here until he and his bride have had ample
opportunity to produce a child, but I do not want him wasted while he
waits," Amara says to Chloe. "Add him into your shifts."

Chloe nods quietly as she watches Aric enter her decorated cell.

"And, Chloe..." Amara says, "Your mother will be helping me with a project tomorrow. I want you to join Agnes and I when we stop for lunch."

"Is the project something I can help you with instead of my mother?" Chloe asks, stopping some strong emotion as it flits across her face.

"Just join us."

"Of course, Queen Amara," Chloe says.

Aric is in the cell now, and he's turned so that Chloe is at his side. Amara is on the other side of the decorative iron as the guard locks them inside. She walks away from them down the hall and it's suddenly quiet.

Aric turns to face Chloe, lust rolling away from her and crashing into his body in waves of magic that I can see at work. I can also feel Aric's body responding, shifting closer to her.

"Aric," Chloe says assertively, and I can see her gift shutting down. The waves of bright white magic stop leaving her body and pull themselves back into her pattern, flowing there, waiting to be let out again. "Penelope and Alexa are in Atlantis."

"Great," Aric says. "My ex-mother may have once convinced me that it was a gift to marry Penelope, but now I know it was just a cruelty, trying to ruin the one good and steady relationship in my life," I can feel Aric's throat is tight as he speaks, and his words come quickly. "I will not have sex with Penelope, and I am sorry, but I do not want to have sex with you either. Your gift will not work once we touch."

"Penny has told me all about your gift, Aric. And if you do not want to have sex, we will not have sex. If you prefer, we can spend our time together helping you learn to control who you use your gift on," she says. "You might be surprised by how often you end up needing to touch someone else while they use their gift."

"Really?" he asks.

"Of course," she says. "Most of the people I encounter would come willingly even if it weren't required. My gift...even the sex is typically seen as...an incentive. Everything has been done through artificial insemination for decades now, anyway." Chloe gestures toward the raised bed and under the bedding, there's a mini-fridge and a small shelf holding several empty plastic cups. "My job is primarily to help with collections, however my clients want to go about that."

"And you can cover for me?"

"I have three other appointments tonight—all eager regulars," she says. "I will just split one of those."

"Okay...then yes," my Aric voice says. "Please help me."

* * * * *

I pulled back into my own mind and sat up on the couch, shifting so I could see Penelope. "Hazel and Lukas are still okay, but..." it felt weird telling her about Amara's plans for her. I also felt a deep sense of shame as jealousy wormed into my mind when I thought about Aric with Penelope. Nobody deserved to be thrown in a sex cage. "But she's moved Aric to a breeding cell. Chloe's with him. Actually she's trying to help him with his gift, but—"

"Let me guess. Amara plans to throw me in there with him," Penelope said.

Her accurate guess shocked me, but she did know my evil aunt well. "Uh...yes...? How did you know?"

"She had us married, I ran away, so of course she needs to assert her power over me and force the situation," Penelope said.

"I hate that she did that to both of you."

"Well," Penelope yawned, "Balius and I have an early morning, so I'm going to head to bed."

"Sure," I said, suddenly uninterested in heading our separate ways. In addition to not wanting to be left alone with my nerves about tomorrow, I didn't want to be away from Penelope. My world could have ended yesterday, and it could end tomorrow as well.

But now, instead of at least getting to hold her close as I waited to walk into danger without her, I walked toward my own cold and lonely room, to wait alone.

"Goodnight," I said to her, and when we were both standing, I pulled myself against her so I could at least give her a goodnight kiss. She returned it happily, speeding my pulse and making it even harder to pull away and walk to my lonely room.

After changing from my ridiculous party dress into a simple white nightgown, I crawled into bed and plopped back onto the large mound of pillows, but I couldn't stop thinking about Amara killing my sister and about being too late. And I also started worrying that I'd sleep through Penelope's errand, missing my window.

That was an easy fix. I'd just go ask Penelope to wake me before she left in the morning.

I slipped out of my room, crossed the hall, and knocked on her door. A small part of me acknowledged my relief at having an excuse to go to her.

"Come in," Penelope called from inside her room.

I walked in and leaned against the closed door. The room was dark except for a low glow around her bed, where a few wall-mounted candles burned. She was sitting up, wearing the same gown she'd worn that night back in Fairbanks. Why did that feel so long ago?

"Well, don't just stand there." She patted the bed. "Come sit by me."

I walked over her stone floors with my bare feet, enjoying the cold feeling against my flushed skin. My heart sped as I settled in beside her.

"What's up?" she asked.

The butterfly nest inside of me stirred, wanting more than I came here for. I ignored them when I asked, "Can you wake me before you go?"

She nodded and smiled at me. "Of course."

"And can you hold me tonight?" I nearly whined it. "I can't stop seeing Hazel dead. I need to get her back, Penelope."

She reached around me and held me as I pressed my face to her shoulder and cried, overwhelmed by the changes in my life. I'd gone from an awkward and desperate hazard to myself living with the Nymphs to this person who was using magic to steal swords and navigate prophecies. I was still desperate, but my motives had changed. I was no longer trying to prove myself but trying to save the people I cared about.

Penelope let me stay like that, with her, until my eyes were puffy but dry, and then she slid down into the pillows and pulled me in against her. I fell asleep with my ear over her heart, soothed by the steady rhythm of it.

Chapter Thirty-One

PENELOPE WOKE ME WITH a few warm kisses to say goodbye before taking off to deal with Sebastian, but those kisses led to me pulling her back into the bed so that I could hold her for a little longer, wanting to remember the feel of her close to me.

When I finally let her leave on her errand, I rested my head back on the pillow and mind shared with Amara to see if it was time to go. She clearly wasn't the early riser that Penelope was, so I went to my room to get dressed while I waited. I pulled on breeches, a blouse and riding boots before heading out to eat something and check on Amara again.

Someone had left out a pitcher of smoothies, so I filled a glass and finished it sitting on a couch before finding Amara's mind a second time.

* * * * *

I look out of Amara's eyes across a food laden table at Chloe's mother and Helen. The table is in the courtyard, near Helen's mounted maps, and the sun is shining bright on Agnes's golden hair. Her whole body is radiating the same bright glow as her light blue eyes, and when I examine her gift, I can see not only the pattern of it within her, but that her pattern dances around and through her flesh, I suppose putting her gift of beauty to work all the time.

Helen's pattern is currently dormant, simply weaving the shape of her magic within her, and still it sets her rich brown skin aglow, almost as brilliant as Agnes. The idea that a gift for beauty exists in the Godline seems a bit silly to me. They're already inhumanly attractive.

"It is time, Agnes," my Amara voice says. "For you to show complete loyalty to our people."

Agnes's face is worried. "Have I angered you, my queen?" she asks.

"Of course you have angered me. You would not be living in the breeding chambers otherwise, traitor," she says calmly, standing up. "But this act will redeem you, Agnes. I am mere steps away from saving our people, and your sacrifice will be part of that."

"My queen, I did not anticipate this...honor. I have people I wish to bid farewell." Several glinting tears fall along her cheeks.

"What I must do will take us all day," Amara says. "You will be conscious and alert for quite some time before..." her voice trails off without finishing that statement. "We will send for your daughter when we pause for lunch so that you can say your farewells then. Otherwise, I will have supplies for letter writing brought down for you. Helen will join us after lunch when she returns from a tax collection in the Royal Community. She can deliver any letters you write. We have a long day ahead though, so come now." Amara's final words come out with a slight roll of power from her gift.

I can feel it form and exit her lips. It shakes the dishes and foods and then envelops Agnes, pulling her to her feet.

Amara and I are polar opposites when it comes to controlling our magical talent.

* * * * *

I pulled back into my own mind, feeling sick. Amara was sacrificing Chloe's mother for her gift. Again, I resolved to take any opportunity to save people if one revealed itself. It was time for me to go.

When I reached the stables downstairs, it was thankfully empty except for a few horses eating in stalls. I crept down to Xanthus's stall.

"Are you still up to do our plan?" I asked. "I know it's a day late, but they're still alive. There's still time."

"Of course, I am up for it!" he said. "Let us prepare and depart immediately."

Xanthus directed me through the steps of how he liked being saddled before I climbed onto his back and he took off through the open barn door and into the sky, headed toward the palace. I enjoyed the feeling of weightlessly surging through the sky, even as I watched my dangerous fate grow closer.

We landed alone, outside the double doored main entry to the palace after being in flight for less than a minute. Xanthus had brought us down at the top of a wide staircase. The building was too massive to take in entirely, but the entry was all smooth white stone with detailed designs carved into it. There were other colored stones and even gems embedded into the white. Several classic Greek columns ran along the exterior but on closer inspection, it seemed to incorporate much more than a single architectural style. Maybe it had become this over the many centuries of its existence.

I slid off Xanthus and pulled out my supplies, dipping my poncho into the Nymph potion as directed and then swallowing the rest of it before covering myself with the poncho.

"Is it working?" I asked him.

"Well, I cannot see you."

"Okay, we have to hurry, then. I only get five minutes like this," I said. "Remember to meet me at the balcony but don't linger too long. If you don't see me come out, I was either caught or found a chance to save someone. Either way, you get back home."

He nodded solemnly just before he reared up and began kicking the doors loudly with both front hooves.

"Let me inside now!" he yelled. "I have complaints!"

"What is the meaning..." A guard stomped out, face stormy. When he saw the black stallion in front of him, he stopped talking and attempted to change his expression. "How can I be of service?" He stood in the open doorway, looking at Xanthus. There wasn't room for me to pass by him safely.

Xanthus must have realized this. "I am coming inside," he yelled. "The sun bleaches my glorious coat!"

"Of course, sir." The guard pulled the door wide and waited for Xanthus to pass into the entry chamber.

I slipped in close behind Xanthus. The guard gave his back legs a wide berth, so I was well clear before he walked inside, closing the door behind him.

"I have many complaints," Xanthus continued on his rant. He planned to keep it going for just a few minutes before leaving so that he could pick me up. "My primary complaint is that Sebastian seems to be the queen's new favorite! I saw him leaving through a portal while I was out flying the other night! Why has the queen not asked me to go to Earth? I fly also, and she knows I like Earth!"

I'd already crossed the open space of the entry and was climbing up the staircase that led to Amara's room.

"Well, Xanthus, sir..." the baffled guard began. "Sebastian traveling is news to me. Perhaps the queen does not send you to Earth because they are not used to horses like you..."

"Like me? What does that mean? Did she tell you she did not like me?" Xanthus was spilling a continuous stream of nonsense at that poor guard. If the circumstances had been different, I would have cracked up watching him, but I was slipping down the empty hallway as quickly as I could walk without making the poncho crinkle and his words began to fade near the end of the hall.

I nudged open Amara's door and slipped inside, pushing it shut behind me. I leaned against it and quietly took in the room. It was a cheery space in the bright morning sun.

I looked at the large tub in the floor, at the bed on the far wall, the closed French doors, and then the full wall of books. I walked over to them, browsing along the shelves around eye level.

The bookshelf felt more vast when I was actually in front of it, and at least a few minutes passed too quickly as I searched the center shelves for the right book. The poncho was no longer invisible, and I ripped it off. I was leaving out the balcony anyway, so it shouldn't matter that I was visible again.

Finally, I found it.

I pulled out the burgundy book titled Populus ex Progenies Immortalis and found the edges of the stone blocking the hidden cubby. It slid out easily. Then I reached into the hole and felt around with my fingers. Thankfully, they ran into the cool hard metal handle of the heavy weapon. I pulled on it, and its weight surprised me, the tip of it falling to the floor with a clunk as I gripped the hilt.

It was time for me to meet up with Xanthus, but first maybe I could check on Amara and see if there was any way for me to save Hazel, save anyone.

I turned back to face the door and cried out as I nearly ran into a palace servant girl in a simple beige tunic and apron. She must have come to do whatever chores this magical self-cleaning room needed done, and she seemed as scared of me as I was suddenly running into her.

"It's okay," I said, reaching a hand gently toward the girl.

She took my hand in hers, and in the same moment I thought to study her pattern, I felt her magic consume me.

I was suddenly so dizzy I dropped the sword on the floor with a loud clatter and got down on my back to try to stop the room from spinning.

I looked up at the girl weakly, struggling to focus on her. "Why djid..d you do zzat," I slurred.

Then Helen was standing over me as well, with a guard at her back. "Welcome, Alexa," she said, voice saccharine.

Then she turned to the girl. "Go now."

The girl sighed heavily and left.

Helen leaned down, and I rolled to keep her in view. She picked up the sword dropped at my feet. "I find my most loyal allies come to me when they are young and traumatized. That does not make their early days less trying, though." She stood with the sword, feeling how it balanced in her hand. "Beautiful," she said, as she examined it. "You naughty child. Best we put this back where it came from." She walked over to the shelf and slid it back into its hidden nest, replacing the stone and the book.

Then she turned to the guard, "Bring Alexa back to the experiment chamber for me." Her eyes met mine. "Silly girl. Did you think I would not sense the rot of Nymph magic in my own house?"

The guard tossed me over a shoulder and followed Helen out of the room, down the hall and a flight of stairs, past the guard in the entry room, and down more stairs. When the passage leveled out, we went through a door on the opposite side of the hall and into the room with Hazel. My plan wasn't a total loss. I could talk to my sister again.

The guard carried me over and threw me in an empty cell. I rolled over onto my other side so that I could see the room.

Helen was standing at the stone table, facing Amara. Agnes was lying between them.

"It is a good day, my queen." Helen gestured over to me lying in my cell.

"Lex?" Hazel called to me. "Alexa! No!"

"Silence!" Amara screamed, sweeping her arm in the direction of my sister's voice. There was a thumping sound, a groan, and quiet.

"Haz...Ha...Haze!" I tried and failed to call her name.

Amara turned and smiled in my direction. "What has been done to her?" she asked curiously.

"Drugged," Helen said. "It made capture quite simple."

I wondered why Helen was lying. Maybe it wasn't a lie. For all I knew, that girl could have drugged me based on how I was feeling.

Helen turned to the guard who was hovering at the door. "Take guards down to the Royal Stables. Post a watch over the Immortal Stallions, and do not let them leave their stalls. The queen will deal with them when she has time. Then bring Chloe here and find Sebastian. I felt his gift flicker in the stables."

The guard nodded and started walking for the door.

"And, " Helen called at him. "My daughter is somewhere close, in the stables or in the community. Do not come back here without her. Her groom awaits her in their marriage bed."

I groaned and desperately hoped that Penelope would evade capture. I did this without her, so she'd stay out of this place. It meant nothing if she ended up here anyway.

The guard left and Helen turned back to Amara. "After Chloe has said her farewells to her mother, it might be best to bring her into the breeding chambers full time from now on. Those stallions were helping this child and Penelope, which means the horsewoman was as well."

"What a shame," Amara said. "Perhaps I should take the gift of the daughter instead of the mother," she mused.

"Please no," Agnes cried. "Spare my daughter. Please."

"Remember your goal to collect gifts from older generations, when possible," Helen said. "Allowing you to replace the region leaders with a younger, more loyal following."

"Of course, you are correct, my truest friend and advisor," Amara said reverently. "I have just finished the next cycle of blood sharing with Agnes. I need rest. Agnes should still be quite well enough to join us, and she deserves some final moments with her child, even if they are both traitors."

"Excellent idea, my queen," Helen said, hooking her arm through Amara's elbow and leading her toward the door. "I'll send a guard to assist Agnes."

I watched them leave the room and then another guard came in and helped Agnes to her feet. She was quite weak but able to walk with his support. It was better than I could do now, and what was happening to her would eventually kill her.

When the room was empty of villains, Hazel called to me again. "Lex? Are you okay? Why are you here?"

"I...I...." My speech seemed to be getting worse. I rolled over to face her direction and saw Lukas peering down at me. I tried to smile. Then I used my bottom hand to prop up the other and moved my fingers around so that I had a fist and a thumb sticking up.

"Uh...I believe she is trying to hold up her thumb?" Lukas said uncertainly.

"Helen said she was drugged," Hazel said loudly, from the other side of him. "Sleep it off, Lex," she called.

That sounded like the only good idea at the moment. I closed my eyes, which were already so heavy, and the fog that I'd been fighting against rolled over me.

Chapter Thirty-Two

HELEN

IN HELEN'S BODY NOW, I–Helen walks next to Dagan, toward Amara and Dante. Amara leans against Dante, who's propped against a wide purple trunk of one of the golden-apple trees.

"Good morning," Helen says. "You must be one of Kyra's girls."

"I am Amara," she says with a friendly smile. "Who might you be?"

"Oh, I am no one special, just a childhood friend of Kyra's, returning after quite a long while away. I am Helen," I say. "I have come back because my boy seeks work as a royal guard."

Amara glances at Dagan. "He will make a fine guard. My mother and sister are more involved in the business of ruling and the palace though. I am sure you have heard the latest prophecy gossip about my family." Her expression says this is a sore spot for her.

"I must admit that we have been a bit reclusive. The last news I heard was that the next queen had been born. Was that nearly three years ago? Have we had peace that long already?"

"Please, join us." Dante gestures toward a large basket. "Help yourself to refreshments. I believe Amara is in a mood to visit. She does love gossiping with new people. That is how we met, after all."

"Not quite, Horse Thief," she laughs at him and then looks at Helen. "I will tell you all about my family drama if you promise to tell me stories of my mother in exchange." She smiles deviously.

"An excellent trade," Helen says, sitting down on their blanket. Dagan remains standing, and Amara watches him curiously.

"He likes to stay alert," Helen says.

"Excellent commitment," Amara says. "I suppose you already know that when my father sacrificed himself, the Olympians rewarded our people with another prophecy."

"Is it true that he really burned up every one of those deadly blades?" Helen asks, sounding interested in the gossip.

She nods. "Yes, all but the one he left to my mother for protection, but even that is tucked away, only to be used in an emergency."

Instinct seems to take over, and even in my near blackout state, I work my way forward through the conversation a little more quickly. Amara is just telling Helen about how her mother had been pushing

Markos and his brother onto Amara and her sister ever since the prophecy betrothed them at age ten. I slow down when they start talking about Dante.

"So, shall I assume this fine young man is not one of the prophesied brothers?" Helen points at Dante.

"No, he is not, thank the gods!" Amara laughs. "But Dante here is part of the story."

"Please tell," Helen grins conspiratorially.

"Well, my sister followed the prophecy like she was told. She married her assigned man and had Irene almost immediately. That was a couple years ago. And, as you know, little Irene brought an end to the fighting among our people."

"Yes, but how does young Dante fit this tale?"

"Once the strife curse was over, my mother no longer had an excuse to keep me cooped up in the palace, so I left. I wanted to see the rest of Atlantis and the human world. So, I did, and I brought Dante back with me." She blushes and turns her face toward the young man behind her. She kisses his lips softly. "We are in love."

"That much, I see," Helen says.

"The prophecy is satisfied. Unfortunately, Mother insists I marry Markos anyway. She seems to think our marriage will appease the gods and somehow cause them to gift more Godline births."

"Do you think she could be right?" Helen asks.

"Markos sure does. He harasses me on her behalf daily." She rolls her eyes. "But I do not want Markos."

"Have you told Kyra about Dante?" she asks.

"Of course, I have, but she will not even discuss it with me because he is human," Amara says. "After today, though, that will all change." She presses a hand to her belly. "Our healer just confirmed I am having Dante's son."

"What wonderful news!" Helen exclaims. "I am certain Queen Kyra will finally hear you with this good news. I must get Dagan to the palace before it gets too late, but we live at the old farmhouse behind the orchard, and I would love to have you over to pay you back with a story of your mother."

"I cannot wait!" she says happily. "How about tomorrow? I come to the orchard every day for Dante. He is living in a barn near your farmhouse, I believe. Finding work in Atlantis as a human can be difficult."

"At least I am near my love," he interjects, smiling and kissing her cheek.

"Until tomorrow, then," Helen says, getting to her feet. She walks past them in the direction of the palace with Dagan at her side.

* * * * *

I felt my body on the cool floor, but I kept my eyes closed while I processed what I'd just seen. Yet another memory of a sweet and gentle Amara. A woman nothing like the monster of today. But now I've started to see the connection to Helen. Dagan was raised by Helen, and he was a monster. Helen is Amara's most trusted advisor and she's evil too. How could Helen possibly have that kind of influence on people? On an immortal and powerful queen? I knew I was still missing something vital.

"Wake up, Alexa." Irene reached between the bars, shaking my arm.

"I'm up," I groaned, pushing myself off the floor.

"Good. You're okay." Hazel was standing against the bars of her cell, which made me want to cry with relief.

I took in my surroundings with a clearer head. Lukas was sitting quietly, eating from a tray.

Irene was sitting on the ground outside my cell, hugging herself. Behind her, across the room, Agnes was lying on the stone table again, but this time one of her arms hung limply over the side, and even from here, I could see that she'd lost all her color and taken on the ashy pallor of someone drained of life. I felt sick that I slept through all that suffering.

I scooted toward Irene and she pushed a tray under the bars of my cell. It had dried fruits, bread, and a cup of water. I shoved it to the side.

"Is she dead?" I asked her, sure that I already knew.

Irene nodded.

"Do you know how many more people she's going to kill before she becomes whatever it is she's creating?"

"She only lets me in here when she is not working, but she must be very close. She has killed many in recent weeks," Irene replied. "Listen, Alexa...I am very sorry that I spent our reunion telling you to leave. I was a little late to realize that. I tend to let fear control me, but I have been working on it."

"It was you that asked my parents...uh...Fern and Reed, to make me think I was human, right?" I asked.

She dropped her eyes to the ground. "I did. Again, I am sorry...I thought maybe they could keep you from manifesting a gift, maybe never face this day."

"I understand what you were trying, but it didn't work at all, and it's been a rough adjustment for me to learn my entire life was a lie." Even as I said the words, I felt an anticipation at speaking with my birth mother. She is a Godline princess and the bearer of some great prophecy. I might not want to let her off the hook immediately, but I wanted to know her.

"I only hope I have a chance to make it up to you," she said. "I must go before she comes for me, but I will come as often as I can."

"I'm glad you came," I admitted.

She pushed to her feet and dusted off her pale brown skirt before turning and leaving the room.

I took the water from my tray. I was thankful it hadn't fallen over when I'd dramatically shoved it aside before. I was parched.

"So, what happened, Lex? I thought you'd gotten away from Dagan," Hazel said.

"I did. We did. I don't want to detail it here and the details don't matter, anyway," I said. "But then I came here to save you."

"That's going well." She tried to smile at her lame joke attempt, but it slipped away almost instantly.

"I'm sorry for going in your head again, Hazel," I said. "And I'm sorry I made you feel like you weren't a good sister. You're everything to me. Always. I love you. I was a jerk!" The thoughts flew out of my mouth.

"Yeah..." She stared at her feet. "And I'm sorry I yelled at you right before getting kidnapped. That was unfortunate."

"I deserved it." I grinned. "I was being a selfish idiot."

"Lexa?" Hazel asked me.

"Yeah?"

"Thanks for coming after me. I wish you hadn't, but I'm happy our last words weren't a stupid fight."

"Me too," I said.

"And I love you too," she added.

"We should sleep," Lukas said. "It is not easy to rest when Amara is in and out during the day."

He and Hazel found spots next to each other on either side of the bars. They were holding hands through the gap again.

"Good night, Alexa," Hazel said.

"Good night," I said.

When I rested on my back, closing my eyes, all I could think about was Penelope. As soon as I thought to search for her mind, I was just there and my heart sank.

* * * * *

Penelope lies on her back as well. She is on the soft cushion of a bed rather than the cool, hard ground. Her arms are crossed in front of her as she stares at the stone ceiling in the candlelight.

"I am so scared, Penny," Aric's voice whispers from beside her.

She turns on her side so she can see him. They're both fully clothed and on top of the blankets. "I'm afraid too, Aric. I know they are eventually going to force us to do what they want. When that happens, it is all just varying degrees of suffering."

"What are we going to do?" Aric asks.

"I wish I knew," Penelope sighs. "Try to get some rest." She reaches over and ruffles his hair.

* * * * *

Then I came back to my own mind. Things were bad, everyone was scared, but at least in this one moment, all of my people were still alive.

* * * * *

I was woken by a white-hot ring of shock suddenly around my neck, stabbing like knives. The pain would have made me scream, but it was also so tight I couldn't breathe. And it was lifting me, forcing me to get my feet underneath me or be strangled.

Once I was on my feet it loosened just enough for me to draw several shallow, ragged breaths. When my eyes stopped watering, Amara came into view on the other side of my open cell door.

Her pale skin gleamed as much as her familiar green eyes, probably from the new gift she'd just murdered for.

When I studied her magic, she seemed more like the Giftless people I'd seen, the shape of her just filled with the bright white light. So many patterns crossed and twined together that they were impossible to untangle and distinguish from one another. I had a feeling it would be very dangerous to ever attempt controlling her gift. Gifts. One of the gifts from within her was flowing from her outstretched fingertips to my neck.

"This way, Alexa," she said. Her invisible leash led me toward the wall where Hazel and Lukas had been chained before.

My heart sped in terror. When I reached the wall, the electric lash instantly shifted from my neck to my wrists and ankles. It yanked me around, stretching my arms and legs into the X shape, and pulled my back up against the cold stone of the wall. The leather straps secured themselves snugly around each of my outstretched limbs so that I couldn't move at all. Then the stabbing, hot pain retracted from my body, leaving me shaking.

"What are you doing?" I cried.

"My darling son, I believe you have met Aric, was kind enough to tell me all about your little gift, or I should say gifts. While I look forward to exploring your magic, it seems a bit dangerous to keep unchecked, but also much too dangerous to exchange blood until I know more." She walked up to me so that her lips were close to my ear. "Not to worry. I have created a solution for just such a situation."

She walked away from me for a moment and returned with some sort of metal ring. "Thanks to one of my new gifts, I have the ability to work wonders with metal." She was speaking loudly enough for me alone to hear her, even though the only other people in the room were also prisoners. "I was able to remove a small filing from my very special sword. Maybe you have seen what my sword can do in one of your visions?"

"Yes, I know about the sword." I said, a little surprised Helen hadn't told her about that part of catching me. Helen was keeping secrets from Amara, but why?

What was she going to do to me with that ring?

"Good, then you know how it works. It normally uses the wound it inflicts to eat up your gift energy and eventually your life energy as well. The graver the wound, the faster the death."

I watched as she took control of the ring with magic, pulling it open to create a large C. Then she shoved it around my neck, closed it, and used some magic that heated the metal at the opening point until it burned painfully against my skin, ripping a scream from my throat as it fused closed into a ring again. In seconds, my magical sense kicked on involuntarily. I felt the thing closed around my neck pulling at the source of my magical pattern, and it only increased as time passed. It was a ripping pain that started deep inside of me and stretched everywhere my blood flowed. The anguish was most in my head, making it impossible to focus.

"The inside of this collar is imbued with the tiniest trace of the Immortal Death," Amara continued, touching the outside of the collar where the evil magic eating metal was buried. "My research has shown it will render you magically and even physically impotent. But do not worry. Its effects are not permanent in this form. I still wish to learn about your magic."

The pain had leveled off at an incapacitating mind and body ache, making coherent thought almost impossible. All I wanted in that moment was to be lying on the floor of my cell in a ball and rolling with the pain, but Amara made no move to take me off the wall.

"I have work to finish," Amara said, standing right in front of me. I think she was trying to meet my eyes, but it was hard to know for sure due to my own inability to make mine focus on any one thing too clearly. "We tried the breeding laws first, but I knew a century ago that was not going to be enough. I even sent our people to Godline owned fertility clinics on Earth, but that failure nearly always resulted in Giftless children. Now, I am within days of finishing my plan, decades in the making of harnessing the magic of the prophecy for myself and returning gifts to the Godline."

"Then wh...what?" I grunted.

She was silent for a moment. Finally, she replied. "Then our people will be saved."

"It's you...they...need s...saving from," I said with great effort.

"Shut up!" The electric sting of her magic slashed across my face. "You know nothing. Just wait and see how wrong you all are!"

Just then Helen walked into the room wearing one of her golden gowns. Even with my inability to see straight, I could tell that much. A guard followed her in, pulling a woman by the arm.

Amara turned to face them. "Come lie on the table, Cassandra, mighty prophetess." Her sarcasm broke effortlessly through my haze.

I couldn't control my gifts, but it seemed my magical sense was stuck in overdrive now that something was trying to suck the pattern right out of me. I saw the white shape of magic stretch from Amara's fingers to Cassandra's neck. In fact, I saw it much more clearly than my eyes could see my physical space right now.

Later, when Amara was taking Cassandra's gift for the third time that day, I couldn't not see what happened as the gift energy transferred to Amara's body. I couldn't ignore the screams that came from Cassandra as her blood was pulled into the queen along with her gift. I watched as the gift rebuilt yet again, pulling from her pool of life magic to mend it.

Worst of all, I had to see and feel what Amara did after hours of repeatedly taking Cassandra's magic. I witnessed the destruction as she pulled the gift out a final time and then pushed every bit of power she'd spent the day gathering back into Cassandra's body, but I could see that the gift wasn't just Cassandra's anymore. It was Amara's.

It poured back into the magical pattern within Cassandra. Her pattern was bursting with the white magic, and when Amara called the gift back to her, it came running for its new home, tearing Cassandra's pattern out with it. I watched as the gift, the pattern, and horrifyingly, the entire pool of her life magic slipped easily into Amara's body. My true vision was clear enough to see Cassandra's lifeless body next to Amara who was both physically and magically aglow.

She turned to the guard who was standing silently near the door. "Clear her away, Sebastian. I do not want to spend time mastering this gift first. I will take the final gift tomorrow."

So, they found Sebastian. Right, and Amara was going to kill someone again tomorrow.

"And put her away," Amara waved in my direction before walking out of the room.

Sebastian walked over to me and began unbuckling my limbs. "You are not so dangerous, now," he laughed.

When I was free of the straps holding me up, I slumped to the floor, too weak with pain to hold myself up.

He grabbed me under the arms again and flew us up near the ceiling of the cavern. "Look how useless you are when you are not messing with my gift," he taunted. Then he darted down and tossed me into the open door of my cell.

It hurt to be tossed on the ground from several feet up, but it was nothing compared to the chronic draining as my gift was stretched tight between its source and the magic eater trying to slurp it down. My magic was exposed and raw and almost useless.

Almost useless. Almost. My magical sense was fully active but paralyzed like the rest of my gifts. If I could even gain a little movement. A little control. A little more power.

With great effort, I found the well-worn connection to Aric's mind. Once I found the path within the magic, I only had to follow it.

* * * * *

With a great relief, I'm looking out of clear eyes that are able to focus, and my pain is reduced significantly now that I'm removed from the strain on my magic. The physical pain of it being pulled apart is back with my body.

I'm sitting, as Aric, against a wall looking up at the bed, where Penelope is perched.

"I think they're distracted," she says. "I'm worried Alexa is the distraction." She's wringing her hands. "I hate feeling helpless!" she whispers loudly.

"Tell me about it," Aric says.

I feel a sudden swell of my heart, seeing Penelope again. Thankful she's okay, I focus my attention on Aric.

I need his ability to amplify. Now that I can see the magic, I understand how to make his gift do that. Every time Aric shut down someone's gift, his gift was pulling it into some sort of infinite space within his pattern, to be saved for future use. It was sort of like what Amara had done, storing up gift energy for a day, except Aric had been storing it up with every touch ever. I just needed to pull from his reserves.

From within his mind, I carefully connect to Aric's pattern, and begin pulling stored energy from it. Keeping a path open for it to follow, I backtrack into my own mind again.

* * * * *

The physical pain crashed over me, staggering my thoughts. I almost lost the path tracing back to the extra power, but I pulled at it again, just as it was slipping away.

When I pulled the power into my pattern, it gave me a moment of slack, long enough slack to maneuver into a vision. With no time to waste, I went in search of intel on Helen, for something I could use to stop Amara.

Chapter Thirty-Three

MY EYES OPEN TO a vision, and my pain is subdued again. I can barely feel the connection I created with Aric's gift.

I'm in Helen's body, lying on a bed in what's now Amara's room, and for a moment, as I look at the green eyes and silver hair of the woman lying next to me, I think I'm with Amara, but then Helen speaks to her.

"I do not know, Kyra," she says. "I was planning to go back with the Olympians. My whole family is going, and—"

"Helen," Kyra says, reaching out to stroke Helen's cheek. "You will have me. We can rule this place together." She rolls onto her back and stares up at me—at Helen—with desire. "This could be our bed."

"How did they decide to put you in charge when you are still learning your gift?"

"Apollo convinced the others that as his daughter and as an Immortal with a Demeter-given gift, I was the most powerful of their descendants to stay behind, which will suit me to lead until the gods can agree to an official ruler.

"If they decided I was not suited to rule as a daughter of Dionysus, what makes you think they want me sharing the role with you?"

Kyra groans. "Oh, just stop fretting and stay with me, Helen! It does not matter that your gift is not suited for ruling or that you do not have the Immortal blood because you will be with me and the world will be ours." She sits up in the bed, her sheet falling away from her bare skin, long silver hair spilling over her shoulders. "I need you," she whispers.

I know Helen ends up staying, so I pull on the connection to Aric's gift again and travel forward in Helen's timeline, searching for something else. It takes a lot of time and effort to shift between visions, and I fall into useless moments much more often than not. Each time I shift, I have to find my connection to Aric again and pull more of his magic.

There are many, many years of visions with Kyra and Helen ruling together. Most of the visions during that time fall into one of three categories—Kyra and Helen in bed together, Kyra and Helen around Atlantis dealing with the aftermath of curses left by the gods, and Kyra and Helen fighting about how to keep the curses from killing everyone.

It feels like hours have passed before I finally settle into a vision with information that might relate to Amara.

* * * * *

I open my eyes to one of Helen's fights with Kyra. They're standing on the cobbled road, uphill from the community flower garden which is filled with finely dressed people and tables heaped with food.

"Please, do not marry him, Kyra." Helen's face is wet with tears. "You are already pregnant with his twins. You do not need any more from him to fulfill that revolting prophecy."

"The prophecy calls for our marriage, Helen. Ambrose has a role that the gods have not made clear to us yet."

"You said we would rule together," Helen yells. "Now you betray me because the prophecy has named the first child of your children as our rightful ruler?"

"We ruled for seventeen centuries, Helen!" she shouts. "Seventeen hundred years ruling a cursed people. Cursed by the Immortal Death, cursed with Strife, and cursed to have our gifts slowly dwindle from our people. This prophecy is the beginning of the gods finally ending the curses. How can I turn away from that?"

"How can you turn away from me?" Helen asks her. "You are the only reason I stayed here in the first place! I wanted to go home with our families, but you promised me a life here."

"This is not fair, Helen! I am not turning away from you. I am choosing our people. I thought you would understand after the pain we have seen," she yells again. "And just because I must share my bed with someone else does not mean I want you out of my life. There are plenty of rooms in the palace." She tries to smile at me and brushes a tear off my cheek with her finger. "Please come to my engagement party, Helen. You can support me even if it is no longer only the two of us."

Helen looks—I look past Kyra to the group of people gathering in the garden and then toward the forest just to its left. The forest that eventually leads to a hill covered in portals between Atlantis and Earth. I watch as scores of men with swords come out of the trees and flood into the garden, slashing into every party-goer that falls in their path.

Kyra turns toward the disturbance, eyes wide. "What in Hades?"

Helen grabs her hand. "You cannot go! I have made a terrible mistake."

"What have you done, Helen?" she screams, pulling herself free from my grip.

I move forward through the vision, trying to get past the brutal murder of all the men, women, and children at the engagement party. I stop after the guards have arrived and the surviving humans have run off. I'm drawn in by a familiar event, one I saw in a vision months ago. But it's from Helen's perspective this time.

I see Kyra and a woman in white standing in the distance. They're walking along the bodies from the party, which have been gathered in rows. The woman in white puts out her golden light, but this time I can see the white gift magic within that light. It spreads through the pile of bodies, making the whole area shine. I watch the light fade from the pile and then from the woman herself before she deteriorates into nothing right where she stands.

My body—Helen's body gives a loud sob at the sight of it. Then the dead begin slowly moving, untangling themselves, standing up and looking around in fear and confusion. From this distance I can hear general cries erupting from many of the people. I assume they're a combination of cries of fear and surprised relief.

Kyra is helping a blond-haired man to his feet. She helps him to sit at one of the tables and fusses over him for a while. He suddenly stops her, grabbing her hand and talking to her intently about something. She falls into the tight hug of his arms before they share a long, deep kiss.

And then she's walking back toward me—toward Helen. When she gets to Helen, her face is red and angry.

"You did that?" she yells, pointing an arm back toward the party.

"I did not mean for that to happen," Helen says, dropping her eyes to the ground. "I found a human with an Immortal Death Blade and showed him a portal...drew him a map...so he could kill Ambrose."

"How could you be so selfish, Helen?" She's yelling louder still. "And stupid enough to think a human with a weapon like that would not bring a mob?"

"I have never been sorrier."

"Words!" she scoffs. "I suppose I can thank you for revealing such a grave security weakness. We are far beyond the days where humans should be allowed to cross into our lands freely."

Helen reaches toward her hand, but Kyra bristles and takes a step back.

"And I should thank you for my wedding present. Today's event has motivated my betrothed to give me a world free from the curse of the Immortal Death. He has vowed to find and destroy all of the swords. No matter how long it takes. That is what he gives to me and our twin daughters," she says angrily. "Never in all our years ruling did you do such a thing for me."

"We began our rule as children!" Helen yells. "Children with a cursed queendom. They set us up to fail, Kyra. We never should have let them leave without us!"

She shakes her head and sighs impatiently. "It does not matter. I was wrong about us being able to stay together, Helen. I cannot raise my girls around your poison. You are a danger to the prophecies that will save us."

"You cannot just cast me out!" Helen cries. "I stayed here for you, and I have ruled all this time, just the same as you."

"And what did you offer through your rule?" she spat venomously. "Constant reports about the supposedly dwindling magic of our people? Useless!" She bore into Helen's eyes with the bright green of her own. "And I will be sure our history does not remember the ugly days where I allowed you and your inferior gift to play at ruling. Only the time of the prophecies—the time of my family dynasty—will be remembered."

"Please, Kyra...don't—"

"I want you out of my home and out of my life, Helen. You may remain one of our people but stay on the other side of the mountains. Unless you would prefer a cell below the palace."

Helen sobs again, and this time it doesn't stop. She falls to her knees and Kyra turns away.

"Be gone by morning," Kyra says before walking toward the distant crowd.

* * * * *

I begin shifting forward in Helen's timeline again, pulling at my connection to Aric's magic so that I have enough strength to work with my gift. I wonder if Aric can feel what I'm doing and suddenly worry I might be hurting him, but as I examine his magic, it seems to function normally, so I choose to trust he's okay. Still, I handle his gift with extreme care.

There is a long span of time—many months, or maybe years—where Helen is primarily living alone in a small house on the outskirts of a community somewhere beyond the mountains. She takes a lot of walks alone during this time, and it's on one of her walks that I come across another moment of possible significance. It is the moment Helen found Dagan as a little boy.

I roll through the next long chunk of Helen's life, skipping over Dagan's upbringing where she nurtures his every violent tendency until he becomes the sadistic hunter that came for me. I stop on a vision where Helen first brings Dagan into Amara's life. It is the first time Helen crosses back over the mountains in about twenty years.

They find lodging in the Royal Community, and Helen spends days watching the palace activities. She uses her gift to track Kyra and her daughters through their magic. She talks to people all over the community, taking in all the latest palace gossip.

I even come across more than one vision where she's naked and straddling a younger man with rich brown skin and glinting dark eyes, who I only realize is Markos because she cries his name often as she's screwing him in the little farmhouse where she's living.

Then one day Helen takes Dagan out for a walk in the orchard at the same time Amara is there. I skip beyond the happy picnic talk between Helen and Amara because I just had this vision. Instead, I follow the memory a little farther than the last time. I follow it until Helen is alone with Dagan in the orchard.

"What now?"

"Now you get hired as a palace guard and join the rest of my loyal assets inside the palace," she says. "I will prepare you for tomorrow when you get home tonight. If you play your role correctly, that young princess behind us will soon be queen, and you will be her loyal guard, her lover. Whatever I need you to be."

"Whatever you require of me."

* * * * *

It's become clear that Helen is somehow involved in creating the monstrous version of Amara—the Amara we're currently all trying to survive. Helen had some plot with Dagan against the younger, kinder Amara, who seems to have disappeared sometime after Helen entered her life, but I need more information to put the pieces together.

My connection with Aric flares to life again as I pull from his gift and move forward in Helen's memories. I stop on the next afternoon, a few hours after Helen had Markos electrify the metal fence surrounding her hen house in exchange for a love potion. Amara and Dante had just shown up at Helen's door when I stop shifting forward again.

"Come inside!" Helen calls down the steps at Amara and Dante.

Amara is dressed in a simple gown that matches the pale pink bouquet of flowers in her hands. She holds them toward me as she comes inside. "These are for you, from the palace courtyard."

Helen takes the flowers with a smile. "Did Markos ever find you? I just ran into him outside of my henhouse of all places. He said he was looking for you but hurried away before I could question him further."

Helen walks across the open interior of the house, past a set of benches and into the kitchen. She pulls out a ceramic vase and deposits the flowers.

"He is persistent." Dante and Amara take a seat together on one of the benches.

"It is my fault," Dagan says, walking into the room from a short hall behind the benches. He sits across from Amara and Dante. "Markos introduced himself to me during my first shift this morning. I mentioned that you both had plans here today, that Helen had hired Dante to add some nests to her hen house while she and Amara visited."

"Dagan!" Helen chastised him. "I have not even asked Dante about the job yet."

"I will take the work!" Dante said, standing eagerly.

"He is a prize, Amara," Helen says. "The henhouse is out back. All the supplies for six new nests wait for your skillful hands just inside the fence."

"I will get right to work," he says, leaning down to Amara, first with a soft kiss on her lips, then one for her belly.

She giggles and pulls his face back up for a longer kiss before he goes outside.

"I am concerned the young man, Markos, is preparing to act in desperation, following you around like that."

"Oh, he is harmless, Helen," she says. "Though, it is strange he came here to find me. I gave him several hours of my time over lunch today where he attempted his worst proposal yet. He only brought one bottle of an overly sweet drink, an imported Nymph tonic, I believe. It was delightful at first, but he brought nothing else and fed me glass after glass of the stuff as he made his case for our marriage." She's laughing softly and shaking her head. "I am honestly still a bit queasy from all that sugar, but I took the opportunity to remind Markos about my son. Perhaps he will finally move on."

"Do not tell that man anything more about Amara," Helen tells Dagan as she sits across from him, next to Amara.

"I would not dare." He bows his head. "Forgive my mistake, Princess."

"Of course." She smiles at him.

"You say Kyra is pushing your marriage because of prophecy?" Helen asks.

"She is entirely inflexible where the prophecy is concerned," Amara says.

"May I confide in you?" Helen asks her.

"Of course," she says. "I can already tell that we are meant to be close friends."

"I do hope so." Helen reaches out and gently squeezes Amara's hand. "I left this community after your mother's obsession with the prophecies started getting people killed. She had Markos's mother killed for refusing to let him move to the palace to serve the prophecy. I could not stay to watch her let the prophecies harm anyone else."

"I did not know that," Amara says, looking devastated. "I know her obsession with prophecy, but I did not know she had people killed."

"I fear she will never stop until you are giving Markos the children of prophecy."

"Do not fret, Helen. I will run away to Earth with Dante before I let that happen. Now please tell me there are some less evil stories about my mother. I was hoping for something to bribe her with, but possibly not murder."

"Of course, we had many delightful centuries—"

"Ow!" Amara yells and doubles over.

"What is it, Love?"

"Something...wrong," she whispers. "Cramps...they worsen with each moment." Her breathing labors as sweat forms all over her body.

"Get her some water, Dagan!" Helen orders abruptly.

He rushes over to a basin in the kitchen and returns with a ceramic cup for Amara. "Drink this."

"Thank you." She sips from the water before handing it back to him so that she can hunch over in a renewed wave of pain.

That's when I see the blood wicking through the light skirt of her dress.

"You are bleeding, Amara." I point—Helen points down at her lap.

"No!" she screams. "Get Dante, please!" She's reached up between her thighs and her hand comes out soaked with blood. Her cries of pain are joined by a devastated sobbing.

"Get him, Dagan!" Helen yells.

And he rushes outside.

Helen is standing now, stroking Amara's hair as she cries, still doubled over.

"Amara, Love, this does not happen to our pregnancies naturally. Have you consumed anything unknown?"

"Of course not. I want this baby more than anything," she sobs.

"Think, Darling. I can try to mix a remedy if I know what you have consumed."

Amara makes a wordless cry of physical and emotional pain before she replies. "There is nothing. Only that sugared drink with Markos."

"You said he knew of your child before your lunch today."

"Yes," she breathed. "What has he done to me?"

"I wish I knew, Love," Helen says. "It seems he sought a way to remove your new family. I am so sorry."

In another several long moments, Dagan comes crashing back inside, but calms his expression before speaking steadily. "Dante is dead. Markos was fleeing the scene when I came around the side of the house. By the time I checked on Dante, the murderer had disappeared into the orchard somewhere."

"Well go find him, Dagan!" Helen says. "Go do your job. Alert the other guards."

He nods and rushes back outside.

"Take me to him. Please!" Amara begs, even as she hunches in pain again. "Please!"

Helen helps her stand and follows her as she goes outside. Amara puts her arm over Helen's shoulder before she tries to go down the steps alone, which is good because she stumbles under another wave of pain. Her legs and skirt are covered in blood at this point, but she's only focused on finding Dante.

They find him on the ground, one hand still on the fence surrounding the henhouse. He's not moving, and as they get closer, it's clear that he's no longer alive.

"No!" Amara runs toward him.

Helen immediately runs after Amara and grabs her just as she's kneeling and crawling to him.

"Do not touch him!" Helen yells. "It appears Markos left his gift inside of Dante. Look." Helen points at his hand on the fence.

Little white arcs appear with careful inspection.

Amara collapses on the ground next to her dead lover, sobbing more violently than ever.

* * * * *

I shift forward in Helen's memories carefully after that, watching Helen spend the rest of that evening taking care of Amara. She bathes her and dresses her in a clean white nightgown. She feeds her and strokes Amara's hair as she rests.

I stop again when Dagan returns.

"I am very sorry to report, Princess," he says. "The queen has rewarded Markos's act with marriage to you first thing tomorrow."

"What? No!" she cries. "Everything you feared about my mother and the prophecy is true! I will never be safe from it. Markos will never face consequences for what he did to me. Instead, my mother gives me to him like some prize!" Amara's face flashes with anger.

"Unless you are queen," Helen says.

"They would never allow that. Irene is to be the next queen."

"You misunderstand me, Amara. You cannot wait for anyone else to allow you anything. Look what that did to your true love—your baby."

"I need to take the throne," Amara sits up, something shifting in her expression. Her eyes meet Helen's, face emotionless. "I must eliminate anyone in the royal family who follows the prophecy."

"And then, as queen, you can make sure no one suffers because of prophecy again," Helen says. "Whatever it is you need to do tonight, I will testify that you were with me all night."

"I can take you to the palace, Princess," Dagan says. "I have a horse just outside."

"Take me now," Amara says. "I know what I must do."

"Of course," Helen says. "Send for me when you are finished. I can help with your transition, find someone to testify that they saw Markos commit the act. If he cannot face justice for the murder of your family, he will face it for the royal family."

* * * * *

I move forward in time once more, stopping when Dagan returns to Helen later that night. They're back on the benches in Helen's living room.

"The next part will take time, Dagan," Helen says. "We have broken the princess down, and tomorrow she will be queen. She will come to me for advice and you for comfort, and we will not let her down. When she relies on us completely, and after I have helped her frame Markos for her family's murder, I will begin to twist that shattered child until she thinks the cruel and vengeful things she does are to save her people. I need you there at her side, fueling her, helping transform her with me."

"Whatever you require of me...Mother."

"I am a mother now." Helen presses her hand on her stomach. "I took advantage of Amara's prophecy with Markos and seduced the young man. Ivy has confirmed I will have a son."

"Congratulations," he mumbles.

"Thank you, Dagan. I believe once the queen is quite devoted to me, I will convince her to punish Markos by turning him into a breeder and allow interested parties the gift of children with him. I myself would appreciate the convenient way to create more loyal followers right in the palace."

"You have thought of everything," he says.

At this point, I have plenty of information to make Amara rethink what she's doing, but how do I prove any of it? I panic, having a sense that many hours have already passed. A sudden jolt of pain pulls another mind into connection with mine. I follow it and settle in the mind where the pain is sourced. The eyes are closed, but I can sense the pattern in this body in distress. Suddenly the pain in this pattern is so severe that I snap back into my own mind.

Chapter Thirty-Four

MY EYES OPENED IN my cell. I sat up with a groan, the pain of my pattern strung tight, hitting me anew. I still felt hazy from the collar on my neck, but I heard Hazel screaming and crying from the wall. I saw her across the room, strung up in the X manacles as she continued to cry out. Then I saw Lukas on the stone table. Amara was standing over him, completing the final steps of ripping the gift out of him. I saw the magic as she pushed his gift back into him and called it all back, along with his pattern and his life.

All I could do was watch in horror as his life faded away and Hazel became a limp and sobbing heap in her straps. I must have cried out myself because Amara suddenly looked at me.

"Welcome back, Alexa." She glanced at the door where Sebastian was posted. "Bring her over. She is no threat in that state."

"Yes, my queen." He walked over and opened my cell. He stepped in and grabbed my arm. I was too weak to do anything but glide along the floor like a rag doll as he dragged me to Amara.

By the time he'd deposited me at the feet of Amara's silver gown, I'd enough view of the room to be fairly certain Helen wasn't there. I had to convince Amara that Helen wasn't her friend and that all these violent experiments were meant to be a distraction, a manipulation, a way for Helen to pull the strings of power.

"W...w...wait." Great. Convincing her of anything like this was going to be nearly impossible.

"Save it!" she yelled at me. "This Nymph will be the first subject in my project to return gifts to our people."

"N...no!" I yell. "Y...you...were...s...se...t...up!" I stuttered out a sentence. Please let her listen.

"The gods may have finally sent a prophecy to end the last curse...they may even intend you to do it with all those special gifts of yours...but I beat them to it this time. Now watch as I change history!"

I tried to grab at her skirt to stop whatever she was going to do, but she kicked me to the ground. Then she walked the few strides that put her directly in front of Hazel, who was still crying, but with terror in her eyes to go with the grief.

With my magical sense still distended and open, I could see Amara bringing the patterns within her to life. The bright whites of each different gift expanded and blurred until she was pulling from each of them toward her hands.

"Please stop," Hazel cried. "Please."

I slumped forward and drug myself toward Amara again. "M...m...me," I cried out. "Test...m...m...me."

She ignored me, and Sebastian dragged me backward by the feet, letting my chin smack the stone floor as he pulled my balance from my arms. The blow had me groaning with a new pain.

Amara suddenly reached one of Hazel's hands with a knife she pulled from somewhere, and then she sliced her own, magic loaded hand and pressed it to Hazel's open wound. Amara began pushing the mass of the twelve gifts into Hazel.

That was when the screaming began. Hazel's body bucked as she tried to get away from what was being done to her, and long ragged shrieks were tearing out of her throat. The gifts were being shoved inside of Hazel's body.

Hazel was already made up of her bright green-yellow magic. There was no place for the white magic to go. The white magic seemed to be blotting out Hazel's natural magic wherever it touched, leaving an impenetrable void behind it, still not making room for the white magic.

As I watched with dread, I realized two things. First, Amara had absolutely no idea what she was doing. If she understood the patterns of the gifts she was wielding and Hazel's natural magic, she'd realize she had zero chance of success. I was pretty sure Amara's Frankenstein pattern of stolen gifts would never be able to pass magic into anyone.

My second realization was that she was killing my sister quickly. I needed to do something now. A minute from now would be too late, but how could I stop someone with so much power when I could hardly sit up?

And then I had another desperate idea and began acting as quickly as I could. I closed my eyes, reached for the worn connection with Aric, and slipped into his mind. Thankfully he and Penelope's biggest issue was boredom—I didn't think I could take another emergency.

It felt like a well practiced skill as I began pulling Aric's extra power back into myself. Once I had that connection, I used the extra energy to first open a connection to Amara, slipping briefly into her mind.

At that moment, I almost lost it all because I was suddenly staring at Hazel's face, twisting in pain...cries gone quiet in her weakness. I was losing her. I had to move faster. I gripped more tightly to Aric's power and slipped back into my own mind holding the path to Amara open.

Then I focused with everything I had, recalling my recent memories of Helen. I pushed those visions out along my connections with all the strength I could muster. I felt it pushing into Amara's mind, and even as I continued to pull magic from Aric, the vision slipped back along our connection to him too.

I showed them Helen revealing her plan to Dagan three hundred years ago, but I didn't stop there. I couldn't leave any question if this was going to work. I found the vision of Helen setting Markos up for Dante's murder, showed Helen tricking Markos into using the poison on Amara's unborn child.

Amara paused in her gifting efforts on Hazel and gave an anguished cry at the reminder of her lost love.

I showed moments where Helen revealed the lies she'd told Amara, how she'd used Dagan to help twist Amara. I called forward moments showing Helen building her following amongst palace guards, like Sebastian. I showed Helen grooming her spies, like the girl who incapacitated me. And I showed her how deeply Helen regretted staying behind when the gods returned to Olympus—how little she actually cared for Amara.

And then the strain of so much magic running through my collar-incapacitated body finally overtook me, the pain redoubling, but thankfully, everything quickly faded into the dull blackness of unconsciousness.

* * * * *

When I woke, my head was clear, and all my pain was gone. The collar was no longer on my neck...no longer sapping my strength and distorting my gift as it tried to eat it away. I sat up and took in the room. Sebastian was in one of the cells, and Amara was seated on the ground in front of me, holding her knees against her, sobbing just like the woman who lost her lover and unborn child three hundred years before. I saw Lukas's body, still on the table, and then my eyes moved to the wall.

I began hyperventilating at the sight of Hazel's limp form, and even as I wept and struggled to take in breath, I searched for her magic, her life, but she was filled with blackness.

Amara's head was hanging, and I knew she'd seen every vision. "I...I am so ashamed," she whispered. "I forgot who I was...let myself get twisted up inside...murdered those who loved me...I...I am a monster." She lost her ability to speak as she sobbed violently, barely able to form her next words. "I would give my life to bring back your sister—all of them."

And just like that, another probably stupid idea occurred to me. "I think maybe we can. Bring her back, I mean." I wiped my eyes and attempted to clear the thick tears from my throat and nasal passages.

Amara looked up at me with weeping eyes. "How?"

"I'm not sure yet. I need to see...and take the gift of a woman who died just before your birth."

"You really are the one—" she started.

"I don't know about all that shit, but I'll try anything to get her back." If we were moving forward with a plan, I didn't have to think about my sister that way. I kept my eyes away from the wall. "I can access and even understand gifts, but I really can't control them. You seem to have no problem taking control of new gifts and making them do what they're supposed to. When we work together—connect our gifts—then maybe we have a chance of bringing Lukas and Hazel back."

"You mean, you will be the source of the gift, but I will wield it. Can that be done?" she asked, still sitting wrapped in on herself like a frightened child.

"I don't know, but we have to try at least."

"Perhaps, but what gift could possibly help?"

"There's a woman who had a gift for healing, but she also learned to bring back the dead...only it came at a price."

"Price?"

"Every time she did it, she lost a part of her own life. Eventually she turned to dust, but she had healed like hundreds of people by then. I just need to save two. Surely, I'll survive it."

I didn't bother saying aloud that I'd rather die trying to give Hazel a chance than to live forever knowing I'd caused this.

"I don't think it will affect you since I'll be the source of the magic," I added. "And I don't care about losing some of the immortal life I didn't even know about before now."

"How can you risk so much?" Her voice had a slight tremble.

"Listen, I'm doing this with or without you." My words cut at her. "Fair warning. I am extremely dangerous when I try to control gifts that aren't mine."

"I will help you," she said. "What is it you need?"

I stood up and walked to Lukas and Hazel, stretching my hands between them, touching both.

Amara stood up shakily. Her eyes lost and far away, probably thinking about the things I'd shown her.

"Hurry up!" I yelled at her.

She walked over to me, pulling her knife out of some hidden pocket.

"Put that thing away," I snapped. "We can share magic without blood, just come touch them." Nothing like joining forces with a recent ex-villain. "I need a boost from Aric for this. Hold on." I closed my eyes to find him.

"So that is how you used your gift on me," she said. "Remarkable."

"Yep." Pulling from Aric without an evil collar on my neck was as easy as breathing. It scared me how easy it was, and reminded me of the awful things I had unintentionally done with my magic. At least Amara would be doing the heavy lifting in the control department this time.

With Aric's power flowing through my pattern, I found the moment that woman healed just one dead person, and I let her pattern flow within me, bringing it to life with my own and Aric's magic. "Okay, Amara," I said. "I'm going to give you access to the gift. Use it to bring them back."

She nodded seriously, now facing me with her hands pressed next to mine on Lukas and Hazel. And I opened the connection between our minds again, letting Amara feel and see the gift alive within me.

She immediately began pulling it into herself and toward her hands, forming a bright gold ball of magic in each. Then she was pushing it into their bodies, letting the warm light spread throughout them. As she continued to press the gift into them, I pulled life magic from the endless pool within me, and I began lacing it throughout the gift that Amara was wielding. The well of life magic might perpetually renew itself, but as we worked the gift together, my well began shrinking.

As focused as I was on Aric and Amara—on Hazel and Lukas—only a small part of me registered what I saw happening behind Amara. Helen had walked into the room wearing a full skirted black dress.

She walked up next to Amara, watching us curiously. "What a convenient and riveting distraction," she said, as she pulled the Immortal Death out of a fold in her skirt and drove it into Amara's side.

Amara screamed in a shock of pain, and the light of the gift flickered as I felt the magic within her begin to slip toward the wound and into the sword. She seemed to shake off the effects of her looming death, continuing to press life into Hazel and Lukas, but after a few more seconds, the strength, all the magic, and her well of life energy had been completely consumed by the sword. Amara fell to the stone floor, dead.

"No!" I screamed. Seeing the last chance to bring back my sister ripped away from me snapped my mind into a different place, and before I could think what I was doing, I dove into Helen's mind, lighting up her pattern. I forced her gift to sense every gift in this room, active or not, and every gift below the palace. I kept pushing her gift, increasing the radius until she was seeing every gift in Atlantis. I wrenched her gift open as if I were tearing a pipe in half to keep the water flowing. And it flowed, letting every other gift fill her consciousness, leaving her no way to stop it—at least until it had time to heal. And then I slipped back into my own mind.

* * * * *

Helen had fallen into the fetal position, gripping her head and screaming. She could live with that pain for a while; it was nothing compared to the pain of losing Hazel a second time.

I grabbed Helen by the arms and dragged her into the cell next to Sebastian. "What the fuck was the point of all that pain you caused?" I yelled at her. "You don't even want to be here, so why hurt so many people just to rule a place you hate?"

She couldn't answer me, and I didn't care about her answers, anyway. I just didn't want to think about the death behind me.

But I had to.

It had taken losing Hazel to realize how much I'd been taking for granted with our relationship. She couldn't be gone now—now that I knew. I'd always been good enough for her. I didn't need to become some perfect person to belong.

I walked back to the wall and forced myself to look at Hazel through tear blurred eyes. I gripped her shoulders in my hands and recalled the resurrection gift pattern to my body. I imagined what I wanted more than anything, and then I pushed magic into my sister. I tapped into the pool of my life magic again and pushed that into her with the borrowed magic.

"Come back, Hazel," I yelled and pushed more of myself into her. "Please don't leave me!"

But when I searched her with my magical sense, she was still dark inside and all the light I was pushing into her—all that life and resurrection magic—it was disappearing into the blackness.

I let the resurrection gift go, let it dissipate and I stopped pulling on my own life. And then I slumped to the ground and cried. A long time passed, I didn't know how long, lost in my grief and the dimly lit cave of a room.

I tracked time in the number of times I cried myself dry, curled into a ball of silent remorse. I thought about all the experiences that I wouldn't get to have with my sister and then started crying all over again.

Something finally shook me out of the cycle. Maybe it was when I saw Amara and realized she'd died trying to atone for just one of her atrocities. Or maybe it was the idea of Amara's atrocities that reminded me I had friends in the breeding chambers. Whatever it was, I got up, took my sister down off the wall and rested her carefully on the floor.

I kissed Hazel's forehead and then went through the door into the hall at the bottom of the stairs. I went through the door into the breeding chambers to find Penelope, Aric, Chloe, and whoever else needed to be set free.

But when I walked into the wide hall between the breeding chambers, I encountered a large crowd of people. There were many faces I didn't recognize, but behind all of them, where the hall widened to create the opening for the cliffside windows, Xanthus and Balius loomed over everyone else, and Chloe sat above it all on Balius's back.

Penelope pushed through the crowd, followed by Aric. I felt completely numb as she ran up to me and wrapped me in her arms.

"The resistance came through," she said. "Everyone here is ready to fight the queen, but..." She took in my stricken expression. "What happened?"

I stared blindly at the crowd behind Penelope as I let her hold me but finally brought myself to speak. "We're all free. I don't know who's in charge here anymore—"

"You did it? You stopped Amara?" Penelope asked.

I nodded and then whispered in her ear before I began sobbing against her. "But they're dead, too."

It took me a while before I was able to stand on my own again and walk back into the murder room. I didn't want to go, but I couldn't just leave her there.

Penelope found Mica and Matthew and told them what had happened. She left them to move our resister army back outside through the palace interior. Then I followed her and Aric back into Amara's experiment room. It was good we didn't run into Amara or

Helen loyalists on the way because I was in the head space to keep frying people's gifts.

I was last into the room and ran into Penelope after she'd stopped short just inside. My breath caught at the sight of Lukas and Hazel standing hand in hand over Amara's body, looking down at her.

With my magical sense, I could see that they were both filled with an infinite tangle of bright white gift patterns. Something had gone wrong. I tried to go into Hazel's mind to figure out what was going on, but I slammed backward into my own mind as if I'd hit some sort of barrier.

"We will not tolerate that, Alexa," Hazel said.

"These minds are quite full enough," Lukas said.

"What's going on?" I asked, panicking about whatever Amara and I had done. "Hazel, are you okay?"

"Hazel is fine," Hazel said. "In fact, Hazel and Lukas are and will be, the only immortal bodies to walk this mortal world."

"What happened in here?" Penelope asked, looking as confused as I felt.

"Alexa did bring them back, but in Amara's final moments attempting to revive them, she pushed every gift within her into the resurrection magic, allowing these vessels to host our visit."

"We have given these bodies the ability to give gifts to every new child created within the Godline. A tedious task that none of us are much interested in," Lukas said.

"And Hera is ready to lift her curse against births," Hazel said.

"But the Godline search for immortality ends today," Lukas said. "The Godline is as close to immortal as our descendants on Earth will ever be."

"Are you saying...you're one of the Olympians? And you're using my sister's body to talk to us?"

Hazel nodded. "I am Athena." She gestured at Lukas. "This is Artemis."

"We felt a direct conversation was needed," Artemis said. "Hera sent a prophecy blessing Kyra's daughters with fertility and that ended in murder. Every one of us combined our magic to send a prophecy of peace into Irene, create a fair and kind ruler for the Godline. And she was traumatized by murder and a life of mental torture. We sent a prophecy giving Alexa and Aric together the resources to rule the Godline and return gifts to the people and Amara murders some of our longest-lived descendants, stealing their gifts to spite us."

"So now we are here, fixing things once and for all," Athena said, kneeling down to touch Amara. "Artemis, I believe this one has much yet to learn. Let us make her our new vessel for prophecy."

Artemis gave a minute nod. "My twin can revive her in a moment, but first I need to share a few things with Alexa."

I took a step closer to Lukas's body—to Artemis. "You gave me one of your gifts, didn't you?"

Artemis nodded. "Apollo and I decided to give you the gifts that, once mastered, would allow you to see and understand every gift, from every line."

"And Aric," Athena said, turning to look at him standing on the other side of Penelope. "I gave you a gift from my line to complement Alexa's gifts. Together, once your gifts were mastered, you two were meant to share the gifts of our line with everyone again without ever hurting anyone."

"But now, Alexa," Artemis said. "Things have changed. You were never meant to attempt a resurrection. You gave up much of your eternal life with that magic, leaving you at risk of mortality."

She walked up to me and touched my head, making a thick lock in the front of my hair turn white. "If your hair turns completely white, you will begin to age like a normal human."

"How long before that happens?" I asked, feeling more panicked by this news than if I'd just been made a normal human again right away.

"Maybe never. It depends on how you use your gifts," Artemis said. "Do not try to bring back the dead again. Do not attempt to give gifts to others—you are no longer suited to that without your eternal life fully intact."

"Anyway, that is why we gave you these immortal rulers blessed to give our gifts," Athena said.

"And be careful how you use gifts outside of your own gift lines. There may be risks," Artemis finished.

I didn't know what to say so I just stared at them both. Then I grabbed the chunk of white hair next to my face and stared at it. How was I even supposed to feel about all this?

"I will get Apollo," Artemis said. "Goodbye, Alexa." Artemis closed Lukas's eyes for a moment, and when they opened again, Athena nodded at him.

"This is our brother, Apollo," Athena said.

Apollo stepped over to Amara's body and leaned down to touch her. A blinding light burst from his hand and spread through Amara's body. He made it seem so much easier than what Amara and I had done, and in seconds, Amara was groaning, and sitting up, holding her head.

"Prophecy is now your only gift, Amara," Athena said. "You will spend your eternal life spreading our official rulings and our messages."

Amara nodded meekly.

Then the two Olympians possessing our loved ones turned to us again.

"Lukas and Hazel are now responsible for ruling the Godline, so they should work to restore order and begin blessing the unborn with our gifts," Apollo said.

"And respect our prophecies," Athena said sternly.

Then Athena picked the Immortal Death off the floor and followed Apollo to the locked cell holding Helen.

She was no longer screaming in agony or holding her head, so her gift must have been healing itself from the damage I'd caused. She faced the gods staring down at her.

"You never should have stayed behind," Apollo told her. "Your father feels the best punishment is to leave you here."

Helen didn't quite start crying, but the emotions crossing her face seemed to be a mixture of deep pain, regret, and exhaustion all at once. She nodded—eyes downcast.

Suddenly the sword in Athena's hand filled with light, brighter and brighter until it was nothing more than a luminous white, nearly too powerful to look at. When it finally dimmed again, the blade was gone.

"Farewell," Athena said.

And just like that, my sister slipped back in behind her own eyes, and Lukas looked out of the eyes Apollo had closed.

I ran to Hazel and wrapped her in a hug so tight that she finally laughed desperately, "You're crushing me, Lex!"

Epilogue

I WENT INTO THE wardrobe of my weekend bedroom and started changing from my Atlantean pants and tunic style top into my Earth clothes. I was back to my trusty jeans and T-shirt even though I'd gotten all my expensive clothes out of storage months ago. It only took my sister's death and resurrection for me to finally get better at recognizing what was important.

Just before pulling my shirt on, cool hands drifted along the skin of my sides and clasped each other around my stomach. Penelope leaned in and kissed my neck, and I dropped the shirt I'd been trying to put on. I turned so I could hold her too. She kissed me softly, and even after six months of life with her, it took everything in me to keep from peeling the rest of my clothes back off and jumping into the bed we'd been sharing.

"Can't you stay for one more day?" she asked.

"You know my Wednesday morning class takes attendance, requires participation and all that stuff, but I'll be back on Friday."

"Fine." She liked to pretend it made her upset, but we'd both been happy with our current arrangement.

"You could always come with me this week. Aric might finally be home."

Aric and a Giftless friend of his from childhood had reconnected and were now exploring Earth together. They'd become more than friends based on the way they were acting last time they stayed with me in Fairbanks. He was my roommate, but I only saw him between extravagant trips.

My Fairbanks apartment and Aric's trips were being financed by the royal accounts of Atlantis. It turned out that the California tech company owned by the Atlantis crown was one of many such investments. Apparently, Helen had convinced Amara to create profitable companies all over Earth and put Godline people in key business and political positions as well. All in the name of the hunter program.

Amara had been a huge resource for information like this, so much so that she'd been released from her cell a few times to assist with information during the leadership meetings. She'd completely changed after our time together and her resurrection in the experiment room, but the long memory in Atlantis still wasn't ready to award her any level of forgiveness.

"I can't leave Markos for that long yet," Penelope said. Once he'd been set free of the breeding chambers, Penelope had finally gotten to meet her birth father who was struggling to adapt after losing three hundred years to his captivity.

Penelope had left Atlantis only twice. Once to pack up her place in Seattle and on one visit to Oread Basin with me. After the dust settled on Lukas and Hazel's immortality and the end to the Queen's Laws, the four of us had gone back home for a weekend to see Mom and Dad.

It had been both a joyful and heartbreaking visit. Our family was alive and reunited, but just as Lukas lost his ability to shift to animal form in exchange for immortality and a gift giving ability, Hazel lost her Nymph magic. They'd both loved who they were before the change, so other than still being alive, it was a huge loss.

After our visit home to Oread Basin, Mom and Dad had decided to move back to Atlantis to be closer to Hazel, and to support her as she dealt with the grief of losing her Nymph magic.

I slipped into Hazel's mind at my thoughts of her.

I look out through Hazel's eyes as she walks into the queen's room, coming face to face with Lukas.

"Are you okay?" she asks, reaching her arms around his waist so that she can hug him and press her cheek against his chest. He's warm through the T-shirt fabric. Lukas hasn't started wearing Atlantean clothing, despite being one of the new rulers.

"I still struggle to be around so many people, and to be stuck in this form," he murmurs.

"I'll order a guard to keep people out of the courtyard if you want to get some sunlight," Hazel says.

Lukas leans down and brushes his lips to hers in a gentle kiss. "I love you, Hazel."

"I love you, Lukas." Hazel's voice is filled with pain.

I slipped back into my own mind, feeling terrible about my sister's fate, wishing I had a way to help her...and then realizing, very suddenly, that there might be a way. With a quick search through my exponentially growing memories, I concluded that I might be able to give my sister back some of the Nymph magic that had been taken from her.

I looked into Penelope's luminous brown eyes. "I forgot to tell you," I said. "Hazel asked me to come with her on her tour of the Nymph villages this summer."

"She's finally getting to visit the Nymph villages like she wanted before. Good," Penelope said.

"Yeah, but it's more extensive than that," I said. "She also wants to start trying to find all the Godline people living on Earth, create a sort of official census."

"In a summer?" Penelope asked. "That seems impossible."

"Yeah, we'll see, but we'll be taking Xanthus and Balius to speed up the travel part."

"Still, there must be thousands of them, many of whom have been hidden from Amara's knowledge. How will you find them all?"

"I have no idea. Maybe word of mouth or something," I said. "I don't think Hazel really cares that much about finding everyone right away. I think she just needs some time to process and learn about her new self."

"I am so happy that you will be adventuring with Hazel this summer." She grabbed me around the waist from the front this time and softly kissed my lips. "But I will miss you."

"Me too, but there are portals all over the world, so you better expect me to visit," I said before kissing her again.

She moved her lips across my cheek and breathed her next words in my ear. "You have gotten a lot better at touching gifts during your mind shares. I think there is a lot to explore, even when you're far...far away."

Then she kissed me again, but this kiss was filled with heat and passion and removed my last ounce of discipline. Clothes flew off and sprinkled the floor in a path to our bed. "Why don't we practice that right now?" I whispered.

* * * * *

For the first time in my life, I felt pleasure when I gazed across the ridgeline shortcut that connected our village to the far side of the mountain range. Hazel was crossing with ease, just like she had countless times in her life.

This time was special though, I thought as I watched the yellow-green Nymph magic filling up Hazel's body, even if I could see it fading already. Before we left Atlantis for the summer, I'd pulled magic from a

Gem tree and channeled it into Hazel. At the rate it was dissipating, it would be gone by the end of the summer.

So, I chose to enjoy today, and today Hazel was smiling at me from across the ridgeline.

"You can do it," she called at me. "And if you don't, you'll survive the fall, so that's okay too!" She was laughing at her own stupid joke.

"I've got something to show you," I called. I hadn't only been studying how to use my magic to help Hazel.

I shifted through my memories to find the gift pattern I was searching for, brought it into my body and gave it life. I pulled on the gift pattern, and it pulled at the air around me, lifted me up, free from the earth. When I stepped, it was into the space next to the path. I hovered over the jagged rocks far below and my borrowed gift told the air to carry me. I pressed into my next step and took off, flying across the ravine and landing next to my sister all in the same breath.

"Well, that was something," Hazel smiled. "Let's go get ready. We get to see Nepal tomorrow!"

The feeling of belonging that had always been there between us flared with new life and my heart swelled. I pulled Hazel into a tight hug. "I love you!" I smiled.

And then I led the way home for the first time, allowing the borrowed magic to help the air catch my feet when the earth failed me.

The End

About Angela Graves

Angela Graves is a fifth generation Alaskan who spends her time skiing and horseback riding through the Interior wilds. When she's not outside, she leads a classroom full of rambunctious elementary students. Angela enjoys supporting young writers in their creative journeys and singing with her local rainbow choir. In the evenings, you can find Angela playing rowdy board games with her wife, her partner, and her daughter and cuddling with her fur babies. Angela loves sharing queer stories from her beautiful community.

Note to Readers:

Thank you for reading a book from Desert Palm Press. We appreciate you as a reader and want to ensure you enjoy the reading process. We would like you to consider posting a review on your preferred media sites and/or your blog or website.

For more information on upcoming releases, author interviews, contests, giveaways and more, please sign up for our newsletter and visit us at Desert Palm Press: www.desertpalmpress.com and "Like" us on Facebook: Desert Palm Press.

Bright Blessings

Made in the USA
Columbia, SC
16 November 2024

46693752R00163